Ice Dance

Ice Dance

A Figure Skating Novel

Kent Castle

authorHOUSE®

AuthorHouse™ LLC
1663 Liberty Drive
Bloomington, IN 47403
www.authorhouse.com
Phone: 1-800-839-8640

Published by AuthorHouse   03/13/2014

ISBN: 978-1-4918-0179-6 (sc)
ISBN: 978-1-4918-0180-2 (e)

Library of Congress Control Number: 2013913265

www.KentCastle.org

Author's Note

This is the first book in the *Ice Dance* series, which tracks the adventures of a US pairs figure skating team from their rocky startup through their entire career. *Genesis* covers the formation of the team and their early struggles. Later books take them through the contests and all of their later adventures. The story is fiction, but the references to the artistic sport of figure skating are accurate.

The chapters are organized in chronological order, and they contain subheadings to serve as guideposts for the reader. A set of maps at the end of the book shows the locations where much of the story takes place.

Chapter 1

Introduction

Quiet Fantasy

Dean Steele was gliding through a silent fantasy wonderland, a peaceful expanse of pure white. All alone in his thoughts, he weaved and bobbed among snow-covered trees and scurrying animals of the forest. Warm sunbeams caressed his face and faint scents of the pine and cedar tempted his nostrils. Until, that is, his flight of fancy was terminated by the rude blast of the buzzer on the hockey scoreboard. It signaled the end of the public skating period at the Lone Star Ice Palace, an unpretentious, somewhat dilapidated ice skating arena located in the city of South Houston, Texas.

For the past hour, Dean had been floating through an uninhabited wilderness in his mind, gliding gracefully across the small ice sheet, alone in his thoughts. Now unsteady children in jeans and rowdy teenagers wearing hockey skates began to intrude into his world.

At the far end of the arena, a door opened, exposing an angry looking Zamboni machine. The beast lurched out onto the ice, threatening to devour any skater so unwise as to be tardy leaving the enclosed area.

Dean made his way through the amateur skaters to an opening in the boards. He pulled plastic guards from his jacket and slipped them over his blades as he stepped out onto the tattered black rubber mat that covered the cold, cracking concrete floor. Somewhat aimlessly, the muscular 26-year-old figure skater made his way to a secluded area of the rink where he sat down alone on a wooden bench. He paused for a breath, and a return to reality, before beginning to unlace his custom-made black freestyle skating boots.

An Intrusion

Suddenly an alien object appeared in his field of vision, something that clearly did not belong. He blinked to see if it would go away, but it persisted. Upon further study, the object became a woman's high-heel shoe, fashioned of brown alligator skin and tipped, at toe and heel, with shiny metal. Above the shoe a light colored pants leg disappeared out the top of his view. Slowly, Dean raised his head, following the leg upward with his eyes. He encountered well-rounded hips, a matching jacket, a white silk blouse, a purple scarf, and eventually a well-made up face framed in soft yellow-blonde tresses.

"Hello," the face said, smiling meekly.

Dean blinked. "Hi," he said. So striking was her presence that he could not decide whether the smartly dressed woman was strangely out of place in this modest skating establishment, or if instead the surroundings had suddenly become completely inappropriate for their clientele.

"You're Dean Steele, aren't you?" she said, smiling in a warm, non-threatening way. Still perplexed by her unexpected presence, the young man merely nodded his response. "I'm Millie Foster," she said. "I've been watching you skate. You're quite good." She paused. "May I sit down?" she asked, raising her eyebrows with the query.

Dean shifted over a bit to make room for the woman on the bench. He had not expected such polite formality from one of the patrons of this unpretentious and decidedly informal ice arena.

"You've competed, haven't you?"

"Long, long ago," he replied, "In a galaxy far, far away."

"The U. S. Nationals in 1991, right?"

Dean stopped what he was doing and looked at the woman. "That's right," he said. It had been a long time since he had heard a stranger mention any of his skating competition to him.

Dean looked at the woman sitting beside him. She was extremely attractive and in good shape for her age, which Dean guessed to be just on the south side of forty. Her beige pantsuit was tasteful and expensive. Her hair and makeup were expertly done. She looked like she belonged in one of the tall office buildings in downtown Houston.

"You won a medal," she said, with an air of significance in her voice.

"Bronze," he said, rather dryly, resuming the activity with his skates.

"Behind Todd Eldredge and Paul Wylie," she replied. "That's pretty good company you keep!"

"They were good," he said, slipping on his street shoes.

"Dean," she began, "I'd like to ask you a favor." When he raised his head, she gazed into his eyes with a polite, pleading look. Puzzlement covered his face.

"My daughter is a skater," she said, "A competitor. She's sixteen, and quite good, actually. But her father and I have some decisions to make regarding the future of her career." She softened her look even more. "I was hoping I could chat with you about it and maybe get some new perspective on the situation." She looked at him, grinning shyly. "I'll buy the coffee."

Dean's head filled with questions. There were any number of coaches, instructors, medal winners and contest judges in the Houston skating community, and she probably knew them all. Why would this woman, so obviously affluent, come down to this modest ice arena to seek out a men's singles skater who had not competed for nearly a decade? How could his advice on her daughter's career possibly rival that of the professionals, to whom she would easily have access?

Coffee

"It's a deal," he said, showing her his smile for the first time. He decided that the entertainment value of unraveling this mystery woman would most likely be worth a brief investment of time. "But I make no representations as to the value of my advice."

"I'll take my chances," she said, grinning almost girlishly. "Put your bag in the Mustang, and we'll go to Starbucks in my car."

That she had known his name, and even something of his competition history was quaintly surprising. But knowing what kind of car he drove was downright eerie. He wondered what was in store for him this afternoon as he finished packing his skate bag. As they walked out together, Dean spotted Willie, the aging black man who owned the aging ice arena, as they passed the office. "Just a minute," he said to Millie, and stepped inside.

"You need a driver this weekend, Big Man?" He asked. Dean sometimes drove the Zamboni for Willie.

"Oh, no, Dean," Willie said, grinning self-consciously. "I'm all covered. But thanks anyway."

"OK, Big Guy," Dean responded, grinning.

"So, who's your friend, Dean?" Willie asked, looking through the glass at Millie. "She's not exactly a regular around here."

"Uh, I don't know, exactly," Dean replied. "But I think I'm about to find out."

Willie partially suppressed a grin. "Don't do anything I wouldn't do," he admonished.

"Willie," Dean grinned, "There isn't anything you wouldn't do!" The older man laughed.

The two went outside into the warm, early September, 1998 air that hung like a net over Houston. A recent cold front, a preview of the fall, had pushed the oppressive Houston summer aside and introduced one of the two truly pleasant months of the year, April being the other. The fresh Canadian air that came down through North Texas had a cool smell they had not experienced for almost six months.

Dean held back slightly as he and the mystery woman walked toward the unpaved parking lot. Millie walked directly to his Mustang, not noticing that she was leading the way. Dean puzzled on this a bit as he locked his skate bag in the hatch and accompanied the woman to her white Mercedes. He got in on the passenger's side.

"What do you do for a living, Mr. Steele?" she asked, as the engine awoke with a roar.

3

"I'm a computer programmer for a small biotech company during the day," he said, "And I'm working on a Master's degree in computer engineering at the University of Houston at night."

A Call

Her cell phone rang. "Hello," she said. "Hi, Honey . . . . No, I'll be late . . . . I know, but I have a meeting with a client . . . . Tell Dad I'll be home in a while . . . . Uh-huh . . . . Not tonight, Honey . . . . I know . . . . I know . . . . I know . . . . But not tonight. It'll have to wait." The small phone went suddenly silent. Millie pulled a dial tone away from her ear.

"Was that the skater?" Dean asked.

"Yes," she answered, "Her Royal Highness, Miss Shannon Elaine Foster, quite possibly the most spoiled rotten, self-centered young female on planet Earth."

"By the way," he said, "Have I been elevated to the status of client? And if so, what is it that I'm a client of?"

Millie laughed. "No, young man," she said, looking at him as she drove. "It's just easy for Fred and Shannon to understand if I say I'm meeting with a client, that's all." She grinned slyly. "It's my generic excuse for not catering to their every whim." The small phone rang again. "Hi Honey," Millie said, glancing at the caller ID screen. "I know you will, . . . I'm sorry, Honey . . ." She put the phone down.

"She's only hung up on me twice," Millie said. "I expect this is a three-hangup disappointment." She looked at Dean. "What about you? Do you have someone you need to report in to?" She held up the small phone, as if to offer it.

"Not tonight," he said. She paused after that brief answer, allowing adequate time for him to elaborate, but when he did not, she suppressed the urge to press for detail.

The phone rang again. "Yes, my darling daughter," Millie said. "I know, Sweetie. We'll just do it later." She put the phone down. "I was right," she said, "Three hang-ups."

"Will she go for four?"

"Not likely. If I refuse her three times in a row, she usually just gives up and threatens either to run away and live with gypsies or eat a bug and die." She looked at Dean. "You've never tried to raise a teenage daughter, have you?"

"That's a joy I've been able to avoid so far," he replied.

"Well, it's a no-win situation. She demands protection and affection, but she's headstrong and independent. If we give her some slack, she feels abandoned and unloved, but if we step in with some guidance, she resents 'being bossed around.'"

Millie pressed a button on the phone. "Oh, Mick?" she said. "This is Millie Foster. Would you . . ." She paused. "I'm fine, Mick. Would you be a dear and put a sign on that back booth for me? I'll be there in just a second . . . . Thanks, Sweetie."

The Coffee Shop

When they arrived at Starbucks in Clear Lake City, the woman took Dean's order for decaf Cafe Latte and spoke briefly with the young man behind the counter. Then she led Dean to a remote booth sporting a "Reserved" sign. After they sat down, Dean became aware that she was eyeing him with a subtle grin on her face. Then she caught herself and assumed a less informal countenance.

"Shannon usually trains at Sharpstown Ice Center on the West side of town, but she sometimes skates at the new Texas Ice Stadium in Friendswood," she said. "She's really quite good, and she loves to skate. She works really hard at it. She looks great on the ice, she's got grace and speed, and . . ."

"Everything but a triple Lutz[1]," Dean finished her sentence for her.

Millie's face wilted into a pained admission that he was right. "She's built like I am, as you may have guessed. She's too tall," she continued, "To win against those midget Asian acrobats that are taking all the medals in singles competition these days." She inhaled, as if to muster her courage. "Dean, I want to talk to you . . . about . . . an idea I have." Another pause. "Since you've been around skating for a while, I'd welcome your advice."

Dean frowned slightly, still curious why she would seek advice for her daughter's career from a retired men's singles skater who'd had a less-than-stellar career in competition. If Millie noticed his puzzlement, she didn't show it.

"Shannon can have a tremendous career as a professional skater," she continued. "She can be a star in the Champions on Ice Tour, I just know it. She's that good. She's absolutely enchanting on the ice. People simply love to watch her skate." Millie looked down at her hands in her lap. "But . . . she'll never get the chance . . . unless she wins a medal in the senior division." She stared at her hands in silence. "A contest medal is like a union card these days."

"Is that what happened to you?"

Millie's body jerked visibly when the question hit her. "No . . . no, I never competed. Well, a few times. Small contests. I never won anything. I was never that good." She shrugged nervously. "I skated professionally for several years, though."

"For whom?"

"Ice Capades. I was in the Ice Capettes line, and I did a couple of specialty numbers in the show." Dean acknowledged her accomplishments with a nod. "But I wasn't star material though," she added. "I tried out for a few featured roles in the Ice Capades, but I never got them. I was just . . . an average skater."

"I thought you said you did some numbers."

"Well, just some little parts. I was Dumbo once in the Disney Cavalcade, and I was one of Cinderella's sisters." She looked at Dean with an embarrassed smile. "It was no big deal." Millie's embarrassment faded as subdued anger took its place. This conversation was not going the way she had planned.

The Daughter

"Shannon plans to enter the USFSA[2] contest series this year. She won silver at Junior Nationals last year, and she'll be skating in senior ladies' singles now. She's good, and she'll work very hard. But I don't think she'll come back from Nationals with a medal. The judges are looking for acrobatics these days, and Shannon's style is more classic." Dean looked at her understandingly.

"Shannon's a good jumper," Millie said, "She has three solid triples, and she's working on two more. But she's nearly seventeen, and she's maturing. She's having to adjust to changes in her weight distribution. That's kept her from landing her triples consistently. I don't think she can win a medal in the current environment in U.S. figure skating. She's more artistic than athletic, and they don't reward that the way they do gymnastics on ice." She sighed. "It's such a shame."

Dean moved his head slowly up and down as he considered what she had said. "Ladies figure skating has become the land of 'The young and the breastless,'" he said. "Lipinski, for example—no hips, no breasts, no problem. She jumps like a gazelle and spins like a top, and judges find it easier to score skating by counting jumps and stumbles than trying to put a gauge on artistry."

"I know. I just hate the way figure skating is going these days—jump, jump, jump! Where's the beauty in that?"

"How tall is she?" Dean asked.

"Five five," Millie answered, subtracting two inches from her daughter's true height.

"How much does she weigh?"

"Around a hundred and ten," she replied, this time subtracting ten pounds.

"Women that size land triples," Dean mused, "Nicole Bobek is 5' 5" at 120 lbs. Andrea Gardiner is 5' 5" at 128. But it's a lot of work. You can't make a woman's body spin as fast as a girl's, so the main problem is leg strength. They can't jump high enough . . . to stay in the air long enough . . . to complete three revolutions. Tonya Harding had positively beefy thighs in '91 when she landed her triple Axel."

"Shannon can do it" Millie said. "She's a hard worker. I just think . . . well, with those Asian kids jumping like bullfrogs . . . she'll have a tough time winning a medal."

"And you need her to win a medal so she can turn pro, right?" Dean considered that a perversion of the amateur figure skating competition system. The woman did not sense his disapproval.

"My idea," Millie continued, "Is to have Shannon enter either pairs or ice dancing. She would have a fair chance then. I think she could win a medal. Then we, her dad and I, could get her in either the Stars on Ice or Champions on Ice tour. I know she'd become a star right away. She could have a wonderful career in the pros." Dean listened quietly, forcing Millie to continue her story. "There are just so many girls skating these days," she sighed.

"I counted it up one time," Dean said, suddenly becoming more animated. "At the 1999 Southwest Regionals in Wichita, 193 women and girls competed in all classes. There were 33 men and boys, 12 pairs, and only five ice dance teams. Most of the pairs and dancers got byes to the Sectionals and didn't even skate at the Regionals."

"I know," she said. "It's a girl's sport."

"There's a real shortage of senior couples in USFSA[2] ice dance right now," he continued. "They just seem to break up when they get to that level. I heard there's only five US senior-level dance teams actively competing now."

"Well, at least it shouldn't be too hard to win a medal," Millie said.

"You really have to pay your dues in dance," he said. "They won't let you onto the podium until you've been at it for several years, no matter how well you skate your dances. And ISU[3] ice dance judging is in such a mess right now that the IOC[4] is considering throwing ice dancing out of the Olympics."

"After what happened at Nagano?"

"Yeah. The judges had the medals all handed out before a blade ever hit the ice. The Canadians got screwed, and the Olympics people got real upset."

"And the soap opera!" Millie said. "I can't keep up with those Russians swapping partners and spouses every other week."

"And the catfights in public," Dean added, grinning. "Maya Usova once bounced Pasha Grishuk's head off the bar at the Spago restaurant in Hollywood. There were rumors of seductions, sabotage, dopings and every damn thing else!"

"Maybe pairs is better for her," Millie observed.

"Dance has more to do with footwork and less with athletics," Dean said, "And it's terribly restricted on what you can do in a routine. If she's a good singles skater, pairs would be the natural progression."

Millie nodded. "The problem with all this," she continued, "Is the partner. Most boys who skate play hockey. Shannon doesn't know any boy figure skaters who are good enough at the dances, or who could hold up their end of a pairs program." She paused to inhale. "There is one boy she has skated with some, and he's a good skater. But he's not a great dancer, and he isn't strong enough to lift a girl her size without straining."

Millie's Idea

Millie looked at Dean, nervously fondling her pearl necklace and waiting for him to say something. He didn't. "I've been watching you skate," she continued. "You have poise and power in your moves. You have tremendous strength. You look like a bodybuilder."

"You think I could coach her pairs partner?" Dean asked. "Maybe train with him in the gym to help him build up his strength?" Finally something began to make sense in this bizarre episode. "I've never really done any coaching before . . . not officially anyway."

"No, Dean," Millie continued, looking intently at him. "You're strong enough to lift Shannon with ease. You're mature enough to be a reliable and responsible pairs partner for Shannon."

Dean was visibly shaken. "What? You want me to skate with your daughter?" He was both surprised by her idea and shocked by her audacity. "You think she and I could win a pairs medal at US Nationals?"

"Shannon is a great skater," she responded. "She's graceful. She's a doll. People love her . . . love to watch her skate. She captivates an audience."

Millie paused. "And you. You control the ice when you skate. Not like those prissy little fags." She blushed at the boldness of her statement. "You know what I mean. You skate with such power that the sheet belongs to you. You hold the audience in an iron grip. You two would be dynamite together! You could be the best there is. You could win a medal at the US championships and go to Worlds'. You might even go to Salt Lake City in 2002. You could skate in the Olympics, Dean!"

Dean's face registered puzzlement at this detailed analysis of his skating style. Millie blushed as she realized she had again given herself away. Dean's raised eyebrows asked silently for an explanation. "I'm sorry, Dean," she said. "I haven't been totally up-front with you." She took a deep breath and exhaled a sigh, as if preparing for a confession. "I didn't want to scare you off before I even got to tell you my idea."

He took a sip of coffee while waiting for her to resume. "The truth is," she continued, "I've followed your skating for years." She smiled sheepishly. "I have all your contest programs in my video library. You were my hope for a new style in men's singles. I was devastated when you retired, but when I found out you were living here in Houston, I was elated." She looked embarrassed. "I don't know why I didn't say that at first. I guess I was afraid if I approached you like a gushy fan, I'd scare you off. I apologize for all the subterfuge."

"No problem," Dean said, his face indicating an understanding of her position. "You probably played it just about right."

"You would make the perfect, perfect pairs partner for Shannon. You're attractive, physically strong . . . lots of muscles. You look like Arnold Swartzeneggar, for Pete's sake! You could lift Shannon easily, where other boys would have to strain. She's not as petite as some . . . well, most of the pairs girls."

"How much did you say she weighs?"

"About one-oh-eight to one-ten," Millie lied. She knew Shannon had recently topped 120.

"Most pairs girls are four-eight to five-two and 85 to 100 pounds," Dean said. "They rarely go over a hundred pounds."

"Shannon's grace comes from her height," Millie said. "And she is maturing into a beautiful young woman. She has the same magic as Katerina Witt. With a physically strong and technically competent partner, she would shine like a star!"

"What does Shannon think about this? Would she rather dance or skate pairs?"

Millie looked down. "I haven't discussed it with her yet. She's still working on her singles routine."

Dean exhaled a disgusted groan. "It seems to me, Mrs . . . . Foster, that you've got the cart about a mile or so out in front of the horse, here. If she wants to skate singles, she'll never make a pairs skater."

"I can make her see it my way. That's no problem. It's the best thing for her. She'll go for it when I explain it to her."

"What does her father think?"

"He agrees with me. He'll support the project, no matter what it costs."

Dean inhaled through clenched teeth. "I see." He had seen more than one promising young athlete's career derailed by overbearing parents.

"Pairs is more dangerous," Dean said. "Her head would be as much as ten feet off the ice if she fell, not just five."

"That's why I want her to skate with you. I know you won't drop her."

"And, in side-by-side spins," he added, "She could catch a sharp steel blade in the face at about thirty-five miles per hour."

"Not likely. You're both are too good for that."

"It happens," Dean said. "Elena Berezhnaya was practicing camel spins with Oleg Shliakhov in '95, and his blade smashed into her skull. She even lost her ability to speak for a while. She had two surgeries and they thought she might never skate again."

"Yeah, but she was back on the ice in three months, working with Anton Sikharulidze, and they won the World's in '98 and again in '99.

Dean shrugged. He had no further objections to raise.

"So, Dean, are you interested?"

"Well, it's not exactly what I had in mind for the next two years of my life. I'm working on a master's degree now, and that makes more career sense that skating. Besides . . ." He looked at her from underneath his eyebrows, "Been there . . . done that . . . got the T-shirt to prove it!" He inhaled. "And all the scars!"

"So, is that final? I mean, is there no way you would even consider it as a possibility? You have absolutely no interest in competing again?"

He sighed. "If I were gonna make a comeback, I'd have done it in '96. After Kerrigan got whacked[6], there was so much interest in figure skating that they were having some sort of trumped-up competition every weekend. A lot of mediocre skaters made a lot of money back then."

"No urge to compete now?"

"Oh, I wouldn't mind competing at Nationals again if I had a decent chance of winning something. I'd never enter the men's singles event. I'm old news, and too many judges hate me. But pairs could possibly offer some kind of opportunity. And pairs skating is a different kind of challenge. I've never really done that before. It might be fun to carry a girl around in the air."

Millie relaxed for the first time in minutes. A faint smile curled on her lips.

"What jumps does she have?" Dean asked.

"She has all her doubles, including the Axel, and her triple loop and toe loop. She can sometimes do a triple flip."

"Lutz?"

"Not the triple. And sometimes her double Lutz comes off the wrong edge."

"She does a 'flutz?' She changes to an inside edge for the takeoff?"

"Yeah, but it's very subtle."

"Judges these days will usually see the edge change," Dean said, "And they'll count it as a flip, not a Lutz." Millie sighed. "Triple Salchow?" Dean asked.

"She has tried it, but never landed one. And judging from her double Salchow, she may never get it. Her weight distribution has changed in the last year and a half, and getting three turns in the air, after an edge takeoff, is a problem for her."

"She would need to develop upper body strength for skating pairs," Dean said. "That would shift her CG back upward and help with the jumps."

"CG?"

"Center of gravity—her balance point. It shifts downward when a girl becomes a woman."

"I would think it would go up," Millie said. "Shannon has sprouted breasts."

"I guess that was inevitable," Dean said, glancing at Millie's ample bosom. The woman blushed subtly when she picked up his comment on her anatomy. "The weight of those is more than offset by muscle weight gain in her hips and thighs," he continued. "She's more bottom-heavy now than when she first learned to jump. The Asian girls don't usually suffer such a weight shift."

"Well, whatever it is, she's had trouble holding on to her jumps."

"Does she work out with weights?"

"Heavens no. I mean, she gets plenty of exercise—swimming, jogging, playing sports, but she's not . . . muscular, like you."

"She would need to work out in a gym three days a week to develop the leg and upper body strength required for jumps, lifts, and throws."

"Wouldn't that just make her hips and legs that much heavier?"

"Whole-body workouts would build up her upper body as well as her legs, but it would also burn fat off her hips and thighs. She would get bigger above the waist, but stay about the same down below. The result would be a higher CG, and better jumps."

"OK, if that's what it takes, she'll do it."

"Has she ever been injured?"

"Just bumps and bruises."

"Anything that made her stop skating for a while?"

"No."

"Sprains or pulled muscles?"

"No."

"Is she built like you?"

"People say we could pass for sisters!" Millie said, grinning. "Of course, she doesn't have my boobs yet."

Dean smiled. No sixteen-year-old girl could possibly look as voluptuous as this woman. "If she looks like you at sixteen," Dean said, "She must be the prom queen!" Pleased by his compliment, Millie smiled.

"Since she doesn't have the narrow hips and shoulders most girl jumpers have," Dean continued, "She won't rotate as fast. She'd have to jump higher, to stay in the air longer, to make three turns. That requires leg strength, and that only comes if you have strong tendons." He paused. "May I examine one of your ankles, Madam?" he asked.

The Examination

A grin slowly developed on the woman's face. Moving slowly and deliberately she reached down and slipped off her right shoe, then she extended her stocking-clad foot to him under the table. Dean cupped her heel in his right palm and grasped her Achilles tendon between his thumb and forefinger.

"Small tendons are the bane of figure skating," he said. "It seems the Foster women have tendons like suspension bridge cables."

Millie smiled. "Is there anything else about . . ." Foster women anatomy' you'd like to know, Sir?" she asked with a coy smile.

"Well, weak joints are always a problem. Your ankles are substantial. Perhaps I could examine your knee?"

"Help yourself, Doctor," she said, shifting slightly to yield him access to her right knee. Dean supported her foot with his left hand while his right hand slipped slowly upward, following the tendon into her calf muscle, which he squeezed, and then on to her knee. He pressed the woman's knee between his thumb and fingers. "You have quite a sizeable joint here, Madam," he observed. Then he rolled her kneecap around beneath the skin, squeezing the tendons that came out of it at top and bottom.

"Push down with your heel," he requested. Millie complied, forcing two tendons to pop up on the backside of her knee. Dean felt them and the muscle in between.

"Are you making a pass at me, Mr. Steele?" she grinned, eyeing him wryly.

"Madam, I expect you have enough 'pass receiver' experience to judge that for yourself." She smiled. Then he moved his hand back to her foot.

"Are you a student of reflexology, Young Man?" she asked.

"Why, no," he said, partially suppressing a wry grin. "It's not on my curriculum." He hooked his thumb around her big toe and pulled down gently until he felt a slight "bursting." According to the science of reflexology this stimulates the pituitary gland, releasing her hormones. Then he gently massaged the point on the bottom of her foot that supposedly connects to her ovaries. Grinning subtly, she gave him a "shame on you" look. He then gently pressed the point on the inside of her ankle that supposedly corresponds to her uterus.

"My goodness," she said, "I'm being seduced in public!"

Vaguely embarrassed by his flirtatious behavior, Dean released the woman's foot from his grip. "How are her spins?" He asked as she slipped the gold-tipped shoe back on her foot.

"Great," she said. "She spins like a top, really fast and always right in one spot. And her position is marvelous on laybacks and sit-spins. She can even do a Biellman[5]."

"How are her school figures?"

"Very good. She practices figures once a week. Besides, figures aren't compulsory anymore, even for singles."

"True, but they still call it 'figure skating'. She'll need to skate figures more than once a week to keep the edge precision and ankle strength she needs."

"You know, this sounds like the conversation I'd be having with a prospective coach for Shannon, not a pairs partner."

"I expect, in my case," he said, "The line between partner and coach might sometimes blur. I've been around this game long enough to form a few opinions about what works and what doesn't. Maybe that's something you'd have a problem with."

Millie paused, not to decide, but to formulate her answer. "One advantage of having you is we get both a partner and a coach for the same price." She gave him a cocky smile.

Dean grinned. "Always the bargain hunter," he mused. "I'll bet you clip coupons, too."

Millie laughed. "Heavens, no! I just use plastic money." They laughed.

Then Millie's face took on a mischievous grin. "Are you always this forward with strange women you've just met, Mr. Steele?" she asked. Dean was somewhat taken aback by her question. "I mean," she continued, reading the confusion on his face, "You've known me less than an hour and you've already massaged my foot and fondled my knee." She was grinning subtly at the challenge she had issued.

Dean thought for only a moment before deciding to throw the challenging tease back at her. "Normally not," he replied. "I seldom encounter a woman so . . . easy." He grinned victoriously. Since her face registered amusement rather than insult, he decided to push it a bit farther. "Quite early on I spotted you as both naïve and vulnerable, a tender lamb ready for slaughter. I knew that some trumped up talk of tendons and joints would almost certainly get my hands on you, and from there the rest would be easy."

"It sounds as though you already have me seduced, Sir," she said coyly.

"I think we both recognize the irony in that, Madam," He said, returning to seriousness. "I could never compete at your level."

"It's all part and parcel of 'Ice Mom,' I'm afraid," she said. "We domineering stage mothers have to submit to all manner of degradation in the name of our daughters' skating."

"Lucky for us," Dean said, "The dirty old men's club." They laughed.

About Dean

"You call your Mustang 'Matilda,'" Millie said, changing the subject. "You rebuilt the engine yourself. It's a hot rod. Very fast."

"You work for the FBI?" Dean asked, looking at the woman with a puzzled squint.

"No," she grinned, "But I have a copy of just about everything that's ever been written about you," she replied. "I even have a Dean Steele scrapbook." She looked at him across the small table. Her eyes seemed to ask, "What do you think about that?" Dean looked at her with slightly raised eyebrows. "I'm serious," she said. "I spent one whole afternoon copying all your performances onto one video cassette." A girlish smile looked out of place on this intensely professional woman's face as she sipped her coffee. "I'll admit it," she grinned, "I'm a fan."

Dean tried to decide if he was being manipulated, or if she was completely sincere. He couldn't, but he knew this was more nearly the real Millie Foster he was now seeing. He had kept her off-guard during their earlier conversation. Now she was in control again, cool and professional. He marveled at the difference in her deportment.

"So, what do you think of my idea?" Millie asked, changing the subject again. She was more relaxed now, her confidence and control fully returned. Dean sensed that she was convinced she would have her way, no matter how long it took.

"Well, I haven't seen your daughter skate," he said. "And I don't know if she has the discipline required to get ready for a contest like Nationals." He paused. "I hear she's spoiled and self-centered." He eyed her with a challenging grin.

"Don't worry," Millie replied. "She'll do fine. She's a very tough competitor, and she loves to skate. She works like a horse, too." Dean sensed that Millie believed that, but would have said it even if she had not. "Even though she does sometimes frustrate her mother," Millie admitted.

Stage Mother

"It concerns me that this is not her idea," Dean said, peering into her eyes.

"I know what you must think," Millie said, addressing the objection with professional salesmanship. "You think I'm the overbearing stage mother, pushing my daughter into a career she doesn't want." She looked at Dean, waiting for him to respond. He refused to allow his face to communicate either agreement or disagreement. "All right, I do take an interest in Shannon. Any mother would. I just want her to be happy . . . and to have the career she deserves. I'm only trying to help her."

Dean looked at her gritting his teeth to keep his countenance as near expressionless as he could.

"OK," she said, laughing. "I guess I just gave the classic stage mother speech, didn't I? It sounded just like Rose in 'Gypsy'."

"Act two, scene six, I believe," Dean said grinning. He had exploited Millie's weakness. She was a compulsive talker. She couldn't tolerate silence in a conversation and would compulsively fill it with an awkward comment.

"OK, you win," Millie admitted. "But let me say in my own defense that Shannon and I are very close, and my 'stage mother' influence has worked out quite well for her, thank you very much!"

"I'm sure it has," Dean said, a hint of sarcasm tipping off less than total agreement.

Millie was amused by his mildly audacious response. "You've only seen bad stage mothers in action," she said. "You've just never seen 'stage mother' played well." She smiled victoriously.

"OK," Dean said, indicating some remaining skepticism. "Maybe there is such a thing as a 'good' stage mother." He smiled.

"I knew you'd be like this," Millie blurted. "It's so consistent with the way you skate. Silent but powerful. Taking control, but not exerting it overtly. And that annoying self-confidence that falls just shy of conceit!" She looked into his eyes and smiled warmly. "When you skate, it's like you're the bad little boy who just raided the cookie jar and got away with it. And you just wink at the audience because they know you ate that cookie, and you are absolutely unrepentant! You skate around just for the fun of it, doing what feels good. You might pop a triple jump, or even a back flip, for God's sake, just for fun. Or you might just skate a lap around the arena as fast as you can, but nobody's going to tell you what to do!"

Finally Millie caught herself. "Look at what you're doing to me," she said. "You're charming me . . . disarming me, keeping me off guard. You've got me babbling like a schoolgirl." She gave him a vulnerable smile.

"You sell, don't you?" Dean said, realizing he was watching skillful salesmanship in action. This woman was accustomed to negotiating what she wanted, and, from the looks of things, generally getting it.

"No, I manage an office downtown."

"Then, I was wrong. You don't sell. You negotiate for a living."

"It would be perfect," Millie continued. "You and Shannon together would charm the pants off the audience and the judges. She can skate 'sweet and innocent,' or she can skate 'bitch.' She's a born show-off. She's always the center of attention." Millie drifted off into a private fantasy of flowers being thrown onto ice and medals being hung around necks.

Despite the carefully planned sales pitch, Dean detected a basis of sincerity beneath her maneuvering. Her concern for her daughter's happiness seemed genuine, though perhaps somewhat misguided. Dean believed happiness could only come from making one's own decisions, no matter how well intentioned a domineering parent might be.

Dean's Past

Abruptly, Millie awoke from her dream and returned her attention to the coffee shop. She stared into Dean's eyes.

"Why did you quit?" she asked. She seemed only briefly embarrassed by the boldness of her inquiry. "I was just sure you would win a medal at the U. S. Nationals in '92 and go to the Olympics at Albertville."

Dean was reluctant to be overly influenced by Millie's expressed interest in him, but yet it seemed somewhat more than simply a ploy to get him to agree to her plan.

"I fell in love," he answered.

"Who is she?" Millie asked, grinning with piqued interest. "What kind of girl captured the heart of Dean Steele, the cold and powerful ice-man?"

"Engineering," Dean replied. "I got into my junior year at UT[7] and found out there's a whole different world out there."

Millie's face registered surprise. "What's so special about engineering?"

"It's being able to control the physical universe." He became more animated. "First you learn the rules, then you decide what you want to happen, then you use your knowledge of the rules to make it happen. And it always does. It's amazing to be able to build a three-mile bridge, or put a satellite in orbit so that it sits directly above one point on Earth. It's almost like being God."

"It sounds like skating to me," Millie said, pleased with herself for finally bringing her quarry out of his shell. "You decide what medal you want, you work up your routine, and you go out and get it."

"There's a difference," Dean said. "With engineering, you are working with the laws of nature. Those are God's laws, and they always work—precisely." He inhaled.

"With skating, the rules are made and administered by humans. By volunteer judges, often from nine different countries. And there's no consistency to what they do. They can't see the whole arena from where they sit. They can't use video replays. They're biased toward their own country. Some are even dishonest. All in all, it's a bit of a mess."

"I know," Millie said. "But it works. I mean somebody always wins."

"Sure, but who? How is it decided?" He sighed. "You work your butt off for six months developing a program. Then you have four and a half minutes, under intense pressure, to skate it perfectly. If you screw up, you lose instantly, and rightly so. But if you do well, and other skaters do too, then it's up to nine biased people, and a ridiculous scoring system, to sort out the winners and losers."

Millie stared at him intently as he paused.

"One day, sitting in a structural mechanics class, I found out what engineering is really like," he continued. It's like having God sitting at the judges' table. Right then I realized I wanted no part of a sport based on such a shaky foundation. So I quit. Right then."

"But you still skate," Millie observed. "You must not have deserted the sport completely."

"Now I skate because it gives me a quiet place to think. I like quiet time alone. I work out all kinds of understanding when I'm alone. And when I skate, I'm totally alone. And it's peaceful. Hell, that's why I started skating in the first place. Competition was merely a distraction for me."

"Well," Millie said, "I wish you hadn't quit. I loved to watch you skate your programs."

Secret Passion

Bolstered by Dean's sudden openness, she began to speak more frankly. "Sometimes, when I'm at home by myself, I put your tape on the big-screen TV, turn the sound up loud and watch you skate for hours."

She stared deeply into his eyes. "I get a physical reaction," she admitted. "I get goose bumps. Sometimes it makes me shiver and tingle all over." She paused, looked down at her hands, then back at him. "You have so much power on the ice. It's amazing. No other skater has ever touched me like that."

Dean paused to visualize this woman, sitting alone in her expensive home, watching his ten-year-old videos on a big-screen TV.

She blushed. "You know . . . I never thought I would even meet you in person, much less end up telling you about my secret passion."

Although he knew he was the target of a determined sales campaign, Dean sensed that her admission had been sincere. He sensed that it had been both painful and enjoyable for her to tell him about her fascination with him and his skating. Although somewhat embarrassed by her confession, Millie was now considerably more relaxed with her secret out of the way.

"I hope you can understand why I was a little less than candid when I first approached you," she said. "If I had hit you with the whole enchilada all at once, you would have run for the hills to get away from this crazy woman."

"No," Dean said, "It's not so bad to find out that someone appreciates what you've done."

"I really think you cheated the sport by dropping out. You had a special mark to leave on skating. You could have sent it back in the right direction."

"What direction is that?" He looked intently at her, preventing any evasion.

Millie inhaled. "Romance!" she said. "Real romance. Boys and girls. Love! Lust! All the things that make life real."

"As opposed to what?" he probed.

"As opposed to aging fags in fluffy collars acting like silly schoolgirls," she replied bluntly. "As opposed to pairs skaters who don't seem to notice each other and ice dancers portraying some ridiculous parody of male/female love, when the real thing is so beautiful."

"I see," Dean said.

Why did you Quit?

"So, why did you quit? I mean really. What happened to turn you away from the sport you love? And don't try to convince me you don't love it."

"Well, it became clear that I wasn't likely to win any medals, no matter how well I skated. And people who don't win medals don't leave marks."

Millie looked into his eyes. "What really happened that drove you away from your sport?" She seemed to know that his earlier explanation had only scratched the surface. "Come on, Dean, level with me. God knows I've bared my soul to you!"

Dean sighed as he resigned himself to telling her the truth. This woman was very persuasive. "Because of the way I'm built," he began, "I sometimes attract attention from the gay guys in the sport. Most of the gays are really nice people, but they have their share of nut cases too." He paused. "It's well-known that I'm straight, but every once in a while one of the fairies decides he's the one destined to convert me to the joys of queerdom."

"Oops," Millie interjected. "Big mistake!"

"Some years back," he continued, "One of the male judges decided he wanted me as his lover. He told some of his gay friends about it, and they told some friends, and pretty soon everybody but me was in on the little secret. I was civil toward him at first, partly because he was a judge, so he thought I was warming up to him. When I finally saw what his intentions were, I was disgusted and upset. I told him to buzz off, and it embarrassed him in front of his friends. He became very bitter after that."

"So you had an enemy at the judges table?"

Dean sighed. "It was worse than that, actually. He didn't just mark me down on his own sheet. He spread vicious lies about me throughout the judging community. Made-up stories about what a poor example of an athlete I am. He recruited his friends into an 'anti-Dean' campaign. He got some really damaging statements into newspaper articles, things that were pure fantasy. Not exaggerations of the truth, but complete and total fabrications."

"Like what?"

"One reporter friend of his wrote that I was ill-tempered and mean, and that I had injured several hockey players in a bar fight. He said at the Broadmoor invitational that I skated like a goalie, and I looked more like a gorilla swinging through the trees than a figure skater. He actually said my knuckles dragged on the ice."

"My God! How did that make you feel?"

"It didn't do much for my self-confidence, or my reputation either, for that matter. I tried not to let it affect me, but it did. I actually two-footed a double Axel at the Nationals in '91 because he was glaring at me from the stands. I know that's why, and I hate myself for letting it happen."

"That's terrible. You might have taken the gold."

"The worst part was that I developed this reputation inside the judging circles, as a clumsy oaf who ought be playing hockey instead of figure skating. He complained so long and loud about my skating that each judge was afraid to give me good marks, for fear of voting out of line with the other judges."

"What do you mean?"

"After hearing him rag about my skating, they expected I would get low marks. Then, if one gave me good marks, he would look stupid because his marks were out of line with the others. With each judge thinking that way, the marks came in consistently two to three tenths below where they should have been, based on my skating. After that, if any one judge had given me decent marks, he would have been called on the carpet by the ISU representative. Of course that just proved it, then, and it became common knowledge that Dean Steele is 'not as good as he looks'."

Millie shook her head. "Your marks always seemed low to me, but I thought I was just in love with your skating and probably missing some technical points that the judges could see."

"Maybe so, but I've studied the tapes, and there are definite cases where another skater clearly made more errors and got higher marks from most of the judges. I'm being objective here. It's not just sour grapes. It's not supposed to happen, but it did."

"Anyway, when I discovered that engineering is largely devoid of those vagaries and human frailties, I decided to invest my effort there. Now I just skate to be alone."

"That's so sad," Millie said. "So sad for the sport. You had so much to give it." Her face sagged briefly.

"Did you ever try to get back at him?" She had recovered her objective demeanor.

"I tried once to talk with him, maybe establish a truce, but by then he was so bitter, and so intent on my destruction, that I realized it was hopeless. I never could find a way to counteract what he was doing behind my back." He paused. "There was one thing, though."

"What was that?"

"At one point he found out he was HIV-positive. He planned to keep it a secret, out of shame, I guess, and maybe so as not to cramp his love life. But shortly after he was told, I found out too, from a friend who worked at the clinical lab in the Medical Center. I happened to see him, the judge, in the parking lot the next day, so I walked up to him and said, 'We're gonna miss you.' That's all I said, but I said it like I knew what was happening, and it had quite an effect on him. He didn't think anyone knew about it. But he assumed if I did, everyone did. And this almost made it seem, if you're at all superstitious, like I had something to do with it. Anyway, he soon went public with it, and he kind of dropped out of skating after that. I heard he died a few years back."

"I knew there must have been something pretty serious to make you quit."

The Pairs Team

They got in Millie's Mercedes and drove back to Willie's Ice Palace where Dean's Mustang was parked.

"So, what do you think of my idea?" she asked. "Would you consider competing again, or are you too far gone?" Millie knew the challenging remark would stir his competitive nature.

"I don't know." Dean sensed that not even a flat refusal would deter this woman. She was determined to implement her plan, and would do whatever it took to make it happen.

"Well, I think you and Shannon would make a terrific pairs team. The audience would just love you both."

"I'd need to see her skate," Dean said pensively. "That would be the next step."

"She has a lesson, just before the 5:30 public skate session tomorrow at the Texas Ice Stadium. Check her out."

"Let me think about it overnight and call you tomorrow," he said. "Where can I reach you?"

"Oh, I'll call you," she said. "I know your number."

Reflection

After returning home, Dean pondered the evening's events. His life rarely brought him in contact with rich people—those who, by effort, skill, or blind luck, had come to control substantial wealth and then chose to indulge themselves in it. He had little in common with them, and he envied them even less.

This woman was wealthy, beautiful, strong-minded, and very sexy—obviously quite a good catch for the fortunate Mr. Foster. She represented almost everything he disliked about contemporary American culture—mindless chatter on cell phones and afternoons spent at shopping malls spending money on faddish items that serve no real purpose. But still he found her interesting, perhaps because she went to so much trouble to be a caricature of the Nuevo Riche.

Dean vaguely regretted his boldness in examining her ankle and knee. It was particularly unprofessional of him to make that reflexology play, even though it was done in jest. If there was to be a professional relationship with her and her daughter, he wasn't getting it off to a very good start. If she had indeed been following his press, she would know of his reputation as an unpolished renegade. He had done little to correct that impression. Still, he considered the odds to be varnishingly small that anything substantial would develop out of Mrs. Foster's skating fantasy. So what if some rich woman from River Oaks considered him crude? It wouldn't bother him if all the women in River Oaks hated him.

He was amused that Mrs. Foster would tease him about touching her knee, as if it were some great privilege for a commoner to touch the queen. But she had, on two occasions, accused him of flirting with her. She had even stretched the point to do so. Perhaps, arriving in her late thirties, she was having to confront the twilight of her youth and beauty. Perhaps having a championship skater, unmarried and ten years her junior, make a play for her filled some need that diamonds and furs couldn't satisfy. Whatever her psychological situation, he had to admit he enjoyed flirting with the wealthy woman from River Oaks.

On several occasions over the next 24 hours Dean noticed his thoughts returning to his encounter with the Ice Queen from River Oaks. There was something intriguing about her, and he could not spot exactly what it was. Something had captured his attention and reserved a small part of his thoughts for this woman. She kept returning to his mind at odd moments.

Surely an ice mom, even a wealthy one, deserved no special place in his mind. She was a fan of his past skating, but he had long since ceased to be affected by that kind of attention. She was intelligent, a skilled conversationalist and a worthy opponent in verbal jousting, but that still did not explain it.

Slowly Dean began to realize what it was. In a number of subtle ways she was . . . sexy. Very sexy. Of course she had the obvious assets: large bosom, trim waist, broad hips, and the mandatory fluffy blonde hair. But that failed to explain the uniqueness of her appeal. It was the whole package, he reasoned. It was the look of her, the sound of her, the scent of her, the moves, the facial expressions, that all added up to captivate the attention of a man. He could not be in her vicinity without primitive regions of his brain responding to her as a potential sex partner. Whether it was deliberate or unintentional on her part he did not know, though he suspected it was no accident.

Dean was mildly amused by this. He was normally attracted to women slightly younger than he. That this older woman would so stick in his mind was a curiosity.

But he had responded to her. He had flirted with her, almost as he might have with a younger, unmarried woman.

Perhaps, he reasoned, her age brought with it experience, and she could more fully appreciate the points he was making than a younger woman might. She had a knack for making him feel comfortable, even safe around her. Perhaps this paved the way for a brief flirtation. Still, he couldn't deny that this older woman had something arresting about her, something that made him enjoy the time spent in her presence, something that calmed and comforted him.

"Maybe I just miss my mommy," he chided himself. But he quickly realized that the promise of maternal nurturing was not what attracted him to Mrs. Foster. Through the mist he could see pure sexual desire at the base of his attraction to her. He sensed that something buried deep in his brain had been stirred by this woman, possibly for the first time in his life.

All of this was merely interesting, though, since it was unlikely that he would ever see her again, and even if he did, little in the way of personal interaction would ever come of it. But he couldn't deny that her interest in him, and her patient understanding of his past defeats at the hands of figure skating had comforted him. And for some reason, or perhaps many reasons, she was sexy—very sexy.

A Call from Millie

At 10:15 the next morning his phone rang.

"You're going to do it, I just know it," Millie's voice said. "I've been dreaming about it all night."

Dean inhaled. "OK, I'm willing to check it out, watch her skate, see if it looks like it might work. But I seriously doubt that it will make any sense in the long haul."

"Great! Here's what you need to do. Strike up a conversation with her at the rink and take it from there. You can lead her into skating with you, and then broach the idea of competing together."

"Wait a minute," Dean said. "You said you would talk her into it. Now are you saying you want me to . . . 'pick her up' at the rink?"

"I think it would be better if you struck up a friendship with her first. That way it wouldn't seem like an arranged partnership. She's very independent-minded. She would accept it better that way."

"You're changing the rules on me, Lady. Now you've got me caught up in a plot of intrigue, here. This is shaping up like a con game now."

"Oh, don't be so dramatic! I know what's best for her. I'm her mother. This way it'll just avoid her getting all upset for a little while. Besides, she'll feel better about it if she thinks it's her idea, not mine."

"I'd like it better if we all went into this with eyes open and cards on the table," he said. "I wouldn't want a partnership that started out on a deception."

"Nobody's deceiving anybody. Just pick her up at the rink and let your interest in skating lead to a partnership. She'll be there for her freestyle lesson this afternoon from 4:30 till 5:30."

Dean felt like he was being pushed into the role of the dirty old man, slyly entrapping an innocent girl ten years his junior, and doing so in collusion with her mother. He had misgivings about it, but it was an interesting prospect. He figured there would be more surprises in store for him if he became involved with this family, and life was a bit dull at that point, anyway.

---

1. Triple Lutz—A jump in which the skater, while skating backward on a left outside edge, digs in her right toe-pick, jumps into the air, rotates three times to the left, and lands on the right foot, skating backward on an outside edge. Named for Alois Lutz who invented the single Lutz jump.
2. USFSA—United States Figure Skating Association, the body that regulates top-level figure skating competition in the United States. It is headquartered in Colorado Springs, Colorado.
3. ISU—International Skating Union, the body that regulates top-level figure skating competition in the world.
4. IOC—International Olympic Committee, the body that regulates competition in the Olympic games.
5. Biellman spin—The skater spins upright on one foot, holding the other foot, with her hand, in position behind her head. Named for its inventor, Denise Biellman.
6. Skater Nancy Kerrigan was clubbed on the knee at the Detroit Ice Arena on January 6, 1996 by an associate of Tonya Harding's ex-husband.
7. UT—The University of Texas at Austin.

Chapter 2

Shannon

Dean wasn't quite finished adding the new image enhancement capability to the Accumedical Data Systems software package when it came time to leave to meet the skater girl. He hated to leave the program unfinished overnight, but he sighed and saved his files and shut down his computer anyway.

During the brief drive from his office to the Texas Ice Stadium Dean wondered why he was doing this. Some frantic ice mom wanted a partner for her sixteen-year-old daughter. What are the odds that he would give up his programming job, and graduate school, to go back into competitive figure skating? "Approximately zero," he thought.

He formed an image of the girl in his mind as he drove. He had known a lot of girl skaters over the years. He knew this one had medaled at Junior Nationals. He figured her skating was probably competent but uninspired. Girls at sixteen don't skate with emotion. Mostly they are too busy remembering what move comes next and regretting the last mistake. It's like a recital with Mom and Dad in the audience—just get through the routine with a minimum of errors.

Dean pictured what Mrs. Foster might have looked like at sixteen. She could have been quite a gangly teenager before her body filled out as it had so well. He figured she was a "late bloomer," a swan in adulthood who sprang forth from an ugly duckling teenager. What do girls look like at sixteen anyway? He tried to remember. Braces? Pimples? Flat chests?

Dean realized this mission was a waste of time. Reluctantly, he had to admit to himself that he was only doing it to mollify the very persuasive rich woman from River Oaks. She was, one could say, entertaining, and, somehow, he wanted to see her again. This was the price he had to pay for another encounter with this woman whose appeal he could not quite identify. He felt even worse after that realization. "She's a married woman, Dean!" he chided himself. Besides, he didn't particularly care for rich people.

He considered turning the car around and going back to finish up the program. He could tell Mrs. Foster that he had to work late on an important project and couldn't make it. He knew, though, that she would not be deterred. She would simply set up another time for him to watch her daughter skate. He resigned himself to go through the motions. Nothing less would deter this determined woman. He took the FM 2351 exit off the Gulf freeway and pulled into the parking lot at TIS.

The Girl

Dean sat in the upstairs lounge at the Texas Ice Stadium and watched four skate school groups and three private lessons. It was no trouble to spot the girl who had medaled at Junior Nationals. Besides the coaches, she was the only one who looked to be as comfortable skating as she would have been walking. Anyway, Millie had shown him her picture.

Dean watched Shannon Foster skate for a while before he decided whether or not he would approach the girl. She flowed smoothly and gracefully across the ice, confident and competent in her moves. Her edging was silent and solid, and there was a minimum of snow kicked up as her blades cut clean groves in the frozen surface. While the other skaters wore looks of intense concentration as they practiced their moves, this girl looked like she was doing it for fun, and without thinking about it.

She was well-proportioned with long arms and legs, and her height accentuated her grace. She had good strength and timing. She was very shapely for a teenage skater. Her relatively broad shoulders rose from a small waist that sat above well-rounded hips and thighs. Her bustline, Dean noticed was quite ample, a rarity for a skater. He could see how this recent development, obviously inherited from her mother, would affect her ability to jump.

He imagined her in pairs competition or ice dancing. Millie had a point. Shannon's style was well suited for it. Her build was appealing too, but she had a good four inches and twenty pounds on most of the tiny girls that skate pairs. She could dance, but the emphasis in competitive ice dancing is on footwork, and this would not allow her to put her athletic abilities into practice. Pairs skating would be a better vehicle for her, he thought, but it would require a very strong partner to lift and toss this sizeable young woman.

There was another thing. More than once Dean saw it flash into view briefly, then disappear. It was a special look, an extraordinary combination of grace and beauty that Dean called "the magic." It would ignite like an invisible blue glow around the girl and then vanish just as quickly.

"The magic" is a rare commodity that few skaters can produce, but it can be devastating to an audience. It can hit an observer like a sledge-hammer blow to the upper chest. It transforms figure skating into an emotional experience as the watcher is swept up by the skater and carried out onto the ice in his mind. Dean recalled watching Elizabeth North, when she was in top form, light up the ice with her magic. It only happened when she was in the perfect state of mind. She would lose herself in the emotion of the music and the skating and grab the audience by the heartstrings, leading them around the arena like so many children following a pied piper. The experience left them dazed and drained—the esthetic equivalent of a sexual experience.

The beauty of Elizabeth North's skating had brought a lump to his throat and a tear to his eye on more than one occasion, although he never let her know she was the only one who could do it. They were dating at the time, a poorly kept secret in competitive figure skating circles. Liz, a Canadian champion, had gone on to skate professionally, and he was programming computers. She took it hard when he decided to quit skating, and they broke up soon after. Often he had wondered what might have happened if had he not hung up his blades, but never did he regret it. His temperament was that of an engineer, not an artist. He would never fit in with the pro skating crowd.

Seeing a brief glimpse of the magic rekindled his affection, all but forgotten, for the esthetic, athletic sport of figure skating. Memories of tear-stained faces that he had encountered as he left the ice came peeking back into his memory. It was a world about as remote from computer programming as one could imagine, but it had always refused to leave him alone. A vague mixture of joy and pain circulated through his thoughts as he tried to press these memories out of his mind.

Though totally unaware of it, this girl had the ability to unleash a powerful emotional force inside an ice rink. Probably she would never develop it to any useful proportion. That brief glimmer would most likely die quietly in the vagaries of a teenager's attention span. Perhaps basketball would snuff out the glow. Or maybe just "hanging at the mall" would be sufficient to kill it. Dean shook his head as he thought how many hard-working professional skaters would gladly die for ten minutes of this magic. It seemed a waste that God had squandered it on a brat from River Oaks.

Meeting Shannon

At the end of the lesson period, Dean waited to see if Shannon would take off her skates. If so, he would arrange to "bump into" her for a brief conversation before she left the arena. But there was a public skating period next, and it soon became obvious that she would stay and use the time to practice after her lesson.

Dean put on his skates and made a few warm-up laps around the arena. "Hi," he said, skating up to where Shannon Foster stood beside the boards. "Can you help me out? I'm working on my jumps, and I need someone to spot me on a couple."

"Sure," she said, looking at the husky skater. "What do you need?"

"Just watch a couple of my jumps and notice if my arms are level on the rollout or if my blade comes down off-edge and skids on the landing."

She watched him do three double jumps. The first one was a double toe loop and Dean deliberately lowered his left arm. She pointed it out to him. On the second jump, a double Lutz, he held his arms level but skidded his left skate on the rollout. She pointed that out to him as well. His third one, a double loop, was properly done.

"That was a good one," she said. "How about checking out my camel for me?" She was acknowledging that she and Dean were the only elite competitive skaters on the ice.

"Go for it!" he said.

She skated around and went into a camel spin in front of him. He watched her as she dropped into a sit spin, then rose into a layback spin. Her spinning was both fast and long in duration. Her skate stayed precisely in one spot on the ice as she whirled, and her position was very good.

"That was pretty good," Dean said, sensing that she was proud of her spins. He figured that she was more showing him her spins than seeking advice.

She beamed. "Nothing to improve?"

"The only thing you might try would be to throw your head back a little more, and point your toe harder on the layback. That might make it look a little more sexy." Dean didn't critique her spins very strenuously, since his purpose was to get acquainted, not to train the girl.

She was surprised that Dean had come up with a critique. She looked at him puzzled, then skated away. For an instant he thought he had lost her. Soon she came back around and did a layback spin in front of him, this time with head fully back and toe pointed. It looked good.

"Bravo!" Dean said when her spinning stopped. "Now, there was a sexy camel!" She grinned, indicating that the idea of looking sexy appealed to her. "Wanna take a break?" Dean asked. "I'll buy the Gatorade."

"Sure," she said. They put on skate guards and tromped over to the cold drink vending machine.

Introductions

During the break they sat in white molded plastic chairs on the thick black rubber mat alongside the arena. They could see the skaters through the scarred Plexiglas shield that protected the fans from flying hockey pucks.

"By the way," he said, "My name is Dean Steele."

"I'm Shannon Foster," she said. "I live over in River Oaks."

"Do you compete?" he asked.

"Yeah, Junior Ladies. I silvered at Nationals last year. You?"

"Senior men, back when dinosaurs roamed the earth," he said. "Before your parents were born."

She grinned at his joke. "Win anything?"

"A little bit of cheap metal at Nationals," he said. "Nothing very shiny."

She grinned at his modesty. "I don't recall seeing you here before. Where do you skate?"

"I usually hang out at the Lone Star Ice Palace in South Houston. It's not near as fancy as this, but the owner is a good guy. He gives me ice sometimes."

"He lets you skate for free?"

"No. He lets me have the sheet from five to six AM all by myself. That way I can jump and skate at full speed without running over a bunch of kids." He turned to face the girl. "He shuts down at ten-thirty and Zams the ice and shuts off the refrigeration until the surface softens. Then he refreezes it slowly overnight. By five it's barely frozen and perfect for figure skating. Soft and smooth, like liquid glass."

"That sounds really neat, but the ice here goes for two hundred and fifty bucks an hour. Why does he let you have it for free?"

"Well, I pitch in and drive the Zamboni for him sometimes. I've done other favors for him too. He's a friend. I think he's kinda adopted me as a charity case. Besides, his ice is less expensive, and nobody else wants it at 5:00 AM anyway."

"I'd like to try that soft ice sometime," Shannon said. "They keep it pretty hard here for the hockey crowd. Could you get me in?"

"Sure. It's my time," he said. "I could have a broomball tournament in there if I wanted to."

"What a waste of good ice that would be!" she said. They laughed.

First Dance

They had just about finished their break when the "couples ice dance" skating session was announced. "Wanna show these folks a thing or two?" Dean asked her. He knew she had passed most of the USFSA compulsory dance tests.

She smiled. "Sure."

They took to the ice and skated together in the Kilian position[1]. The music was a ¾ time waltz. Without speaking, Dean led her into the waltz position[2], with her skating backward. Then they started to turn, alternating who was skating backward. As they gained confidence, they skated faster and faster, passing the other couples on the ice and leaning deeply into the turns. They moved to the music, expressing the nuances of the melody with the movement of their bodies.

"You're smooth," Shannon said, noticing his perfect ice dance posture and the fact that he skated without ever taking his eyes off her.

"Dutch Waltz?" Dean asked her, knowing that she had long ago passed the USFSA test on this preliminary-level dance.

"Of course," She said, smiling. They did the sixteen steps of this simple dance two times through.

"Willow Waltz?" he asked, suggesting a bronze level dance.

"Anytime," she replied. They skated this twenty-two step dance twice through. Their bodies moved in synchrony as they glided swiftly around the arena. Most of the other skaters stopped to watch them move. Soon all eyes were on them as the arena was lined with stopped skaters. Few of them had ever seen ice dancing of this quality, except on television.

"American Waltz?" he asked, suggesting the more difficult silver level dance.

27

"Of course," she said, smiling confidently. They skated this sixteen-step dance twice through. The steps of this dance are simple, but the amount of rotation involved makes it difficult to skate correctly. With Dean's strong lead, Shannon felt confident in the dance, and they whirled smoothly around the rink.

"Viennese Waltz?" he asked, suggesting the waltz at the gold level.

"OK," she said, now somewhat less confident at skating this more difficult dance with a new partner.

Dean led her gracefully through the twenty-four steps of the dance, and then rolled out into straight skating.

"Let's do that one again," Shannon said, pleased with how smooth it had felt. They repeated the sequence then skated over to the boards to catch their breath. The stopped skaters who lined the rink applauded. After about a minute the music stopped, as did most of the skaters.

"Tango time," the announcement came over the public address system. The skaters looked at Shannon and Dean.

"I think we're on," Dean said. They skated out to a starting position as tango music flowed from the speakers.

"Canasta Tango?" Dean asked, figuring they would start with the simplest tango, the one at the preliminary test level. Shannon merely smiled. They skated the simple fourteen-step dance twice through. They skated the slightly more difficult pre-bronze level Fiesta Tango, and then the silver-level Tango. "Shall we go to Argentina for the gold?" Dean asked, suggesting the rather complex gold-level Argentine Tango.

"Why not? Shannon replied. They skated this difficult thirty-one-step dance twice through. They were not quite as smooth doing the cross-foot stroking and deep edging required by this challenging dance, but their audience didn't know the difference.

"Enough is enough for me," Dean said as they rolled out of the second sequence of steps. As they made their way to the opening in the boards, the assembly applauded again. As they tromped back to the benches, Millie came trotting up excitedly, with a video camera and bouncing boobs.

"That was just beautiful!" she exclaimed. "I got it all on video. Your dad will be so excited!" Then she looked at Dean. "Who's your friend, Shannon?"

"Oh, Mama, this is . . ." She looked at him blankly. "I don't remember your name."

"I'm Dean," he said. "Dean Steele." Millie stuck out her hand and Dean shook it. "I'm Millie Foster," she said, "Shannon's mother." Millie looked at Shannon. Y'all looked like you've been skating together for years. I thought it was Gordeeva and Grinkov out there."

"Grinkov's dead, Mother," Shannon replied.

Millie gave her a frown. "Why didn't you tell me you had a freedance partner?"

"I only met him five minutes ago, Mother," Shannon said, with an edge of teenager's disgust in her voice. Millie ignored it.

"Well, y'all looked wonderful. Everybody thought so. Did you hear 'em? They applauded you!"

Shannon was becoming embarrassed by Millie's gushing. "It was no big deal, Mother," she said. "We were just skating together. Just doing regular stuff."

"Wait till your Dad sees this. He'll be so impressed!"

"Young man," Millie said, looking at Dean, "Would you like to come over to our house for dinner tonight? You could meet Shannon's father and watch the premier of my video of y'all skating together."

Dean looked at Shannon. She gave him a sheepish look and a smile that seemed to say, "That's my Mom. She's always doing stuff like this." Dean took that as an invitation from the girl as well.

"Thanks. I think I'd like that," he said.

"Good," said Millie, "I'll go on ahead. Shannon, you ride with . . . Dean, and show him how to get there." She left in a flurry of excitement.

"Your Mom's a whirlwind," Dean said. Shannon rolled her eyes. "Does she do this a lot?"

"Do what?"

"Hand you off to strange men she doesn't know."

"I guess she figures if you're a skater, you're OK."

"I've known a lot of skaters," he said, "And very few of 'em are what I'd call 'OK.'"

"Good point," she laughed. "Am I in big trouble?"

"Quite possibly," Dean said. "We'll know when we see how bad that video looks. It could well be the end of your skating career." They laughed.

The Ride to River Oaks

Shannon and Dean traded skating boots for street shoes and went out to his Mustang.

"Cool wheels!" Shannon said as Dean unlocked the door for her. "It's an old 'stang, right?"

"1967 Shelby GT 500 Mustang," he replied.

"How fast will it go?"

"I don't know. Probably not quite as fast as when it was new."

"How come?"

"The guy I bought it from had blown up the original engine, which was a real beast. I bought it cheap and put a new 4.6 liter double overhead cam V-8 in it. That was only a Lincoln engine back then, but now Ford puts it in the new Cobra Mustangs."

"Did you soup it up?"

"Some. Twin turbochargers help a little. I basically blew my allowance on it."

"Just take I-45 north into downtown and then take Allen Parkway west," she said.

"Check," Dean replied.

"How long have you been skating, Mr. Dean Steele?" the girl asked, after the car was rolling down the freeway.

"I started ice skating when I was nine," he said, "But I had been roller skating since I was five or six. How about you?"

"Oh, Mom waited till I was almost three before she put me on the ice," Shannon said, grinning. "She skated professionally for a while, 'till she met my dad, so it was always assumed I'd skate."

"I see."

"But I loved it though. I couldn't get enough of it." She looked at him. "How did you get started?"

"Well, I grew up in a small town in East Texas. There was literally nothing to do there but whittle and spit until, one day, one of those portable roller skating rinks came to town. It was basically a circus tent with a hardwood floor. The whole thing would fold up and fit on the back of a truck. That's when I discovered the joy of moving around without having to walk." The girl looked at him, waiting for the rest of the story. "Well, the guy who owned the portable rink had only planned to stay there for two weeks," he continued, "But he ran out of money, and he had to sell his rig to one of the locals. The guy who bought it made it into sort of a permanent rink, and, from then on, there was something to do in town." The girl continued to look at him expectantly. "I hung out there most of the time," he continued. "My parents gave me skates for Christmas. Since I wasn't big enough to play football, and I didn't particularly enjoy riding bulls, I found that skating was about the only way I could get any kind of recognition."

"You're a big guy, Dean," she said. "I'd think you'd make a great football player."

"I was a skinny kid. I didn't get . . . big . . . until college."

"So when did you turn in your wheels for blades?"

"I went to live with my grandparents in Dallas when I was nine. There was an ice rink near their home in North Dallas. Once I got a taste of ice-skating, I never looked back. And my grandmother was a dancer. It wasn't just a hobby, or a profession with her. It was a religion. She came to all my ice dance lessons. She made sure I took lessons all the time. She would always say, 'Don't skate to the words, Dean. Don't skate to the music. Skate to the beat!' She would even make me practice patting my foot to the beat. She always said, 'The drummer is your only friend.'"

"So you're an ice dancer? I thought you said you competed in senior men's singles."

"No, I'm not a dancer. But my grandmother made me pass all thirty-one compulsory dance tests, though.

"Wow," Shannon said. I've only tested up through gold. That's twenty-two dances, I think."

"Right. But I earned a lot of spare change serving as a dance partner for girls at their test sessions."

Shannon grinned. "So, you were a taxi dancer?"

"Hey, I figured if their moms wanted to pay me for it, I'd dance with 'em." He inhaled. "I was just about the only dance-qualified boy skater in the area. Most of the girls didn't want to skate with their coach at the test sessions, so I had a thriving business going there. I always had more money than my friends. I got so good at the compulsory dances that I could usually drag a girl through 'em, even if she was kinda shaky. Once the word got out, I was much in demand." Shannon was pondering what he had said. "So what about you?" Dean asked. "What does Shannon Foster do to fill up her day?"

"Skating mostly," she said, "And school. I'm a junior at Bel Aire. But I skate from six to eight every morning. I get out of school at three, and I'm back on the ice, Except I take dance lessons five days a week. Ballet two days and jazz dance the other three. And I take a gymnastics class at school. I used to take karate, but now it's gymnastics."

"Busy lady!"

The girl's attention went back to Dean. "So, if you were a skinny kid, how did you get so big?"

"When I was a sophomore at UT . . .,"

"You went to UT?" she interrupted. "The University of Texas at Austin?"

"Uh-huh."

"That is so cool! I'm gonna go to school there," she said excitedly.

"I don't doubt it."

"So what happened?"

"Well, two of the guys in my dorm had been weightlifters in high school. I started working out with them, and I cleaned up my diet and started taking vitamins, and pretty soon I wasn't skinny anymore. I guess it came at about the right time for me, when my hormones were doing their thing. Anyway, I gained some weight, and I've been doing it ever since." They rode in silence for a time. "What does the future hold for the talented Miss Foster?" Dean asked, smiling at the girl.

"Huh? Oh, I'll compete at the senior level, I guess."

"Gold at Nats? Will I see you on TV? Maybe Champions on Ice?"

"Ha! Sure. Just as soon as I outskate Michelle Kwan!"

"OK, silver maybe?"

The girl gazed off into space. Then she sighed. "I suppose I might someday win a medal. But there's a whole crop of young kids coming up, and they're really good. They jump like Tara Lipinsky. I doubt if I'll ever medal at Nats."

"So, what then? How will you spend your next sixty years? What's your most probable scenario?"

"You're an engineer, right? You always plan everything out."

"It's a compulsion."

She laughed. "OK, let's see. I'll go to Nationals three or four times and finish as high as fourth or fifth. Then I'll get into the cast of one of the Disney on Ice productions and skate professionally for a while. Then Mom will pick out some boring accountant guy for me, and I'll get married and live in River Oaks. Oh, and I'll have kids too. I just don't know how many. Mom hasn't told me yet. Then I'll live in a nursing home for a while, and then I'll die." She looked at Dean and grinned. "How'd I do?"

"Not bad, but you left out the grandkids and the part about the ice follies at the nursing home."

She laughed. "OK, what about you?"

"What about me?"

"Come on! We did me. Now we have to do you!"

Dean sighed. "OK, here's one. I get a PhD in computer science and go to work for NASA or one of the NASA contractors in Clear Lake City. I work my way up to Project Manager for telemetry data systems on the Space Shuttle and retire after twenty years. Then I get an adjunct faculty position somewhere and try to teach punks like you something. I die a miserable failure."

She laughed. "That'll work," she said. What about a family?"

He chuckled. "Well, I'll date a model, an actress, a rock singer, and a lady lawyer, and get dumped by all of them. Then I'll marry a molecular geneticist and spend my off days catching fruitflies for her experiments."

Shannon was giggling. "Any kids?"

"Yeah, three. One of each."

She laughed. "You'd have to have four, Dean. A boy, a girl, a gay guy, and a lesbian."

"No, I meant a blonde, a brunette and a redhead. My geneticist messes around." Shannon giggled for a while then became silent. "So, did you ever think about ice dance or skating pairs?" Dean asked.

"I've always worked on a singles program," she said, "Ever since I was a kid. I never paid much attention to pairs skating, I guess."

"Well, how is your singles program going?"

"OK, I guess. I can jump OK. I have my doubles and a couple of triples. I kinda lost 'em when I started filling out, you know, as a woman, but I'm gettin' 'em back. I'm workin' on my triples now."

"So, what is your strongest point, I mean, what would clinch the gold at Salt Lake City for you?"

"Ha! Well, let's see. Not my jumps, probably. I mean, I can land 'em, but it's not all that . . . precise, you know? I have trouble getting it perfect. Other girls are better."

"OK, so what about spins?"

"My spins are OK, I mean, I spin good. It's OK."

"So, what is your very best move on the ice. I mean, what are you better at than anybody ever?"

"Anybody ever? You mean like Peggy Fleming, and all?"

"Yeah."

"I guess it would be like, you know, skating the music. Sometimes I feel like I'm conducting the orchestra when I skate. It's like the music flows out from me, and I'm performing it for the audience. It's like . . . they can not only see my skating, but hear it too. And feel it. I sometimes think the audience is out there with me, like I'm their tour guide, taking them through a beautiful routine. It's . . . I don't know, like I'm carrying them with me when I skate." Dean listened in attentive silence. "Does that sound crazy? Like I'm a nut or something?"

"No, young lady, you sound more like a skater than just about anyone I've ever heard."

"Really?" He gave her a smile.

River Oaks

They drove to an address in the exclusive River Oaks section of West Houston. "Is this where you live?" Dean asked, awed by the estate spread out before him as they drove up to a gate.

"It's my foster home," the girl replied.

"You're adopted?" Dean asked, somewhat puzzled. He had gotten the distinct feeling from Millie that Shannon was her natural daughter. Shannon looked at him and began to grin. Dean frowned at her as he reviewed the situation.

"Oh," he said. "Shannon Foster lives in the Foster home. Very funny!"

"Gotcha!" She laughed. Dean looked at her in mock disgust. Then he grinned. "Just punch in 6721," she said. He pressed the number into a keypad, and the gate slowly opened.

"Guess who!" Shannon said as they walked into the den.

"Uh . . . Bonnie and Clyde?" Millie pretended puzzlement at the query.

"No, Mom! It's Jane Torvel and Christopher Dean[3], only without the funny accents."

"Well, aren't we honored!" Millie responded.

"This is Dean," Shannon said to her father as he rose to his feet. "Senior men's freestyle. He medalled at Nationals in the Ice Age."

"Pleased to meet you, Son," Fred said, shaking his hand warmly.

"Where have y'all been?" Millie asked. "I can't wait to see this!" She shoved the cassette into an opening in a wall of electronics.

"We got caught by a mob of autograph seekers, Mom," Shannon answered, grinning at Dean.

"They broke down the barricades and overpowered our bodyguards," Dean added. The two skaters laughed.

"Dad, you're just gonna love this!" Millie said as the tape began to play.

The Video

They watched in silence as the somewhat shaky video of their skating began to flicker on a giant screen TV. After a few moments Shannon leaned over toward her mom. "He's real smooth," she said quietly.

"I can see!" Millie replied enthusiastically.

In a moment Shannon and Dean began an ad-lib critique of the program. "Now here's where Dean crashes into the hockey goal," Shannon said, giggling.

"No, this is where Shannon runs over those two kids."

"Here's where Dean skids into the rail."

"No, this is where Shannon smashes her nose on the Plexiglas."

"Aren't they beautiful, Dad?" Millie asked. "Doesn't it look just like the Olympics?"

Dean and Shannon chuckled simultaneously. "Which year was that?" Shannon asked. "I must have missed that one."

"I think it was the 1997 Winter Olympics in Tijuana," Dean replied. He and Shannon looked at each other and giggled.

"Actually, this is Campbell soup's 'Three Stooges on Ice,'" Dean said. "But it's just Shep and Larry. Moe was out sick that day." They laughed.

"Oh, come on, you two!" Millie said. "Y'all looked great out there, especially for two people who just met. Y'all are naturals skating together!"

"You're right Mom," Shannon said. "It was a very successful program . . . . We skated almost two whole songs, and nobody got killed." She and Dean looked at each other and snickered.

Dinner

"You know what?" Millie said during dinner. "Y'all ought to work up a little routine to do together. You could perform it at the Christmas pageant and other skating club events like that. The club would love it. They're always needing skaters for some kind of exhibition. Y'all are undoubtedly the best they've got."

"Sure, Mom," Shannon said. "We could do our famous 'flip, flop and fly' routine." She grinned at Dean. "He has a great butt slide."

"Oh, but it's nothing compared to your back outside fanny drop." They laughed.

"No, I'm serious," Millie said." The audiences would love y'all. You heard 'em today. Y'all were a big hit!"

"Oh, Mom. That was just the first time those people had ever seen two people skate together without falling down. We're not exactly Torville and Dean for Pete's sake."

"More like Laurel and Hardy," Dean said. They laughed.

"I'd say we looked like Tinkerbelle and Godzilla skating together," Shannon said, grinning.

"More like Brian Boitano and Annie Klutz," Dean added.

"No, Nancy Kerrigan and Dick Van Dyke is who it was," Shannon responded.

"No, Scott Hamilton and Carole Burnette," said Dean.

"No, Dorothy Hamill and Arnold Swartzeneggar on ice."

"Oh, get serious, you two," Millie said, interrupting their impromptu comedy routine. "Y'all looked great together. I really think you should work up a program for the club. There's all kinds of opportunities where you could perform it."

"What music would we use?" Shannon asked, still grinning.

"How about the 1812 overture?" Dean suggested. "We could time our falls to coincide with the cannon fire."

"Boom—splat! Boom—splat!" Shannon said, slapping her hands together to simulate a skater's fall. She and Dean laughed as Millie rolled her eyes in disgust.

After Dinner

Dean and Fred sat in the living room after dinner was finished. Millie and Shannon cleaned up the dishes.

"What kind of work do you do, Dean?" Fred asked.

"I'm a computer programmer for Accumedical Data Systems in Clear Lake City," he said. "We write software for archiving the pictures in radiology departments."

"You mean, like X-ray films?"

"Yes, but it's mainly the digital images like MRI and CAT scans."

"Must be interesting work."

"It is. I get to work with some of the sports medicine people at the Texas Medical Center. I get to see the X-rays and MRIs of lots of sports injuries."

"Where did you go to school?" Fred inquired.

"I got a BS degree in computer science at UT," he said. "I'm working on a master's at U of H now."

"Millie used to skate," Fred said after a pause. "Did you know that?"

"Uh, no," Dean lied, even though Fred was in on the charade.

"Yes, she was an Ice Capette when I met her."

"I'll bet she was good."

"Well, she was the prettiest thing I'd ever seen, on or off the ice. I fell in love with her instantly." Dean smiled. "My biggest problem was convincing her to quit skating and marry me."

When the evening was over, Dean said goodbye to the Fosters and drove back to his apartment in Clear Lake City.

The Day After

Dean's phone rang early the next morning. "What did you think?" Millie's voice asked. "Isn't she great?"

"She's a cute kid, and quite a nice little skater," Dean acknowledged. "We rather quickly got comfortable skating together. She's sharp, and she has a sense of humor."

"I knew y'all would hit it off." Millie said, excitedly. "She seemed to really like you too. She's wearing an extra little grin this morning, after her 'chance encounter' with Mr. Dean Steele. I think she's been bragging about you to her friends." Dean didn't respond to her comment. "So, are you ready to start working up a pairs program for Regionals?" she asked.

"Not just yet," he replied. "Your daughter's a charmer, but I don't think I want to put myself back into that particular pressure cooker."

"I see. Well, let's meet for lunch and talk about it. Write down this address." Dean did as he was told.

Private Ice

"Willie, I need a favor," Dean said to the owner of the Lone Star Ice Palace.

"Whatever you want, Dino," the man replied.

"I'd like to have the early ice one day this week, if you can spare it. I want to show it to a friend."

"That rich woman I saw in here the other day?" he asked.

"Her daughter, actually," Dean replied. "I'm . . . working on a deal."

"Well, you can have it tomorrow, no, day after. I'll sign you up for it."

"Thanks, Buddy," Dean said. "I'll make it up to you."

"You already have," Willie said.

Shannon

"Hello," Shannon answered her cell phone.

"Is this Shep Foster, star of Campbell soup's 'Three Stooges on Ice?'" Dean asked.

"Yeah, Shep here" she giggled. "Is that you, Larry?"

"Yeah. Moe's feeling a lot better. He should be back in the act in a couple of days."

"How you doin' Dean?" the girl asked with a giggle in her voice.

"I'm all right. I survived my dinner at your 'foster home' OK."

"Good. That was the most fun I've had in a while."

"Hey, I've got a deal for you. Would you be interested in private ice tomorrow morning?"

"Oh, you mean, the soft ice at that other place where you skate?"

"Yeah, Lone Star. And we'll have it all to ourselves."

"Cool deal!" Shannon said. "When is it again?"

"Five AM. Better turn in early tonight."

"OK, I'll see you there."

"Oh, and if you have music for one of your programs, bring the tape."

"OK, bye, Dean."

Early ice

Shannon was waiting in her car when Dean drove up. It was ten till five. He parked, walked over and peered into her window. "Anybody awake in there?"

"Just barely," she answered. Dean unlocked the side door and they went into the modest building that housed Willie's ice sheet.

"You have a key to this place?"

"I'm practically family," he replied, "Even though I show up a little bit too pink in all the family portraits."

They put on their skates and stepped out onto the ice. Shannon bent down and touched it. "This is really nice ice," she said. The girl pushed off and glided across the perfect surface. "This is wonderful," she said. "It's just like glass! And it's like you and I are the only two people in the world."

"We are," Dean said. "Everyone else is asleep."

Shannon amused herself by floating serenely upon the perfect surface for a time. Her blades cut their paths so smoothly that they did little to mark the glassy stratum. Dean watched her graceful movements with a careful eye. Being there together on that deserted sheet of ice promoted a camaraderie between the two skaters. They had each, through countless hours on the ice, developed a very special skill. They were figure skaters competent to compete at the national level. They were different from other people. They could do things almost no one else could do. They were unique. It created a warm feeling of confidence and pride that both felt, but neither mentioned. A bond developed in the cold silent air.

"Give me your tape and I'll put it on," Dean said when she skated up to him. "Willie has a decent sound system here."

She pulled a cassette out of her jacket and laid the garment across the rail. Dean took the tape to the sound booth. Soon her music boomed out to fill the arena.

"This is wonderful," she said as she skated into her routine.

Dean watched the girl skate her program. She was graceful, even inspired as she glided through her moves, jumps and spins.

"Now you," she said after her music finished. "I want to see your stuff, Mr. Senior-level Skater."

"I'd rather skate with you," he said, extending his arm.

"Well, OK. But you gotta show me your stuff before time's up, OK?"

"Will do," he said.

The Pair

Dean and Shannon skated together for about twenty minutes. They said very little, communicating with graceful movements of their bodies. Within minutes they had melted into one being, flowing as a single unit throughout the arena. Dean's lead cues became so subtle that Shannon was practically reading his mind. Not once did they stumble or lose their balance. It was what ice dancing was meant to be, a graceful flow of two bodies moving as one on the ice.

Dean Skates

After a short break, Dean put his music on and started his program. It included some moves of his own design, moves Shannon had never seen done before. Then he skated forward, coming directly toward her. He moved his weight to his left foot, and extended his right foot and both arms behind him. Then he brought his free leg and both arms forcefully forward and up. His left toe pick bit into the ice, and his left leg pushed hard, launching him into the air. He crossed his ankles and snapped his arms in tight against his body, causing him to spin rapidly in midair. He rotated three and a half times and landed smoothly, right in front of Shannon. He emerged from the jump skating backward on the outside edge of his right skate with both arms and his left leg extended.

"Dean!" she screamed, skating after him. "Was that a triple Axel? My, God! That was a triple Axel!"

He skidded to a stop. "Of course it was a triple Axel."

"Holy Shit! And there was nobody here to see it!"

He looked into her eyes. "You were here to see it," he said. "I did it for you."

"Oh, my God, that is so awesome! I'd love to be able to do a triple Axel!"

"You can. It just takes a little practice. The right kind of practice."

They sat down on a bench and took off their skates.

"Hungry?" Dean asked.

"Starving," the girl replied.

"Follow me to IHOP," he said. "I'll buy." The girl complied.

Breakfast

When they entered the IHOP restaurant on NASA Road One, they were met by a waiter who was a friend of Dean's.

"Hi, Dean," he said. "Who's your friend?"

"Moses," Dean said, "This is Shannon. She's a skater."

"Hi, Shannon," he said. "Come this way."

"That guy's name is Moses?" Shannon asked after they took their seats.

"Yeah," Dean said. "He once parted the Red River."

A laugh exploded from the girl. "Uh, I believe that was the Red Sea, Dean," she said. "And I bet it was his great-grandfather."

"No, it was this guy," Dean replied with a straight face. "He walked down from Oklahoma wearing a robe and sandals, and he parted the Red River. It was amazing. It made all the papers."

"You wouldn't shit me, would you Dean?" She was still laughing.

"Hey, ask him if you don't believe me."

"Moses," Shannon said when the young man returned with their coffee, "Where did you come from?"

"Idabel, Oklahoma," he replied.

"And how did you get down here?"

"I walked."

"So, what did you do when you got to the Red River?"

"I just walked across. It was . . . low tide." He gave Dean a mischievous grin.

Shannon held still a moment, then burst out laughing.

"My . . . Father didn't give me bus fare," Moses added. "So I had to improvise."

"You guys are so fulla shit!" she giggled.

"Hey, I just report the facts," Dean said.

Shannon's giggling continued throughout breakfast.

---

1. Kilian position—the lady stands to the man's right, facing forward. Their left hands are clasped, and their right hands are on her right hip.
2. Waltz position—the lady faces the man, skating backward. His left hand clasps her right. His right arm encircles her waist. Her left hand is on his right shoulder.
3. Jane Torvel and Christopher Dean—Famous British ice dancing couple.

Chapter 3

Lunch Date

Damien's

Dean drove up to the address Millie had given him. It was on Smith street, just south of downtown Houston. "Good afternoon, Mr. Steele," the Valet parking attendant said as he opened the car door. "We'll take good care of Matilda."

Dean walked in, preparing to explain to the Matire'D that he had reason to be there. "Good afternoon, Mr. Steele," the man said. "If you will come with me . . . ," Dean followed him through the restaurant to a secluded booth where Millie sat, smiling up at him. She was stunning in business suit and silk scarf, the perfect combination of business chic.

She held out her hand, which Dean took and kissed. "You look charming, Ms. F." he said.

She smiled. "I hear you and Shannon skated early yesterday," she said after he took his seat. "She won't shut up about it. You have my daughter thoroughly charmed. She's practically bored her friends to tears bragging about her private session with the brawny boy skater."

"Yes," he said, "We did have a good session."

"Do you find her comfortable to skate with?"

"Remarkably so," he replied. "We seem to have the same moves."

Millie summoned the waiter and placed their order. "Have you read Christine Brennan's book, 'Edge of Glory'?" Millie asked, as the waiter left.

"I've read both of her books," he replied.

"Do you remember what she said about U.S. pairs skating?"

"Not verbatim, but I think it was . . . less than complimentary."

"Well," Millie said, reaching into her purse, "I just happen to have that book with me." Dean grinned as she popped the paperback open to a bookmarked page and began to read.

"U.S. pairs hardly ever won anything. They never won any Olympic gold medal, and won only two world championships, one in 1950, the other in 1979 . . . . When U.S. coaches put two American skaters together as a pair, they often perform like singles skaters who just happened to wander onto the ice surface at the same time. They tend to be remote, unemotional and downright boring. U.S. pairs are like U.S. marriages; about half of them work, and even the couples who don't separate occasionally have problems."

"She goes on to say that the top U.S. pairs teams were mainly brothers and sisters, and, from 1914 to present, only two of them were actually married couples."

"That's probably why the Russians have been so successful," Dean said. "Most of their pairs are . . . really pairs . . . like G & G¹, for example."

"Dean," she said, gazing into his eyes, "Don't you see what an opportunity this represents? You and Shannon can bring romance back to U.S. pairs skating!" Dean pondered what she had said, then nodded at least partial agreement.

"You can almost certainly make it to Nationals," she continued, "And you might even be U.S. pairs champions in a few years! It's entirely possible. Y'all could set the pattern for pairs skating in the US, and Lord knows we need it!"

"Not impossible, I guess," he mused. "But an awful lot of things would have to go right."

"The age difference won't show up on the ice," Millie continued. "Shannon's body is maturing now. With makeup on she won't look like a child. And you're not siblings. You two could skate a very romantic program."

"But it would take one Hell of a lot of work," he added.

"Let's play a game," Millie said after the waiter brought their drinks. "Let's pretend you've thought it over thoroughly and decided not to skate pairs with Shannon. And now you've come to tell me the bad news, and explain your reasons, OK?" Dean peered at her suspiciously. "Oh, come on," she chided. "Just for fun. Humor me, you dear young man!"

Dean sighed his resignation. "OK, so what's your first reason for deciding not to do it?"

"Well," he said, thinking as he spoke, "I don't want to get back into that pressure cooker. Life is nice and calm just being a programmer and an engineering student. No contests, no judges, no press. It's simple and fun."

"Good!" Millie said, "Excellent reason. What's number two?"

"It wasn't my idea," he said. "I mean, it was brought to me by someone else."

"A total stranger," Millie added, with an ominous look on her face.

"OK," Dean agreed, "So it's not the result of . . . it's not the normal evolution of my future. It represents a ninety degree turn in the direction of my life."

"Right. Now, what's number three?"

"Well, no offense, but it's a bizarre situation. I mean, Ice Mom approaches retired skater about skating with Daughter, only Daughter isn't in on the plan yet." He frowned. "That's not the normal sequence of events."

"Fair enough, Millie responded. "Number four?"

"It would delay my graduation, and cut my whole career short, by probably two years. So it would cost me at least two years of lifetime income. And that comes off the far end, where, presumably, I'll be earning the big bucks."

"Good. What about number five?"

"I don't know what I would be getting into. I mean . . . ,"

"Who are these people?" Millie interjected. "How do I know what strange business I would encounter getting mixed up with this weird skating family from River Oaks?"

"Something like that."

"Number six?"

"We might not win anything. Shannon and I might not work well together, or one of us might get injured, or we just might not be as good as the other skaters, or the judges might not like our style . . . ,"

"OK. That brings us up to ten."

"And if we don't win," he continued, "There'll be a lot of unhappy people. People who've sunk a lot of time, effort and money into this partnership, only to have their hopes dashed and their expectations disappointed. It would put a lot of pressure on us, and it could result in a lot of hard feelings down the line."

"OK. That's eleven. Number twelve?"

"The age difference. I'm ten years older than Shannon. We have different viewpoints and different interests. That might make it hard to work together, long-term."

"All right. What's number thirteen?"

"Can I rest a minute?"

"What's the matter, Champ? Running out of objections so soon? And you were doing so well there!"

"Well, that'll have to do for now. If I think of any more on the way home, can I mail them in?"

"OK," she laughed. "You're being a good sport. Let's move on the second part."

"When do we start having fun?"

"Oh, I'm having enough fun for both of us," she replied. He raised his eyebrows at her. She was relaxed and intimate with him, as if they had been friends for years.

"Now, pretend you've thought it over thoroughly and decided to go ahead and skate pairs with Shannon. And now you've come to tell me the good news, and explain your reasons."

"Doesn't this mean I'm doing your selling job for you?"

"Just humor me, you sweet young man. What's reason number one?"

Dean sighed deeply and closed his eyes. "Well, first there's Shannon herself. She's a great little skater. There's magic in her moves. And she's easy to skate with. She flows like molasses. I think she's a natural pairs skater, if there is such a thing."

"Oh, yes," Millie said enthusiastically, "No doubt about it. What's next?"

"Well, I think I'm well-built for pairs. I'm probably the strongest boy skater in the business. Now, that didn't profit me much in my singles career, but it could work to our advantage in pairs skating. We could do bolder moves, even given

Shannon's size and weight, than most of the other couples. We could be like Brasseur and Eisler[2], only with a full-size girl."

"Dean," Millie reassured him, "We can get Shannon's weight down. She can diet. She's a little heavy right now. She can lose several pounds."

"She'll lose some fat," Dean said, "But she'll also gain muscle weight. She needs to work out more and build strength. I expect she'll come in at just about 120 to 122, unless she goes on an all-Twinkie diet, of course. But it's not a problem. I can lift 120. And half the secret to a good lift or throw is the girl's initial jump. With strong legs, she'll be able to jump halfway there." He paused to think. "The only factor to consider is her momentum," he continued. "I won't be able to snap her around quickly, like I could a smaller girl. But that only means we'd have to do big, smooth, graceful moves. All in all, not a real problem."

"OK, What's next?"

"Well, I think we have the opportunity to develop a unique image for our act. Look at Isabelle Brasseur and Lloyd Eisler[2]. They do amazing things in pairs. He tosses her all over the rink. But he's a foot taller than she is. Her cute, petite size is an interesting contrast to his size and bulk, but it still looks like he's skating with his kid sister.

"Lloyd's a big guy, but I'm stronger than he is. I could toss Shannon, even at her weight, almost as well as he can throw Isabelle. But Shannon is almost as tall as I am. It would give a totally different look to the act. Two same-sized skaters doing really athletic throws like that. I would love to do Eisler-type moves on a full-sized woman."

"I knew it!" Millie said, "I knew you could throw Shannon!"

"Being the same size," Dean continued, "We could sell a romantic number better. It's a 'man and woman' thing, not a 'big man and little girl' thing. Even though I'm a lot older, we'd look like a believable couple from the bleachers."

"Sounds great to me," Millie said enthusiastically.

"You know," Dean mused, "I know that audiences always go for the 'Little girl's dream' number." Millie's face registered a slight confusion. "You know, where a tiny pre-pubescent girl, all alone on the ice, skates her little heart out to music like, 'If I believe in myself, all my dreams will come true.' Lipinsky did it really well when she was an amateur, and so do a dozen others. But Shannon can't do that one. She's too mature. She's too big, and she's too old. And, frankly, I've seen that one done enough times, and done well enough, that it's no fun for me anymore.

"I prefer more adult themes," he continued, "And pairs skating offers an ideal vehicle for dealing with romance themes. You know, good old-fashioned boy/girl, heterosexual, love themes. Something that 95% of the population can relate to. I'd like to help bring a little more of that back to the ice."

"I wish to God somebody would," Millie said, "I get so tired of the gay influence always creeping into skaters' programs. It's just so overdone these days."

"Well, if Shannon and I skated together, we'd almost be forced to do the boy/girl thing in our programs."

"Thank God!" Millie said. "Now, what's your next reason?"

"I was in Las Vegas once, at the Hilton hotel, where they were having a bodybuilding competition. One of the contestants came walking through the casino and down a corridor leading to the theater where the contest was being held. With him was one of the fitness magazine models, a really voluptuous, muscular, athletic-looking girl. Their outfits weren't anything special, but they looked really good.

"The reaction of the people in the casino was amazing. These two kids were like Pied Pipers. Like a herd of dazed robots, people fell in line behind them, just to watch them walk. People would pull away from slot machines, leaving a tray full of nickels, just to follow 'em down the hall! I felt it too. I even got caught up in the mass hysteria.

"So, pretty soon, about thirty people were following these two kids down the hall, without even knowing why. They were just watching this couple walk. Probably neither one of them would have created a sensation by themselves. But together, they were spectacular. There is something magical about a pair of beautiful, muscular bodies, male and female."

"Amazing!" Millie said.

"Now, I can look like that guy. And in six or eight months, with regular workouts and good nutrition, Shannon could look like that girl. I base that on what she looks like now, and what her mother, grandmother and aunts look like."

"Ah. So that's why you wanted to see pictures of Fred's mother and sisters the other night." Dean smiled in admission. "And does this mean that you've 'scoped me out' as well?"

"Better than that," Dean replied. "I've felt you up, remember?"

"I wondered why I got such an enthusiastic hug," she said.

"You have surprisingly little fat for a woman of your age and figure. Your shape is largely defined by your muscle structure, and you have a strong skeleton and thick tendons." He paused. "I was even able to verify that your boobs are real," he joked. She gave him a playful, "Shame on you," look. "Shannon would need to work out with weight on a regular basis," Dean continued, "But she needs to do that anyway, just to have the strength for lifts and throws. So we could kill two birds with one stone—strength and beauty." Millie was lost in thought, so Dean took a sip of coffee. "By the time we get into serious competitive position, Shannon and I could be, well, pretty phenomenal looking. I think we could have the same effect on an audience that these two kids had on that casino. And the judges couldn't ignore that."

"You're giving me goosebumps," Millie said.

"Now, I'm not saying that looks can substitute for good skating. But if a pairs team has both the looks and the skating, then they have a fighting chance of beating this ridiculous judging system."

Dean realized he had lost his audience. Millie was off in a dream world imagining what he had described. He paused, yielding right-of-way to her fantasy. "My God!" she exclaimed at last, "It's wonderful!" She clasped his hand with hers and squeezed it as excitement overcame her. "You kids would be just simply great!"

"Well," he said, "It looks like I've sold you on the idea. Now, who's gonna sell me?"

"Dean Steele, you cannot possibly look me in the eye and tell me you aren't going to do this! Any idiot can see that your positive reasons outweigh your negatives ten to one!"

"Well, I can't look you in the eye and say I will, either. I honestly haven't decided."

"OK, OK. Have it your way. But this is just too good an opportunity to pass up. Take another day, or another minute, or whatever, and then tell me you'll do it. But don't wait too long. The anticipation is tearing me up! I've got so many ideas for costumes and programs!"

"You'll be the second one to know," Dean said.

They finished their meal and parted.

Decision

Millie gathered up her purse and walked out of the Texas Ice Stadium, toward her car in the parking lot.

"Millie?" a voice called out softly from the darkness.

"Dean!" she said. "Did you just get here?"

"I was hoping I'd catch you," he said.

"How are you?"

"I'm good," he replied. "I've made my decision." Millie walked over to where he stood in the darkness.

"Well, finally!" she said, forcing a joke to conceal her anticipation.

She moved close to him. "So, what's the word, Tiger?" Are you in?"

"I've decided . . . ," he paused. Millie's heart was racing. "I've decided that my destiny is to kick butt in pairs skating."

It took Millie a few seconds to decode his comment. "Then, you'll do it?" she asked, fearfully.

"Yes, Ice Queen, I'll do it," he said.

Millie grabbed him in a bear hug. "Oh, God," she said, "This is the happiest day of my life!"

The two figures stood silently in the dimness outside the ice stadium, the woman desperately clinging to the young man. Soon Dean felt her beginning to tremble. Then her heard her begin to sob.

"I'm sorry," she said, "But this is just so . . . ,"

Her sobs became louder and her hands went under his jacket and began to move up and down along his back.

"Hold me tight," she pleaded. "Really tight." Dean tightened his grip on the woman. "I never dreamed . . . ," She moaned as he held her quivering body. Dean became aware that her hands were exploring his arms and back, even his buttocks, as she continued to sob openly. "Let me touch you," she whispered. Dean was not sure what to make of that request. "I want to feel your strength." The woman's hands continued to explore Dean's back, from his neck to his buns, as she continued to cry. Dean was unsure what to do. It seemed to be some sort of emotional release for her, so he simply stood there as she drained herself. Finally her sobbing subsided. "I want you to press me against this wall," she said timidly, "And hold me as tight as you can. I need that right now."

Somewhat confused, Dean obliged by rotating her around until he faced the wall of the ice arena. He took a step forward, pressing her back against the cool concrete block structure. He slipped his arms inside her fur coat and gradually increased his grip on her body as he leaned against her. So explosively did she resume sobbing that Dean thought he might have injured the woman. He soon realized that her emotional release was not yet complete. "I can't help it," she sobbed, "I can't help it."

For long moments Dean held the sobbing woman in a firm grip, pressing her against the cool concrete wall. Gradually she regained her composure, and finally she opened her eyes. "I'm sorry you have to witness a breakdown so early in our association," she said, "But the pressures of the past few days finally got to me."

"I understand," Dean said. "It's not a problem. You're entitled to it."

Millie opened her mouth to explain further, but then decided that more words would only cloud the issue. They both knew what had happened. She turned toward her car. After a few steps, she turned and walked back to Dean. She took his left hand in her two. "Thank you, Dear Boy," she said. "You've made me so very happy." She tiptoed and gave him a tender kiss on the forehead. Then she got in her Mercedes and left.

---

1. G & G—Ekaterina Goordeva and Sergi Grinkov, Russian Olympic pairs champions, husband and wife.
2. Isabelle Brasseur (5' 0", 95 lbs.) and Lloyd Eisler (6', 180 lbs), Canadian and world champion pairs skaters
3. Mutt and Jeff—comic strip characters, Mutt short and Jeff tall.

Chapter 4

Telling Shannon

The Approach

Shannon was flattered when Dean took her to a restaurant for a snack after her afternoon skating session. Somehow she didn't think it strange for him to offer since they had been spending some time together, due to their interest in skating. Besides, she liked the effect it had on her friends.

"I've got an idea I want to run by you," he said.

"What's that?" Shannon asked, mildly interested.

"What would you think about you and me working up a pairs program together? I mean for competition."

Her jaw dropped. "Are you serious? You can't mean it!"

"Sure. I think we might make a great pairs team. What do you think?"

"I thought you were just a recreational skater now," she said, eyeing him suspiciously, "I thought you got tired of competition."

"I did. But with the right partner, I just might jump back into the competitive fray. I'm not totally over the hill yet, you know!"

"I can't believe this! You really want to skate with me? In contests?"

"I've given it some thought recently, and I think it might make a lot of sense. I think you and I skate well together. We have . . . something . . . unique to show an audience."

Shannon was flabbergasted. She looked at him wide-eyed and open-mouthed. "Dean Steele wants me to be his skating partner?" she said, as if trying it out for credibility.

"I sure do," he said. "You and I could make history on the ice, Kid." He said in a W. C. Fields voice as he wiggled his eyebrows Groucho style.

"Shannon Foster skating with Dean Steele? I can't believe it!"

"We'd be . . . 'totally awesome'," he grinned, acting pleased with his use of teenage diction.

"You're such a good dancer. You could have any girl skater you want, Dean. Why me?"

"Well, first of all, there hasn't exactly been a line at my door."

"If they knew you were available they would! There's a million girls out there looking for partners."

"And second . . . you're the one I want."

"Why me, of all people?"

"Because our styles are compatible. We say the same kind of things when we skate. And you're, shall we say, not just another Tinkerbelle with blades. You have . . . stature, so to speak. And, besides, I love tossing big girls around!"

She ignored his slight. "So, when did you decide all this?" she asked, somewhat regaining her composure.

"Oh, I've been kind of thinking about for a couple of weeks," he said.

"Well, how long do I have to decide?"

Dean looked at his watch, "Oops," he said, "You're minute is just about up!"

"My Mom would have a cow!" she said, grinning disgustedly at his joke. "She's got her heart set on me being a singles champion."

"Naw, I'll bet she could deal with it."

"No, really, she'd lose her water!"

"Not so, Kid. She's already cool on the idea."

"What? You've talked to her about it?"

"Yeah. She's completely OK with it. Her and your dad too. If it's what you want to do, that is."

"That doesn't sound like them. They usually just tell me what to do."

"Not this time. Maybe you're . . . dare we say it? . . . growing up!"

"Wait a minute. You talked to my parents about this before telling me?"

"Uh . . . yeah."

"Why?"

"Well, I wasn't sure I wanted to do it until now. It's a big step for me. I'd have to postpone my education, and a lot of other stuff. I didn't want to ask you to be my partner one day, then change my mind the next. It wouldn't be fair to you. I just waited 'till I was sure I wanted to do it, and that your parents would go along with it, before mentioning it to you."

"So, how long have you been talking to my mom about this?" she probed.

"Oh, a week or two, maybe."

"You must have started right after we met."

"Yeah, about then." Dean was beginning to sense danger in the air.

"OK, exactly when did you first talk to Mom about skating with me?" She was becoming exasperated.

"I think it was the day before we skated together that first time at TIS."

"Before you even met me? What did you do, see me across the ice and then run ask my mom if you could skate with me?"

"Not exactly."

"Then what, exactly?" The girl was becoming upset.

"Well . . . ,"

The Upset

"Wait a minute! Was it your idea?" she asked suspiciously. "Whose idea was it to begin with, Dean?"

"Well, actually, your mom may have been the first one to mention it." Dean quickly regretted having been so honest with the girl.

"So my mom came up to you, a total stranger, and said, 'Excuse me, Sir, but could I trouble you to skate with my daughter? She can't cut it in ladies' singles, but maybe, with you help, she could make it in freedance.'"

"That's not an accurate account of what happened."

"OK, then," she demanded, "What did happen?" She was fuming.

"Millie was familiar with my skating history. We'd never actually met before, but she knew me from the old competitions. She recognized me at the rink one day, and we got started talking about skating. She told me all about you . . . more than I wanted to hear, actually." He paused to look at her, but she didn't laugh at his joke.

"Eventually," he continued, "She said she thought your style and mine were ideally suited for a pairs team. At first she didn't want you to give up your singles career, but then she really got excited thinking about what you could do as a pairs skater. I thought about it for a while, and I decided it's a great idea. So good, in fact, that I'm now willing to jump back into the boiling water, if you'll jump in with me, that is."

"Nice try, Asshole, but no sale!" the angry young woman snapped. "You picked me up in the rink that day, after you and Mom had been talking about it, but Mom acted like she didn't know you! And you skidded out of the double toe loop you asked me to spot, but you have a fuckin' triple Axel! Then you hung around for two weeks, acting like you had an interest in me. I can't believe I didn't see what was going on. I am such an idiot!"

"I did have . . . do have an interest in you, Shannon. Really."

"No you don't. They warned me it was fishy, that you didn't really like me."

"Who warned you?"

"The girls at the rink, and they were right. You're just working for my mom. You're just a hired hand, like the fuckin' pool man!" The girl fumed. "I am such an dunce!"

"I like my version of the story better," Dean said. "It's a lot closer to the truth."

"So, what did my parents promise you to be my so-called 'partner'?" Shannon asked disgustedly. "A new car? Will you get a shiny new Mustang out of the deal? Or is it a scholarship to engineering school? Are they gonna send you to MIT?"

"They said if I were your partner, they'd buy my ice," Dean replied calmly.

"They bought your ass, not your ice, Buddy-boy! You belong to them now. You're just another one of my mother's pets. You'll get a food bowl that says 'Dean,' right between the dog and the cat. You're disgusting!" She turned away fuming.

"Nobody buys me, Shannon," he said quietly. "Nobody owns me. There's an opportunity here—an opportunity to do something really worthwhile."

"Fuck you! And fuck my mom too! I hate her for doing this to me!"

"OK, Shannon, why are you so upset about this? What is it your Mom and I did that's so bad?"

"You don't know?"

"Well, kinda, but I may not be seeing everything you are. Maybe you can just explain it to me."

"She always does this," the angry girl began. "All my life, she's . . . Every fuckin' time . . . ," Shannon fought back tears of anger.

"Every time I try to have an independent thought. Every time I try to be me, just a little bit, she steps in and squashes it! I guess when I'm eighty she'll be coming to my nursing home, picking out my bathrobe for the day and feeding me my oatmeal."

"I see what you mean," he said. "It's a bitch."

Shannon continued to fume. "It was so cool, that first time we skated together. I was so proud with everybody watching. And I was so happy when you said you wanted to skate partners with me." Tears welled up in her eyes. "I thought I was finally being recognized for being *me*. I thought somebody had finally seen a little glimmer of Shannon Foster shining out from under my mom. Now she went and ruined that too. God damn her!"

"OK, but . . . what did she actually do? I mean, how did she ruin it?"

"Don't you see?" Shannon said through angry tears. "I thought this was *my* deal. I thought you were *my* friend. I thought *I* had found Dean Steele on my own. I thought you wanted to skate with *me*. Now I find out you're just another agent in Millie Foster's secret service." She glared at him. "You're just a puppet with my mother's hand up your ass, making your mouth move."

Dean turned his head slowly and looked behind him. "I wondered what that was!"

"This whole thing was engineered by her," Shannon continued, ignoring his joke. "I had nothing to do with it. I was just dumb little Shannon, as usual, walking merrily down whatever path the Ice Queen lays out in front of me. I feel like Chelsea Clinton, for God's sake. I have no life of my own. I'm not even sure there is a Shannon Foster. I think I'm just a wind-up doll in Millie Foster's toy box. She takes me out, shows me to her friends, and puts me back."

"I see what you mean," Dean said, nodding slowly. "That's a bitch."

Shannon looked at him. "Don't forget whose side you're on, soldier. Your assignment is to sweet-talk me into something here. You better do you duty to the Ice Queen, or you might not get your . . . fucking Ph.D."

"I don't think MIT gives advanced degrees in sex anymore."

A subtle smile began to curl up on Dean's face. "Military duty can be a real pain," he said. "If I fail this mission, I'll have to bite my cyanide capsule."

"This is not the time to be making jokes, Corporal," Shannon said. "You have a very pissed-off girl on your hands here!"

"You know," he mused, "When I joined the elite Royal Special Services Secret Agent Corps, I never knew it was going to be this tough. I usually only have to swim for miles underwater and blow up bridges and stuff. But this is the toughest assignment of my long and colorful career on Her Majesty's Secret Service."

"Oh, yeah?" she said, mildly intrigued by the reckless tack he was taking.

"Damn right. I have to seduce a hard-headed young woman into a star-studded skating career."

"Seduce?" she said. "Are you trying to seduce me?"

He shrugged, pleased that the emotionally charged word had gotten a rise out of the girl. "It amounts to that, I'd say. I have to subvert your carefully laid plans of being an anonymous nobody and drag you kicking and screaming down into the degraded slime of international fame and fortune as a big-time figure skating star. I have to draw you away from the warmth and comfort of second-rate mediocrity and debase you with championship titles and gold medals around your pretty little neck. It's sick and twisted, I know, but I have my duty to Queen and Country."

"Mediocre? Second-rate? Is that what you think I am?"

"Actually not. If I were forced to admit it, I'd say you're actually a very good skater. You can win some titles skating singles. No doubt about it. You'll have to retrain after your body gets filled out, to get some triples, so there won't be anything very soon. But there's a place for you in the singles record books if you work hard.

"But where you could really shine . . . ," He paused for effect, "Is skating pairs with me. Pairs is what you and I both were made for. I only recently realized that. I'd never go back into competition as a singles skater. But pairs gives us an opportunity to make a mark on skating."

"So, how are you going to seduce me?" She still had an interest in that concept.

"Shit, I wish I knew! I have to somehow convince a self-centered little brat to stop thinking about herself long enough to help a washed-up boy skater get back on his feet." He shrugged. "This is not an easy sell."

"Well, you're blowing it big-time by calling me a brat, you jerk!"

"See, I'm no good at this type of mission. I should be out blowing up bridges, or something."

"Huh!" Shannon sneered.

"So, how would you approach it? I mean, what would you do in my situation? Remember, I'll be executed in the most painful manner if I fail."

"Just eat the poison pill," she said, "It's your only way out."

"Oh, come on. Surely there's some desperate tactic I could try before I bite the big one."

"No, it's too late. You and Mom have made me too mad. I'll never get over it."

"Damn! I was hoping there was one more low-down, sneaky, dirty, rotten, underhanded trick I could try before I suck the cyanide."

"No, I think you and Mom have already covered 'em all."

"I guess I'm dead meat, then. Look for me in tomorrow's obituary column. It won't be a pretty sight."

"Couldn't happen to a nicer guy, either." She stuck out her tongue.

"Hey!" Dean said. "There is one trick I haven't used, but it's so evil and underhanded I don't know if even I have the guts to try it."

"Get Mom to help you. I'm sure y'all could stoop to anything!"

"I don't know. It's really evil."

"What is it?" She was becoming curious.

"What if I just . . . No, not practical."

"What's not practical?" Her voice contained frustration.

"I was just thinking, what if I explain the situation to her rationally and let her make up her mind as an adult? Is that just completely hopeless?

"Nothing like that's ever been tried on this girl before!"

"Well, we're desperate here, and desperate times call for desperate measures."

"You could give it a shot. But the answer's gonna be 'No!'"

"Well, if it's hopeless, then I won't bother trying it."

"Well, you gotta try something, and you don't have a better option!"

"I guess you're right. So is there a tiny chance it might work?"

"No. It won't work. It's just the only thing you haven't tried."

"All right, but I need some glimmer of hope to work from. Some microscopic chance that she might fall for it."

"Well, I've done a lot of dumb things my Mom wanted me to do. I guess it's possible I might do one more."

"Great! So here goes. Are you listening?"

"It's either that or walk home," she said, disgustedly.

"Oh, goody!" Dean said, "I just love a receptive audience."

Shannon looked at him from beneath eyebrows raised in disgust.

"So, here's the deal. I'm five-eleven, 200 pounds. I'm stronger than anybody in the business right now. You're five-seven, 120 . . . ,"

"I don't weigh a hundred and twenty!" she said, insulted.

"OK, but you will when you get in shape."

"I am in shape!"

"Not the kind of shape you're gonna be in."

"If you think you're talking me into something here, you need a session with a shrink!"

"Hear me out, oh, Fair Lady. It gets better, I promise."

"It better get a lot better," she said, "Or I *am* walking home."

"As I was saying, most pairs girls come in at four-ten to five-oh and 85 to 100 pounds. That's half what their partners weigh, and a foot shorter. Look at Brasseur and Eisler, for example. They're great, but it's Mutt and Jeff[5] all over the ice."

"Mutt who, and Jeff who?"

"Forget it. What I'm saying is . . . you and I make a normal size couple. You're big enough to look me in the eye. We're more like an ice dance team. But I'm strong enough to lift and toss you anyway. I'll bet we could do any of Isabelle and Lloyd's moves, even their triple lateral twist, or the one-handed star lift. And it wouldn't look like I'm skating with my kid sister!" Shannon stared at him suspiciously. "In a year or so, you're gonna be knockout gorgeous. I've scoped out the women on both sides of your family . . ."

"You checked out my aunts?"

"Oh, yeah. Grandma too."

"You fondled my grandmother? Ohoo, gross, Dean!" Shannon shook her head, suppressing a grin.

"Hey, it was fun! Anyway, we would be one of the most athletic looking, physically attractive couples on the ice."

"Sexy?"

"We'd have to be careful not to be *too* sexy," Dean said, noting her sudden interest in the subject. "We wouldn't want to shock the judges. But the audiences would love us. We're strong, we're beautiful, we're straight, and we're the same size. They could easily imagine us getting it on."

"Is that what you want?" she asked indignantly. "People watching us skate and imagining us fucking?" Dean read her to be considerably less disgusted by that concept than she pretended.

"Romance, my naive compadre. It's romantic if it suggests love and lust. We'd be believable as a couple. You're a full-blown woman . . . and I'm not a fag."

"Except that you're a generation or two ahead of me."

"Well, you'll look older with makeup on, and all my wrinkles and liver spots won't show at a distance. Besides, we could leak dirty old man rumors about me. That would cause talk and suspicion and fill up the cheap seats."

"You have a warped view of why people watch skating, Mr. Steele!" The girl was only partially able to conceal her fascination with what he was saying.

"True, but I came by it honestly. A skating act is romantic and exciting if it looks like foreplay. Do I need to explain that term to you?"

"I know what 'foreplay' is, you jerk. After all, I am sixteen."

"Ohoo, the voice of experience!"

"If you think you're calming me down, Asshole, it's not working!"

"All I'm saying is, we could work up a really romantic, even sexy program. People would love it. Even judge-type people." He paused. "I'd never go back into competition if it was just two people skating together. The world doesn't need just another pair. But there are some things I'd like to say on the ice . . . romantic things . . . things that have never been said before." The hard look on Shannon's face softened a bit at the prospect. "We'd wear costumes that show off our bods," he continued, "But tastefully, of course. And we'd skate out romantic fantasies. We'd grab the audience by their heartstrings and give 'em a yank." She stared at him blankly. "And we could work out some really nifty lifts and throws." He leaned over toward her and whispered emphatically, "Moves the world has never seen."

Shannon wrinkled her mouth skeptically. "Like what?"

"Well, like . . . you lifting me."

"Oh, as if, Dean! You weigh 200 pounds! Like I'm really gonna carry you around in the air!"

"You can do it. And it would be . . . spectacular! It would knock the audience on their asses."

"You've been taking too many steroid pills," she said.

Dean gripped her shoulders. "Skate with me, Shannon. We can make figure skating history!"

The girl blinked. Her face began to melt into a soft glow. Then she caught herself. "That's Mom talking, isn't it? She told you to say all that stuff to me. You don't want to skate with me. You just want a new car and a scholarship to Caltech."

"Adoption," Dean said.

"What?"

"Say hello to your new brother. When Fred and Millie die, you and I split the estate, 50/50."

"That's really sick!" Shannon exclaimed.

"Just kidding," Dean said. "My lawyers couldn't get them to go for adoption."

"Not funny!" Shannon replied, suppressing a giggle. "Take me home!"

"As you wish, my princess," Dean said. They got in the Mustang and left.

When they arrived at the Foster home, Dean said, "Look Shannon, I really think it's a good idea for us to skate together. It doesn't matter who came up with the idea, only if it's the right thing to do. Keep that in mind."

Shannon didn't reply, but got out of the car and slammed the door. As she walked toward her front door, Dean called inside on his cell phone.

"She's mad," he said when Millie answered. "Leave her alone for a while. Let her cool down and think about what I said."

Millie hung up as Shannon walked in. "Hi, Honey," she said. The girl didn't answer, but went straight to her room and locked the door. In a few minutes Millie knocked on Shannon's door. "Shannon? Are you OK, Honey? Is something wrong?" There was no response.

Millie immediately phoned Dean, who took the call in his car on the way back to Clear Lake City. "What did you say to her?" she demanded. "She's locked herself in her room and won't even answer me!"

"I told you, she's mad—at me and at you. Just cut her some slack. She'll be OK in a day or two."

"A day or two!" Millie roared. "She's never refused to talk to me before."

"She has something to work out for herself," Dean said. "Just stay out of her life for a minute or two. It'll be OK."

"I can't believe this! You were supposed to talk her into the pairs thing, not make her mad at her mother, for Christ's sake!"

"So, I screwed up. Shit happens! Just leave her alone about it for two days. If she doesn't go along with it by then, you can stand me up in front of a firing squad. Goodbye, Millie."

Shannon and Dean didn't talk the next day. The girl was cool toward her mother, and she refused to discuss her skating at all.

Millie called Dean. "I think you really screwed this up," she said. "I've never seen Shannon like this before."

"Good," Dean said. "My plan must be working."

"Look, Dear Boy," Millie scolded him, "I hope you know what you're doing. If I have to step in and force her to do this, it's gonna be messy."

"It's already messy!" Dean said. "Just let her have the time she needs. We'll live with her decision."

"I don't want to live with her decision," Millie roared. "I want her to live with my decision!"

"That's the problem," Dean said. "Goodbye Millie."

Shannon's Call

"Hello," Dean said.

"Hi," came the response from the telephone. "It's Shannon."

"Hey, Hot Shot! What's happening?"

"Nothing much. What's with you?"

"I'm OK. What's on your mind?"

"I've been . . . thinking about what you said."

"Yeah? How's it going? Have you decided yet?"

"No, I've . . . got some questions for you."

"OK, shoot."

"I'd rather do it in person. I want to watch your eyes when you answer."

"Oh, yeah. It'd be too easy to lie to you over the phone, right?"

"Well, I just think it's important."

"No argument. You want to meet somewhere?"

"No, I'll come over there. What's your apartment number?"

"Hang on," Dean said. "Maybe we better meet in a public place."

"How come?"

"Well, this is a bachelor pad in a singles apartment complex. It might not be appropriate . . ."

"You don't think I can handle myself?"

"No, it's just that you're accustomed to an orderly family environment. This place is inhabited by all manner of degraded perverts."

"No problem. You don't even have to pick up the beer bottles off the floor. Just give me the address."

"OK, but I hope you're not too grossed out by what you see here. It's . . . not a pretty sight."

Shannon's Visit

Dean opened the door, and Shannon walked in. "Ohoo, tacky!" she said, perusing the decor of the den and entryway.

"I warned you," Dean said. "Men are animals, and they revert to the beast when there's no woman around to keep 'em civilized."

"I can tell," she said. "But I saw some women downstairs."

"Oh, those aren't women. Those are the party girls that hang out in singles apartments. And they do not bring civilization to the premises!"

Shannon looked at the beer bottles arranged on the floor. "Do you drink beer?"

"No."

"Then where did these beer bottles come from?"

"The dumpster out back."

"You went dumpster diving?"

"You said you expected to see beer bottles on the floor."

Shannon grinned, pleased that he had gone to some trouble in anticipation of her visit. "OK, Steele," she said, picking up some of the bottles. "I can see you need some help here."

"See? You're proving up a sociological theory here. Women compulsively instill civilization into the savage world of the single male."

"Cut the philosophical crap and help me carry this stuff out to the trash." They filled a trashcan with beer bottles and took it out to the back.

"See? You've only been here a few minutes, and already you've injected a healthy dose of civility into my depraved den of debauchery."

"Ha!" Shannon said. "It'd take a battalion of nuns to do that."

Skating

"So, what about my idea of us skating pairs together?"

"I don't know. You make it sound good, but I don't know. You've been lying to me a lot, haven't you?"

"Yeah, about almost everything."

"About really wanting to skate with me?"

"Well, everything but that."

"About thinking we could be a really great pair?"

"Actually, that was the other thing I forgot to lie about." She looked at him, puzzled. "Well, let's sort out the pros and cons, OK?" he asked.

"How?"

"I'll ask you a some questions. Maybe the answer will come out of that."

"OK, so what do you want to know?" she asked, coolly.

"Well, give me one reason why you wouldn't want to skate with me."

"OK . . . because Mom put you up to it," she said defiantly.

"Good. Now give me a reason you would want to skate with me."

"We might win some medals."

"All right. Now give me a reason you wouldn't want to skate with me."

"Because I'd have to give up my singles program."

"OK. Now give me a reason why you would want to skate with me."

"We might look really good out there on the ice."

"Fine. Give me a reason why you would not want to skate with me."

"Because you're a jerk, and you're always messing with me and making me mad!"

"Fair enough. Now give me a reason why you would want to skate with me."

"Because you're . . . always messing with me and making me mad." she grinned.

"Good. Now give me a reason you wouldn't want to skate with me."

"Because you're old, and mean and set in your ways, and I can't get you to do anything I want you to."

"Right. Now give me a reason you would want to skate with me."

"Because you're old, and mean and set in your ways, and it'd be fun trying to get you to do things." She grinned again.

"Good. Now give me a reason you wouldn't want to skate with me."

"Because you're a dirty old man, and I'm an innocent young girl, and I'd never be safe around you."

"Right. Now give me a reason you would want to skate with me."

"Because you're a dirty old man, and I'm an innocent young girl, and I'd never be safe around you." She giggled.

"Good. Now give me a reason you wouldn't want to skate with me."

"Because you say I'm just a kid and I'm not sexy on the ice."

"Right. Now give me a reason you would want to skate with me."

"Because you say you can make me look beautiful and sexy on the ice."

"OK, any more answers?" Dean noticed that she seemed to be finished.

"I think that about covers it."

"OK, do we now have the basis for a decision? Can you now make up your mind?"

"I don't know."

"Well, don't wait too long. Nicole Bobek is on hold on line two."

"No, she isn't, you shit! . . . Is she?"

"Actually, I think she may have been cut off by now, but Kristy Yamaguchi is due to call back any minute."

Dean looked at her. "So come on, Ms. Foster. What's it gonna be? Are we a team, or do I send you home right now and sink back forever into the degraded slime of the Piccadilly Apartments? Are you going to pull me out of this debauched lifestyle, or leave me to degenerate further?"

"I want . . ." she paused. "I want . . . you to look me in the eyes and tell me why you want to skate with me."

"OK, Kid. That's fair." He sat her down on the couch and took her right hand in his left. He put his right hand on her left shoulder, pressed his face close to hers and looked into her eyes.

"I have this plan, you see. I want to make you the most beautiful and the sexiest girl that ever cut a grove across a sheet of ice. And then I want to hold you up in the air as high as I can and show you to the whole world. I want to yell at 'em, 'Look what I've got! This is my partner, and she's fuckin' beautiful! And if you don't like it, you can kiss my ass!'" He paused. "That's basically why I want to skate with you."

Wide-eyed, Shannon gasped. "If you'll practice with me, and work out with me in the gym, and eat like I tell you to . . . in the next two years you'll develop into the most gorgeous woman ever to hit the ice, from Sonja Hennie right on up to present day. And whether we ever win a medal or not, the audiences will absolutely love to watch us skate."

Shannon was wide-eyed. "We'll be Hercules and Venus on the ice. A god and a goddess. I have moves nobody else can do. You have the magic. I've seen it. Together we can be spectacular. Whether the judges will recognize it or not is still a question, but the audiences will love it, and if that's all we ever get, I can damn well live with that!"

"I used to compete," he continued, "And I got a lot of attention from fans. People would stare at me and whisper to each other in restaurants. And when I'd come off the ice after a program, people would just gape at me in awe. And I wasn't as big then as I am now."

"But I never had the knockout effect of a senior pairs team. When one of the pairs would walk down the street, people would just fall all over themselves. There is something magic about a man and a woman who can skate well together. It just knocks people on their asses."

"Now, I'm not saying I like people staring at me. It gets to be kind of a drag after a while. But the point is, you can speak to twenty thousand strangers at once with your skating. You can reach them down where they live, intimately. You can go right to their hearts and inspire them to do better in their own lives."

"There's a certain look skate fans sometimes get on their faces. Whether they're kids or grandparents, and it's always the same. It's an, 'Oh, my God . . . that is so beautiful!' kind of a look. Their mouth drops open and their eyes gape and glaze over. You know that you have stirred them very deeply inside. We can give them that look, Shannon, thousands at a time."

Shannon's Decision

The girl grabbed him in a bear hug. "Oh, Dean," she said. "You're so wonderful!" She held him tightly for a time.

"So does this mean 'yes'?"

Finally she released him and looked into his face. "Of course it means 'Yes!' I'd die to skate with you, Dean Steele. Any girl would!" She took on a more serious look. "The last two days have been so miserable, not seeing you. I reached for the phone a hundred times to beg you to skate with me. I had a thousand thoughts I wanted to tell you. I had a million questions I wanted to ask you. Everything I did was just so . . . empty because you weren't there anymore. It was horrible!"

She donned a lighter look. "I've never known what it was like to have a brother, a big brother, 'til now. It's wonderful! I get a free look at being an adult. I get to see things my parents would never show me."

"Hang on, Tiger!" he interrupted. "I'm not volunteering to become your sibling. Just your skating partner. I was only joking about Fred and Millie adopting me."

"I know, I know. But it's the same, don't you see?" She sat up straight on the couch. "Lots of times I've wanted a big brother to show me things a girl my age can't usually see. Like this cool bachelor pad, for instance. I'd never get inside a place like this on my own!" She paused. "And to look out for me and teach me things. And, OK, to give me a hard time, and tease me a lot like you do. I never had that . . . not until just the last couple of weeks with you. And it's great! And then, when we weren't talking . . . it was just terrible. I missed you so much!"

"Shannon," he began, "That's all fine, but you shouldn't read too much into this. It's true that we'll be spending a lot of time together, and we'll have some fun, but I'll never be your brother. We'll be a pairs team, but not a family. It would be a mistake to go into this with the wrong expectations."

"Oh, I know you won't change your name to 'Dean Foster,' for Pete's sake. But it doesn't matter. We'll be working together everyday. You can't help but treat me like a kid sister, anyway. It's a compulsion with you. So I get a big brother for free, see?"

"There is some truth to what you say, but as a skating partner, I could never fill the role of a brother. I'd still have my own separate life. You'd be a part of only one aspect of my life, and I'd only be involved in one part of yours. I'll never be a part of your family."

"Whatever," she said with a teenager's disgust. "But it'll be a lot closer to having a brother than I've ever been before. Heck, in some ways it might be better. I won't be quite so eternally stuck with you, like I would be with a real brother."

"Look, Kid. I like hanging around with you a lot. No shit, it's fun. And I think we can make a dynamite pairs team. But don't go into this deal thinking I can fill the role of some fantasy brother you never had. That would just set us both up for a big disappointment."

"Oh, don't make me sound like a psycho. I'm only saying that having you as a partner would be kinda like getting a big brother as a bonus, that's all. I can learn a lot from you, about a lot more stuff than skating!"

"OK, if you say so. I'll even take you to the zoo, if it'll make you skate better."

"The zoo!" The girl looked at him and experienced a rush of excitement. She pressed her lips to his in a kiss that became increasingly passionate. Her tongue pressed its way past his teeth. Finally Dean pulled away.

"Hey, Wonder Woman, just because I'm your skating partner, doesn't mean you get to lick my tonsils!"

She giggled. "I'm just excited, I guess. I get to skate with Dean Steele! The other girls will be so jealous!"

"Shannon," Dean said seriously. "It's not a bargain. You'll have to work harder than the other girls do, harder than you ever have before. I'll be a slave driver. We have an awful lot of work to do, and a short time to do it. We have to learn all the pairs moves and pass all the pairs tests."

"I don't care, Dean. I'll do whatever it takes to skate with you."

"OK, partner," he said.

Planning

Dean and Shannon went skating at Willie's to celebrate their new partnership. After a vigorous session they took a break on the benches. "So, what do you think of my skating, now that we're partners?" Shannon asked.

"Well, I probably shouldn't tell you what I really think, at least not for a long time."

"Why, is it really bad?"

"No, it's really good."

"Then tell me! Tell me now!"

Dean grinned at her girlish enthusiasm. "You know, I scouted you for quite a while. I checked you out really good."

"OK, so tell me what you found out!"

"I'll tell you what. I'll give you my scouting report, OK?"

"Cool!"

"All right. You're a very competent skater. You have all the moves. You do everything correctly. You've obviously learned all your lessons."

"I hope it gets better than that!"

"Just hold on," He scolded. The girl frowned impatiently.

"But every once in a while, I see . . . the magic."

"The what?"

"The magic. Do you know what that is?"

"Uh, I guess so . . . No. What is it?"

"The magic is a rare and precious substance that sometimes circulates around a skater. It's like the sparkles that follow Tinkerbelle around when she flies. It's like the glow from a fireplace after the flames have died out. It's an invisible energy field that radiates out from a skater and warms everyone in the whole arena."

"Wow! And you see that in me?"

"Sometimes. It's not always there, but I've seen it more than once."

"So, tell me more about this magic."

"OK, but you better be ready for some really deep philosophy."

"Go for it, Sophocles."

"Well, a skater is basically out there, marking the passage of time with movements of her body. And sometimes, when she makes a movement that is perfect, absolutely perfect in every detail, it establishes a mental connection with someone who's watching, because they're imagining a perfect move, subconsciously. And for a moment, the two of them are locked together in the time stream, seeing, hearing, and feeling the same thing. The skater, then, allows the spectator to feel what it's like to glide across the ice, in a perfect path through space and time. For a brief instant, it's like the spectator and the skater merge together into a single being. Then the spectator can not only feel what it's like to move gracefully across the ice, but can see it from the outside while she does it. That's the magic, as best I can describe it."

"Gee," Shannon mused. "So, is that like what I was talking about? I mean, taking the audience with me, and all?"

"Yes, I think it is."

"Wow." she said.

"And the magic is why people come to ice shows, whether they know it or not. It's what there is to like about figure skating."

"So, what do you think about us as a pairs team, Dr. Freud?"

"Well, if you'll create the magic, I'll hold you up in the air while you do it, and we'll be pretty damn good!"

"Do you think we can win something?"

"I think we might could, eventually, win it all."

"Holy shit! You mean . . . gold at nationals?"

"Yep. We have a shot. No guarantees, of course. The big question is how the judges will like our style. We'll be . . . different. They don't usually respond very well to 'different.'"

Shannon paused to contemplate the almost forbidden thought. Then she waxed serious. "So, really, Dean, are we doing the right thing, skating together?"

"Well, we are . . . if we have several things going for us."

"Like what?"

"Well, first we both have to really enjoy doing it. It has to be so much fun we'd rather practice our act than eat pizza."

"OK, what else?"

"We'd need a lot of support. I mean money, time, ice . . . a lot of stuff from a lot of people."

"OK, Mom and Dad will fix that. What else?"

"We have to be able to win something. I mean . . . to have a decent shot at a title or a medal or something significant. Otherwise it's not worth getting back into the rat race."

"But you said we have a shot a being the best."

"Maybe. But there's one more thing."

"What?"

"We'd have to get along well together."

"Well, we haven't had but one big fight in the two weeks we've known each other. Maybe we're compatible."

"Maybe. But being a skating partner requires extreme dedication to another person. You and I are from very different worlds. I'm a lot older, and a lot more cynical."

Age Difference

"I know. I think of you as my grandfather." Shannon said matter-of-factly. She held a straight face long enough for Dean to give her a puzzled look. Then she lost her composure and burst out laughing.

"I got you that time, didn't I? My grandfather! You thought I really meant it!"

"Well, it did sound a bit extreme."

"No more extreme that what you said. You think I'm just a kid. That's bullshit. There's no significant difference in our ages."

"How do you say that? I was nine the day you were born."

"Well, first," she explained, "Girls always mature faster than boys. And girl skaters mature even faster, because they don't have a normal childhood. And I'm mentally older than my age anyway. All those together easily make up for nine years." Dean grinned at her logical construct. "The biggest problem I can see," she continued, "Is me having to put up with your immaturity."

"I see," Dean said, pensively. "And do you think you have the patience to stick with me while I mature to your level?"

"Oh, you'll never catch me, because I'm continually maturing all the time. I'm already worlds more mature that I was yesterday."

"It must be a dizzying experience, maturing at such a pace."

"I just find that my perspective changes on a daily basis, as I become increasingly able to take a broader view of life."

"I should have paid extra for the bullshit-resistant boots," he said. "I think these are done for." He stomped his cowboy boots on the floor.

"See? That's exactly my point. There you go being immature again. It's very trying for a woman of my age and experience."

"Too trying to take a shot at some gold medals?"

"Not *that* trying!" she said emphatically.

"Seriously, Shannon, you are mature for your age. I'm constantly amazed at the wisdom you come up with . . . or maybe stumble upon."

"Really? She softened. Then she caught herself. "Or are you bullshittin' me again?"

"No, not at the moment. I really do get a kick outta you. You come across as the typical spoiled brat clueless teenage chickie-babe, but there's a brain behind those baby blues."

"I just do that for Mom and Dad," she explained. "They desperately want a spoiled brat for a daughter, and they're so good to me," she shrugged, "I feel obligated to give 'em one."

"Well, would you be able to be their spoiled brat, and my dedicated and mature skating partner at the same time?"

"In my sleep, Dean!" She gave him a bored look. He grinned. "After all," she continued, "Spoiled brat is harder since I have to act it out. Mature adult just comes natural."

"I see," he chuckled.

Chapter 5

Dean Quits

The Boss

Kevin, Dean's supervisor, was on the phone when Dean poked his head into the doorway of his office. Kevin motioned him in with his free hand. Dean moved a pile of computer printout and sat down on the only other chair in the small room. Kevin was defending his request to hire another programmer to the Division Vice President.

"Damn!" Kevin said as he put the phone down, "We've got another rush project to do for Baylor, our customers are finding user interface bugs in AccuScribe 4.0 the first week after its release, Compaq just hired away one of our best programmers, and these assholes think we can get by without replacing him!" He looked at Dean. "What's happening, Buddy?"

"A funny thing happened on the way to the ice rink," he began.

"OK," Kevin grinned, "I'll bite. What happened?"

"I met this woman who wants me to skate with her daughter."

"Does she know what a lady-killer you are? I'd never let you near my daughter . . . if I had a daughter."

"She and her husband are willing to fund a try for the national championship in pairs skating."

"I thought you already won that."

"No, I took the bronze in men's singles. I've never skated pairs in competition."

"So, are you gonna do it?"

"Yeah, I think so, but it'll take a lot of time. I'll have to cut back my work hours."

Kevin inhaled. "I see." He frowned. "How much?"

"Probably to half time."

"Ouch!" Kevin said. "This is not a good time for that, Amigo."

"I know, but it's a real opportunity. All the pieces are there to put together a real solid try for the championship."

"Maybe I could get you a raise," Kevin said. "I've been trying to upgrade the compensation package for our whole group. I keep telling corporate that's part of the reason we're losing good people."

"It's not the money, Big Guy," Dean responded. "Besides, these River Oaks people will be putting big bucks into this project. You couldn't match it anyway."

64

Kevin sighed. "OK, Dean. Do what you gotta do. I just hope you don't mess up your career chasing a kid's dream, that's all." Dean got up and left. He had an empty feeling in the pit of his stomach.

The Professor

That evening, after his operating systems class at the University of Houston, Professor Atkins called Dean aside for a chat. They walked down the hallway to his office.

"I've just accepted a faculty position at UT Austin," the man began. "It's a full professor's chair in the Electrical and Computer Engineering Department, and it comes with a fully equipped lab. I'll be moving over there in three weeks."

Dean was stunned. Atkins had been at the University of Houston for almost ten years, ever since he finished graduate school at Carnagie-Melon. He had been a good advisor, and Dean wondered which of the other profs he could get to supervise his master's thesis.

He paused when he saw Dean's perplexed look. "Don't worry, Dean," he said. "I'm not abandoning you. I've gotten you into the PhD program at UT. All your graduate courses from U of H will transfer to UT. You can skip the Master's degree. Just take a few more courses, write a thesis, and you'll be 'Dr. Steele.' You'll have to pass their qualifying exam to be admitted to candidacy for the doctorate, but that shouldn't slow you down much. Oh, and there's a research fellowship for you. It pays almost what you make at Accumedical, and it's tax exempt." He smiled. "I'm not one to leave my graduate students high and dry."

Dean was stunned. "That's great," he mumbled.

"It's a good move for me," the professor said, "They have a research program in wavelet analysis going on over there. And it's a good move for you. I've always hated to see you working on a Master's degree at night. You ought to be working full time on a PhD. It's a much better career strategy."

"Can I think about it a day or two?" Dean asked.

"OK," Atkins said, "But it shouldn't be too hard a choice to make. I just assumed you'd jump at it."

"Thanks," Dean said. "I really appreciate you looking out for me."

"No problem," he replied. "Just get back with me in a day or two. There's some paperwork we have to submit to the UT graduate school office. This is kind of a miracle we're pulling off here, and we have to give the university administration its due."

Dean left the U of H campus in a state of shock. It would be a dream to work full time on a PhD thesis at the well-equipped UT campus. Besides, he knew Austin, and he loved that unique blend of state capital, university city, and small cowboy town. He missed the hills and lakes that Houston lacked. Austin also had a thriving music industry, with numerous night clubs and recording studios. He saw

Houston as an overgrown oil boomtown. The summers were oppressive due to the humidity, everything was too far apart, and the freeways were constantly under construction.

Having a PhD in ECE[1] from UT Austin would open up a world of employment opportunities for him. He would be qualified for a faculty position at almost any university in the country. He could get a job managing the research department at a big electronics firm, or even work in the space program at one of the NASA research centers. He got little sleep that night as visions of his new career possibilities danced in his head.

Millie

"So, what's so important, Dean?" Millie said, sliding into a booth at Starbucks.

Dean looked up with dejection and pain on his face. "I've got some bad news, Millie."

"What is it, Dean?"

"I've been thinking it over, this whole deal. I think I've been kidding myself. It doesn't make any sense for me to go back into competitive skating at my age. Skating is for kids, and I don't have the patience anymore. I need to get on with my career, and my career is engineering. This whole thing is a kid's dream. It's time I started acting like an adult."

"What are you saying, Dean?" Millie was concerned.

"I'm saying I've thought it over. I've realized that this pairs skating project is basically not a good idea. In fact, it's a really bad idea. It'll just get us all excited for a while, and then leave everybody hurt and disappointed. It'll cost a lot of money, time and effort, and in the end, it will all have been a waste. Everybody loses."

"What happened to change your mind?"

Dean looked down. "I talked with one of my profs yesterday. He's moving to UT Austin next semester. He has a research assistantship for me. It pays a decent wage. Almost all of my graduate coursework at U of H will transfer to UT. I'll skip the Master's degree and go directly into the Ph.D. program in computer engineering. It's a really great opportunity."

"So, what are you really saying, Dean?" Millie was very concerned.

"I'm saying I've decided not to skate anymore. I mean compete. I know it's a blow now that all these big plans have been made, and I'm sorry for all the trouble I've caused. I know Shannon will be disappointed too, but in the end she'll be better off. This ill-founded pairs arrangement would just end up denying her a real skating career. She needs a situation that makes sense, whether it's singles or pairs."

Millie inhaled, suppressing rage. "Are you sure about this, Dean? I mean, have you made up your mind, or are you just undergoing a brief period of 'buyer's remorse'?"

"I wouldn't mention it, Millie, if weren't final. I apologize for the trouble I've caused you and your family. Y'all have been very kind to me. "But I have to stop it before I do any more damage. It's just a bad idea—bad for you, bad for Shannon, and bad for me. We'd be fantasizing if we thought otherwise."

"I see. You think you can just turn it off like a light switch? Here today, gone tomorrow. 'Sorry folks, I've got to go out and be an engineer. You can throw away all your plans to be a part of a great skating project? I'm off to build bigger and better computers!'" Dean looked at her coldly. "What is it, Dean? You want more money? You think you sold out too cheap? Is that it?"

"It has nothing to do with money."

"How much do you want?" she asked, ignoring his answer. "What will it take to make you come to terms here? Just spit out your number, Mr. Steele."

"Millie, you're not tracking me here."

"You think I can't meet your price? I'll write a check for ten thousand dollars right now. You think I won't hock my furs and jewels to give my daughter the career she deserves?" She glared at him. "I'd rob a fuckin' bank, Dean, you can believe that! I'm not about to let go of this dream. It means too much to Shannon . . . and to me."

"No sale, Millie. Money is not the issue here. It's my life, my career I'm thinking about, and this skating thing is . . . just a fantasy. We've got to give it up before it causes a lot of people a lot of pain."

"Then what is the real issue? What do I do to get you back on track?"

"Two years of my life, Millie. Can you add two years to my life to make up for spending the next 24 months pursuing a hopeless dream? Can you compensate me for two years of working my ass off just so a panel of nine self-important assholes can tell me how bad I am?" He paused. "Sorry, madam, but I'm a member of a rare and endangered species . . . homus libertarius . . . people Millie Foster doesn't own!"

"You've been taking too many steroids, Mr. Steele. They fucked up your brain."

"I don't take steroids, Mrs. Foster, and my brain is working fine."

"OK, Dean, have your fun," she snapped. "Insult me. Flex your muscles. Rant and rave for a while. But then get back in line! We have a lot of work to do to make this thing happen, so don't waste too much time with your petty fit of . . . career . . . or whatever it is." She got up to leave.

"Goodbye, Millie," he said. "We won't be seeing each other again."

"Take a day off, Dean. Take two days off. Go down to Corpus Christi. Lay on the beach and get your head straight. But I want your butt back on the ice on Monday!"

"Sorry," Dean said after her as she walked away. "Sorry," he said again, almost in a whisper.

Shannon

Shannon was sitting on his front steps when Dean arrived home the following afternoon. "Hey, Kid," he said. "What are you doing here?"

"Mom says you're having second thoughts about skating with me," Shannon said.

"How long you been here?" he asked.

"Oh, a couple of hours," she replied. "I didn't know where you were, so I just waited."

"Shit, Shannon. This is not a good place for a young girl to hang out."

"Oh, everybody was real nice," she replied. "Several kind gentlemen offered to take me in."

"I'll bet they did!" She didn't smile. "Is your mom mad?"

"Oh, awful! She's like an old bear with an arrow in her ass. Nobody can talk to her without getting their head bit off."

"I can imagine."

"Can I have some water?" the girl asked timidly.

"Sure, Tiger. Get whatever you want outta the fridge."

Shannon pulled a diet Sprite out of the refrigerator.

"So, why did you do it, Dean? I mean decide to quit."

"It's a long story, Shannon. It might not make much sense to you."

"Because I'm a kid? Is it because I'm not a guy, you think I can't understand?"

"No, it's just got a lot of personal reasons mixed up in it, and those might be hard for you to see. It has a lot to do with what I want out of life."

"OK, but can you tell me about it anyway?"

"I can try. After all, I'm the one who talked you into this deal in the first place. The least I can do is tell you why I'm quitting." They sat down on the black leather sofa in Dean's den. "I took a look at how much effort we would have to put into working up a program," he began, "How much time and money it would take from everybody. And I looked at the chances of us winning a long series of contests and getting up to the Nationals, or Worlds, or the Olympics. I calculated the probabilities, and they're dismally small."

Shannon sipped her drink as she listened attentively.

"So what would happen is, a lot of people would put in a lot of time and money . . . and we'd lose, and everybody would be disappointed and sad, and you and I would feel terrible. All that time and money would have been wasted."

"But you said it yourself, Dean, there aren't many senior pairs teams out there."

"But there are a few, and they're really, really good, and they're well established in the sport . . . well known to, and well respected by the judges. Most of 'em have been skating together for eight or ten years." He paused. "It only takes three of 'em to keep us out of the metal . . . only four to knock us out of advancing to the next contest." He paused. "It's really unlikely that a recently formed pairs team from Houston can beat the Canadians and the Russians. They're just too good."

"OK, she said, "I can see that. But why not give it a try? What do you have to lose?"

"I've got a really good opportunity to enter the Ph.D. program at UT next semester. My prof is going there and he wants to take me with him."

"You want to be a doctor?"

"It would qualify me for some really interesting jobs."

"Couldn't you still do it after we go to nationals?"

"Well, I doubt if I could get into their Ph.D. program without Dr. Atkins' sponsorship. And even if he still wanted to do it two years from now, it would take two years off the end of my professional career," he said. "I'll retire at sixty-five, right when I'm making the most money. If I start my career two years late, that slips everything back and essentially cuts off the last two years of my earnings. It works out to a lot of bucks."

"So, when would you get out of school and start this career? How old would you be?"

"Well, if I get a Ph.D., it would probably be another two years. I'd be almost twenty-nine."

"OK, so you'd be working as a professional engineer for . . . umm . . . thirty-six years before you retired, right?"

"Yeah, about that."

"But if you skate with me for two years, you'd only get to be an engineer for thirty-four years, right."

"Yeah."

"OK, so what could you do in thirty-six years that you couldn't do in thirty-four? You could put in one extra hour a week and catch up by the time you retired, anyway. So, what's the big deal?"

Dean was amused by her arithmetic. "Actually, it'd take a little over two hours a week to make up two years in thirty-four, but you do have a point."

"And look at this," she continued. "If we don't do this, I'll always wonder what it would have been like. Would we have won gold at the Olympics, or would we have fallen on our butts at the Southwest Regionals? What would the history books have said about Foster and Steele? Were they the greatest pairs team ever to slice the ice, or were they Bozo and Bimbo on skates? Would the big-name pairs just laugh at us, or would they sweat their asses off, afraid we'd cream their butts in competition? We'll never know."

She looked at Dean. "You're the 300 pound gorilla on skates. You're Arnold Schwarzenegger out there. You're Rambo on ice, for Pete's sake. And I'm . . . well . . . I'm something. I'm the opposite of you, and that could make a great pairs team. You're big and mean and I'm sweet and innocent, or at least I can skate that. You're a responsible adult and I'm a spoiled kid, or at least I can skate that. Anyway, I just think that together we have something people will like." The girl paused to look out the window. "I'd like to know what the answer is. I'd like to find out how good we can be . . . where we fit in to all this. No matter what the answer is, I'd just like to know . . . before I settle down into the boring suburban wife and mother role. I'd just like to know where Foster and Steele fit in."

She turned around. "And as far as all that money and expense goes, Mom and Dad are determined to spend a fortune on their only daughter, one way or the other. It's their main purpose in life. Nobody can stop 'em. If it's not skating pairs with you, it'll be something else that makes even less sense. They'll find a way." She inhaled. "And you should have seen 'em when we first got together. It's the most excited they've ever been in my whole life! And when you quit, they went downhill real fast. This pairs project is like drugs to 'em. They love it. So even if we place dead last in every contest, they'll still love every minute of the chase." She paused to reflect. "If we don't do it," she said, "They'll just sink back into their dull, boring lives. God, I hate that!"

"But you can have a singles career," he said. "That was the plan before I came along and messed everything up."

"Sure, I can skate. But I'm not cute and petite like Lipinski, or as slender as Kerrigan. I'm not as sexy as Bobek, or as shy as Ito, or as sophisticated as Witt. And I can't jump like Kwan or Yamaguchi. I'll always be somewhere in the middle. Just another 'pretty good' girl skater. Yuck! Who needs it? There's no gold in them hills."

"But Foster and Steele," she continued, "Now there's something the world has never seen before. Two pairs skaters almost the same size. A guy who can toss a 120-pound girl around like she was a feather. It would blow their minds."

Shannon turned to face him. "Wouldn't you like to walk up to Lloyd Eisler and say, "I can toss my girl as high as you can, and she weighs one-twenty!"

Dean inhaled and shook his head. "How old are you, again? I haven't heard a thirty-year-old make sense like that in a long time."

"Don't you wonder, Dean? Don't you wonder what would happen when Foster and Steele hit the ice?"

"Sure. But I've also calculated the odds, and anything that's even remotely probable ain't very appealing. All the most likely scenarios involve a lot of sweat and expense, no reward, and a heap of heartache."

"But the reward would be finding out, don't you see? Knowing where we stand. Even if we fail, we still get to find out. Are we second behind Meno and Sand[2], or are we sixteenth, behind a dozen stumbling teenagers. That's what's so cool about it!"

"But, Shannon. We won't win any medals!"

"So, who cares? So what if we don't win any medals? They just collect dust in a drawer anyway!"

"But I thought that was the point. We gotta win some medals, or it doesn't count."

"Wrong, Dean. What counts is how we skate. What counts is, do we put that warm smile on the audience's faces? Does watching us light up their eyes and inspire them to do better in their own lives? To heck with the judges and the titles and the medals. That's not what it's about. It's about saying something to an audience. Something you can only say on skates. Something that stirs them deep down inside."

"But you need to win medals so you can skate professionally."

"I don't worry about that. I don't have to be Peggy Flemming, or Michelle Kwan. Mom will marry me off to some boring rich kid, and I can skate whenever I want to. The Stars on Ice tour is a drag anyway. You spend your whole life on a bus full of skaters. Who needs it?" She paused. "So don't worry about me," she continued. "You have to do what's best for you. I'll get by. I'm the Ice Princess, remember. Mom and Dad forbid me to be unhappy. It simply isn't permitted at my house."

"But, don't you want to skate pairs?"

"Oh, Dean, when you asked me to skate with you, it was the happiest day in my life, even if I did get mad because you and Mom tricked me. I think it would be Heaven on Earth." She paused. "But it's more important that you do what you have to do. I wouldn't be happy if you weren't happy, and I couldn't bear to know that you were giving up something you love, just to skate with me. I couldn't stand that, and I'd never forgive myself."

"Damn, Kid! I never thought you'd feel that way about it."

"Do you remember what you said? You said we could speak to their hearts, Dean. The audience, I mean. You said we could inspire them to overcome their problems and do better in their own lives."

"Yeah, but that was just bullshit to get you to agree to the Ice Queen's evil plan."

"Well, bullshit or not, it changed my whole attitude toward skating. I've been a different person ever since, don't you see? That's why I want to skate with you, Dean Steele. I could never do that by myself, or with any other partner, either. I'd just get caught up in that competitive, judging, backstabbing thing where everybody ends up mad at everybody, and nobody really wins. But with you . . ." She swallowed. "We could rise above all that and reach for the audience. It wouldn't matter if we got five-nines or three-nines. We would know we had shown them something." She looked into his eyes. "I don't want you to do it for me, Dean. But if you want to do it . . . for your own reasons . . . and if it's right for you . . . I'd really, really . . . really love to skate with you. If not, then I'll always wonder what it would have been like, being Dean Steele's partner. I'll tell my grandchildren about how close I came to doing something really spectacular."

"Shannon, nothing Millie said had the slightest effect on my decision not to skate. But I'll have to admit, you've opened my eyes a little here. You have the real reason, the pure reason in mind. Everybody else wants to do it for all the wrong reasons, and I had fallen into that trap too. But you . . ." He choked up.

"Heck, Dean, I just repeated what you said to me."

"I suppose, but I had forgotten it. You brought it home to me again." He regained control. "Tell you what. Give me another day to chew on it. If Brian Boitano or Kurt Browning call up, beggin' you to skate with them, tell 'em to buzz off, OK? Tell 'em you haven't been released from your current partnership yet. I've got to work this out in my head. Once I figure out what's right, it'll all come out OK."

"You've got my number," she said. "I'm open 24 hours."

Shannon and Millie

"Where were you?" Millie asked.

"Talking to Dean," the girl replied.

"That little shit! What did he say about me?"

"Your name didn't come up."

"Well, what did he say about you?"

"I'm not going to tell you. It was a private discussion."

"Well, you're just a bundle of news, aren't you Young Lady? What's going on?"

"He's thinking about it."

"About what?"

"About skating with me, of course!"

"I thought that was already decided. He bailed out on you. He left you standing at the rail with no partner."

"He's thinking about it."

"You think he might come back?"

The girl looked at her mother. "He will come back," she said. "Tomorrow at six."

"How do you know?"

"I just know. He'll come back."

"Shannon, don't let this man break your heart again. It's a tough world out there. Despite what Daddy and I do, you'll get some bad breaks. You have to learn to roll with the punches."

"Tomorrow at six," she said, "He'll come back." She went to her room.

Dean's Decision

Shannon was waiting on Dean's steps when he came home.

"Hi, Partner," she said, confronting him calmly but boldly.

He looked at her, partially suppressing a grin. "Hi, Young Lady," he replied. "Can I buy my skating partner a diet Sprite?"

"Sure." They grinned at each other. "Not that it matters," Shannon said, grinning wryly as they entered his apartment, "But I'm the happiest girl in the whole wide world, right now."

"Not that it matters," he repeated, grinning.

"Right," she said, looking at him calmly, "Not that it matters."

"So, how did you know?"

"Know what?"

"That I'd decide to skate after all."

"I just knew."

"But how did you 'just knew'?"

"It was simple. First, I knew you'd eventually do what's best for you . . . and you should. And second, I knew that skating with me is the best thing that could ever happen to you. No rocket science there." She held a straight face.

"I see," he said, grinning to himself. "Nothing like a partner with self-confidence."

"You're a lucky guy, Steele." She grinned. He rolled his eyes.

River Oaks

Shannon and Dean walked into the living room of the Foster home. "He followed me home, Mom," she said. "Can I keep him?"

"Dean!" Millie exclaimed. "What are you doing here?"

"I want you to meet my new skating partner," Shannon said. "His name's Dean."

"Thank God!" Fred exclaimed. "Welcome back, son."

"So, Mr. Steele," Millie said from beneath cocked eyebrows, "On what terms has the lost sheep returned to the fold?"

"Essentially unconditional," he said. "Win or die trying."

"And what brought about this amazing change of heart?"

"Your daughter is a very persuasive young woman," he said. He sensed that Millie was displeased that Shannon had succeeded where she had failed. "I would like to discuss some ground rules, though," Dean said, "Just to maximize our chances for success."

Millie frowned. "Sure," Fred agreed. "What's on your mind?"

"Well, first I'd like to have MRI scans done on Shannon's knees and hip joints and her lower back, and I'd like to be able to go over them with the radiologist."

"Why? Do you think there's something wrong?"

"Oh, no. But if she does have some slight weakness there, we can work around it to avoid an injury that might shut us down." He paused. "And if there is some serious weakness, then we shouldn't go ahead with it. It'd just lead to pain and disappointment.""What about you?" Millie asked. "Would you submit to an MRI scan?"

"Sure, I'd love it. But you'd have to pay for it. It falls well outside my health care budget."

"Well, that sounds like a good insurance policy to me," Fred said. "We can rule out any cause for worry about weak knees and such."

"OK, but you'll need to grant the doctor permission to show me her scans. As you know, my company writes software to process MRI and CAT scans. I'm conversant with it."

"No problem. What else are you thinking of?"

"Well, I assume, from what you've said all along, that you don't intend to do this thing on a limited budget. I mean, you'll want to do whatever increases our chances, even if it costs a few bucks."

"Well, this thing is gonna cost a fortune anyway," Fred said. "It doesn't make sense to cut corners."

"We'll spare no expense for our daughter's happiness," Millie corrected him.

"OK, I'd like to have all our practice sessions videotaped. That way we can see ourselves skating together on an ongoing basis, and continually refine our style. We have to get real good together, real fast. I have a friend who'll do it for a reasonable price."

"No problem. Millie will set up an account with the guy," Fred said. "What else?"

"I'd like to be able to buy private ice at Willie's arena whenever we need it."

"Oh, good heavens!" Millie said. "You don't have to skate at that dreadful place anymore. We'll buy all the time you need at TIS or Sharpstown."

"Their ice goes for $250 an hour," Dean said. "It's not necessary. Willie's place is modest, but his ice is excellent. If you'll just set up an account . . ."

"No problem," Fred said. "I'll fix it so the bills are paid automatically every month. We'll even put up a cash deposit if necessary."

"No. Willie won't require that."

"What else."

"OK, this might be a little tricky. I know you have a long relationship with Shannon's coach. He's good, but he's not a pairs coach. Besides, I don't think he'd like working with me. I think . . ."

"No problem," Fred said. "We'll get y'all a new coach. You and Shannon can pick him. And if he lives someplace else, we'll rent an apartment in Houston for him."

"I think we can find a good coach locally," Dean said. "But we'll also need help from a good choreographer. Our routines will have to comply with all the USFSA rules. We don't want to lose points because we did too many jumps or went two seconds over the time limit. I know a choreographer who has a digital sound editing setup that can stretch and compress songs without changing the pitch. She can cut our music together to make it fit the timing of the routine."

"No problem," Fred said. "We'll use her. What else?"

"I think Shannon has had enough ballet for now. I'd like for her and me to take dance lessons from this French woman I know, Cecile. She moves like a cat. Damnedest thing I've ever seen."

"OK, new dance lessons. What else?"

"Shannon and I will need new boots," Dean continued. "She'll need softer ones than what she now skates in."

"I'd think she would want stiffer ones for pairs," Millie said. "She'll be landing harder than in singles."

"Skaters with stiff boots don't develop ankle strength," Dean said. "They depend on the boots for support, and weak ankles in stiff boots are a recipe for injury. I'll work out some exercises to strengthen Shannon's ankles."

"Then why won't her regular boots work?" Millie asked.

"They don't allow her to point her toe well enough. It'll make a big difference in how we look . . . and in what Dick Button says about us, for that matter." He grinned.

"OK," Fred said. "New skates for everybody. What else?"

"I'm fresh out of demands," Dean said. "That should give us a fightin' chance."

"That's what I want to hear!" Fred said. "Let's do this thing!"

"Oh," Fred paused. "One more thing. I'd like to put you on the payroll. Either my company or Millie's. At least half time so you'll qualify for health insurance." He looked at Dean. "I'd like to ask you to quit your programming job. I'll match your salary, even give you a little bump."

"Let me think about that one," Dean said.

"Are you afraid of becoming too dependent on us?" Fred inquired. "Getting sucked into the Foster family a little too deep?"

"It's not that," Dean lied. "I just . . ."

"You said you were in for the duration," Millie said. "So prove it. Quit your job."

Fred looked at her harshly. "Easy, Millie."

Dean inhaled. "Let me talk to my boss. See what we can work out."

"Just quit, Dean," Fred said. "It's the best thing. This is gonna be more than a full time job."

They chatted for a while longer, and Dean went home.

The Bowl

"Shannon," Millie called as her daughter walked by the door to the kitchen. "Do you know anything about this?" She pointed to the floor in the corner where their pets ate their food.

Shannon was surprised to see three food bowls there. She reached down and picked up the middle one, a bright red, totally clean plastic dog food bowl. She turned it around and let out a shriek when she saw the word "Dean" in white letters. Millie looked at her expectantly. "Beats me, Mom," she replied. "I didn't put it there. Ask Dad." She walked away giggling.

Millie

Millie got Dean alone the following day.

"I'm not going to apologize," she said, "For all the horrible things I did after you decided to quit. It would take too long and hurt too much. But I do want to explain something to you. I want you to know why I went off the deep end so badly."

"Millie, you didn't . . ."

"Shhh," she stopped him. "Let me speak my piece."

Dean silenced himself.

"I was so excited when I found out you were in Houston," she began. "I knew I'd find a way to meet you. Then I got the idea of you skating with Shannon. It was a dream. And when you finally agreed to it, I was in Heaven. My life had finally been fulfilled. I was all set to stroll down the yellow brick road and live happily ever after with you and Shannon skating together." She paused and took on a more somber look. "But when you started having second thoughts," She inhaled, "I thought I could turn you around, ease your mind, make up for any objection you had to the arrangement. I would have done anything."

She looked down. "But you came up with something I couldn't fight. Your engineering career was a rival I couldn't compete with." Her face drew up. "When I finally realized I had really lost you . . ." Her eyes moistened. "It ripped the soul right out of my body, Dean. I went numb, emotionally and physically. I couldn't feel anything anymore. It was as if I had lost everything." She mopped her eyes with a tissue. "I couldn't deal with it. I went stone cold inside. I felt nothing. Not anger, not frustration, not even sadness. I ceased to exist as a human being. Then everything I did just made the situation worse. I started making mistakes at work, at home, everywhere. I was a total mess, and I'm still not over it. I'm still stuck in the nightmare to some extent. But I think I'll recover pretty soon."

She placed her hands on his cheeks. Her eyes welled up with tears. "I just want you to know . . . that I was so totally destroyed, that I couldn't function. That's why I acted so terrible to you. I would never, in my right mind, do anything hurtful to you. So please don't think of me as that woman you saw the past few days. That wasn't me. It was an empty shell that only looked like me. Can you understand that, Dean?" Her eyes pleaded for understanding.

"I understand, Millie," he said. "You had a right to feel the way you did. I let you down."

"No, no, that's not it," she said. "I had no right to act that way. But it wasn't me, Dean! That's what I need you to understand. My heart had been ripped out, and there wasn't anything left but a shell. Please don't think that was me, the real me, because it wasn't. The real me was knocked unconscious, and my body was running on automatic. And the autopilot . . . isn't very nice."

"I understand what you're saying, Millie. You were suffering from traumatic emotional shock. I know that really wasn't you."

She embraced him. "Thank God," she sobbed softly. "Thank God."

---

1. ECE—Electrical and Computer Engineering
2. Jenni Meno and Todd Sand, US national figure skating champions

Chapter 6

Millie's Visit

Millie's Entrance

Dean answered the door. Millie entered with a condescending look.

"Good afternoon, Madam," Dean said. "Welcome to my modest homestead."

Millie looked at him and grinned. "Nuevo Tacky," she said, "I might have known."

"You disapprove of my humble digs?"

"Not at all. I suppose this is the only way an unmarried 26-year-old man can live."

"I only chose this place because it's close to schools and churches, and they have bingo on Wednesday nights."

"I'm sure," she laughed, giving him a distrusting look. "And the hot and cold running women had nothing to do with it?"

"Oh, they only run hot, here," he replied. "It's in the lease agreement."

Millie sneered and walked into the den, examining every detail and passing judgment silently on what she saw. Dean found himself mildly irritated by her haughty and insulting behavior.

"Just wondering," she said, "Where's the velvet painting of Elvis?"

"It's in the bathroom, of course," Dean replied, now visibly irritated. "You'll see it when you go in there to throw up." Millie laughed. "You've got to understand that these apartments are actually elaborately designed woman traps," he said, finally choosing to retaliate.

"And how does that work?" she asked with newly aroused curiosity.

"Well, when a woman of any refinement sees the tacky decor and the messy surroundings, she's overcome by a compulsion to straighten it up and inject an element of civility. As a result, she stays too long and eventually ends up in the bedroom, degraded and defiled. It's all been worked out over many years of intensive research and development."

Flirtation

"A woman trap, huh? Come with me, young man. I want to check this out." A haughty prance took the woman directly into Dean's bedroom. She turned with her back to the foot of his bed and pulled him over in front of her.

"So, if you wanted to catch this woman in your trap," she said, taking his right hand, "What you would probably do," she placed his hand on her left shoulder, "Is put your hand right here," she looked into his eyes from beneath raised eyebrows, "And push. Am I right?" A knowing smile seemed to ask, "What do you think about that?" The two stood looking at each other for a long moment.

"I hate to have to tell you this, Madam," he said, exerting a gentle pressure that shifted her weight onto her heels and pressed her calves into the bed, "But the Nuevo Tacky is beginning to take its toll on you."

"Oh, it's not the decor, Dear Boy," she responded, "However charming that might be. I'm afraid I've been caught in your trap for about eight years now, and all my struggling to escape only gets me in deeper. By now I might be hopelessly ensnared. Will the trapper now collect his pelt?"

They stared at each other. Dean was mildly put off by her overt flirtation. It flashed through his mind that this might be a test of his moral fiber. He was, after all, the man to whom she had entrusted her daughter. "I think it's time," he said, taking her right forearm in his left hand, "For our stalwart heroine to muster her strength and break free of her bonds, just in the nick of time." He used her right arm to swat his right hand off her shoulder. "See? I knew you could do it."

Without taking her eyes off him, Millie shook her head in amazement. "You know, you aren't doing much for my ego, Mr. Steele," she said.

"Fortunately," he mused, "Egotism is a testosterone-induced disease, and women are generally immune. Besides, you strike me as one who suffers no lack of self-esteem."

"Perhaps." She inhaled. "But to place myself on the altar and be rejected . . . is somewhat of a blow."

"There's been no rejection here," he said, realizing that he had embarrassed her. "Merely a concern as to what may be an appropriate course of action, given the circumstances."

"Then you admit to a modicum of temptation, Mr. Steele?"

"I'd say it's more an intense desire to behave shamefully, Ms. Foster."

The woman smiled, obviously pleased by his admission. "Tell me more," she said. This last exchange had considerably lifted her spirits.

"Well, I can illustrate with a preview of what came to mind . . . if you would not be offended by some slightly inappropriate activity."

"Oh, I'd love to see it!"

Dean took the woman in an embrace. He exhaled near her ear as he squeezed her. Then he gave her a tender kiss on the cheek.

"You are an amazing woman, Madam," he whispered. "And I very much appreciate what you're doing to make this skating project work." He kissed her cheek.

She smiled. "And how do you intend to show your appreciation?"

"I'll send you a box of candy," he said, releasing her.

"Less than I expected, I must say," she remarked.

"It's the most appropriate means available," he replied.

"I look forward to it," she said. Then she walked into the living room and sat on the couch.

The Ice Moms

"You know," Millie said, gazing out the window, "The women in the figure skating club are a lot friendlier to me since you and Shannon paired up."

"Yeah? Why's that?"

"Because Shannon's not competition for their daughters anymore. One less skater to take the medal away from their girls." She paused. "I get invited to all kinds of social functions now."

"Do you go?"

"Heavens no! I don't want to spend my time with those silly bitches."

"You could probably be an officer in the club, what with your newfound popularity."

"God forbid! They just sit around and talk about what ought to happen, then they go home and watch the soap operas and forget all about it. They couldn't execute a plan if their lives depended on it."

"Well, I'm happy that you now have so many warm new friends."

"All except two. The women who are figuring out how to kill me."

"Who's that?"

"The mothers of the two pairs girls, Shirley and . . . what's-her-name."

"What's their problem?"

"They know that you and Shannon will beat their asses off in competition. Shirley and her partner, Tommy or something, just slipped down a notch, no better than second at the Regionals. The other little girl just lost her chance to go to sectionals."

"Another figure skating tragedy," Dean mused.

"Shirley's mom took me aside. She gave me some sage advice from a veteran pairs girl's mother—just for my own good, of course."

"That was kind of her."

"Right! She advised me that Shannon is too big to skate pairs. Her boobs are too big for a pairs girl. You two would do better in ice dance."

"Did she convince you?"

"Ha! I listened intently, of course, to the wisdom of one who's been there. Then I described to her in detail how her daughter would probably take third at Regionals and finish way down the list at Sectionals. I said if she goes to Nationals this year she'll be sitting in the bleachers." An evil smile had developed on Millie's face.

Dean began to grin. "You enjoyed the Hell out of that, didn't you?" A laugh exploded from Millie. Dean's grin widened. "You're a sadistic bitch, Ms. Foster."

"Are you shocked, Dean?" she asked, laughing. "They don't call me the Ice Queen because I'm generous and kind!" They laughed together.

Bitches

"I suppose you know," she said coyly, "That I'm not the only bitch in the Foster family."

"I'm shocked!" Dean said, obviously faking surprise.

"My dear daughter is cut from the same cloth. That clueless teenager act of hers is a con game. She's a conniving bitch, with the best of 'em."

"I wonder if that could be genetic," Dean mused.

"Of course it's genetic," Millie grinned. "She got it from her father."

Dean laughed. "I think Fred Foster is the most honest, straightforward, what-you-see-is-what-you-get guy I've ever met," he said.

"Well, maybe it's just a random mutation then," Millie suggested. They laughed again. "Seriously, Dean, the good-old-boy gene is recessive. The bitch gene is dominant. That poor child never had a chance."

"You make it sound unfortunate."

"Oh, it is. Not for her, but for any man she encounters. That girl will leave a trail of devastation throughout the male population."

"So is that my lot in life? A helpless pawn to the merciless manipulation of the Foster women?"

"You'll do well in the role, Dean. Being manipulated by a woman is one of the few natural talents men have."

"You don't seem to hold the male gender in high regard."

"Oh, I respect 'em. How the weaker sex ever came to dominate the society has always been a mystery to me."

"It's a facade," Dean said. "Men don't really run the show. Not if you look at the big picture."

"You're wise beyond your years, Young Man," Millie grinned. "Few of your gender realize that. Men are blessed with a special blindness that makes female manipulation invisible to them."

"I'd have to agree," he said. "So should I resist? Or should I just give up and accept my fate?"

"Oh, resist, for sure, Dean. That's what makes it fun!"

"I hope I can keep you ladies well entertained," he said.

"I'm sure you will," she responded, with a knowing grin.

A Song for the Queen

"I made up sketches of some ideas I have for skating costumes," she said, pulling sheets of paper out of her briefcase. Dean raised his eyebrows as he looked at the drawings.

"Aren't I good?" Millie asked, smiling confidently.

"Yes, Ma'am!" Dean said. "This is brilliant."

"So, what does the Ice Queen get as a reward for all her hard work?"

"What hath a poor knave that might appeal to Her Grace?" Dean inquired.

"Get out your guitar and play me a song. No, sing me a song," she said. "A love song!"

"Your command is my wish, Your Highness," he responded, reaching for his instrument.

"Mushy," she said. "Make it one of those mushy old love songs."

"One bowl of mush coming right up!" he said. "Eggs sunny side up." He fingerpicked the intro to the Dolly Parton song, "I will always love you," and then he began to sing. Millie smiled softly as he delivered the song to her.

"Oh, that was so sweet!" she said when it was over. "That's such a sad song."

Dolly

"Dolly sang it in the movie, Best Little Warehouse in Texas." She had written it years before, but it fit perfectly into that scene with Burt Reynolds. She didn't have to change a thing."

"That's right," Millie said, "Dolly Parton did sing that song. But I didn't know she wrote it."

"She's quite a talent."

"You admire her, I can tell."

"As a songwriter and singer mainly. She's written a lot of good stuff."

"Most men have a Dolly Parton fantasy, Dean. What's yours?"

"I can't tell you, Millie," he teased.

"Come on, Dean! Tell me. I know you have a Dolly Parton fantasy!"

"OK," he said, acting reluctant and embarrassed. "I'd really like to sing a duet with Dolly Parton sometime."

"I'll bet you'd be good! And I bet I know where you'd like to do it. On stage at the Grand Ole Opry in Nashville, Tennessee! Am I right?"

"Actually, I would prefer the shower of a small motor home," he said.

"Oh, God, you're terrible!" She laughed as she threw a pillow at him.

"With a bar of soap to serve as a shared microphone," he continued.

"Disgusting, Dean!" Her laughter took the form of a girlish giggle. It was the first time Dean had seen it come to the surface. He was definitely amused.

"Oops! Gotta go," Millie said. She gathered her belongings and left.

Reflection

Dean pondered the encounter after the woman left. She was obviously flirting with him, even teasing him, but why? Perhaps she wanted a little attention from a younger man as she faced the onset of her forties; something to reaffirm her appeal before it began to fade. Perhaps she simply enjoyed teasing a virile, unattached young man. He would be an easy target for her charm.

Dean wondered what she would have done if he had responded more aggressively to her flirtation and perhaps tried to kiss her. Undoubtedly some frivolous foreplay would have been tolerated, but how far would she have let it go to prove her point, and what would she have done when she decided he had gone far enough? Perhaps she would have enjoyed cruelly rebuffing his advances. He was glad he didn't attempt to find out. Running afoul of this woman would be a burdensome complication for the skating project.

Chapter 7

Media Fight

Shannon and Dean arrived at the Texas Ice Stadium for a meeting with her parents, their coach, their choreographer and Walt Mason, a friend of Fred's who is an executive with a downtown Houston advertising and public relations firm. Millie had reserved the upstairs VIP room for the meeting.

The bartender brought in soft drinks and sandwiches. Through the glass wall they could see a freestyle class practicing on the ice below.

Walt stood up and looked out at the skaters. Then he turned around to address the group. "I wanted us to get together to discuss how we handle the media," he said. "I have some ideas that should get the ball rolling."

"OK," Millie said, "Let's hear it!"

"All right," Walt continued, "It's a five-pronged approach. I want to get TV sports behind these kids as soon as possible—get 'em on the local 6 and 10 o'clock sports segments a couple of times first. That'll do more to get the ball rolling than ten newspaper articles. I think I can get Harry Snow at Channel Thirteen to put 60 or 90 seconds of ice skating in between baseball and the NBA. He's new in from Denver, and he knows figure skating. I think he'll do it."

Millie and Fred were getting interested.

"I have to sell him on the idea that the next big, up-and-coming local skating stars are a pairs team. They usually expect a girl skater to be the hot item, you know, Lipinsky, Yamaguchi. But I can sell him on a pairs team as the next hot item to come out of Houston. It fits into the new 'Houston figure skating dynasty' idea. Everybody in town's up for that, particularly with the Oilers gone and no NFL team. It fills the void. We're now competing with Canada for producing top-ranked skaters."

"Harry's new at Channel Thirteen," Walt continued, "And currently he's the sports anchor. But he's looking to make his mark. The news anchor slot will be up for grabs when Dave Ward retires."

"How are you going to convince Harry Snow that there is anything here worth covering?" Dean asked. "We haven't won anything yet."

"That doesn't matter," Walt continued, undaunted. "'New Houston pairs team prepares to win contest!' That'll get us 30 seconds of prime time sports easy. I can build it up from there."

"I knew I'd like this guy," Fred said. "Walt, you're a genius." Millie added.

"By the way," Walt added. "The name of the team. I'm thinking we go with Dean and Shannon, you know, Steele and Foster, since Dean has a history in the sport. "He looked at Fred and Millie with a question on his face. "But that's just an idea."

"What's the advantage?" Fred asked. Millie wrinkled her brow. She had assumed her daughter's name would be listed first.

"Because Dean is known in skating. His name's in the books. You know, with medals and trophies. The team name begins with a known quantity. It gives the media something to grab on to. 'Dean Steele, 1991 national bronze medalist, now skating as Steele and Foster . . .'."

"I can see that," Fred said. "Besides, he is the older one." Millie nodded, beginning to accept the idea.

"Hang on a second," Dean said. "Most teams put the woman's name first, like Torvel and Dean." The Fosters raised their eyebrows pensively.

"Besides, this is a totally new act. We don't want it to get tangled up with anything I did or didn't do ten years ago."

The group was lost in silent thought. Finally Millie spoke. "You have a record to be proud of, Dean. It could only help the act. Besides, Randy and Tai put the boy's name first."

"I think 'Shannon and Dean,' or 'Foster and Steele sounds good," Dean said. "And it will avoid anyone thinking, 'Has-been men's singles skater now attempts comeback with unknown teenage girl in tow.' I just think it's fresh, and it's cleaner."

Walt deferred the question to Fred and Millie. "Sounds OK to me," he said. "Sure," added Millie, "Whatever y'all want."

"Fine," Walt said. We'll go with 'Foster and Steele.' It has a . . . rhythm to it."

Fred and Millie nodded at each other. They were happy with having their daughter's name placed at the top of the list.

"OK, so next I'll have to cultivate a columnist," Walt continued, "For sustaining support. There are two I know at the Chronicle. I'll work 'em both 'till one of 'em proves out. But I think Charlie Liebowitz will be a gold mine. He can really make it happen for us."

"What do we get out of the newspaper thing?" Fred asked.

"Ongoing support. Constant occasional mention of their names. It builds recognition and familiarity. It sustains reputation. Over a period of time they become a household word. It'll help at contest time, too. The media will have heard of them. Even the judges will be affected by it."

Fred nodded.

"Third," Walt continued, "I want to put up a 'Shannon and Dean' Web Site. It'll be professionally done, lots of pictures, background info, even streaming video of their best skating. The younger fans will love it."

"Oh my God!" Millie exclaimed. "You mean I can log on and watch them skate right there on my computer?"

"Any time of the day or night," Walt said, "In living color."

"Wow!" Millie said.

"The Figure Skating Club already has us on their web site," Dean said. "Their webmaster has given us a page of our own. It's quite flattering."

"Oh, they're just using y'all to build up the club," Millie said. "It's a new club with no big name skaters, so they have to boost you two."

"The Foster and Steele web site will make that club site pale by comparison," Walt said.

"Next is the 'Shannon and Dean Fan Club'," he continued. "Membership card, autographed pictures, newsletter, favored seating, special exhibition events for club members only, the works."

"Now there's a winner!" Fred said.

"But the last leg of my plan is personal appearances. Both on and off the ice. Skating exhibitions," He paused. "And celebrity appearances. The TV coverage is the key. Even if we have to tape it ourselves and let the stations work the tape into a slack spot in their air time. I know a two-camera video team that does really good work. Fast-paced editing, lots of motion and excitement. Just the thing for a short, compact news spot."

"What type of . . . 'exhibitions' are we talking about here?" Dean asked.

"Well, first, events held here at the Ice Stadium. That's the hot new thing. And you and Shannon can skate an exhibition as the featured entertainment. The more affluent parents are all wanting to do their kids' birthday parties that way."

"And what type of 'celebrity appearances'?" Dean asked.

"Lots of opportunities there. Grand openings, parades, you name it. Everything that shows up in the 'Weekend' section of the Chronicle. Even a strategic lunch at Anthony's or a precipitous entrance at the ballet. It all works together to build your image. It gets everybody noticing you, talking about you."

"So, you've got us cast as the clowns at the kids' birthday parties, and as the ribbon-cutters at supermarket openings. Anything else?"

The room went silent. Everyone looked at Dean. Finally Millie spoke.

"Dean, Honey . . . Are you, . . . not in agreement with the media management thing? I mean, . . . don't you think the media aspect of your career needs to be handled properly?"

"No argument there, 'Mom.' But the media . . . It's like a fire-breathing dragon. Once you wake it up, you have to keep feeding it, because if you ever let it get hungry, then you get burned."

"What are you saying?" Walt asked. "What's this 'feeding the dragon' thing you're talking about?"

"I mean that once you show up on their radar scope, once you become 'news,' they expect to write something about you every few days, or weeks, at least. And if you don't keep giving them something good, then they'll start writing bad stuff about you."

"Whoa, wait, hold on a minute," Walt said. "Nobody's gonna be writing anything bad about you two. I'll take care of that. You just skate, and look pretty, and win trophies, and I'll give them plenty of good stuff to write about."

"It doesn't work that way," Dean said. "If we're opening stores and hosting birthday parties and going to interviews, . . . then we aren't practicing. And practice, lots of practice, is the only hope we have of ever winning a medal."

"But there'll be plenty of time for practice," Walt said. "Just leave the scheduling to me. Interviews only take a few minutes. You'll be back on the ice in no time."

"I've been down that road, remember?" Dean said. "I never lost less than half a day to a five-minute interview, and I did a bunch of 'em. Dealing with media people is a mammoth time-waster. And it eats up the most valuable practice time of the day."

"But that was in the past," Walt interrupted. "You didn't have me. I'll make sure it takes a minimum of time away from your skating. After all, we want you to win."

The room again filled with silence, until Millie chased it away.

"I think Dean may have a little different viewpoint on the whole idea of media management than the rest of us do. Am I right, Sweetie?"

Dean curled his lip and nodded slowly. "You could say that," he replied.

"Well look," Millie said. "Before we go racing off in one direction, lets take a minute to let Dean put in his two cents worth." She sounded like a second grade teacher lecturing the kids about fair play at recess.

Nodding heads indicated reluctant agreement from Walt and Fred. The others present were welded solidly into the role of spectators.

"Go ahead, Honey. Give us your ideas."

Dean got up, collecting his thoughts as he walked across the front of the room. Finally he spoke.

"There are two kinds of media coverage," he said. "There's good media, and there's bad media."

Walt, the PR professional, rolled his eyes to the ceiling and sighed.

"A skater can get either kind. Just look at Tonya Harding. She got awful press for a while."

"Oh, come on." Walt exploded. "That's got nothing to do with our situation here. She beat Kerrigan with a rubber hose[1], for Pete's sake."

"No, Walt, She hit her with a club, not a rubber hose!" Millie said. "Just keep quiet and let Dean finish."

"What I learned, and I got both kinds of press, is that the only worthwhile media comes directly out of accomplishment. Let them write about something good that you did. Not what you plan to do, or think you can do, or hope you might do. Not like DiGeorgio, Tara Lipinsky's agent, calling a press conference to announce that someday she'll do a quad jump. That, friends, is bullshit!"

"So for that reason I think it's way too early to wake up the sleeping giant who runs the big printing presses. If we do actually win something, and there's no telling how long that will take, then we'll have plenty of media attention. It's automatic. They swarm on you like piranha. Walt will have a full time job just keepin' 'em off of us. They'll put on snowshoes and bring cameras and microphones out on the ice while we practice."

Walt couldn't stand it any longer. "Without my help," he fumed, "You couldn't get your name mentioned in the Austin Asswipe right now. So don't worry your little pointed head about TV crews cluttering up your front lawn, Hot Shot."

"For Pete's sake, Walt!" Millie scolded. "Be nice! We're all together in this thing."

Dean was unaffected by Walt's comment, primarily because he considered the man to be of a subhuman species.

"If we wake up the media monster before Foster and Steele actually do anything, like at least winning bronze at a regional event, then we won't have anything to say at the interviews. We'll sit down at a table with the anchor, we'll smile, and then not have any answers to his questions. It'll just make us look stupid."

"Dean, Honey, you and Shannon would never look stupid on TV!"

"Not to you, Millie," Dean said, "Because you love us. But all those beer-and-corn-chips sports fans out there, and the figure skating judges in the TV audience too, won't be so easily pleased. It's a very bad idea to go on TV when you have nothing to say."

"But you can say plenty," Millie objected. "You two would make wonderful guests on, . . . Leno or Letterman, much less on a Houston TV sports show, for Pete's sake!"

"Millie, we would be introduced as accomplished pairs skaters, and the fact is . . . we haven't accomplished jack shit! Not yet, anyway. We'd be setting in motion a process that could eventually eat us up alive."

"How so?" Fred asked.

"We would be continually racing to catch up with our larger-than-life TV image. And I don't want to live like that." He paused. "And the pressure at contests would be horrendous. We'd be there trying to make good on all the promises we'd been making on TV. That kind of burden could sink our boat."

Walt let out a groan.

"Just look at Kerrigan in '96," Dean continued, "In the middle of that 'Nancy-Tonya' thing the media was doing—before the attack. She had 16 network cameras pointing at her every time she went to the john. She was so distracted, it's a wonder she even landed a double toe loop."

"Obviously he's had a bad experience with the media in the past," Walt said, with a disgusted "Why me?" tone in his voice. "And he couldn't stand the glare."

"What do you think, Sweetheart?" Millie asked Shannon.

"I just wish y'all wouldn't fight like this," she said. "It makes me feel all funny about everything."

"Come here, Darling," Millie said, stretching out her arm. Shannon sat down beside her mother and cuddled up. Millie put her arm around her daughter and patted her shoulder.

"The right time to 'manage the media,'" Dean continued, "Is after you've accomplished something. Then the whole circus almost makes some kind of sense. You did something people want to know about, and the media tells 'em about it. Otherwise, it gets real crazy, real quick. You haven't done anything anybody cares about, but you're right there in their face, anyway, talking about it. That doesn't make people like you. It makes you a joke."

"But Dean," Millie interjected. "Wouldn't it be nice to come home and see you and Shannon, skating, all over the TV?"

"That depends. It depends on what they're saying about us while they're showing us. They could be saying we just won gold at Salt Lake City. Or they could be saying we just killed any hope of the USA winning a medal at Worlds. They could be saying we're under investigation for selling cocaine to second graders. They could be saying we're aliens from Pluto who came to Earth to poison the water supply. The point is, that old 'any media is good media' idea is total bullshit—at least for us."

"Oh God!" Walt exploded. "Why couldn't she pick a boy her own age?"

"Because," Dean answered, with jaw clenched and fire shooting from his eyes, "None of the boy skaters her age can hoist her sweet little ass overhead with one hand free and a smile on his face. That's why you have me, and it's the only God damn reason I'm here!"

Walt buried his face in his hands. Millie's face took on a pained look. Fred was in total confusion.

"And one more thing," Dean pressed on, "If I may be so insensitive as to verbalize it at this little pep rally. When the house lights go out, and the music starts, and the spots light up, it's not 'us' out there on the ice. Its just Shannon and Dean. For the four and a half minutes that really count, you folks are spectators. And all this other stuff, while it is vitally important, is not worth a damn if those four and a half minutes aren't absolutely . . . , totally . . . , fucking perfect. So let's not lose our perspective here. Everything has to evolve from the programs that

Shannon and I skate. No amount of 'media management' will substitute for clean skating. No TV interview will correct a two-footed landing or a busted spin. No PR hype will cover up for us sittin' down hard on the ice. The skating has to be perfect. And that requires much more practice than there is ever time for. Nothing can be allowed to interfere with that."

"I can't argue with that," Fred said, more in an effort to defuse the moment than to agree with the concept.

"The point," Dean continued, regaining his composure, "Is that when you do something, the media will seek you out. And that's a legitimate thing. It even kinda works, if you don't mind a bit of a freak show. But the harder you try to get their attention, the more they ignore you. If you try to hide from 'em, they'll show up in your shower with cameras and a boom mike. It's one of those things that works backwards in this universe."

"We just want what's best for you two, Millie said, "For the team."

"Do you?" Dean asked. "Is it for Shannon's sake that you want to see her face on your TV, or is it for your own reasons? Ask yourselves that question, all of you. Why are you in such a Hell-bent hurry to make the world notice this girl? Is it for her . . . , or is it for you?"

A dark, eerie silence rolled into the room and settled like a thick fog, squeezing out the air and permeating the pores of the concrete block walls. The clock jarred to an abrupt halt, leaving the room and its occupants suspended in time and space. It may have been seconds, or possibly hours later that Millie broke the spell and breathed life back into the seven frozen bodies.

"Dean, no matter what we say or do, or how it may sound, we all, every one of us . . . we just really want this pairs program to succeed. We want you and Shannon to skate, and win, and be happy. We happen to think that media coverage is a part of that, but if you don't, then OK. We'll work around it. The point is, you two have to feel good about it, so you can skate well. That's what's important."

"Well, media is a part of it, all right," Dean said. "As soon as we win some metal that's any harder than lead, they'll be underfoot everywhere we step. I'm just pointing out there can be such a thing as too much media coverage, too early. And I know Walt doesn't share that concept. In his business, there's never enough. But too much exposure, too soon, could push Shannon and me into a trap that would prevent us from achieving the one thing that will ensure the success of this experiment. And that's clean skating and winning. We have to win, and we have to win first. If we do win, then camera cables will be ruining your flower beds. If we don't, you couldn't get our names in the . . . 'Austin Asswipe' if all seven of us ran down the street naked."

"By Gosh, I think he makes a lot of sense," Fred said. "We should build this thing on a strong foundation. Give it time to develop and mature. Then, when the right time comes, we'll take 'em by storm! And it'll be us in control, not those media crackpots."

"There's another factor at work here," Dean continued. "The judges."

The room once again went silent.

"If they hear all over the place how good you are, they'll be expecting a clean performance, and if you don't skate clean, they'll be disappointed. If you skate a 5.7 program, say, they'll give you a 5.6, just because you weren't as good as they expected. But if they think you've been having trouble with your jumps, or artistry, or synchrony, and you skate a 5.7, they'll give you a 5.8 because you exceeded their expectations. So an effective PR campaign could actually keep us from winning."

"Walt, you've been strangely quiet for a while," Millie said after a thundering silence. "What's your spin on all this?"

"I think it's a mistake not to manage the media from the word 'go'. Where the media's concerned, if you don't control it, it'll control you. But if you want me to soft-pedal the buildup, then I'll go slow with it. I'll play it however you want."

"OK, then," Fred said. "I think we've got a plan. Let's go for a beer!"

As the meeting was breaking up, Walt came over to Dean. "I hope you weren't offended by anything I said . . . , didn't take it personal . . ."

"No problem," Dean interrupted. "I know how it is in your business. You're just doing your job, and you're good at it."

"Well, I just want to make sure you kids get the attention you deserve." He held up his palms. "When the time comes."

"That's great," Dean said, grinning warmly.

Millie waited till nearly everyone else was gone, and she pulled Dean aside for an extended hug. During the embrace she spoke softly into his ear, "Dean, we don't just have you here because you can lift Shannon. You're a part of the team now. Understand? You're part of our family now. So don't ever think you're expendable, OK? You're not just one of the hired hands. You're the central pillar of this whole thing. It all revolves around you. Understand? So, don't go feeling like an outsider. Promise?"

"Yes, Mom," he said, with a grin. She gave him a peck on the cheek and a wink.

"This is a dream come true for me," she whispered. "I just want it to be perfect for you two. You may not know this, but I think you got a raw deal before, and I want the world to see how good you really are. I want it for you as much as I want it for Shannon."

Dean smiled softly at her. "But not as much as you want it for yourself," he thought to himself.

Out in the parking lot, Walt got in the back seat of Fred and Millie's Mercedes. "I don't mean to butt in where it's none of my business," he said, "But is Dean really the only boy Shannon can skate with?"

"Well," Fred began, "I don't see . . ." His words trailed off as he looked at Millie.

"Better get used to it, muchachos," Millie said. "The only male skater that would be any better for Shannon lives in England, and he's already got a partner."

"Christopher Dean," Fred mused.

"Besides," Millie continued, "You don't know how lucky I was to find him right here in Houston." Then her face took on a sly grin, "Or what I had to do to recruit him!" She winked. Fred smiled at her little joke.

"OK," Walt said, giving up that line of pursuit.

In the car on the way home, Fred asked Millie, "What was that little deal with you and Dean over in the corner back there?"

"Oh, I was just reassuring him," she said. "Keeping his spirits up. I can't have him getting upset or nervous right now." She paused. "Keeping him calm is part of my job."

"Ahh," Fred mused. "Always working, aren't you, Mom?"

Millie's face melted into a self-satisfied smile. "Always," she said to herself.

Sports Illustrated

Walt had driven up from Bel Aire and left his car at the Foster home in River Oaks. When they arrived home, Millie went inside, and Walt approached Fred.

"There's another angle we can work," he said. "It's just an idea, and I didn't want to let the girls in on it till I had gone over it with you."

"OK," Fred said.

"What would you say if I could get Shannon in Sports Illustrated?"

"Wow!" Fred said.

"Well, I know one of the editors there, and here's the deal. You know SI has become a skin mag."

"You mean, just because the country's premier sports magazine prints more skin than Playboy? I hadn't noticed," he joked.

"Right. Well they sell newsrack copy like gangbusters on those issues, but then it falls off. And subscription revenues alone don't keep the shareholders happy. They have those swimsuit issues spaced out to make their quarterly numbers look good, but the roller coaster revenue gives them a big headache."

"I can imagine."

"What happens is, the issue after the swimsuits sells pretty well. Probably guys hoping for more. But it's not there. So the next issue sucks gas, big time, no matter what's in it. They don't even put a full roll of paper in the presses. And even then, most of the newsstand copies come back for recycling."

"Ouch!"

"So what they do is, they cover female sports, much more than they ever did before. And it's all from the skin angle. Women's bodybuilding, for Pete's sake. They never considered that a sport before."

"So, what does . . ."

"OK, like I said, I know this editor at SI. He has an eye for women. He knows what the newsstand buyers want to see. And, so help me, God, Shannon is it. I kid you not. I mean, she's got that wholesome, athletic look they want. She's fresh, but she's flowering womanhood. I can sell her to this guy. It'll be a short feature on her, or her and Dean, I guess. And it'll go in the issue right after the swimsuits."

"Humm."

"Look, the Chronicle sports section goes out with yesterday's trash. But SI goes on the bookshelf. People come back to it, months, even years later. Sportswriters dig it out when they're writing their columns. Once she gets in SI, she's permanent."

"OK, but what kind of pictures are we talking about?"

"Hey, it's Sports Illustrated, remember? It's not Penthouse for Christ's sake. Just a skating outfit. You know, what Yamaguchi wears. Short skirt, big hair, and makeup. They'll love it. We're probably talking one portrait, plus a full-length shot, and two skating shots, with her up in the air, or something."

"Well, that sounds . . ."

"He'll let me write the copy," Walt interrupted. "I'll just take a stack of photos and let him pick out three or four to use. Hell, you can cull the stack before I go to New York. I would never do anything to compromise Shannon."

"I think it's . . . ," Fred said. "To get her in Sports Illustrated would be . . ."

"OK, we need to get pictures made. Hell, we need photos for all that other stuff anyway. I'll just work with the photographer to make sure we get some shots that SI will want."

"OK, Walt. Go for it."

"Thanks, Buddy," Walt said. "And lets wait till I have a commitment from SI before we tell anybody, even Dean. Our secret, OK?"

"Right!" Fred said. "No sense going through all that explanation before we know we have a deal."

Walt flashed him the 'thumbs up' sign.

Shannon

Dean took Shannon home from the meeting in the Mustang. On the way they stopped at Starbucks for coffee.

"So, what did you think about the big meeting?" he asked the girl.

"I don't know," she replied, disgustedly. "I just wish it wasn't such a big deal. Everybody was so tense!"

"I guess there's a lot at stake," Dean said. "At least they seem to think so."

"But, you know what's weird?" Shannon said. "I mean, you're back to normal now, but for a while back there, it's like . . . , you were my dad's age. You turned into one of them. It was spooky!"

"Does that mean you've guessed my secret?"

"What secret?"

"That I'm a space alien who can change his age just by turning this little knob concealed in my belt buckle."

"Yeah, I knew that," she giggled.

"Damn. And I thought I was being so careful!"

"But really. I thought you were my age, I mean basically. But you were mixing it up with Dad and Walt like a forty-year-old. I've never seen you like that before."

"So which is the real Dean Steele? Is it that cool teenager snappin' his fingers and poppin' his gum? Or is it the solemn businessman, workin' a corporate takeover deal? There's a signpost up ahead. It's the twilight zone!"

"Get serious. Sometimes I think I know you, but other times I don't know who you are."

"That should make your skating career very interesting. Never knowing who you'll be skating with next."

"Come on. Tell me who you are. I mean, really."

"I'm just what you see. I'm who you think I am. I'm just smart enough to not let Walt screw up our practice sessions, that's all."

"Well, don't ever get weird on me, OK?"

"Cross my heart and hope to lose my tentacles."

"Clown!"

"So, come on," Dean coaxed. "Don't you have any opinions on what we were talking about? It was just me speaking for the skaters. I was kinda outnumbered by the rabid publicity seekers."

"You did great. I thought you put 'em all in their place."

"OK, but did you agree with what I said? Or would you rather go into full-time publicity-seeking?"

"Umm, I pretty much liked what you said. It makes sense. We gotta win first. But I do think we should do some exhibitions. I mean, they're good practice for competitions, you know, with people watching, and stuff. Practicing by ourselves is not the same as, you know, lots of people watching."

"You've got a point, Kid. Why didn't you speak up?"

"Nobody wants to hear what I think."

"Whoa. Is that what you think? Really?"

"Sure. You and Mom run the show. I just do what I'm told. It's OK, though. I don't mind."

"Oh, oh. Danger, Will Robinson! Houston, we have a problem! Bold and vibrant male skater has wimpy mouse for partner!"

"Hey, I'm not a wimp!"

"How else do you explain your last statement? 'You and Mom run the show. I just do what I'm told'," he whined.

"There's nothing wrong with that. I don't need to be in the big middle of everything!"

"Only one problem. My contract guarantees me a headstrong, independent skating partner who can think for herself. I may have to file suit!"

"You don't have any contract!"

"Sure I do," he teased. "You don't think I'd trust the Ice Queen on a handshake, do you?"

Shannon laughed. "That would be dangerous."

"But seriously, this is supposed to be a team. I shouldn't have to run the show all alone. You have ideas too."

"Yeah, but nobody wants to hear 'em."

"OK, let's get to the bottom of this. Who doesn't want to hear your ideas?"

"Nobody. I mean, everybody . . . doesn't."

"Name one."

"You."

"Wrong answer. Another name, please."

"Walt."

"Screw Walt. He's an retard whose brain has been eaten by maggots."

"He thinks Tonya Harding beat Nancy Kerrigan with a rubber hose," Shannon added, giggling.

"Well, your Mom didn't have it much closer!" They laughed.

"Ignore Walt. He thinks Houston produces as many champion skaters as Canada, Russia and the Ukraine all put together. So who doesn't want to hear your ideas?"

Shannon got quiet. "Mom," she said softly.

"Who?" Dean asked, pretending not to hear.

"I said, 'Mom'."

"I'm sorry, who?"

"My mother!" Shannon said loudly.

"Oh," Dean said, feigning surprise. "Why doesn't your mother want to hear your ideas?"

"Because she already has her mind made up, and it wouldn't make any difference what I think, anyway."

"Oops. Bad sign. I can see we're going to have to fix this. Otherwise, when my lawyers get through with your Dad, you'll be living in a tent, watching rock videos on a kerosene-powered TV set."

"What's with you?" Shannon asked, becoming defensive. "Why do you all of a sudden want a bitch for a partner?"

"I have a bitch for a partner. I want a woman for a partner. A woman with a brain."

"I have a brain," she said emphatically.

"OK, that's a start. Now if we can just get you to use it a little."

"Jerk!" she said, grinning. "I use my brain, . . . every day or two."

"OK, then connect it to your mouth, so people can hear from it occasionally."

"What do you want me to say?" She was both irritated and amused by this exchange.

"Whatever you think. Analyze a situation logically, form a rational opinion, and express it eloquently. That'll do."

"What, you want a college professor for a skating partner?"

"No, but is an intelligent human too much to ask for?"

"OK, Mr. Smartass," she challenged, "What do you want my opinion on?"

"All right," he said, accepting the challenge, "Diamonds as an investment vehicle."

"Bad idea," Shannon replied. "The price is held artificially high by the cartels who're hoarding 'em. If they ever decided to unload, you'd lose your ass."

"Wow!" Dean said. "That was pretty good."

"Try me again," the girl said defiantly.

"OK, how about income tax reform?"

"The tax code has been used by the government to try to encourage some things and discourage other things, to the point where it's a hopeless mess. It has long ago lost sight of just raising money to run the country. It can't be fixed. It has to be replaced with something else. We need a clean start."

"Pretty impressive, Professor. When's your new book coming out?"

"Right after my lecture series at Harvard." She burst out laughing.

"You been holding out on me, Kid. You're not just another pretty face. You're some kind of a damn computer!"

"You underestimate me in so many ways," she said haughtily.

"I think you're an alien, or an android, or a mutant of some kind. No fluffy headed teeny-bopper knows stuff like that!"

"That's gynoid, Sucker. Androids are male, and I'm definitely not male!"

"Brains and a bod. What a combination!"

"Eat your heart out, Peasant!"

"I better call my lawyers and tell 'em to stand down. I've got Albert Fucking Einstein as a skating partner!"

"That's Marie Fucking Curie, Dum-dum. You gotta learn to deal with my gender."

"I stand corrected," he grinned. They looked at each other and laughed.

"So, how do we exploit this new-found intellectual component of our partnership?

"I guess I'll just have to run the show!" Shannon replied, matter-of-factly.

Dean put a pained look on his face. "I fervently hope there's another way."

"OK," Shannon popped off, "You run the show. I'll just do as I'm told."

"What if we both run the show? What if we discuss the issues, and come to an agreement about what we want to do? Then both of us will say the same thing anytime anybody asks."

"Might work," Shannon conceded.

"So, let's start by getting your views on what was discussed tonight."

"OK, so I agree, nothing should be allowed to interfere with practice." She looked at him sheepishly. "That's my favorite part," she admitted. "I love practicing with you."

"OK on the practices. What else?"

"Now, I do want to be on TV. I want to tell all those bitches in my class at school, 'Tune in at six o'clock, cause I'm on the news.' I know that's terrible, but I wanna do it anyway."

"OK, we'll make allowances for rampant, unbridled vanity. What else?"

"I like having our own web page. It's cool. Most kids don't have one. Or it's just some funky personal page if they do."

"OK, the raging vanity extends to cyberspace. What else?"

"Like I said, exhibitions. But good ones, though. Not birthday parties for little kids that are always dropping their ice cream cones. I hate that."

"OK, no ice cream on the floor at expos. Agreed." Shannon rolled her eyes.

"Oh, and the fan club. It's OK, I guess. But only if somebody joins. I mean, I wouldn't want to announce it and have everybody go, 'Yuck!'"

"Good point. No yucking at the fan club."

"And one more thing. I want our billing to make it clear that I'm the star, and you're nobody. I get the big letters, and you get little tiny ones. Something like 'The beautiful and talented Shannon, assisted by What's-his-name'."

"Check. Least talented skater gets top billing. Par for the course in this sport. Anything else while we're tippy-toeing through fantasyland?"

"Yes," she looked into his eyes softly. "I want you to skate with me always. I want to be your partner forever."

Dean smiled. "Just to be safe," he cautioned, "Let's try it for a thousand years before we make any long-term commitments, OK?"

She smiled at him warmly. "This is so cool!" she said.

---

1. The clubbing of Nancy Kerrigan by an associate of Tonya Harding's ex-husband in Detroit on Jan. 6, 1994.

Chapter 8

A Party Gone Bad

A Call for Help

Dean was sitting at his computer when his cell phone rang. "You gotta come get me!" Shannon's voice said. "It's really bad, and I'm really scared."

"Where are you? What's happening?"

"I went to this party with Brandon, and he got really drunk, and he says he's gonna fuck me, and it's really gross, and I'm really scared." She paused. "Can you come get me, please?" she whined.

"I don't run a taxi service for wayward girls, Shannon. Are you really in trouble, or is it just another wild party?"

"Well, Brandon's telling everybody he's gonna fuck me tonight, and he's so drunk I'm afraid to ride with him."

"Who are the adults there?"

"There aren't any. The party moved to somebody else's house, and their parents are out of town or something, and they put alcohol in the vaporizer, and they're inhaling it, and everybody's crazy. Please Dean. I'm just so scared!"

"OK, where are you?"

"I'm hiding in the bathroom."

"Can you put Brandon on the phone?"

"Just a minute." There was a pause as she ventured out of her hiding place. Then Dean heard, "Brandon? Brandon! It's for you."

"Hullo?" came an extremely inebriated voice.

"Brandon? Buddy! How's it going, Dude?"

"Cool, Man. Howze zit wuth hue?"

"Peachy. Hey, man. What you gonna do to that hot date of yours tonight?"

"I'm gonna fuck her, man!" he boasted.

"Cool, Dude! Now give the phone to Shannon."

"Dean?" Shannon's voice said.

"OK, Kid, he's plastered. You can't ride with him. Give me the address and go hide in the bathroom 'till I get there."

Dean's Arrival

It took Dean almost thirty minutes to get to the address Shannon had given him. When he pulled up to the house he saw two young men trying to pull Shannon into a 1970 Dodge Challenger. He walked up to the trio and said, "Hey guys, what's happening?"

"Who are you, Motherfucker?" Brandon asked.

"I'm the motherfucker who's gonna take your date home for you, Dude."

"The Hell you say, Asshole." He continued to pull at Shannon's arm.

Dean gripped his throat. "I said . . . I'm the motherfucker who's takin' your date home, Sonny Boy!"

"Fuck you!" the drunk boy said, reaching back to throw a punch.

Dean's rabbit punch to the boy's solar plexus came so quickly that even Shannon didn't see it. Brandon dropped to his knees, heaving and gasping. "That's gonna hurt real bad when you sober up," Dean said quietly. Then he yelled, "Hey! Can we get some help for my man here? He's tossin' his cookies!" Two of Brandon's friends came over to tend to their vomiting comrade. "Get his keys, Dude," Dean said. "Don't let this drunk bastard drive home."

Leaving

As Dean lead Shannon forcefully to the Mustang, one of the boys came up to them. "Hey, Man," he said, "That's Brandon's date, Man. You can't just take her with you!"

Dean stared at the boy. "You play football. Son?"

"Uh . . . Yeah," came the reply.

"Then if I break a couple of your ribs with a roundhouse kick, you'll miss a few games, right?"

"Uh, yeah. I guess so."

"Or if I take out your knee with a crossfire kick, you'll be on crutches for a month or two, right?"

"Uh, yeah?"

"So, which one do you want? I can go either way. Your call."

"Take the bitch!" he said with raised eyebrows and raised palms as he walked slowly backward.

Shannon and Dean got into the Mustang and drove away. As they exited the neighborhood for the freeway, Shannon relaxed. She gave Dean a sheepish look. "I'm sorry to be such a baby, Dean. I just got really scared there for a minute. He kept telling everybody that he was gonna rape me, and nobody cared! They all thought it was great. They were all gonna just stand around and watch!"

"Well, he was so drunk he wouldn't have anything to do it with," Dean said, "But he sure could have gotten you killed in that 426 Challenger R/T of his. That's way too much car for a drunk asshole to be drivin'.."

"Oh, so when I told you my virginity was in danger you couldn't be bothered, right? You only came over because I was gonna get killed?" She seemed irritated.

"Pretty much." he said. "It's a long drive over here. I need you alive to skate with, Princess, but your virginity? . . . That's expendable. It's days are numbered anyway, from what I can see."

"Fuck you, Dean Steele!"

"Look, Kid, I've seen virginity vanish, and I've watched people die, and, from what I can tell, there's no comparison between the two."

"I should have known you'd give me shit about this. I guess I should have just stayed there and gotten gang-banged by a dozen drunk football players!"

"You deserve some shit about this, Young Lady! You got yourself in a jam and had to call in the Texas Rangers." He looked at her sternly. "You fucked up!"

"I fucked up? How was I supposed to know they were gonna move the party and all get drunk and go completely crazy?"

"A veteran party girl can deal with that, and come out alive, and even keep her virginity intact."

"OK, so I'm not a veteran party girl. Sue me!" He grinned at her. "But I'm your skating partner, Dean Steele, and if I get in trouble, you have to come get me. That's the rule!" She crossed her arms and pouted.

"Shannon," he grinned insincerely, "I'm honored to be the one called upon to come save your precious young ass." He chuckled to himself.

"Are you, Dean? Are you honored?" Her voice was tinged with anger and disgust.

"Indeed I am."

"Is my ass really precious?" She softened a bit.

"It is to me, Princess," he smiled. The insincerity was gone.

"Oh, Dean, this is so cool! You saved me from a fate worse than death."

"Getting screwed is not the end of the world, Kid, as you'll someday learn. But getting killed in a car wreck can spoil your whole fuckin' afternoon."

They rode in silence for a while. Then Dean looked at her and grinned. "What?" she demanded as he continued to grin. "What?"

"I was just thinking." He paused. She waited for him to continue. "You don't look like a kid tonight, all dressed up in party gear. I've never seen you like this before. You look like a woman. You look . . . really good. I can see why those guys wanted to bang you."

"Oh, yeah? Would you stand line to fuck me, Dean?" She took on a haughty, indignant air.

"Why, I'd elbow my way right up to the front of the line!" He grinned.

The girl was both insulted and flattered by his response. This left a disgusted smile on her face. "Dean," she said after a pause, "I thought I was gonna have this really cool date, and it just turned to shit, and it was horrible, and I was really scared, and it turned out really bad." He looked at her, showing precious little in the way of sympathy. "So, I want you to take me somewhere, to make up for it, and all. Please take me on a date, Dean—a nice date. Please, please, please!"

"Don't you think you've had enough dating excitement for one evening, Young Lady?"

"No, Dean, it got all messed up. I want a real date before I have to go home. Please take me someplace really cool! Please, please, please!"

The call

He looked at her, obviously pondering something. Then he picked up his cell phone and punched in a number. "Let me talk to Bobby Joe," he said. There was a pause. "BJ? Dean Steele . . . Cool, you? . . . Good . . . Listen buddy, I want to bring this woman by, but she forgot her purse, you dig? She's twenty-one, I swear, but she's got this intense baby-face. Know what I'm sayin'? And she's strictly zero-point-oh on the B-A-L. Can we do business?" Another pause. "Say what? I don't know, Man. I'm bad outta practice." Another pause. "OK, shit! If you're not expectin' much. I haven't blown my horn in a long time. Square it with the man for my woman, and I'll do your gig. Thanks, Bro."

"Who was that?" Shannon asked.

"A friend."

"What's a B-A-L?"

"Blood Alcohol Level"

"Oh, you told him I don't drink, right?"

"You got it."

"You're gonna take me someplace you have to be twenty-one to get in, aren't you? Way cool, Dean!" She bounced with excitement. Then she spoke. "Why did you tell him I'm twenty-one? He'll know I'm not as soon as he sees me."

"He already knows you're not. But this way, it was me who lied to him. That kinda gets him off the hook. I take responsibility for getting you in. If I had told him you're sixteen, then he'd have to break the law to accommodate me. See?"

"Whatever. I just think it's too cool!"

Billy Blues

They drove to a club on Richmond Avenue, parked behind it, and went inside. A large black man at the door looked at Shannon and donned a hard look as he asked for her ID. "I'm Dean Steele. This is the woman I spoke to Bobby Joe about. Did he tell you?"

"This is her?" He eyed her suspiciously.

"Yeah. Call BJ if you need to."

The man waved them through with a bored snort. They took seats at a table near the stage, ordered orange juice, and listened to the band for a while.

"Now I'm gonna ask Dean Steele to come up and help us do some of them funky ole blues songs," Bobby Joe said. "Some of you remember Dean. He's an ice skater. Excuse me! He's a figure skater. He don't do no hockey."

"Wha' chu been doin' Dean?" he asked as Dean stepped up to one of the microphones. "I ain't seen you in a month of Sundays!"

"I ain't been practicin' the blues, you're gonna find out!"

"Dean's got him a new partner he skates with. Look close and see if you can spot his skating partner." He pointed at Shannon. Bobby Joe looked at Dean. "What you wanna do, Bro?"

"Hey, this is your nickel, remember?"

"Yeah, Dean owes me a favor. OK, ya'll want to hear Dean do some classic Elvis?" The guitar player adjusted his instrument to produce the sharp echoed sound of the late 1950s. "Imagine you're in a cheap honky tonk in East Texas in 1957." The band started into "My Baby Left Me." "You know, a really cheap dive, a place like, well . . . a place kinda like this! Hell, you are in a cheap dive in East Texas!" Bobby Joe played an intro on his keyboard and looked at Dean. After a pause Dean sang the first verse of the Elvis Presley song. Not only did his voice characterization sound reminiscent of Elvis, but so did his movements. Shannon's jaw dropped as she watched her partner doing his thing. Her face seemed to say, "I can't believe you're doing this!"

Bobby Joe played a solo, Dean sang another verse and the guitar player took a solo. Then the band modulated into "Mystery Train." Dean sang it with even more of an Elvis inflection. Shannon put her hands over her eyes, feigning embarrassment. When finally the medley was over, the audience applauded enthusiastically.

"OK, Dean, let's do some blues. What feels right?"

"Maybe you guys can roll me some steam," Dean replied.

"Goin' straight for the good stuff!" He turned to the band. "Steamroller," he said. The drummer began patting his foot on the bass drum pedal and tickling the cowbell with a stick. The bass player jumped in, and Bobby Joe played the keyboard for a while. Dean looked at Shannon grinning from the front row. She was a curious mixture of naïve and sophisticate, of woman and child. She was clearly enjoying this brief taste of adulthood. Dean began singing the song, "Steamroller Blues," as done by James Taylor.

Dean enmeshed himself in the song, much to the delight of the audience and the band. Shannon was aghast as she watched her partner perform in the smoke-filled, dimly lit cavern. She gave him a look that said, "I can't believe you're doing this!" Dean sensed her surprise. As he sang the second verse, he directed the sexually suggestive lyrics toward his young partner.

Shannon found herself overtaken by Dean's attention and the loud throbbing beat. She rose slowly from her seat and began dancing toward Dean. She came up on stage in her short red party dress and high heel shoes and did slow, sexy dance steps while the band played. Her flirtatious movements were directed primarily at Dean. The drummer began to watch her dance closely and accent her movements with percussion. With the loud music behind her, and the enthusiasm of the audience, she became inspired as she performed. The song went on for a long time, with Shannon dancing and Dean ad libbing suggestive lyrics, and the crowd loved it. Shannon's sexy teenager image of naughty innocence gave the jaded crowd something totally unexpected in that raucous environment.

"Dean Steele . . . and Shannon," Bobby Joe yelled into the microphone as they sat down. "Where did you find that girl, Dean?" he asked.

"Junior high!" came the answer from Dean's seat. Shannon's fist impacted his shoulder almost immediately. "Jerk!" she grinned.

"Junior high?" Bobby Joe replied. "Hell, I spent six years in junior high and I never saw nothing like that."

"River Oaks!" Dean yelled.

"Oh, River Oaks!" Bobby Joe responded. "Well, excuse me. Everything's fancy in River Oaks!" He paused. "You know, I used to live in River Oaks.". The band let out a groan of disbelief. "Yeah. Right behind that jewelry store at Kirby and Bissonette." More groans. "Yeah, I had to move, though. I couldn't afford the taxes on my elegant one-bedroom dumpster." The audience laughed. "Anyway, Honey, if you get tired of skatin' with that guy, you can dance in my band anytime." She grinned.

"I can't believe you sang the dirty blues in a night club, Dean."

"I can't believe you got up and danced," he replied.

"Hey, I wasn't gonna miss the chance to dance during my partner's big performance! That's once in a lifetime stuff. I might never get the chance again!"

"I certainly hope not!"

They listened to the band for a while. At one point the drummer and bass player started into the song, "Suzie Q."

"Hey," Billy Joe said, "Y'all wanna see Dean and Shannon again?" Shannon's eyes widened as the crowd applauded. She looked at Dean. He gave her a pained smile, which she took as permission. They took the stage, and she danced to the song while Dean and Bobby Joe sang a duet. Eventually the music modulated into "Be-bop-a-lula" and that went on for a while. At one point, during Bobby Joe's solo, Shannon pulled Dean away from the mike and made him dance with her. They did a few lifts, to the amazement of the crowd. After a while they thanked their host and left the club.

After the club

"You're a pretty good Elvis impersonator, Dean," Shannon said as they walked toward the Mustang. "For a while there I thought The King was back!"

"I guess I've just got rhythm in my genes," he replied.

"You've got something in your jeans, all right Mr. Studly!" She giggled.

"Hey! I'm talkin' DNA here, Little Miss Trashmouth."

"And doin' the blues too. You were makin' up all kinds of funky stuff."

"Blues is easy. All you do is squint and growl some unintelligible noises."

"What was that you were saying? In that song, I mean," Shannon asked as she got into the Mustang. "A burnin', turnin' . . . something. What was it?"

Dean turned to face her. "A churnin' urn of burnin' funk." He gave her a grin.

"That's you, all right Dean!" A churnin' burnin' urn full of funk. Too cool!" She giggled. "Mr. Studly!"

"I can't help bein' what I am." He chuckled.

"I thought blues was supposed to be about hard times and bad luck, and stuff, but you were describing a disgusting sex act in that song!"

"Yeah? Well you and that drummer were just about to demonstrate one! He was makin' love to you with that snare drum."

"They liked me, didn't they?" She seemed pleased.

"You're a natural performer, Princess. You stole the show."

The Call

Shannon's cell phone rang. "Hello?" she said.

"Shannon? Thank God you answered," Fred's voice said. "She answered her phone!" he shouted at someone.

"What's the matter, Dad?"

"Are you hurt bad, Honey? Are you in the water? Can you tell me where you are?"

"My Dad's totally zoned out!" Shannon told Dean. "Dad, what's wrong with you?"

"She's delirious," Fred told someone. "Shannon, can you see any lights? Just tell me if you can see the lights!" He was almost screaming.

"I see lots of lights, Dad. Are you on drugs?"

"Which way are the ambulance lights, Shannon?"

"Ambulance? My God! Is there an ambulance there?"

"Just tell me if you can see the ambulance!"

"My God, Dad, are you sick? Is it Mom? Is she OK?"

"Shannon, please! Just answer my question. Which way are the lights?"

"They're all around me, Dad." She was near panic.

"Shannon, just hold on. We'll find you. Just don't let go!"

"Hold on to what, Dad?" She held the phone out to Dean. "My Dad's completely bonkers!" She said.

Dean took the phone. "Fred," he said, calmly. "I'm going to call 911, but you have to tell me what you took, OK? What drugs did you take?"

"Who is this? One of the Deputies?"

"It's Dean Steele, Fred. Just remain calm."

"Oh, God! he told someone, "Dean was in there with her!"

"Can you see her, Dean? Is she hurt bad?"

"Just lie down and breathe deeply, Fred," Dean said, "The medics will be right there." He looked at Shannon. "Dial star-9-1-1 on my phone. I don't want to let him go."

Shannon took Dean's cell phone but dialed her mother's cell phone number instead. Millie answered.

"Mom?" Shannon said. "What's wrong with Dad?"

"Shannon!" Millie said. "Hold on, Honey, we'll find you in just a minute. Are you in the water?"

"My God!" Shannon said. "My parents have totally wigged out!"

"Where are you?" Millie screamed.

"I'm in the parking lot!" Shannon screamed back.

"She's in the parking lot!" Millie yelled at someone. "Go to the parking lot!"

"Wait a minute," Fred said to Dean. "What parking lot?"

"The one behind Billy Blues on Richmond."

"Then, you weren't in the wreck?"

"What wreck?"

"Brandon rolled his car off the bridge into Buffalo Bayou. Several kids have been taken to the hospital. We thought Shannon was in there too. We're looking for her in the lake."

"Uh, no, Fred. I picked Shannon up at the party a couple of hours ago. She's safe and sound here with me."

"Oh, my God! And we're wading around here, looking for her body. We thought she must have been thrown out when he hit the water."

"Well, I've got her body here on Richmond, and it looks to be in good shape."

"Mom?" Shannon said into Dean's phone. "I wasn't in Brandon's car. I'm here with Dean in Houston. Mom?"

"Thank God!" Millie said.

"OK, everybody," Dean said. "Why don't we rendezvous at River Oaks and everybody can see that everybody's all right, OK?"

"Brandon wrecked his car?" Shannon mused after her parents disconnected. "How weird is that?"

"Not too surprising since he'd been sniffing ethanol."

"God! I hope nobody dies!"

River Oaks

Millie and Fred got home shortly after Shannon and Dean arrived. "You look dreadful, Mom," Shannon eyed the mud that covered her mother to the waist.

"Well, excuse me!" the exasperated woman said, "But wading around in the God damn ocean, looking for your daughter's body, can smear your fuckin' mascara!"

"Gee, Mom, I hope you didn't break a nail looking for me!"

"What happened?" Dean asked.

Millie inhaled. "When Shannon didn't get home on time, we called Brandon's parents. They had just gotten a call from the Sheriff's Office telling them that Brandon's car had gone off a bridge on the West Loop. We naturally assumed Shannon was in there, so we took off. When we got there, the other kids had already been taken to the hospital, and they were pulling the car out of the water. We told them Shannon had been in the car too, so they started looking for her body. Since she wasn't in the car, they assumed she had been thrown out. Dad had the bright idea of calling her cell phone, in case she was still conscious."

"And we'd just come out of the club, and we thought y'all had just totally gone bananas," Shannon said.

"Where in the Hell did y'all go?" Millie asked.

"Well, see?" Shannon began, "The party moved to this other house, and Brandon got drunk, and he just went crazy, and I hid in the bathroom, and I called Dean, and he came and got me, and he punched Brandon and made him puke." She paused. "That's pretty much it."

"I somehow sense there's more to this story." Millie looked at Dean.

"That's about it," he said, putting on an overly innocent grin. Millie eyed him, unconvinced.

"OK, you two," she said at last. "Have it your way. Now why did you call Dean instead of your parents, when the party went bad?"

Shannon took on a deer-in-the-headlights look. "Well, uh, I just figured . . ."

"Yes?" Millie probed.

"Well, I just thought it would look bad if I had to call my Mommy to come get me, that's all. Like I'm just this big baby, or something. But I figure if Dean comes over, it's cool. You know, he's a guy and all."

"Your Dad's a guy, Shannon."

"No, he's not! He's a Dad! I'd never live it down if I called my Daddy to come rescue me from a party. But if my bodyguard shows up and kicks some ass 'cause I'm not gettin' respect, then that's cool."

"Bodyguard?" Millie looked at Dean. "I would have kicked some ass!"

"See? That's just why I didn't call you, Mom! You'd make a big scene and embarrass me to tears. Dean just punched Brandon and made him puke and told Keith he was gonna break his ribs, and we left, and it was all just too cool!"

Millie looked at Dean with raised eyebrows. "A gentle love tap to the upper abdomen," he said. "Crude, but effective."

"He barfed his guts!" Shannon said. "It was so cool!"

Millie groaned. "And what did y'all do after Dean picked you up?"

"Well it was still early, see? And I didn't want to go home yet, so we went to Billy Blues, and I danced while Dean sang all this funky blues stuff."

Millie looked at Dean. "You took her to Billy Blues? That's an over-twenty-one club, Dean. She's about five years too young. How'd you get her in?"

"He has pull with the management, Mom." Shannon answered.

"So, you two went dancing?"

"No, Mother," Shannon said in disgust. "Dean sang with the band, and I did a solo dance number on stage."

Millie eyed Dean harshly. "You let my sixteen-year-old dance onstage at a night club?" She asked.

"She was a big hit," Dean said, attempting unsuccessfully to suppress a grin.

"Dancing in that little party dress? I'm sure she was! I just hope she didn't take her clothes off!"

"Oh, don't worry, Mom. If I did that, we'd never tell you about it."

"You're a big help, Shannon!" Dean said quietly.

After everyone calmed down, Millie got Dean alone. "I'm not sure I like the idea of you sneaking Shannon into a beer joint, Dean. She's too young to be starting all that."

"Uh, excuse me, Mrs. Foster, but it appears I saved your daughter's life. In less pretentious neighborhoods one might get a 'thank you' for such a deed."

Millie sighed. "You're right, Dean. Shame on me. It's just that we got so . . . emotional when we thought Shannon had been in a car accident. I wasn't thinking." She smiled warmly. "Thank you, Kind Sir, for saving my darling daughter's life."

Dean grinned. "You are most sincerely welcome, Madame."

The Hospital

Dean went with Shannon to visit Brandon at River Oaks Medical Center.

"Brandon?"

"Shannon? Are you OK?"

"Yeah, What about you? They said you have a concussion!"

"Yeah, No problem though. There's no brain in there to worry about." She laughed. "Listen Shannon," he said. "I'm really sorry about what a jerk I was last night. I really hate it that Jackie and Joey got hurt. It's a major bummer. But I'm really glad you weren't in there. If anything had happened to you . . . I'd have to kill myself."

"No problem," she said, touching his arm. "I'm cool with it."

"No, but I really messed up though. I really let you down. I was such an asshole!"

"It's OK, Brandon. It was just a mistake, OK? Everybody's gonna be fine."

"I'm sorry, Shannon. I'm really, really sorry."

"It's OK," she said. "Forget about it."

She stepped back. "You remember Dean?"

"Are you the guy?" the boy asked.

"Uh, I'm the one who punched you, Brandon," Dean said.

"Yeah? I wish you'd broke my fuckin' jaw! Then I might not have tried to drive home."

"Well . . . ," Dean said.

"I'm really glad you came and got Shannon," he said. "If I had gotten her hurt or . . . killed . . . I would have just . . . ," He choked up.

"I know, Dude," Dean said. "It worked out OK. A little medicine and a little time . . . and everybody's OK."

They visited the other two injured kids briefly and left the hospital. "You were really nice to Brandon, Dean. I thought you'd give him a hard time, or something, about how he treated me, I mean."

"He's already giving himself a hard time. He got two other kids hurt, he lost his car, and I expect he's getting a ration of shit from his parents. He doesn't need any from me. He's got all the remorse he can handle right now."

"You know, Dean," she said seriously, "If you hadn't come to get me when you did, I'd be in there in one of those beds, instead of walking out with you." Her eyes were big and round.

A grin slowly formed on his face as he looked at her. "Well, aren't I just the perfectly lucky bastard!" He gave her a sharp slap on the bottom.

"Bite me, Dean!" she giggled.

Chapter 9

Millie's Intentions

Dean's Past

Millie Foster and Dean Steele were alone in the lounge at the Texas Ice Stadium. Alcohol had loosened her tongue. Dean was drinking grapefruit juice.

"Why don't you compete in men's singles, anymore?" she asked. "I thought you were great at the '91 Nationals."

"Because I couldn't possibly win." he answered.

"Why not?"

"Because the judges don't like me."

"Why not?"

"Because . . . ," He looked at her. "Why are you so interested in my career?"

"Because you are the most powerful skater ever to hit the ice. With your strength you could do things ordinary guys could only dream of. Now answer my question, Young Man. Why do you think the judges don't like you?"

"Because . . . , I don't play by the rules."

"What do you mean?"

"I don't fit into the mold of the starry-eyed kid who wants to devote his life to the sport in the hopes of winning a piece of metal on a string. Because I want to skate my programs, not theirs."

"Why do you think the judges don't like you?" she repeated.

"Because I'm too old and too cynical for their taste."

"Why do you think the judges don't like you?" she asked again, persistently.

"Because . . . , because I don't like them, and they pick up on it."

"Ahh, and why don't you like them?"

"I have fundamental disagreements with the whole way the contests are conducted. And some of the judges allow personal considerations to affect their objectivity."

"Give me an example."

"The ice dance judging at the Nagano Olympics was so obviously prearranged that the IOC[1] threatened to drop ice dancing from the Olympics if the ISU[2] didn't clean it up."

"What happened to you?"

"What?"

"What happened to you?"

"I don't understand."

"What was it that happened to you that made you lose your confidence and your will to compete?"

"No specific incident. It's just the whole situation with the ISU."

"So, what happened?" she insisted. Dean paused. He looked at her as if trying to decide whether or not to tell her. Millie looked back into his eyes. It was clear she would not be put off in her quest for this answer.

"OK," he said. "There was one judge who always gave me marks a tenth or two higher than the average. We were talking one day, and he put his hand on my leg. I moved it. After that, his marks were 2 to 3 tenths below the average."

"Damn!" Millie said, with compassion filling her eyes. "I knew it must have been something."

"After that," Dean continued, Other judges began to give me lower marks too. The word was out that I was a 'rebel,' that I wasn't 'devoted to the sport.' Pretty soon I was averaging 2 to 3 tenths lower than other skaters at the same level. I was improving, but my marks were going down. It was frustrating."

"That's a crime," Millie said. "Did you try to do anything about it?"

"Well, I didn't call that judge up and ask him out on a date, if that's what you mean. But I did consult with an expert to see how I could improve my image. I worked the PR aspect, and even came up with a flag-waving routine to show my devotion to the sport."

"Did that help?"

"No. It merely gave that judge the satisfaction of watching me squirm. But he still didn't give me decent marks. And the other judges' marks didn't come up much either. That prejudice was imbedded too deep by then. It was an 'everybody knows' kind of thing inside judging circles."

"The other skaters just figured I had done something really bad to piss off the judges. They tended to avoid me after that, I guess so it wouldn't rub off on them, and I didn't have much interest in socializing with them either. I hung out with the more boisterous skating crowd."

"Including Elizabeth North?"

"Yeah. Liz wasn't intimidated by all that. She was already a Hell-raiser herself by that time." Millie looked at him expectantly. "No one in the stands knew what was going on," Dean continued. "The commentators just assumed I had passed my peak—lost my edge. Finally I began to accept that explanation myself. I decided to quit."

"Oh, my God! That's terrible."

"Fortunately, I got my own thinking sorted out eventually. I decided to become the 'Bad Boy' of amateur skating. It worked for me. I had a small but loyal following among the rowdier fans. But I don't know what that image will do for our pairs act—or for Shannon in particular."

"I knew there was an explanation," Millie said. "I have every one of your performances on video tape. I loved your skating. I could never understand why you were always out of first place."

"Well, maybe it's because I'm just second class."

"No, Dear Boy, that's not it. You're definitely first rate." She touched his cheek.

Millie's Motives

He looked at her, studying her face. "Are you . . . ," He paused to consider what he would say. "Are you trying to go to bed with me?" he asked.

"Well," she said, somewhat disarmed, "I had hoped your proposition might be a little more subtle and romantic than that. But I'll take what I can get. And yes, I am 'trying to go to bed with you,' Mr. Steele." She smiled at him coyly.

"OK, let me try that line again." He grinned subtly. "Would you consider a social invitation to visit my apartment?"

"Quite possibly," she grinned.

"And if I offered to show you the bedroom?"

"I just might take a look at it. No, I definitely would look at it."

They looked into each other's eyes for a long moment.

"I hate to be analytical at such an emotional time, but . . . why? Why would you want to get involved with me?"

Millie formulated, then rejected several answers. The urge to confess was intense. Finally she resigned herself to an honest answer. "I have been fascinated by you for a long time, Mr. Steele," she said. "When I watch you skate, something stirs inside me, something that remains dormant otherwise. I want you to wake it up, whatever it is, and let it run wild. I want to know what I have inside me that responds to you so strongly. I want to feel this strange force that only you have the key to unlock."

"I see." He sat silent for a moment, pondering her answer.

That admission felt so good that Millie continued her answer to his question. "And I want to feel your power," she added. "You have such strength pent up inside you. I want to be there when it is released. I want to feel it flowing into me." Somewhat embarrassed by what she had just said, she paused to compose herself.

"You know," he said, not focusing on her discomfort, "You might be disappointed. Even if we turn in a 6.0 performance, it probably wouldn't change your life, except to complicate it. Having an affair with your daughter's skating partner would create all manner of complications."

"I could handle it, and so could you. You're as cool as the ice you skate on!"

"Perhaps. But it would be one Hell of a distraction. It would add to the pressure. I can't dismiss the feeling that it's a really bad idea."

"Well, what about the idea of fucking your partner's mother? Doesn't that have some appeal for a man of the world?"

"You mean, as a conquest? A notch on my gun? A scalp on my belt?"

"Something like that." She flashed an evil grin.

"God, I hope not. I hope I'm not so low that I would enjoy telling my friends, 'See that proud, well-dressed woman in the stands, whose daughter just won the medal? Well, I fucked her last night'."

"I'm sorry!" Millie blurted. "That's not what I meant, really. I mean . . . Oh God, I've said too much. I've said it all wrong." She sighed and collected herself. "I didn't mean to suggest you're that kind of person."

"I know," he said. "And you're right. I would dearly love to have an intimate relationship with you. You are charming, intelligent . . . and one very foxy lady! I'm sure we could make beautiful music together." He looked into her eyes. "If we had met in a bar, and I didn't know your husband or your daughter . . . maybe it wouldn't be such a mistake. You could visit me once or twice a week, and perhaps little harm would come of it. But I just have to question the wisdom of starting all that up right now. We would be betraying so many people, and betrayal usually ends up hurting the betrayer more than the betrayed."

She smiled. "Maybe that's what I like about you," she said. "Always analytical. Always in control. Even when confronted with an emotional woman whose hormones are running wild."

"Don't press your luck, Lady." He smiled softly. "With a little more temptation, I just might change my mind. You could still be dragged into a tacky affair before the evening is out."

"So there are limits to your self-control, after all, Mr. Ice-man?"

"Only when subjected to severe stress." He grinned.

"Is that what I am? Severe stress?"

"You are, indeed. I have an abiding urge to jump you like a big green frog."

She laughed. "And how could a girl resist such romantic language?"

Then Millie waxed serious. "So now you know." She looked at him. "Maybe you already did, but now I've made it official. I want you . . . as my lover. I want the experience of you. I want you to take me somewhere I've never been—someplace I can only go if you take me." Dean found himself without a response. "Don't misunderstand, Honey. Having you skate with Shannon was a very good idea in its own right, and it's working out wonderfully." She looked at him softly. "But the possibility of being intimate with you is what kept me going when Shannon, and you, kept trying to back out."

Dean took her hand in his, pulled it to his mouth and kissed it. They gazed into each other's eyes for a time, and they parted.

---

1. IOC—International Olympic Committee.
2. ISU—International Skating Union.

Chapter 10

Private Eye

"So, tell me, Dean," Millie inquired, "How come you never got married?"

"No irate father with a shotgun ever caught up with me, I suppose."

"Have you ever gotten close?" Dean was silent. "I see," Millie mused. "Who was she?"

Dean inhaled. "A woman who had a choice to make," he replied.

"Sarah Ann Steed?" she asked. "Or should I say, Mrs. Larry Winston Hutchinson?" She looked at him smugly.

Dean turned to face her. His brow furrowed as he regarded her. "What have you been up to, Millie?"

"Oh, I called a friend," she grinned.

"A friend with a PI license?" Dean asked.

"Just a friend who's well connected in Austin social circles."

Dean's face softened. He gently placed his right hand on her cheek and caressed it. Then moved it to her throat. He tightened his grip until she could hardly breathe. Millie kept her hands at her sides as she gasped for air. "Did you engage a private eye to investigate me," he asked.

"Dean, please. That hurts."

"Did you not hear my question?" he asked, holding his grip on her throat. "I'll repeat it."

"Yes!" she blurted. "Please let me go." He released her and looked away. "Fred and I are about to invest a lot of money in you, Dean," she explained, "And we'll be entrusting our teenage daughter to you, to a large extent. It would have been irresponsible of me not to check out your background, just a little bit."

"Just in case I'm well known as the Hill Country Strangler, right?"

"Just to be on the safe side. But Heaven knows we didn't expect to find anything, and we didn't, of course!"

"So what did you find, Mrs. F.?"

"Nothing. Just the usual stuff. Where you went to school. Nothing at all, really. You're a model citizen, Mr. Steele." She showed an uncomfortable smile."

"What about Sarah Steed?" he asked.

"I don't know. She was just a name that showed up somewhere. I don't even remember who she is."

"You're a skilled liar, Millie, but this one isn't selling. What did you find out about her?"

"Well, just that you, apparently, dated her for a while. And then she got married."

"To whom?"

"The Hutchinson boy, I think. It's not very clear from the notes."

"And who was the Hutchinson boy, Millie?"

"I don't . . . ," Dean glared at her. "He was your best friend," she said, melting. "My God, it must have been terrible for you!"

"Where's the file?" Dean asked.

"What file?"

"The fuckin' file on me the PI gave you! Don't ask 'what file?' you lying bitch!"

She flinched. "It's at my office," she said tensely, "In a locked cabinet. No one but me has seen it."

"Get you shit together and get in my car."

"But, Dean . . . I don't see . . ."

"We're gonna go take a look at my file, Millie. Now get in the car!"

"You have a practice now, Dean. I'll bring it home tomorrow night so you can look at it."

"Wrong, Millie. There won't be any more practices until I see that file. And I'm not going to give you a chance to cull it before I see it. Get your ass in the Mustang, right now."

Millie saw she had no choice. She picked up her purse and went outside with him. The twenty-five minute trip to downtown Houston was icy and silent. They went to Millie's office, and she unlocked a file drawer. "Look under 'Dean Steele'" she said coldly.

Dean pulled a thick folder out of the drawer and laid it on Millie's desk. It had dozens of pages of telephone bills, credit card statements, bank statements, and his grades transcript from The University of Texas. It also had newspaper clippings and photographs of Dean and dozens of his friends, including Sarah and Larry, and their wedding.

"You got your money's worth," Dean said. "This asshole did a good job."

"He's a she," Millie said.

"The bitch did a good job," Dean corrected himself.

Dean then turned to the twenty or so pages of typed narrative. He began to read excerpts out loud. "Subject Dean Anthony Steele, white male, 1/27/72, 6' 0" 180. TX D/L 0433678, SSN 447-77-9919." He looked up at Millie. "She definitely got the right guy."

He continued to read. "In 1981, parents, Daniel J. Steele and Margaret Comwell Steele, killed instantly in head-on car/truck collision. One younger brother, James Killian Steele, 3/04/75, also in the crash, died later at the hospital. No other siblings. Subject went to live with maternal grandparents, Charles L. and Ellen S. Comwell, in Dallas, TX. Graduated North Dallas High School, 1990, near top of class."

"Are we having fun yet, Millie? You don't mind if I skip some of the more boring stuff, do you?"

"Let's see, skating . . . skating . . . ahh. Subject linked romantically with several female ice skaters (usually older), most notably Barbara Sontag and Elizabeth North. No homosexual rumors. Many female conquests, both on and off the ice. None led to serious commitment."

"She made a fuckin' soap opera out of my life, Millie. 'All My Children' could get two years out of this."

"Subject had a thing with one Sarah Ann Steed, white female 4/21/74, blonde/blue 5'6" 110, 35C/22/36, 6 1/2D, with moderately wealthy parents. Father an Austin attorney, partner Jason, Jacobsen & Steed. Relationship deeply romantic, lots of sex. Met in English class at UT. Planned marriage, kids, etc. Mom and Dad wanted subject to attend law school after engineering degree, become a patent attorney, and join the firm. Subject had other plans. Daughter eventually sided with Mom and Dad. Big fight. Subject walked. Much weeping and wailing."

"This is fascinating, Millie," Dean said. "I hope my life has entertained you as much as it has me."

"Dean, I never . . ."

"Steed girl eventually marries one Larry Winston Hutchinson, formerly best friend of subject. Much acrimony ensues, friendship explodes."

"This bitch really has a way with words," Dean said. "She could win a Pulitzer."

"Dean, I'm sorry," Millie said. "I never meant to hurt you like this."

"So, what did you mean to do? Mrs. F.?"

"I just wanted a simple background check. She went way overboard on me."

"Bullshit. I'll bet you sent her back to the trough at least three times to get this kind of detail. This report has photos of every woman I've ever had a conversation with. It even has Sarah's shoe size, for Pete's sake! What are you planning to do, Millie, give her patent leather party pumps for her anniversary?"

"Dean, please. Don't make this any worse than it is. I've said I'm sorry. No one but you and I have ever seen that file. Lets control the damage now, shall we?"

Dean began to flip through the newspaper clippings. "I see she got the Austin American-Statesman's account and the San Antonio Light's account of my parent's death. It's too bad she didn't pull the Dallas News. Their pictures actually showed my little brother's blood on the seat."

"Dean, I'm so sorry!"

"Oh, shit! My dog died when I was six, and she doesn't have a clipping for that. I'll make you a copy of mine. And I can call Sarah Steed and get her hat size for you!"

"Dean, please!"

"Fuck you, Millie Foster!" he said coldly. He walked over to the window and looked out at the night sky over downtown Houston for a time. Then he walked over to the desk, closed the file and handed it back to the woman. "It's OK," he said. "Accurate enough."

"You're not going to sit here and make me shred it?" she asked.

"I'm sure your 'friend with Austin connections' has copies," he replied. "Besides, it's all public record. Well, all except the bank records, the telephone records, the illegal wire taps and the photos from the hidden camera in my bathroom!"

Millie put the file back and locked the drawer. Then she stepped squarely in front of him with a sincere look and said, "I want you to forgive me, Dean, right here, right now. Please. I'll do whatever it takes. I made a big mistake, but we have to get past this!"

He rolled his lips together for a moment, looked at her, and said, "Fuck you, Millie Foster." A pained look came over her face as she realized she would not get resolution so quickly.

"I opened painful old wounds, Dean. I had no right. I'd give anything if I hadn't let it slip that I had that file."

"Come on, Millie. You wouldn't have missed this for the world! Watching my face while I rifled through that file? You must have been in Heaven!"

"You really think me so cruel, Dean?"

"You're beyond cruel, Millie. You go way off the end of that scale."

"I'm very hurt that you feel that way, Dean. I care for you very deeply."

"A bug on a string, Millie? Watch him fly! Isn't he cute? Well, this bug is through flying for you, Mrs. Foster. I'll skate with your daughter, but you can stay the fuck out of my life!"

As Dean started the Mustang, Millie said, "I'd like you to just drop me off at home, please. I have an appointment with a client this evening, and there's not enough time to go back and get my car. I'll ride in to TIS with Shannon tomorrow."

Dean was silent. When he reached the Pierce St. elevated ramp, he turned south on I-45 toward Friendswood, instead of north toward Allen Parkway and River Oaks.

"Dean, I need to go directly home now, remember?"

The Mustang roared up the onramp to I-45 south with the turbochargers screaming. When it reached cruising speed Millie inhaled, took her cell phone out of her purse, and dialed a number. "Mr. Greenfield," she said, obviously making a recording, "This is Millie Foster. I'm terribly sorry, but I'm afraid I must reschedule our meeting due to a sudden illness in the family. I hope you understand. I'll call you tomorrow." She put the small instrument back in her bag.

The drive back to Friendswood was mostly silent. "Dean," she said cautiously after a time, "I now know it's not Sarah Steed. It's the loss of your parents . . . and your brother. You haven't fully recovered from that."

"Butt out, Mrs. Foster." he said, coldly.

"You're still in the second stage—anger. You haven't moved to grief and on to acceptance yet. It's a very dangerous situation."

"Who the fuck are you, Sigmund Freud?"

"I know there is still unresolved conflict there, Dean, and it can eat you up from the inside. Please let me help."

"Oh, you're willing to let me pour out my heart, so you can tell me it's all better now? No thanks, Millie."

"Why not, Dean? Why won't you talk to me about it?"

He glared at the woman. "Because you're not human, Millie. You're not of my species. You're not even native to this planet." He paused. She was puzzled. "You're an Ice Queen," he continued. "Ice water runs in your veins. You thrive on other people's suffering, and I'm just another meal."

The woman looked hurt. "Dean, I'd do anything to relieve the your pain!"

"No Millie, you just want to watch me squirm. Well, not tonight." He paused to regard her. "Go back to Hell, Ice Queen!"

Millie remained silent for several minutes, then she tried again, taking a somewhat softer tack. "I don't think I'll be getting much sleep tonight," she said. "Not after this." She looked at him. "What about you?"

He looked at her. "Usually not a problem. I have a special technique."

"Oh? What's that?" It appeared he had softened up a bit.

"I don't count sheep," he said, "I count bleeps."

"I don't believe I've heard that one." She was trying to be pleasant.

"Do you know what a cardiac monitor sounds like? Bleep . . . bleep . . . bleep. Well I do. I hear one every time it gets quiet. Every time the noise level dies down, it's right there. And do you know what the oscilloscope screen looks like on one of those things? That little green dot goes across, always left to right, left to right, left to right, bobbing up and down, up and down, up and down." He began to shake. "Until the bleeps are replaced by that continuous tone."

He paused. "Do you know what 'flatline' means, Millie? 'Flatline?' It means that little dot ain't gonna bob up and down anymore, ever again. It means you're all alone. It means you're nine years old, and absolutely, totally, all alone."

He got quiet. Millie was frozen, afraid to make a sound. Finally he spoke again. "So at night, I just lay down and start counting the bleeps. And I close my eyes and watch the dancing spot. And if I'm lucky . . . very lucky . . . I'll fall asleep before they stop. Before the flatline." He inhaled. "And if I'm not, I get to start it all over and try again. Sometimes it takes hours."

Millie was sobbing. "Your brother, Dean? You were there when he died?"

Dean whipped the Mustang off the freeway onto the FM 2351 exit ramp. "This is your stop," he said as they coasted into the parking lot at the Texas Ice Stadium. As she sobbed, he gave her a gentle smile that slowly turned stony cold. "Now get the fuck out of my car, you conniving bitch!" Convulsing with anguish so hard that she could barely manipulate her key, Millie got into her car and left.

Millie's return

It was just before 8:00 AM when Dean heard a knock at his door. He saw Millie standing there, looking extremely haggard.

"If you won't let me in, she said, "I'll start screaming bloody murder!"

"Come in, Millie," he said, turning his back to the open door.

Cautiously she entered his domain. "I cried all night," she began. "I slept in the guest room so Fred wouldn't hear me. Even so, I think I woke them both up. I can't even keep coffee on my stomach."

She looked at him intensely. "I'm here to have it out with you, Dean Steele. I don't care if you beat me to a bloody pulp, I can't go on like this! I'll take whatever I have to take, I'll do whatever I have to do, to get us back right again. I'll eat that fucking file, page by page, if necessary. Anything, Dean. Anything at all. Just don't let this go on one minute longer!" She was almost screaming by the end of her statement.

"Care for some coffee?" he asked calmly. "Oops, I forgot. Not sticking."

"Just tell me, Dean. Just make a list. What do I have to do to make it up to you? And don't leave anything out. I want the whole program, right now!"

"It's OK, Millie," he said quietly. "No problem."

"No, Dean. It's not 'no problem.' It's not just 'OK.'"

"Yes it is. I got over being upset. I calmed down. I'm all right now." He looked into her confused face. "I'm sorry I was rude to you last night."

"Dean, you can't do this. You're scaring me. What's going on?"

"Calm down, Millie. I'm no longer upset about your background check on me. It makes sense. There's nothing damaging in there. I'm sorry I was harsh on you."

Millie's body flopped limply on the black leather sofa. "I can't believe this! You can't just 'get over it' like that!"

"I did. It's OK now."

"Oh, God," she said with horror on her face. "You've completely shut me out now. I no longer exist in your world. You're numb toward me!"

"No, Millie," he said, "You still exist. Now go home and get some sleep. You look awful."

"Dean, I came over here prepared to wash your feet and dry them with my hair. I'll do any demeaning thing you want me to, to get my place back in your heart. I brought no pride whatsoever with me. I'll eat bugs, if you want me to. I'll do anything."

"No insect consumption necessary, Millie. Everything's OK. Really. We're still friends."

"What happened?"

"I got upset when I found out you had a file on me, and when I saw what was in it, some old memories came back a little too strong. But I got a night's sleep, and I got over it. In the cold light of day, I have to say, what the Hell? What do I care if you know that I called the cleaners at 3:17 in the afternoon sometime in 1994 to check on my shirts? It's old news."

Millie started sobbing. "I can't deal with this Dean. I think you're totally shut me out of your mind."

"All right," he said, "I can see that you need something to get you through this." He sat beside her on the sofa.

"Here's your face," he said, touching her cheek. "What am I going to do to your face? Am I going to slap it with my hand? Pop it with my fist? Are you frightened, Millie?"

"Yes," she said weakly, looking into his eyes.

"I'm just going to kiss it gently. It's a beautiful face. Gorgeous." He pressed his lips to hers gently. Slowly the tension in her melted and she began to respond to his kiss. He continued a gentle teasing kiss until she relaxed, and then the flame of her passion began to blaze. She began to breathe deeply.

At last he pulled away and looked at her. "Satisfied, Millie?" he asked. "Are we back on track?"

"Yes," she said, "I guess we are." She lay down on the sofa and almost immediately fell asleep. Dean draped a blanket across her body. Just before noon she got up and left, still in a daze.

Shannon

"Mom had you investigated?" Shannon asked. "Cool!"

"That wasn't my reaction," Dean said.

"Did it piss you off?" She was grinning.

"I was a bit put out initially."

"What did they find?" she asked eagerly. "Anything really juicy? Lots of assorted affairs?"

Dean burst out laughing. "No, actually, my affairs don't make much of an 'assortment'." He laughed again.

"What are you laughing at, Dickhead?"

"Shannon, the next time you pass a library, go in and get a dictionary and look up the word sordid, s-o-r-d-i-d, OK?"

She frowned. "So what did they find?"

"Oh, just the usual boring stuff," he said. "Speeding tickets, past-due phone bills, and the occasional murder of a nosey sixteen-year-old."

"You wouldn't murder me, Dean!" she said emphatically. "I'm your partner, and you're my protector and defender, remember?"

"I wouldn't bet the barn on that one," he said.

Chapter 11

Ice Show

The Show

"Dean," Millie said. "Most of the club members are going to the Champions on Ice show at the Compaq Center on Saturday night. But we're going down to Galveston and see it at Moody Gardens on Friday night. Why don't you go down there with us?"

"OK," Dean said. "That'll be nice. I like the rink down there better anyway."

"Good," she replied. "We'll pick you up on the way to Galveston."

Backstage

When the show was over at ten, Dean said to Shannon, "I know a guy backstage. Wanna go with me?"

"Sure," the girl said.

"They have security here, since the Tonya—Nancy thing," he said, "So act like you belong to the cast or crew." Shannon looked puzzled.

As they made their way back toward the dressing rooms, a security guard stepped in front of Shannon. "Can I help you, Miss?" he inquired.

"If you can tell me what went wrong with my triple Salchow, that would help a lot!" she snapped.

"The young man looked embarrassed. "Sorry," he said as he stepped out of her way.

"That was pretty good," Dean said.

"How come they didn't stop you?"

"Because I look like one of the guys who drag the electrical cables around."

Shannon followed Dean back to the locker rooms where several cast skaters were milling around. He walked up to one man, put his hand on his shoulder and said, "Hey, Fella, remember me?"

The young man turned around and looked at him. He blinked, then his eyes widened. "Hulk!" he said. "Dean Steele. My gosh, I haven't seen you in years!" They shook hands warmly.

Shannon's face registered shock. "Brian Bartholomew," she mumbled.

"You've gotten better since I skated against you," Dean teased him. "Looks like I quit just in the nick of time."

"And you've gotten bigger. Look at you. You're huge!"

"Well, when I quit practicing six hours a day, I had more time to work out," he explained, grinning.

Liz

"Oh, there's someone who'll be shocked to see you," Brian said. Let me get her. "Liz!" he yelled. "Where's Liz?"

One of the female skaters looked up with a quizzical countenance.

"Liz," Brian shouted, "Come over here!" The petite but stocky woman put down her bag and started walking toward them. "Remember him?" Brian asked, grinning.

The woman looked at Dean. Her eyes widened and her jaw dropped open. "Oh, my God!" she screamed. "Hulkie!" She ran to him with an enthusiastic embrace.

Shannon was wide-eyed. "Elizabeth North," she mumbled.

"Oh, it's so good to see you!" she said. "I thought you had dropped off the face of the Earth!"

"Pretty close," Dean replied. "But you sure didn't. You were foxier than ever out there tonight."

"My God, Dean," she said, feeling his arms, "You're bigger now than you were at Nationals!"

"I didn't stop working out."

"You still skate, don't you? Surely you didn't hock your blades!"

"I still slice some ice occasionally," he replied, "But not like you do."

Dean noticed Brian smiling at Shannon. "Who's your friend?" he asked.

"This is Shannon Foster," Dean said, "From my skating club. Ladies silver at the '97 Junior Nationals."

"Pleased to meet you, Shannon," Brian said. "I remember your program. You looked really good."

"Thanks," the embarrassed girl said.

"Hey," Brian said. "We're going out for a bite. You wanna come with us?"

Dean looked at Shannon. She gave him an open-mouthed stare, as if to say, "You surely wouldn't consider passing up this opportunity!"

"We rode down from Houston with Shannon's parents," Dean said. "Maybe they would go get coffee somewhere while we join you guys for a few minutes."

"I'll take you home, Hulkie, if you get stranded," Liz said. "I can use one of the rental cars."

"Ask them to join us," Brian said.

"OK, Dean said, "Let Shannon and me go see what they want to do. We'll be back here in five minutes." He and Shannon went out to find Millie and Fred.

"My, Hulkie," Shannon said sarcastically, "You sure are huge!" She glared at him. "You slept with her, didn't you, Dean? You fucked Elizabeth North!"

Dean stopped in his tracks. "Listen, Bitch," he said. "You better can that crap right now, or you'll ride home with Mommy and Daddy. That's a promise. I'm not gonna be embarrassed by your bratty bullshit tonight!"

"Sorry." She said.

"Sorry won't cut it, you little shit. Promise me you'll act human all night, or you're off the program right now!"

"I'm sorry, Dean. It was just a smart-ass crack. I promise I'll be good if you let me go out with y'all."

"There'll be severe penalties imposed if you break that promise, Kid."

"I promise," she said. "You won't be sorry."

"OK," Dean relented. They resumed their search for her parents.

"But you did fuck her, didn't you?"

With eyes flashing fire Dean said, "That's it, Kid. You're outta here!"

"No, Dean!" she pleaded. "I'll be good, I promise."

"You'll be good in the back seat of the Cadillac!" he replied.

"No, Dean, let me go. Please! I'll be perfect, you'll see."

"One smart-ass crack, and you'll be skating with a steel pin in your jaw."

They found Millie and Fred and told them the situation. They wanted to meet and congratulate the famous skaters backstage, but they declined to join in the subsequent festivities. Dean and Shannon took them backstage for brief introductions. "One of these guys will drive us back to Clear Lake," Dean said, "And I'll take Shannon to River Oaks from there." Millie and Fred left for home.

The Restaurant

Dean and Shannon accompanied several of the skaters to a restaurant on the Strand in Galveston. On the way, Liz North sat in the back seat, arm in arm with Dean while Shannon rode up front with Brian. "You didn't have to quit, Hulkie," Liz said, after they ordered. "You could have skated pairs with me. I'd love to fly around the arena with you under me."

"The way you skate, Liz," Dean said, "There's not room for anybody else on the ice. I'd get blown off the sheet."

"Oh, I'd mellow out for a pairs program," she said. "I'm not all fire and flash. I can do romantic . . . if I have the right inspiration."

"I'm sure I couldn't keep up with you," he replied.

"Sure you could. And you're probably the only guy who could hoist my beefy little bod up in the sky anyway. If you won't skate pairs with me, I'll just have to stay on the ground."

"You're doing just fine as a single, Lizzie. Don't change a thing."

"I'd give up a row of sixes to see you skate that damn 'Dogtag Dance' again," Liz said, grinning at him with an accusing gaze. Dean blushed.

"So, what about you, Shannon," Brian asked. "Are you going to Nationals as a senior this year?"

"I don't know," Shannon answered, looking at Dean. "I . . . haven't decided."

The eyes turned to Dean. He inhaled. "Shannon and I are working up a pairs routine," he said. "We hope to take it to Nationals someday." Shannon's face only partially concealed her pride.

The table got quiet. "Oh, my God!" Liz said, looking at Dean. "You are coming back? That's wonderful!"

"We'll have to see if it's wonderful or not," Dean said. "So far we're still trying not to bump into each other. We skate a kind of a Laurel and Hardy slapstick routine."

They laughed. "Oh, you'll do great!" Liz said. She smiled at Shannon with a gaze that hardened and lingered an instant too long.

"At least it's pairs," Brian said. "None of us will have to skate against either of you in competition."

"Not that you'd lose sleep over that!" Dean said.

"Will you go to Worlds?"

"Well, it may take several tries to place at Nats and get a seat on the USA team. But if we ever did, we might go for it."

"You'd go up against the Russian pairs," Liz said.

"Nobody beats the Russian pairs," Dean said.

"Well, you two might could," Brian said. "With your strength, and Shannon's style, it's possible. It would make an interesting competition."

"Don't bet your Rolls on it," Dean teased.

"Hey, the big-time doesn't pay that well," Brian retorted. "I still drive a Jeep."

The Bar

After the meal, the group moved to a nearby bar that had a band. Liz disappeared during the band's intermission and returned after a conversation with the bandleader. "OK," she said. "The band knows 'Rodeo.' They play it all the time. Dean's gonna do his ice skating song. It's all set."

"The Hell you say, North!" Dean responded. "I haven't done that song in about a hundred years!"

"Well, you're gonna do it tonight, or I'll know the reason why!"

"I don't remember the words."

"They'll come to you. You sang it enough before!"

The band picked up their instruments for the next set. "I need a guitar to hide behind," Dean said, joining them onstage. The bandleader handed him an acoustic guitar. He pulled the strap over his head.

"How about 'E?'" the man asked. Dean struck an E chord on the guitar, hummed a note, and said, "That'll work." The band went into the intro bars of the

Clint Black song, "Rodeo." Dean looked out at the audience. Liz was grinning broadly. Shannon was wide-eyed. The other skaters were smiling.

"This is a song about a young man who had the misfortune to fall in love with a figure skater," he said. "A girl skater, in this case," he added. They laughed. After another round of the intro, Dean began to sing.

Her eyes are cold and restless,
Her blisters almost healed.
He'd give a row of sixes,
Just to change the way she feels.
But her love is in Lake Placid,
And he knows she's gonna go.
Well, it ain't nobody like you and me,
It's that damned ice skating show.

It's the blades and boots,
It's the triple loops,
It's a cheer from a crowd of fans.
It's the moves you can bet'll,
Sure win her a medal,
If she does the best she can.
It's the jumps and spins,
It's the falls and the wins,
It's the scores and the 'Six point oh!'
It's hello, and goodbye,
At the kiss and cry,
And they call it a skatin' show.

As Dean stepped back to let the band play an instrumental interlude, the crowd broke into enthusiastic applause. Then he sang the second verse.

He tries his best to keep her,
When it's time for her next show,
But her needs are takin' control of her,
And he knows she's gonna go.
She says 'So long, boy, I'll see you,'
With him standin' in the snow.
Well, that young man loves that skater,
Like she loves that damned ice show.

After singing another chorus, Dean held the guitar close to a lowered microphone and finger-picked a chorus of the song. Then he sang the third verse.

It can make a skater crazy,
Just dealin' with defeat.
Daddy sells off everything he owns,
So his girl can still compete.
But a broken lace, and a frostbit face,
Is all she'll ever know.
After years that she spent chasing,
That dream they call a skating show.

It's the blades and the boots,
It's the triple toe loops,
It's a cheer and a 'Give it your best!'
It's the moves she can bet'll,
Sure get her a medal,
Of gold at the next contest.
It's a jump and a spin,
It's a loss or a win.
A horny judge gives a 'Six point oh,'
That determined little slut's,
Out bustin' her butt,
For that damned ice skatin' show.

Yeah, that busy little slut's,
Out bustin' her butt,
For a damned ice skatin' show.

The song ended, on a loud chord, to wild applause. As Dean walked back to the skaters' table, Liz jumped up and gave him a hug and a kiss on the mouth. After they sat down, Liz looked at Shannon, whose mouth was agape. When she caught the girl's eye she gave her a smug, knowing smile that said, "There's more to your partner than you know about, isn't there, Little Girl?" After the other skaters all expressed their approval and the conversation got back to normal, Liz hooked her arm around Dean's neck and dragged his ear forcefully to her lips. "I wondered if you remembered that third verse, you bastard." She grinned at him. "That's what you think of us, isn't it? Determined little sluts, out there bustin' our butts to get a score. You figure we'd fuck a judge to get a score, don't you?"

"It's just a song, Liz."

"Well, I'll tell you one thing . . . ," She mumbled something in his ear that Shannon and the others couldn't hear. Then she pulled away.

"You bastard!" She said. "You've got so many women crazy about you it's disgusting."

"You're the only one that counts, Liz," he grinned, giving her a squeeze.

"Bullshit! You're a rascal, Dean Steele." She planted lipstick on his cheek.

The Ride Back

Liz drove Dean and Shannon back to his apartment in Clear Lake City, with Shannon in the back seat. After they got out, Liz called Dean back. He spoke to her through the open window for a time while Shannon waited on the steps. After a few minutes he tossed the girl his keys. "Go on inside for a minute, Shannon," he said. "I'll be right there." He got back in the front seat with Liz. Shannon went inside and watched the Playboy Channel on TV for about 35 minutes. Finally Dean came in as the rental car roared away. "Ready to go home, Tiger?" he asked.

"Isn't she gonna spend the night with you?" Shannon demanded. "Maybe I should just take a taxi home so you won't have to wait to jump her bones."

"You're risking serious injury here, Young Lady," he warned.

"I just don't want to stand between you and your old flame," she sulked. "How long did she give you to dump your skating partner and get back here? You can make it to River Oaks and back in thirty-seven minutes at full throttle. Don't get a speeding ticket!"

"Bruises, contusions and lacerations." Dean said, glaring at her.

"Oh, Hulkie," She said, imitating the older woman's voice, "You're so big and strong. Hoist my beefy little bod up in the air and carry me off to bed in a reverse platter lift!"

Dean grabbed her by the shoulders. "Are you finished, you little shit?" he demanded.

"She wants you to skate pairs with her, doesn't she? She wants to fan the flames of your old love affair and work up a pairs program for the Champions on Ice show!"

Dean glared at the girl. "Put a lid on it, Foster!"

"You ought to do it, Dean. The money's good. There's no judges—no scores. Just an admiring audience and Elizabeth North gushing all over you every night. And you could carry her 'beefy little bod' anywhere you wanted!"

They faced each other in anger. "You know," Dean said, "The hard part of this is not the jumps and spins, not the judges, not even falls on the ice. It's having to put up with an insane teenager who's Hell-bent on destroying our pairs team before it ever gets started."

"Me? I'm not the one who sat out in the car for an hour talking to his old flame. You left me in here watching 'Dumbo' on the Disney Channel, remember?"

"You're making up a fantasy even Walt himself couldn't come up with. Our discussion had nothing to do with us skating together."

"So, what did you talk about then?"

"It's none of your fuckin' business, you nosey little bitch. You were shittin' in diapers when I was hanging out with those people. You have not the foggiest clue what we went through together in the old days. So if we want to talk about it a little bit, ten years later, you can butt the fuck out!" He inhaled. "I should have sent you home with your Mommy and Daddy."

"If you won't tell me what it was, then it must be bad for us."

"It's not bad for us. It's not good for us. It's not anything for us. It's just none of your God damn business!"

"She's not gonna quit the tour, Dean. If you start back up with her, you'll have to follow her around everywhere that tour goes. You might as well just go ahead and skate with her."

"Where do you come up with this shit? I'm not gonna start anything up with her. She's dating a guy. That's not what we talked about, for Pete's sake."

"Well, if you didn't talk about skating together, and you didn't talk about getting back together, then what did you talk about for an hour?"

"Old times."

"Yeah, right! Precious memories of days gone by. Get real, Steele, I'm not a retard!"

"Unfinished business."

"Oh, yeah? And what was that?"

"She was facing some problems back then. I helped her work through them, or so she says."

"What kind of problems?"

"Fuck you, little girl! That's her privacy we're talking about."

"OK, what did you do to help her solve them?"

"Just listened mostly. She needed someone to talk to."

"Father Dean," she remarked in a catty voice.

"Bless you, and kiss my ass, My Child," he said in a calm, sincere voice.

"So, does she have more problems now?"

"No, she's doing quite well, thank you very much."

"Then what did you two talk about for an hour?"

Dean sighed. "She just wanted to catch me up on how her situation turned out. I guess she wanted to thank me, and let me know my efforts weren't in vain. I didn't know until tonight that she has just about won all her battles now."

"That's heartwarming, Dean," Shannon said sarcastically.

"You cold-blooded little bitch!" Dean replied. "The River Oaks princess. Just because you've had everything handed to you on a silver platter, you've got no respect for someone who's had to work for what they got!"

"Is that what you think?"

"That's exactly what I think!"

"Well, I'm sorry if I gave you that impression. I respect Elizabeth North very much. She's a great skater, and I admire her strength in handling the problems in her personal life. And as long as she doesn't try to take my skating partner away from me, I'll let her live to skate another day. Otherwise, I'll stomp her 'beefy little bod' into a bloody pulp with my Wilson Gold Star freestyle blades!"

"Methinks you fear for nothing, oh, brutal and vicious one."

"Well, she's lucky. She doesn't know how close she came to a horrible death."

"Nor do you, Young Lady."

Shannon's Ride Home

Dean drove Shannon back to River Oaks with little conversation. "You've got to admit it, Dean. That was pretty disgusting the way she came on to you."

"Not at all. Your imagination is running rampant."

"Oh, Hulkie, you're so big!" she teased him. He grinned and shook his head. "What was that . . . dogtag thing she mentioned?"

"That was . . . a number I used to do. It was kind of a joke."

"She sure seemed excited about it. Was it your Nationals program?"

"Oh shit no! I never did that one in front of judges."

"Why not, Dean?"

"It wasn't designed for polite company."

"Was it dirty?" Her face lit up.

"No, not really. It just lacked elegance in a major way."

"It sure must have had something 'Lizzie' liked!"

"She has bizarre taste in skating routines."

Dean's Return

When Dean arrived at the Piccadilly apartments, there was a rental car parked in front of his unit. "I did pretty well," Liz said when he walked up to the car. "I made it halfway to Galveston before I realized I had to come back."

"Would you like to come inside?" he asked, grinning. "Sexy young women aren't safe out here."

"Are you saying I'd be safer in your apartment?" She grinned coyly.

"I'm saying that," he replied, "But it's merely a ploy to lure you inside. Actually, this is a picnic ground compared to what lies in that den of debauchery."

"Color me lured!" she said, opening the car door. They went inside.

"Will you be here long enough to take off your coat?" Dean asked as he closed the door behind them.

"I'll be here long enough to take off a lot more than that," she said. "If you have any eggs, I'll be here long enough to cook breakfast."

"I've got eggs," he said. "All the eggs you're gonna need."

Shannon and Millie

"That was pretty exciting last night," Millie said at the breakfast table, "Meeting the famous skaters like that."

"Yeah," Shannon said blandly. "Dean used to hang with 'em."

"So, how'd it go after Dad and I left?"

"It was great," she said, unconvincingly. "They were really fun."

"You seem to have some reservations on your enthusiasm, Sweetie. What's troubling you?"

"Nothing, Mom. Everything's cool."

"Sure it is! You spent a night out with your idols, and you have nothing to say about it this morning? What happened?"

"Nothing happened, Mom. Just drop it, OK?"

"Have it your way, Honey. Just don't think you sold me that 'nothing happened' bill of goods."

Millie was silent for a while. "Was it Elizabeth North?" she asked finally.

"Did you see it?" Shannon asked. "Did you see how she acted around him? She actually called him 'Hulkie-pooh!'"

"I saw how she gazed at him. She bears the marks of an old flame."

"Shit, Mom! This is all I need right now. Liz North comes roaring into town and takes my partner away from me!"

"Did she try to do that?"

"Same as! She said she'd skate pairs with him if he'd 'hoist her beefy little bod up in the air.' And she couldn't keep her hands off of him all night. It was disgusting."

"How did Dean respond?"

"Oh," she sighed, "He was cool. He said she's doing great as a singles skater." She paused to reflect. "But they sat out in the car and talked for half an hour before he took me home. And he wouldn't tell me what they talked about."

"You have no right to ask, Shannon."

"But wouldn't you want to know?"

"I'm dying to know, but I'd never ask. You have to lead him into telling you."

"He said they were just catching up on old times. She was thanking him for his support back when she had a rough time, or something like that." Millie weighed that explanation for credibility. "Damn, Mom! I feel so helpless! She's Liz North, for Pete's sake, and she wants my partner! And I'm sixteen, and a Juniors skater. How can I fight that?" She paused. "And she's been in his bed."

"Did he tell you that?"

"No, but I can tell by the way she acted toward him. She might as well be wearing a sign!"

Millie pondered that. Then she turned her attention back to her daughter's problem. "Well, just look at what you have going for you, Honey. First of all, he's your partner. He chose you to skate with, not her or anybody else."

"But you talked him into skating pairs, Mom, and I was the only choice he had then. Now he can have his pick of the gold medalists in the world!" She paused. "I'd be ruined if I had to find another partner. Have you seen that USFSA partner search web site lately? What few boys there are on there are too young, too inexperienced, and too little."

"You won't have to find another partner, Shannon."

"God, if Katerina Witt ever winked at Dean, he'd be gone in a flash!"

"Don't be so sure, Honey. Changing partners is a serious decision. It's working out for you two now. If he were to switch partners, even if it were to a champion, it still might not work as a pairs team. He knows that." Shannon's frown indicated a lack of comfort. "And don't sell him short, either. Dean has integrity, and he knows you have to make a plan and stick with it to succeed in this sport. He won't go running after the first gold medalist who looks his way."

"But they had a thing, Mom," she whined. "They were lovers!"

"Are you sure?" Millie asked, recalling the private investigator's file.

"Pretty sure."

"Well, maybe they were just friends."

"It's Dean Steele we're talking about here, Mom. He doesn't know how to be 'friends' with a female."

"He knows how to be friends with you."

"Yeah, but he thinks I'm a child. Liz North is his age, and she has hot pants for him. Like it's really gonna be platonic, Mom!"

"Well, that was a long time ago. If they did have a thing, they may just want to remember it fondly, but not start it all up again."

"I don't know," the girl said, looking dejected.

"But most important," Millie said, returning to her lecture, "You've got to respect yourself. You've got a lot of promise. You're a good partner for Dean. He's lucky to have you."

"Oh, for sure, Mom!" the girl snapped sarcastically. "Like he'd step over three Olympic champions to get to a US Juniors medallist!"

"Stop that, Shannon!" her mother ordered. "Don't ever make light of your accomplishments. You've done very well in this sport. Be proud of that."

"Get real, Mom. Liz North can skate circles around me. And she's an adult, and she's sexy, and she's everything I'm not."

"She'd trade with you, Shannon, in a second. Your whole life is in front of you. Hers is half gone. She retired and came back. Don't sell yourself short."

"OK, Mom, I'll sit here and polish my silver medal while Elizabeth North skates off into the sunset with my partner."

"Don't give up, Shannon. Just be a good partner. Dean will take care of you."

Millie and Dean

"I hear you and Liz North had a lot of fun Friday night," Millie said, eyeing him closely.

"You can hear all kinds of things these days," Dean replied, somewhat irritated by her accusative tone.

"You knew her before last night?"

"We'd met. Remember the file?"

"OK, Dean. If you don't want to talk about it, I understand."

"Thank you," he replied.

Millie held silent for as long as she could. "I think Shannon felt a little intimidated hanging out with all those famous skaters."

"She held her own," Dean responded. "They liked her. Brian remembered her long program at Junior Nationals."

"Good," Millie replied. "I just think she feels a little inadequate after getting so close to people who have gone so far in the sport. It makes her own accomplishments seem small by comparison."

"She'll get used to it. No matter how high you go, somebody's always better."

"I'm sure she will," Millie said. She paused, and then looked at Dean. "What kind of relationship did you have with Liz North?"

"Biological," Dean said. "We're both Homo sapiens."

"All right, Dean. You've made your point. I didn't mean to pry. I just sense that it's bothering Shannon, that's all. It's a little disconcerting for her to find out her partner has emotional ties with a world-famous female skater."

"I sense those 'emotional ties' may be bothering you as well."

"Nonsense. I have no interest in what you did ten years ago. I'm just reacting to Shannon's obvious distress."

"I see."

"I am, however, interested in anything it might mean for the future. Are you and the flashy Ms. North planning to see each other again?"

"If our paths cross."

"But will you be taking steps to make sure they cross?"

Dean looked at her. "You've taken this as far as it's going," he said, with a measure of irritation in his voice. "The discussion of Elizabeth North is closed."

"I see." Millie said. She turned and left.

Dean's enjoyment of cutting off the prying woman was tinged with a vague regret. He had caused her needless worry when he could have dispelled it with a word. "I can always do that later," he thought.

Shannon and Millie

"Liz North hates me." Shannon said.

"Why do you say that, Hon?" Millie asked.

"It was the way she looked at me. She doesn't think I deserve Dean. I'm not good enough for him. I'm too young and inexperienced, or something. I haven't paid my dues enough."

"Are you sure you're not imagining that, Honey?"

"No, Mom. She might as well have just slammed me up against the wall and told me to my face."

"Shannon, I think you may be a little over-sensitive here. It's very understandable. You're younger and less experienced than Dean, and they're old timers, of a sort. Dean used to run with that bunch. They have history together. You and Dean haven't made your history yet. But you will, and it'll be a wonderful history. You just have to be patient, Honey."

"I still say she hates me."

"OK, to Hell with her!"

Shannon grinned. "Yeah, Mom, to Hell with her!" They laughed.

Millie and Dean

Millie dropped off a costume at Dean's apartment. She hung it in his closet and looked at him, grinning slyly.

"Tell me about Liz North," she said. "What's she like in bed."

"Why don't you ask her boyfriend? He plays hockey in Canada."

"I'd rather hear it from you," she grinned. "I expect you know her better." Dean glared at her from beneath raised eyebrows. "What's the matter, Dean? Cat got your tongue?"

"You're in a particularly slutty mood, Ms. Foster. Why are you doing this?"

"I'm a skating fan," she replied innocently. "I need to know the seedy details of my idols' private lives."

"Bullshit!"

"Come on, Dean. What did you two do in bed? What's she like? How does all that fire and flash she displays on the ice translate into the bedroom? Is she the same ball of fire in the boudoir that she is in the spotlight?"

"Let me ask you something, Millie," he said, raising a fist. "Would you file assault charges if I broke your fuckin' jaw?"

"Ooh, sensitive!" she mused. "There must be some really juicy stuff there. How long were you two an item?"

"You were in the Ice Capades troop, Millie. Satisfy yourself with your own 'juicy' memories."

"Oh, our little group was tame compared to your circle of friends." She moved her mouth close to his ear. "What's she like, Dean? Is she as good as she looks on the ice? Does she deliver on the promise? What's it like to have her under you?" She grinned. "I've seen her 'moves in the field[1].' How are her 'moves in the bedroom?'"

Dean turned his head until their noses touched. Then his right hand closed snugly around her throat, restricting the flow in both her windpipe and her jugular veins. He pushed her to arm's length. "Curiosity killed the cat, Millie," he said as the pressure inside her head began to increase. "You're skating on thin ice. You might want to back off a little bit." He glared at her, then released her.

"Have I ever told you," she asked, catching her breath, "How hot I get when you manhandle me like that?"

"I don't believe that topic has come up in conversation," he replied.

"You're so strong," she breathed. "I feel your power flowing all over me. It's frightening, and it's fascinating. And it turns me on like crazy!"

"Look in the yellow pages," he said, "Under 'P,' for 'psychiatrist.'"

"Come on, Dean. Tell me about fucking Liz North."

"Call the first name on the list."

"What noises does she make?"

"Make an appointment for his earliest opening."

"What does she do when she gets off? Tell me, Dean."

"Tell him to cancel all his other patients."

"All right, party-pooper," she said. "You're no fun!" He glared at her. "OK, I'll be nice. Just tell me if you fucked her. I'll settle for that."

"Surely you remember the 'no kiss and tell' rule, Millie."

"Well yes, but she's a big star. You could be forgiven if you bragged a little."

"Goodbye, Millie." She gave him a pouty look of disappointment. "Are you going to apologize for your rude behavior before you leave?" he asked.

"Why bother, Dean? It would be extremely insincere." She grinned and left.

---

1. Moves in the field—elements of basic figure skating skill and edge control. A series of skill tests consisting of progressively more difficult edge and step patterns.

Chapter 12

Halloween

Banana Split

Dean was already at her table by the time Shannon saw him. It was too late to push the banana split over in front of one of the other girls.

"Hi, Dean," she said, nervously. "You know Brittany and Crystal?"

"Hi, ladies," he said. The young girls giggled. He looked at the banana split and then at Shannon. "That looks tasty!"

"Not bad," she replied, almost defiantly. "Want some?"

"No, thanks. It's not on my training diet." He addressed her with a serious look. "Or yours either, for that matter. There's about a week's worth of sugar and saturated fat in there."

"It doesn't hurt to break training every once in a while," she asserted. "Nobody's perfect."

"You're the poster child for that motto," he said. She put on a disgusted look.

"It's mine," Crystal said. "I was just giving Shannon a taste."

Dean sat down beside Crystal, placing his arm around her back. "Nice try, Sweetie. But I saw the waiter bring it to your chubby little friend here."

Crystal became uncomfortable as he squeezed her shoulders between his hand and his chest. "You see," he said intimately, "This banana split creates for me a problem." He paused. "My job is to lift Miss Foster's cute little ass over my head with one hand while scooting across a sheet of ice on two thin steel blades."

He moved his mouth close to Crystal's ear. "And she's not a small girl," he said softly. "So if she puts a few pounds of disgusting fat on her cute little ass, then, one, it won't be cute anymore, and two, I can't lift it anymore. And that means no fame, no glory, and no medals. That would make me very sad."

The girl was very uncomfortable. She turned to Shannon. "Your partner and I don't think you should eat that ice cream," she said.

"Thank you," Dean whispered intimately.

"Lighten up, Dean," Shannon said. "One banana split won't ruin me."

"I'm sure. But it's not really you I'm worried about," he said. "It's the poor slob who has to hoist your adipose ass up in the air."

"Quit complaining, Dean. You're plenty strong. And one ice cream won't make me fat."

"Well, OK. But just be careful what you're eating. Sometimes ice cream gets contaminated with foreign matter."

Shannon defiantly dug her spoon into the mound and drew out a scoop. She was just about to slip the cold mass into her mouth when she noticed a strange color in the dish. She frowned and turned the bowl around to see it better. She shrieked when she recognized dog poop as the extra ingredient.

"God damn you, Dean! You put that in there!" Fuming, she dropped the spoon on the table.

"Good day, ladies," he said as he turned to leave. "Enjoy your dessert."

Halloween Party

"Guess what, Dean," Shannon bubbled, bouncing with excitement.

"I couldn't possibly," he responded dryly.

"There's a costume party at the club next weekend, and Mom said I can invite you to go with us!"

"The club?"

"The River Oaks Country Club. I'm going as Princess Anne. It'll be cool!"

"Way too cool for me, Your Highness. I'm a mere commoner in Her Majesty's court."

"No you're not. You're going as Sir Lancelot!"

"I don't even speak the language."

"It's just English, Dum-dum . . . kinda like with rocks in your mouth."

"I'm not sure I could make a convincing knight. I'm kind of a knave at heart."

"Mom's going as Queen Elizabeth the first . . ."

"No surprise there."

". . . and Dad's going as King Henry the Eighth."

"Who else?"

"We'll get our costumes fitted on Tuesday. It'll be too radical."

"Way too radical for me, I'm sure."

The Party

"Who's your new friend?" Dede Lindstrom asked in a sly, accusative voice.

"Oh, that's Shannon's new skating partner. His name's Dean Steele.

"He sure is cute, Millie. Did Shannon pick him . . . or did you?"

"I . . . scouted him out, and Shannon decided to skate with him."

"He's married, of course."

"No, I believe he's . . . unattached."

"Living with someone?"

"Living alone."

"Millie Foster, you are perfectly disgusting!" she said slyly. "Shame on you!"

"I'm just playing the Ice Mom here, Dede. "Anything for the cause."

"Millie, you have found yourself a boy-toy, and you're being perfectly obnoxious about it! Bringing him here so we can all drool over him."

"It's all perfectly innocent, I assure you," she said coyly. "I selected him because of his skating ability. He won a medal at US Nationals a while back."

"And all those muscles and that handsome face didn't put you off a bit!"

"I . . . didn't notice." She grinned wryly.

"Millie, you are a bitch in heat! "I'm ashamed to admit I know you!"

"No, you're jealous because you don't have one."

"Does he have a brother?"

"I don't think so."

"I wonder if he'd like to come over and . . . clean my pool sometime. I'll bet he looks perfectly wonderful in swim trunks."

"Before you get any naughty ideas in your head, Dede . . . I'll clean more than your pool if you so much as touch him," Millie lectured, grinning. "Besides, his skating takes up all of his time."

"So, how did you do it, Millie? How did you capture so worthy a prize for your personal collection?"

"I offered to sponsor a try for the US National Championship."

"Oh, you got a bargain! I would have offered him a Corvette and a Givinchy wardrobe, not to mention a conveniently located apartment with a king size bed and mirrors on the ceiling."

"Dede, you are an animal! Mr. Steele is a nice young man. He wouldn't think of doing anything . . . inappropriate. He thinks only of skating."

"Even when you wiggle your well-preserved ass in front of his nose, Millie? I've seen your work, remember? Don't play innocent with me."

"Why, Dede! I'm shocked you would even suggest such a thing as me flirting with the young man. The very idea!"

"Are you saying you never spend time with him . . . alone?"

"Well, we sometimes find it necessary to work out choreography for a program, or music, or costume design ideas. And it's often more convenient just to meet at his bachelor apartment in the afternoon when Fred is at work and Shannon is in school. But, of course, I dress very conservatively, and it's all strictly business between us."

"Millie Foster, you are slime! You're getting your bell rung on a regular basis by Tarzan over there, and you won't tell your dearest friend every juicy detail!"

"I assure you, Dede, if anything . . . romantic should ever happen between us, I'll call you on my cell phone the instant he rolls off of me." She laughed.

"Millie, you lie like a dog!" Dede said. "You've got yourself a young stud, and you refuse to share him with your friends. It's an abominable breach of etiquette, to be sure!"

"Look, Dede, just because you would seduce and defile a young man like that, and use him to scratch your deep down itch, that doesn't mean I have any interest whatever in the boy that goes beyond his skating with my daughter."

"Oh, he can reach the deep one, can he?"

"I wouldn't know." She grinned knowingly. "But, knowing you, I expect he has everything you need, all wrapped up in one tight, well-tanned package."

"Oh God, Millie, I'm getting hot just thinking about it! Just send him over to my house one afternoon a week, and I'll be your friend forever!"

"You already are my friend forever."

"OK, then, I'll give you my jewelry."

"Oh, shit, Dede!" Millie laughed. "You'd never part with that gaudy collection of bangles."

"For that . . ." she mused, "I'd be sorely tempted." They laughed. "How did you do it, Millie? What did you wear? Surely it wasn't that slinky red dress with a black choker necklace and that bra that lets your boobs bounce around like basketballs! Please say you didn't stoop that low."

"I don't recall ever wearing that particular outfit in his presence."

"Well, thank goodness for that! So what was it, something tasteful in black, I hope. Black spaghetti-strap dress and black pumps? Pantyhose, or barelegged? And did you nonchalantly bend over in front of him, or just bury his nose between your boobs?"

"I did no such thing!"

"You're a despicable tease, Millie Foster. You tease your husband, my husband and half the gentlemen in River Oaks at least once a day. I hope you had the decency to give the boy what he needed once you melted him down."

"Dede Lindstrom, I am not a tease!"

"I've known you since second grade, Millie Foster. You were teasing boys then, and you've only gotten worse with the passage of time."

"Well, at least I don't do like you. You find out what the poor boy needs money for—tuition, his poor sick mother's surgery or whatever—and then you cram a handful of cash in your pants and send him diving for it!"

"At least I let him have what he needs when he needs it, Millie. I don't tease him up and then revel in his suffering the way you do."

"I'm not going to stand here and be insulted by the likes of you, Dede Lindstrom! Come over here and meet my friends."

Shannon

Dean was dancing with Shannon. "I really feel out of place here," he said quietly. "I don't have anything in common with these people. And the rent on this costume is a month's pay."

"Oh, forget about it, Dean. You're ten times cooler than any of these boring jerks. Rich people aren't interesting, didn't you know that?"

"Uh, no, I must have missed that day at school."

"No, really. They never have any real adventure in their lives. They just spend all their time trying to be interesting, and the joke's on them. When you have everything handed to you, you never have any adventure."

"Who are you, Plato, all of a sudden?"

"No, Dean. I just grew up around these people. They play golf and mix drinks, and wish they were interesting like you."

"Me? Interesting?"

"Sure. Your parents died when you were nine. You were poor, but you worked your way up to US Nationals. You write computer programs for X-ray machines. These people couldn't do any of that. They'd starve to death if they didn't have a maid to cook and a butler to serve 'em food. All they know how to do is stand around and be rich . . . and dull."

"What about you? Aren't you one of them?"

"No, not really. We're not rich. I mean, by these standards. But we have adventure. Mom, Dad . . . even me."

"What's your adventure history, Miss Jane Goodall[1]?"

She gave him a frown. "I won silver at Junior Nationals," she said. "And I've done other stuff. Not much, I guess, but heck, I'm only sixteen. Give me time!"

"Actually, you're right. You are the most interesting girl at the party."

"Really, Dean? Or are you shittin' me again?"

"No, Ma'am. It's a fact too, not just my opinion."

She grinned at him, pleased, but still suspicious. "I guess you know Mom's friends are teasing her about you," Shannon said after a pause.

"What do you mean?"

"They're saying you're her 'new pet.'"

"What's that all about?"

"Don't be naïve, Dean. They're saying you're her lover."

"You're kidding!"

"No, Dean. I can tell by the looks on their faces when they huddle over there. They're giving her a hard time about you."

"Wow! Some nice friends she has!"

"Oh, she loves it! She'll say just enough to keep 'em talking about it all night. It's their favorite game." She grinned. "You're on display here Mr. Studly."

"I knew I was gonna hate this party," he sighed.

The Dance

"Dean," Millie said, "This is De-de Lindstrom. I've known her from the cradle. She is absolutely without class, but she loans money to God when times are tight in Heaven."

"Pleased to meet you, Ma'am," Dean said, grinning as he took the woman's extended hand.

"She lives in that horribly gaudy palace over on Tanglewood Court," Millie added. "She has excellent taste, but only in her mouth."

"I'm just a simple girl with an eye for things that shine," Mrs. Lindstrom said flippantly. She was dressed as a peasant girl, with the credibility of her expensively tailored costume somewhat undermined by audaciously dripping jewelry. "You look very chivalrous, Sir Knight," she observed as she eyed Dean rather closely.

"Strictly an artifact of the costumer's craft," he responded. "In reality I'm knave to the bone."

"I understand you're quite an accomplished skater," she said.

"Something less than that, actually," Dean replied, smiling self-consciously. "What I lack in skill is compensated by marketing hype from the Foster organization."

"Millie says you're a champion," she said.

"Mrs. Foster is prone toward exaggeration," he replied. "As you quite possibly know."

"They're playing a waltz, Sir Knight" De-de said. "I wonder if you'd care to dance with a humble peasant girl."

"I'd be thoroughly charmed," he said, smiling at her. He took the woman's hand and led her to an open spot on the floor. He took her in the waltz position and they began to dance. By force of habit, Dean kept his eyes fixed on his partner as they whirled around the floor. Dancing with a woman was so natural to him, and his lead so sure, that Mrs. Lindstrom was taken aback by how smoothly they glided across the floor.

"You're a very good dancer, Mr. Steele," she said.

"We have my grandmother to thank for that," Dean said. "She supervised my dance instruction with a fist of iron."

"She has my undying respect," De-de replied, smiling. When the waltz ended, Dean started to lead the woman back toward her table. "Oh!" she said. "Do you hear that? They're playing my favorite mushy old sentimental song." The band was playing "In the Still of the Night." Dean took the woman in his arms and they danced to the slow ballad. He pressed her close to him as they glided smoothly across the floor. Then he returned her to the Foster table. "Has anyone warned you about Millie Foster yet?" De-de asked Dean after she deliberately sat down between him and Millie.

"Just about everyone," he said, "But perhaps you have something to add."

"Sometime when you have a couple of hours free, call me up and I'll hit the high spots." She grinned at Millie.

"You should do that, Dean," Millie said. "Mindless gossip is De-de's primary skill. She's quite inventive at it. She could write for the soap operas."

"There's more to Millie Foster than meets the eye, Young Man," De-de confided. "On the surface she appears to be just another vicious conniving bitch, but actually she's a lot worse than that."

"Since De-de prefers to marry money, rather than earning it," Millie said, "She has plenty of time to devote to her favorite hobby—the merciless slander of her oldest and dearest friends."

"How does the generous Mrs. Foster reward you if you win a gold medal?" De-de asked Dean.

"She usually gives me a Big Mac and a coupon for a free oil change," Dean replied, no longer able to stay out of the verbal jousting.

"I'm impressed," De-de said. "But what if it's only a silver medal?"

"No oil change—just the hamburger."

"And for bronze?"

"The medium size soft drink of my choice."

"And, what if there's no medal at all?"

"She usually just rolls up a newspaper and beats me like a dog." The folks at the Foster table laughed.

"All right, Millie," De-de said when the two women retired to the powder room, "Name your price. I'll write you a check and take him home tonight."

"De-de, you're disgusting! I'd never think of selling that innocent young man into bondage in your dungeon."

"Oh, I'd take very good care of him, you can rest assured."

"You'd suck the life out of him and leave nothing but a dried-out shell!"

"But wouldn't that be fun!" she replied. They laughed.

Millie and Dean

"You made quite an impression on some of my friends, Dean" Millie said. "De-de Lindstrom just goes on and on about you."

"Maybe it was my dancing." he grinned.

"I think you flirted with her, you naughty boy," Millie grinned. "You had her hormones just a-bubblin'."

"I doubt it," Dean said. "I suspect she was just playing some kind of mind game with you."

"She offered to buy you," Millie said. "I probably could have gotten $50,000 for your muscle-bound carcass."

"You shoulda took it!" Dean said. "I'm not worth near that much. Besides, I think I read somewhere that slavery has been abolished."

"Not that kind of slavery, Dear Boy. The enslavement of men by women has kept this species from extinction for a million years. That one will never be repealed." She cocked an eyebrow. "And even if it were, that wouldn't stop De-de Lindstrom. She always gets what she wants. It's some kind of natural law." After a pause she spoke again. "If you ever do decide to sell yourself into that particular brand of slavery, don't just go giving away the store. Let me negotiate your deal. She'd offer to lease you a Corvette. I'd make her buy you a Ferrari."

"You mean, I'd have to serve as a wealthy woman's gigolo?" he asked, grinning. "There's worse careers than that."

"Not for you, you rebellious little rascal, you. No rich bitch could ever control you properly."

"Present company excepted?" he asked, grinning because his remark suggested she was both rich and a bitch.

"Present company included," she replied, grinning back and denying neither allegation. They gazed at each other for a moment. Finally Millie broke her eyes away and spoke. "Actually, I suppose I should tell you the truth. I threatened to shoot her dead if she ever laid a finger on you. I have to protect my investment"

"So, you saved me from a fate worse than death?"

"Oh, I just couldn't bear to see you turned over to the satisfaction of her debased and degraded desires." She grinned.

"Well," he replied, "Thanks for the warning. I wouldn't want to get degraded . . . or hit by a stray bullet, for that matter!" They laughed.

---

1. Jane Goodall—Anthropologist who studied primate behavior.

Chapter 13

Trouble with Shannon

Shannon Drives Matilda

It was about 9:30 on Saturday morning. Dean and Shannon were leaving the Texas Ice Stadium after passing one of their pairs skating tests. "Come on, Dean. Let me drive!" Shannon was adamant. "You never let me drive your Mustang."

"And for very good reason, I might add."

"Why not? I'm a good driver! You've ridden with me."

"A life-threatening experience, to be sure."

"That's bullshit! I'm safe, sane and responsible, and you're just an old shithook if you won't let me drive your car!"

"It's a burden I have to live with. Being a shithook, I mean."

"Come on, Dean! Let me drive. Please, please, please!"

"Shannon, this car is not like anything you've ever driven before. It's not set up like a normal car."

"How's that? What's different about it?" She was skeptical.

"The steering is quick. The steering wheel is more sensitive than usual. You might flip it, just changing lanes."

"That's bullshit. I go very easy on the steering wheel."

"The pedals are very close together, so you can use heel-and-toe downshifting. You'd get your fashionable thick-soled casuals all tangled up in 'em."

"More bullshit. My feet fit perfectly well in there."

"You've never driven a car with this power-to-weight ratio. This engine can develop 525 horsepower at full throttle. It's a whole different driving experience."

"So, I'll just go easy on the gas pedal. No problem."

Dean was out of ideas. The girl had performed well at their test, and he felt she deserved a reward.

"So, just let me drive it over to IHOP for breakfast. That's just a mile or two."

Dean sighed. "Will you stay on the service road and keep you foot out of it?"

"Yeah, sure. I can do that."

"OK," Dean sighed, tossing her his key ring. She got in on the driver's side wearing a big grin. Dean grimaced when she held the starter on too long and ground the gear as the engine awoke. "It starts quick," he said, too late to prevent the clashing of gears.

"Sorry," Shannon grinned sheepishly. She scraped the gears only slightly getting the transmission into first gear and raced the motor before releasing the clutch with a jerk and a bark of the tires.

"I thought you knew how to drive a standard shift." Dean commented.

"Just getting the feel of this one," she explained. "I'll be smooth as silk in a second." There was more jerking and the squeal of rubber as she shifted into second gear. When they reached the entrance ramp, Shannon wheeled the car onto the freeway.

"Service road!" Dean yelled.

"Oops, I forgot," Shannon explained. "I'll be careful. It's just three exits."

As the Mustang rolled out onto the freeway Shannon shifted into third gear and slowly pressed the accelerator pedal to the floor. Dean watched the manifold pressure climb to 16 psi of boost as the twin turbochargers began to spin up. "Let off, Shannon," he said as the tachometer climbed toward the high horsepower range of the engine. "Let off!"

Exhilarated by the fierce acceleration and the roar of the engine, Shannon kept her foot on the floor as the car's speed increased. When the engine reached 3,600 rpm, with full turbo boost, the car was going 70 miles per hour, and the rear wheels broke loose and began to spin. The rear of the car drifted to the right, and Shannon instinctively turned the steering wheel to the left, sending the vehicle into a slow skid. "Let off!" Dean yelled as he grabbed the steering wheel and pulled it back right, controlling the skid before the car had crossed more than one lane. "Pull over!" Trembling, Shannon released the gas pedal and the steering wheel. Dean guided the car onto the shoulder as it came to a stop. "Get out!" he ordered.

"Are you mad?" Shannon asked after she got in on the passenger's side.

"Lucky to be alive' is more like it! You put us into a powerslide at 70 on the freeway, Punk!'

"Sorry," she said, in an insolent, "So what?" tone of voice.

They rode in silence to the restaurant. After they ordered breakfast, Dean confronted the girl with her misbehavior. "OK, Hot Rod, why didn't you stay on the service road like you promised?"

"I wanted to see what it felt like to go fast."

"Did you find out?"

"My God, Dean, it was fantastic! I never felt so much power in my life!"

"You almost killed your skating partner."

"I know, and I'm sorry. It just got away from me for a second."

"You put it onto a skid."

"No, I didn't! It just started sliding. Maybe your tires are slick, or something."

"It started sliding because you steered away from the rear end. You have to steer into a skid. What do they teach in Driver's Ed at Bel Aire, how to use the rear-view mirror to put on mascara?"

"OK, Dean, I'm sorry I almost killed us and wrecked your precious car! Are you satisfied?" Her tone was defiant.

"Yes, but not by your insincere, half-hearted apology. I'm satisfied because I know profoundly, deep down in my heart, that Shannon Foster will never ever again drive any car I ever own, from now until the absolute end of time. If I had a golf cart I wouldn't let you drive it. Not even a skateboard!"

"I don't see why you have to be such a shit-face about it! It was only a little skid. You got it back straight in just a second."

"We came close to death out there, Young Lady, all because you didn't keep your word."

"Fuck you, Dean Steele," she pouted.

"Cursing the guy who holds you nine feet off the ice is ill-advised, Princess."

"Oh, so now you're gonna drop me?" She showed disdain.

"It would solve a lot of my problems," he replied, "Especially if you hit head-first."

"Fuck you, Dean Steele," she repeated.

"I wish somebody would," he mumbled.

Mrs. Robinson

Dean had returned from a brief workout in the exercise room at the Piccadilly Apartments, and was in the shower when the doorbell rang. He blotted himself briefly with a towel, slipped on a pair of sweat pants and answered the door. "Hello, Millie," he said as the door opened. The woman let out an audible gasp as her jaw fell open. She did not speak. "Come in." Trembling, she clutched the door frame for support. "Are you OK?"

"I just didn't expect . . ." she stammered. He looked puzzled as beads of water ran slowly down his abdomen. "Oh, my God!" she said. "I'm having some kind of hot flash!"

"Come in and sit down." Without taking her eyes off him she complied. Becoming self-conscious, Dean said, "I was in the shower. If you'll give me a minute, I'll put on some jeans."

"Oh, no!" she blurted. Then she blushed as she said, "It's OK. You're . . . perfect . . . just fine . . . as you are."

"I'm not even dry. It'll just take a second."

"No, Dean . . . please. Just . . . greet me with a hug." She held out her arms.

Somewhat puzzled, Dean moved closer and felt her trembling as he took the woman in his arms. He heard her gasp when he squeezed her. "I hope I don't get your dress wet," he offered. "I didn't have a chance to dry off." Her hands ran up and down his bare back as she clung to him in silence. Finally he pulled away. "Did you bring sketches of you ideas for costumes?"

"Yes," she replied. "Sit down and I'll show them to you." Dean complied. "These are great," he said when she finished demonstrating her ideas. "I am in awe of your talent, Madam!"

"Thank you, Young Man." Again he became self-conscious as her eyes devoured him. "No wonder you skate with such power. I haven't seen muscles like that since the last Mr. Olympia contest!"

"I'm nowhere near their league," he replied

"You're in a league of your own, Mr. Steele. You are . . . magnificent." Her face held a hopeless look as they gazed at each other. He had questions he didn't know how to ask. She had answers she was fearful to yield. After a long moment she spoke.

"When I first saw you a moment ago, standing there, your bare skin glistening with dew drops, wearing nothing but those . . . drawstring pants . . . I had a physical reaction. I almost collapsed on your porch, actually. I was light-headed. My heart was pounding. I couldn't breathe. It was . . . so much more than . . . ." She paused, and her eyes fell to her lap. Dean sat in silence as she mustered the strength to continue.

"I've told you that I sometimes . . . watch your old skating performances. They . . . inspire me. They . . . thrill me. They . . . arouse me." She inhaled and released a long breath. "You stir in me a passion that nothing else can touch. It's a deep passion. It's . . . quite intense. It erupts like a volcano, and it consumes me like an inferno. As you can guess, I dream about you. I fanaticize. I imagine making love with you. I behave scandalously with you in my imagination, and I enjoy it thoroughly." She paused. "So today, after ten years of having you on the TV screen, when suddenly I'm standing in front of your provocatively exposed body, in the flesh, it was almost more than I could handle."

"I should be better dressed when I receive visitors. I knew you were coming. I just misjudged the time."

"No, Dean. It wouldn't have mattered. It was bound to happen. I should have known I couldn't . . . work in your presence harboring this secret." She shook her head slowly. "I knew instantly. You were wet. You were in the shower when I rang. You only had time to grab your sweat pants. You . . . aren't wearing anything under those disarmingly sexy drawstring pants."

Dean's face flashed pink in admission. "I didn't think . . . ."

"You knew, Dean. You knew the sight of you was driving me out of my mind, so you didn't go get dressed. And thank God for that too! Sitting here with you like this has given new meaning to my life."

"What's so . . . ?"

"Dean, I want to touch you so badly I can hardly control myself. And, in those thin drawstring pants you're so completely . . . accessible." Her face developed a knowing grin. "You might as well be naked, my boy."

Dean's face reflected his embarrassment. "I had no idea you . . ."

"I guess you thought only males turned into drooling idiots in the presence of one of the opposite sex. Sophisticated ladies never have scandalous thoughts. Well, most of what you and I do in my dreams would shock Masters and Johnson . . . and you as well, I expect, despite your wealth of experience." Having gotten her secret out, the woman relaxed. "Are you shocked, Dean? Do you find it disgusting that an older woman should find you so . . . stimulating?"

"I find myself . . . without rational comment." he replied.

Millie slid her arm behind him. She moved closer to him and exhaled softly into his ear. "Are you trying to seduce me, Mrs. Robinson?" Dean finally asked.

"Why, no, Benjamin Braddock," she replied, pleased that she had so quickly remembered the Dustin Hoffman character's name from the 1967 movie[1]. "I've been trying to get you to seduce, me." She paused. "And it's becoming quite a chore!"

"Sorry for my tardiness," he replied. "What exactly did you have in mind?"

"Well, I thought that you, being a young, strong and single man, would target this sexy but vulnerable older woman and put some of your manly moves on her. She would resist, of course, desperately holding on to her dignity. But, after a time, your persistence would pay off. Her emotions would get the better of her, she would falter, and, in a moment of weakness, you would take advantage of her."

"What then?"

"Well, you would have your way with her in the most disgusting and despicable manner. But she would find such bliss in your arms that she would instantly become your hopeless love slave. She would henceforth care for your every need with tenderness and devotion."

"I see. It's just a bit difficult to visualize you, the cruel and evil Ice Queen, in exactly that role."

"That's the beauty of my scenario," she said. "The young man's charms tame the cruel and evil Ice Queen and turn her into a docile servant!"

"Somehow I think that's a fantasy even C. S. Lewis[2] wouldn't attempt to sell."

Millie put a pouty, injured look on her face. "I know I'm a hard-boiled case, Dean," she admitted, "But you shouldn't underestimate the power you have over me. You, and you alone I should add, can melt me down and remold me into whatever you wish." Her body undulated as she spoke.

"I wouldn't venture to change a thing about you, Millie," he said. "You're perfect just as you are."

"A perfect bitch, maybe. Come on, Dean. Surely you'd like to mess with the cruel and evil Ice queen. Wouldn't you like to bend her to your will, just a little bit? Wouldn't you like to feel her melting like putty in your hands? Losing her grip on herself and baring her soul to your irresistible power? You can't tell me you wouldn't just enjoy the Hell out of that!"

"I doubt if any of that falls within the realm of possibility," Dean said, still refusing to admit to his interest in the woman.

"Oh, it would happen, Dean. I can guarantee it. You put your sexy moves on me and you'd think the whole north pole had melted. That's a promise."

"You make it sound like an act."

"Oh, no. It would be genuine, I can assure you. I just know the effect you have on me."

"Why do you want to do this, Ms. F.?"

The woman inhaled, then let out a long sigh. "That's not something I should share with you, Mr. S."

"But you will share it, won't you, Ms. F.?" He eyed her intently.

"You bastard," she grinned. "You just keep pulling intimate confessions out of me, don't you?"

"I somehow get the impression that confession is good for your soul, Millie, or at least it's good for your sales statistics."

Grinning, she shook her head. "You look right through me, don't you, Mr. Dean Steele, bold and honest boy skater?"

"So, what's the answer to the question?"

"I forgot the question," she said evasively.

"The question was, 'Why do you want to do this?'"

"OK," she said with resignation, "If you must know." She paused and looked at him, affording him the opportunity to let her off the hook. He didn't take it. "Dean, there is a fire inside me. A flame of emotion and sensuality. It smolders most of the time. Sometimes it flares up a little, then dies back down to glowing embers." She looked at him to see if he was following her train of thought.

"Go on," he said.

"Sometimes just a touch from you, or even just a glance, can make that little flame erupt into a raging inferno." She raised her eyebrows. "You turn me on, Dean." He looked at her in silence, prompting her to continue. "I want to feel that inferno, Dean. I want to be burned to a crisp in that oven. I want to see just how hot it can get in that furnace, even if it melts me completely." She fell silent. "So, there you have it," she said. "The Ice Queen's secret. What do you think?"

"It makes sense," he said. "I should have known it would."

"So, are you interested?"

"In joining your scenario?"

"It's not something I can do without you, Dean," she said, grinning.

"I suppose not."

"So?" she demanded her answer.

"What you propose sounds like great adventure indeed," he said. "I just think it comes with serious complications, given our current situation."

"It would remain a secret, of course," she said, almost flippantly.

"That would be one Hell of a secret," he mused, "Since your husband is my financial backer and your daughter is my skating partner."

"A secret is a secret, Dean. It's quite simple. You just don't tell anybody."

"It's never simple, Millie," he said. "People are very perceptive where sex is concerned, especially people who know us well. There are hundreds of subtle ways we could arouse suspicion without knowing it."

"You sound like the voice of experience, Dean. Have you had affairs with married women?"

"This is your confessional, Millie, not mine."

"Ooh, touchy on that subject!" She grinned knowingly.

"I just think it would put the whole pairs skating project at risk," he said.

"OK, Mr. Straight Arrow." she grinned. "We'll do it your way . . . for now." She smiled at him. "But maybe you give this crusty old Ice Queen a hug?"

Dean softened, relieved that Millie did not feel serious rejection. "I think I'm entitled to hug the Ice Queen," he said. "After all she's done for me."

He took her in his arms. "You're a charming woman, Millie," he said. "Soft and warm beneath that icy exterior. Sensitive and sexy."

She sighed as she pressed her body against him. He moved his mouth to her neck and began to kiss her. He worked his way up to her earlobe with his lips.

"You're stoking the fire, Mr. Steele," she said.

"I can smell the smoke already," he said.

"It's incredible," she said, "The effect you have on me. I'm already burning up, and you've only gotten to my ears. I can't imagine how hot I'd get if you went all the way with me."

"Let's pray we never find out, Madam."

"I suppose," she said, obviously unconvinced.

The Strike

While doing an overhand lift in practice, Dean's arm buckled. Shannon sank slowly to the ice, landing gently on her butt. She skidded rapidly toward a beginner's class of little kids. Unable to get a blade into the ice to slow her momentum, she watched helplessly as she mowed them all down, including the instructor.

Shannon got up and began to help the frightened children get back on their feet. She apologized to the instructor. Then she skated back to where Dean was standing.

"You bastard!" she said through clenched teeth. "You did that on purpose!"

"Did what?"

"Dropped me on the goddam ice! I know you did! I could feel it."

"Something happened to my shoulder," he said. "I couldn't hold you. I went off balance and lost control."

"Save it, Asshole! You laid me down like a bowling ball, right in front of God and everybody. I've never been so embarrassed in my life!"

"Maybe it's your fat ass has gotten too heavy for me to hold up in the air!"

"It's that ice cream, isn't it?" she fumed. "You did that because I ate a Goddam ice cream! Damn you Dean!"

"No, I dropped you because my shoulder snapped and I lost control of your beefy little bod. That's my story, and I'm sticking to it."

"Asshole! You made me take out that whole beginners class. I could have killed those little kids!"

"Now, you might do well to ask yourself this: 'If eating the first banana split sends me sliding across the ice on my butt in practice, what is that second banana split gonna do for me?'"

"You wouldn't dare!" She glared at him in anger.

"Not deliberately, of course, but if your weight goes up any more, I might lose you in the middle of the routine. You could end up doing a belly flop in front of the judges table at 30 miles an hour, right there on ESPN."

"You wouldn't dare drop me during a performance!" she asserted.

"Well, you overindulgent, self-centered little brat, there's only one way to find out. There's an ice cream parlor down the street, and they have 31 flavors!"

"I can't believe this! What does it hurt if I eat one fucking ice cream? And what business is it of yours, anyway?"

"Look up the word 'partner' in the dictionary, you insolent little bitch!"

"I know what it means, God dammit! Besides, I want to be . . . voluptuous."

"Leave 'voluptuous' to May West. You're a skater, not a porno queen. I have to lift your voluptuous little body over my head with one arm. I don't mind lifting muscle and I don't mind lifting bone, but my contract don't say I gotta carry around no fuckin' lard!"

"You don't have any trouble lifting me. You're strong. Besides, one ice cream won't make me gain any weight."

"Bullshit! You're already up at least four pounds from when we started. You're gettin' heavy faster than I'm gettin' strong! You've already got twenty pounds on the next heaviest girl skater here. Just try to find some other guy who can launch your rocket, Miss Priss." Shannon fumed. "Seriously, Kid, you're an athlete. You gotta act like one. You gotta keep your body in shape. And if you don't, you'll find yourself doing that bowling ball act again. Next time you'll go face-down into a hockey goal . . . with an audience. And that's a promise." Shannon glared at him. She didn't have a response. "And don't try sneaking around the ice cream store, either. I can feel it when you gain half a pound."

Shannon softened. "But you make it look so easy. I just thought . . ."

"Look, Kid, just because I have a relaxed smile on my face doesn't mean I'm not straining like Hell down there. I just try not to let it show."

"OK," she sighed, "I guess I was a bad girl. I'll give up the ice cream."

"A wise choice, young lady. You shan't regret it."

She grinned coyly. "Do I have to make it up to you?'

"Just keep your body weight in check. That'll keep me happy."

"No, I just thought that, since I was such a bad girl and all, maybe I have to submit to a disgusting sex act to atone for my sins."

"There's a Catholic church down the street. Go sit in one of the little booths and tell the nice man what a bitch you are."

"But I have a skating partner. You're supposed to hear my confessions. Don't you want to hear about all the tacky things I've done?" Her eyes batted coyly.

"I get to see all the tacky things you do. I don't need to hear about 'em too."

"Oh, but I've done a lot of naughty things you don't know about." She grinned knowingly. "Don't you want to hear about 'em?"

"Like what?" he asked. "Poppin' your gum in class?"

"Oh, it's a lot worse than that, Dean. Loads worse."

The girl was in a playful mood. He was curious what transgressions she might offer up. "Yeah? Well, some other time. Right now we have to get ready for a pairs test tomorrow."

---

1. The Graduate, directed by Mike Nichols, 1967.
2. C. S. Lewis, author of science fiction and fantasy novels.

Chapter 14

An East Texas Thanksgiving

An Invitation

"Guess what, Dean!" Shannon said excitedly.

"I couldn't possibly," the young man replied.

"Mom and Dad are going to invite you to go up to East Texas with us for our Thanksgiving!"

"What's that all about?" he inquired.

"My granddad has this big old farm up between Lufkin and Dibol, and they have this big old funky farmhouse, and all Dad's relatives come in from all over East Texas to have this huge Thanksgiving dinner, and it's too cool, and you're gonna go with us!"

"Sounds like a sure-fire formula for disaster to me," he replied. "Nothing worse that attending somebody else's family reunion."

"No, Dean, you gotta go. It'll be too cool!"

"Sorry, Kid. I've already made firm plans to be bored and lonely this Thanksgiving."

"No, Dean," she pleaded. "You gotta go, don't you see? You'll meet all my cousins and stuff."

"If they're anything like you, I think I'll pass."

"No, Dean," she whined, "It's all set. If you don't go it'll just be terrible."

"Terrible is my idea of Thanksgiving dinner with a table full of strangers who all know each other."

"No, Dean, you'll get to know 'em too. Don't you see?"

"Isn't it just possible that they, and I, are just as well off if I *don't* know 'em?"

"No, you awful person! If you don't go to Daddy Buff's with us for Thanksgiving, I'll just die!"

"If I have to spend Thanksgiving in East Texas with your family, I'll just die!" he replied. "Better you than me."

"Dean, you're being a terrible jerk," she pouted. Then she softened. "Please say you'll go with us. Please, please, please!"

"Really, Shannon, it's not a good idea. I have stuff I need to do here, and I wouldn't add a thing to your family reunion." He looked at her. "I'm not your brother, you know," he admonished.

"No, but you're my skating partner," she said, "And skating partners always have Thanksgiving together. That's the rule."

"Why do I get the feeling this rule book of yours is still under construction?"

"Please, Dean. You just have to go with us . . . or I'll kill myself!"

"In that case, I'm spending Thanksgiving in Afghanistan."

"I'm serious, Dean. You gotta go with us."

"OK, I'll wait 'till I'm invited, and I'll talk to Fred about it, just to see if it makes any sense. Right now it sounds like a really bad idea."

"Great!" she said, bouncing with excitement. "I can't wait 'till my snippy little cousins see you!"

"Now I know it's a bad idea!"

A Chat with Fred

"Dean," Fred said, "Uh, we always go up to my parents' place in East Texas for Thanksgiving. Millie and Shannon and I would like for you to go up there with us this year. We'll go up Wednesday afternoon and come back Friday morning."

"I wouldn't want to intrude on a family gathering," Dean replied.

"Oh, no. You wouldn't be intruding. My sisters always bring a whole entourage of kids and their friends along with 'em. It's a real mess."

"Was this Shannon's idea?"

"Well, she mentioned it first, I guess. Hell, I'm so used to there just being the three of us, I wasn't thinking. But we'd really like to have you go with us."

"Will I have fun?"

"I doubt it," Fred grinned. "But you sure will get a lot to eat."

"You'll get to meet Fred's sisters," Millie said, walking up on the conversation. "Linda and Earlene think their baby brother married poorly."

"I'm aghast!" Dean said, tongue firmly in cheek. "How could they possibly?"

"Oh, they wanted him to settle down in East Texas with some mousy little farm girl and raise a dozen kids."

Dean couldn't restrain himself from pursuing this line of teasing. "How could that possibly be any better than sharing one's life with the charming and vivacious Ice Queen?" He inquired, grinning at Fred.

"Well, they're automatically suspicious of anybody who didn't grow up in East Texas," she explained, "And I'm a West Texas city girl. They tried to die when we got engaged."

"Growing up in Midland makes you a city girl?"

"For them it does," she answered. "Anything over 50,000 is a metropolis. They also think I'm selfish, only giving Fred one daughter and then having my tubes tied. The Foster name will end with this generation, and they'll never forgive me for not turning my body into a baby factory, like they did."

Amused by this insight into the Foster family, Dean continued to press the issue. "What about it, Fred," he asked. "Did you marry the wrong woman?" he knew the answer, since Fred had often commented on how lucky he was to get Millie. Dean simply enjoyed stirring the pot. Millie raised her eyebrows as she awaited Fred's response.

"Smartest move I ever made," he said, rolling his eyes skyward and pretending to offer a diplomatic answer in lieu of the truth.

"No, that was the smartest move you ever made, Country Boy," Millie said, laughing.

Dean was having so much fun he continued to press the point. "So, why didn't y'all just settle down in East Texas?" he asked.

"Did you see the movie, 'Deliverance'?" Millie asked.

"Oh, come on, Millie!" Fred said. "It ain't that bad!" They all laughed.

"So, are you going, Dean?" Millie asked.

"Do y'all really want me to? Seriously?"

"You'll add a much-needed dose of sanity to the festivities, Dean . . . really." Millie said.

"OK," he said. "Save a piece of turkey for me."

Millie

Dean and Millie were out of earshot of Shannon and Fred.

"I expect we'll need to curtail our normally friendly conversation while we're up there in East Texas," Dean said. "We wouldn't want to fuel the gossip machine."

"Oh, it wouldn't take much to get Linda and Earlene talking about us," Millie replied. "They'd just love to get me embroiled in a scandal. It would prove they were right about me all along."

"Then we best have very little to do with one another," Dean suggested.

The Ride Up

Shannon and Dean rode up to East Texas in the back seat of the Cadillac. On the way up US Highway 59 they passed a truck dealership that had a Peterbilt tractor-trailer rig mounted high atop a pair of telephone poles.

"Look at that!" Shannon said. "How'd they get that big old truck way up there?"

"I expect they just drove it up there," Dean said. "Those Peterbilt trucks are real hill-climbers."

"As if, Dean!" Shannon said, grinning at his tease.

"That reminds me of an old saying," Fred said. "'Old truckers never die, they just get a new . . . 'what is it? 'Mack truck,' I think is how it goes. Right Dean?" Fred was grinning mischievously in the rearview mirror.

"I'm not sure," Dean replied, grinning as well. "It may be, 'They just get a new Kenworth.'"

"What about Peterbilt?" Shannon asked. "That'd work." An explosion of snickering blew out of Millie's mouth after a slight delay.

"What?" Shannon said, indignantly, realizing that her three companions were laughing at her. "Old truckers never die," she said, trying it out, "They just get a new . . ." Her face registered recognition. "That's gross, Dad!" she said. Then she started giggling. She liked being teased by her daddy.

The Farm

When they arrived at the Foster farm, Dean was introduced to Fred's father, Buford, who met them in the driveway. The farmhouse was of East Texas classic architecture, big and white and square, with a screened-in porch skirting three-quarters of the perimeter. It was held off the ground by short brick columns. Its peaked roof had a single lightning rod with a metal rooster on it. "This is East Texas, all right," Dean muttered under his breath.

Shannon walked toward a group of three women with Dean in tow. "Who's the fox?" Dean asked, loud enough for the three women to hear.

"What?" Shannon asked.

"The good lookin' one in the middle."

"That's Mamaw, Dean," the girl said, grinning disgustedly. "She's my grandmother!'

"There's hope for you yet, Foster," he said, "If you grow up lookin' like that."

Shannon hesitated for a second, then caught on to what Dean was up to. "Mamaw," she said, "This is Dean Steele, my skating partner."

"Pleased to meet you, Madam," he said, smiling warmly as he took her hand.

"Welcome, Mr. Steele," the older woman said, regarding him closely. "I'm Marybelle Foster. And just remember . . . you can go to Hell for lying just like any of God's other sins!"

"I'll make a note of that," he said, grinning. The woman grinned back at him.

"Oh, uh, this is Aunt Linda and Aunt Earlene," Shannon said, "Daddy's sisters."

"Hello, ladies," Dean said. The two women regarded him pleasantly, but could find nothing to say.

Shannon pulled Dean away to look for more relatives to show him to. "I can't believe you," she said when they were out of earshot. "Flirting with my grandmother!"

"I was overcome by her charm, I guess."

"You were overcome by bullshit, you mean! Mamaw's pretty scary. Most people are afraid of her."

"I hope I haven't messed in my nest already."

"She likes you," Shannon advised. "I can tell."

The Cousins

"Dean has this Mustang," Shannon announced as she and Dean sat amid a cluster of her cousins. "It's all souped up and it's got no mufflers, and it's really loud, and it's really fast, and he lets me drive it!" Her cousins gaped in silence. "Dean and I work out together at the gym all the time," she said, "And he lifts tons of weight, and he's a monster!" She paused . . . "He's just this really great skater, too, and he doesn't drink at all."

The boys were incredulous. "Not at all?" one asked. "Not even a beer?"

The eyes turned to Dean, and he saw he was being forced to answer. "I don't drink motor fuel," he said, somewhat miffed by what Shannon was putting him through. "I don't drink gasoline, I don't drink diesel fuel, and I don't drink alcohol. Those are for cars and trucks. Water is what humans run on. I drink that."

"He lives in this really cool singles apartment in Houston," Shannon continued. "There's all these really wild parties there every night. And these girls? They're always trying to get him to go out with 'em. There must be at least a hundred of 'em!"

The kids looked at Dean in awe. "You know," he said to the group, "That when exaggeration fails her, your cousin goes straight to fabrication, right?"

"No, it's true," she said. "Sometimes I have to help fight 'em off! They're so tacky, and I have to run 'em off!"

"Maybe you can wait 'til you hear a distress call on that one," Dean suggested.

Dean took Shannon aside later. "OK, Kid," he said. "You and I kind of yuck it up and josh around all the time. Our antics could sometimes appear . . . flirtatious to the casual observer. That's OK for a pairs routine, but here in East Texas folks might be offended by any suggestion of romance between persons so widely separated in age."

"You have a point to make, Steele?"

"Let's just cool it a little on the horsing around, OK? We don't want to supply these good folks with their next scandal."

"Oh, come on, Dean! What could they possibly have to talk about that's any better than us?"

"Anything! We do not want to get that rumor started, Kid. Believe me. It would be seriously messy."

"Lighten up, Steele," she grinned. "I won't do anything too scandalous." Her grin told him his suggestion had been all but discarded.

Dean gave Shannon from 6:00AM until 9:00PM on Thanksgiving Day to eat anything she wanted. At 6:10 she had a cup of coffee and a piece of warm apple pie with ice cream on it. This was followed by a hearty breakfast at 8:30.

The Thanksgiving meal was served at straight up twelve noon. The table was large enough to accommodate all the adults and the older children. Shannon's cousin, Lou Anne, was sitting beside her at the dinner table. "Your partner's real nice, Shannon," Lou Anne whispered, "But he's awful quiet."

"Oh, he's just on his good behavior," Shannon replied. "He's really a wild man." The other girl's face showed skepticism.

There was a lull in the conversation as the participants finished up their main course. "I think I'll have a piece of that pecan pie with some Blue Bell ice cream on it," Shannon said rather loudly. "And then some chocolate cake. Better put some ice cream on that too." She glanced over in time to see Dean wince. "Dean hates it when I eat like this," she announced. "He has to lift me up over his head all the time when we skate. He's always afraid I'm gonna get too heavy."

Dean quickly picked up that Shannon was pushing him to respond in front of her relatives. He held his tongue to see how far she would go with it. "It's kinda hard on him, him being so old and all." The forks ceased moving and the chewing stopped in response to this bodacious barb. "He has a really hard time keeping up with me," she added. The table remained silent as everyone waited to see what Dean's response to the girl's audacious challenge would be. Fred's sisters considered that Millie had failed to teach his daughter proper manners, and this they took as an example.

"I just want you to be happy, Princess," Dean replied sarcastically. "If eating like a school of piranha and oinking like a blue-ribbon Poland-China sow floats your boat, then, by all means, let's do that!" He paused to the thundering silence at the table. Pleased that she had evoked this response, Shannon amused herself by scanning the shocked looks on her relatives' faces. "And if I ever have any trouble lifting you," he continued, "Why, we'll just work a forklift into our routine! OK?"

"He's a real slave driver," Shannon said, continuing to push her performance. "And he's mean to me all the time. He even beats me."

"Young lady," Fred's mother said sternly, "I do not for one minute believe that your daddy would stand by and allow you to be beaten by your . . . skater boy!"

"Daddy doesn't know about it, Mamaw," Shannon replied quietly with downcast eyes, as if revealing a painful secret.

The old woman glared at her son, demanding a response. Millie was having great difficulty suppressing her snickering. Under the heat of his mother's gaze, Fred was forced to enter the fray. "Do you beat her, Dean?" he asked, working his way into the joke.

"Not often enough, obviously," came the reply, "And I get permission from her mother every time." Several pairs of widened eyes shot to Millie.

"Well, just don't leave any scars on her, Son," Fred said, suppressing a grin as best he could.

There were a few tense moments of silence before laughter exploded from Millie's mouth. Then Fred started laughing at her loss of composure. Slowly the tension drained away as the others came in on the joke. Marybelle Foster, realizing that she had been taken in by her granddaughter's teasing, decided that she could play the game too. "Why is it you see fit to beat my granddaughter, Young Man?" she challenged Dean.

Thinking quickly, Dean began his response. "You're charming granddaughter, it seems, inherited only half of her DNA from the Foster side of the family, and, perhaps as a result, she is prone toward occasional fits of misbehavior. Now, whether there's any connection there or not I couldn't say, but corporal discipline is a last resort to which I am sometimes pushed, just in order to maintain some focus and direction in our skating project. When I do beat Shannon, it is always with both restraint and regret."

"I see," Mamaw Foster replied. "And who disciplines you when you misbehave?"

"Uh, Shannon's mother usually handles that chore," he replied. "She's quite the expert at inflicting pain."

"Well, if she ever gets tired of it," the elder Mrs. Foster said, "I'll be happy to take my turn tanning your britches!"

"We'll call you if we need you, Madam," Dean replied. Everyone at the table was laughing.

"Did you get what you wanted at the dinner table?" Dean asked Shannon later.

"You mean that piranha thing? Yeah. It was funny. I knew you'd say something cool if I messed with you long enough. Did you see the look Mamaw gave Daddy when I said you beat me? It was too cool! But you left something out."

"What's that?"

"It should have been 'fuckin' forklift,' right? 'We'll work a fuckin' forklift into our act.'"

"Actually, you're right. I'm kinda new around here, so I soft-pedaled it a bit."

Shannon grinned. "It was too cool," she said. "I thought Lou Anne was gonna shit when you said that piranha thing."

"And that's a good thing?" he asked. "You're the laxative girl?"

"Trust me, Dean. It was way cool."

Dean started grinning. "I think the word is out on you, Princess."

"What do you mean?"

"Well I haven't seen this many pickup trucks and cowshit covered cowboy boots since the Houston Livestock Show and Rodeo. I think the local farm boys are stopping by just to sniff you out."

"Ha! Did you hear what Mamaw said? She's never had this many women drop by on Thanksgiving, just to say 'Hi.' I think every single woman in East Texas between twenty and forty came over to get a look at the Houston hunk."

"Did you see the way that Simmons boy tensed up when you announced that I beat you? I think he has the hots for you."

"Oh, as if, Dean! Like I could possibly care what he thinks!"

"I expect he just came to this shindig to see you, Kid. He's had these big moony eyes the whole time."

"Off my case, Steele! Like I would look twice at that clodhopper!"

"You really oughta consider the East Texas farm life, Shannon. Cookin' and scrubbin' and plowin'. It's good, clean fun."

"Bite me, Dean. I'm a city girl, remember? Shopping malls and cell phones. No dirt under these fingernails!"

"You might be missing a bet here. Young Mr. Simmons looks to be real strong and stable."

"You're strong and stable, Dean. I'll just keep what I've got, thank you very much!"

"But you don't 'got' me, Foster, remember?"

"Same as, Steele!" she replied with a haughty air. "I'm the main focus of your life right now, remember? Your whole world revolves around me." She gave him a triumphant look. "Deal with it . . . Skater Boy!"

"I was trying to forget," he muttered.

Bulldozer

Dean was looking at a display of framed photographs on the wall in the den. "See that one?" Shannon said, walking up behind him. "That's Daddy Buff on the bulldozer."

"Yes, I can see it is."

"Daddy, tell Dean the story about Daddy Buff and the bulldozer."

"That story gets a little bigger every time he tells it," Buford Foster protested. "It's easily ten times size by now."

Fred Foster walked over and put his arm around his daughter. "Dad owns 160 acres of pasture land about fifteen miles northeast of here," he began. "The adjoining land on the east side belongs to a man named Rufus Caldwell. He's . . . not well liked in this county." He paused. "Rufus runs cows on his land, and one day he decided to rework the road that goes up between the two parcels because it always got muddy when it rained. Well, he widened the road and moved his fence over onto our property, clipping off about an acre and a half of our land." Dean raised his eyebrows. "So Dad got a surveyor out there to find the property lines, and then he rented a bulldozer and tore the Hell out of that fence and that shiny new blacktop road where it overlapped our land. Well, when the fence went down, Rufus' cows got out and scattered all over East Texas. Dad called him up and said, 'Rufus, I was doing a little dozer work out on my grazing land, and I noticed one of your cows got out.' Rufus spent the next three days in his pickup, pulling a cattle trailer all over the place picking up his cows." He paused to grin. "Nobody else has tried to steal any Foster land since."

"That picture was in the paper, Dean," Shannon announced proudly. "Daddy Buff and the bulldozer."

Millie

Millie found Dean alone in the gun room where Buford stored his guns and reloaded his ammunition. She pushed the door closed and took him in an embrace from behind. "Shit, Millie!" he said as her arms closed around him. "You could start a nasty rumor, here!"

"Did I startle you, Big Boy?"

"I just needed a second to figure out if it was you or Linda or Earlene," he teased her.

"You would be very wise to keep your distance from those two," she said. "I always hate it when I have to murder a sister-in-law."

"I don't know," he said. "That Linda is a fox, and Earlene has been giving me these . . . looks."

"Trust me, Dean," she admonished. "They don't have anything you need."

"As you wish, Your Grace," he replied.

"Shannon was giving you a hard time at the diner table," Millie said.

"You could have stepped in and stopped it," he replied.

"I was having too much fun watching you squirm," she said. "It's my favorite pastime. If I can't do it myself, I'll just watch and enjoy while my darling daughter does it."

"Sadism is a disease, Millie, and you're seriously ill."

"With me it's a hobby," she replied, grinning mischievously. Then she left the room.

The Shoot-out

"Who owns this collection of sissy pistols?" Dean asked as he gazed into the glass case in the den.

"You consider pistols sissy?" Buford Foster asked, walking up behind him.

"No, just these pearl-handled, chrome-plated six-shooters here. They look more like Hollywood movie props than serious firearms to me."

"Do you shoot?" Fred's father asked.

"I took marksmanship two semesters at UT," Dean replied. "I can shoot the whiskers off a gnat at eighty yards. What about you?"

"I squeeze off a few rounds now and again," the older man replied. Then he regarded Dean closely. "You care to participate in a little lead-slinging contest?"

"One of your spreads[1] will cover three of mine, with about an acre to spare," Dean replied. The others in the room were dumbfounded by the audacity of Dean's challenge to the senior Mr. Foster.

"Pick out one of them 'sissy pistols' there," Buford said, unlocking the gun case. "We'll see if you can shoot it as good as you shoot off your mouth, Sonny Boy."

The handguns in question were single-action .45 caliber six-shot revolvers manufactured by the Colt Firearms Company. These pistols were relatively light in weight for the large caliber bullet they fired. Their lack of balance and heavy recoil presented a particular challenge in target shooting competition.

"What are we shootin'?" Dean asked as he took one of the guns out of the velvet-lined case and examined one of the bullets.

"Sixty-five grain copper-sheathed slugs with a 20% overload of Fastfire smokeless powder," Shannon's grandfather replied. "I loaded the brass myself."

"Shit, Buford," Dean said, "It's just a paper target. You don't need field artillery to kill it!"

"It's just a sissy pistol, Son, remember?" The old man smiled to himself.

Buford picked up the matching pistol and a box of ammunition and relocked the case. They walked outside to a shooting range that had been set up in front of a pool bank[2] behind the house.

"Two hands or one?" Dean asked.

"Sissies use two hands," Buford replied. "You call it."

Firing an overloaded 45 with one hand is a profound challenge, but Buford had left Dean no option. "One's enough for me," he said.

"One it is," Buford responded, grinning to himself.

"I'll need six shots to sight it in," Dean requested, "Then it's best two out of three cylinders after that. You can have a warm-up too, Old Timer."

"I don't need no warm-up," Buford responded. "I know these pistols real good. I'm ready for shootin' right now."

"As you wish," Dean said. "I just hope you can keep the holes on the paper with that cannon."

"Just worry about your own pattern, Son," Buford said as they slipped earplugs into their ears.

Most of the Foster relatives and guests drifted out to watch the big shoot-out. Buford Foster was a gunman of some reputation, but he usually practiced in private and traveled to distant shooting competitions, so they seldom got the chance to watch him shoot. Dean fired off six rounds to learn the relationship between the gunsights and the resulting bullet holes. He used binoculars to locate the new hole after each shot. The women and children in the crowd flinched each time the big pistol barked. The recoil carried Dean's right hand high into the air with each shot.

"Age before beauty," Dean said, offering the old man the chance to shoot first.

"Mouth before brains," Buford replied, returning the offer.

Dean wanted to shoot last, but, seeing he had no way to earn that spot, he resigned himself to shoot first. He fired six shots at the first target, and then Buford fired six at his first target. They reeled the two targets in and Shannon added up the scores. Dean's pattern was smaller, and his score slightly higher. "You're in a heap of trouble, Buford," Dean said, "Looks like we won't need to shoot up that last six rounds. I'm takin' you out in two."

"Just keep your eye open and your mouth shut, Boy," the man replied. "This contest ain't anywheres near over yet." The audience stood quietly as each man fired six more shots. Shannon reeled in the targets and counted up the scores. This time Buford's score was higher.

"You got lucky," Dean said. "But I'm through playin' with you now."

"If this was a bullshit contest, you'd beat me hands down," Buford said, "But it ain't. Just fire off six more, Son, and do your shootin' with that Colt, not your mouth."

"You're goin' down, Foster," Dean said. "I'm takin' you out, right now." He fired six more rounds. Then Buford shot six times. They reeled in the targets.

"Granddaddy won!" Shannon announced, "Sixty-one to fifty-six!"

"Damn!" Dean said. "I thought sure I had you on that one." The old man just smiled. They cleaned the two handguns and Buford locked them back in the case. The big shoot-out took its place in the family tradition.

The Dance

"Come on, Dean!" Shannon said. "We're going over to Lou Ann's house. A bunch of kids are over there dancing."

"Why don't you youngsters just run along without me?" he replied. "I'll just stay here and soak my corns and sip my Geritol."

"No chance, Dean. We're gonna show 'em a thing or two."

"I feel a real nightmare comin' on," he mumbled as he got up to join her.

Lou Ann's home was located on an 80-acre farm a few miles away. It was similar in construction to the Foster spread, but it had a large living room that had been cleared for dancing. More than a dozen young people were there participating in an impromptu dance event. The music was supplied by an old vinyl record player and a modern "boom-box" CD player.

Shortly after they arrived, Shannon forced Dean to dance with her. She insisted on performing some of the dance moves they had been practicing, to the amazement of the other kids. Later she began to introduce the girls to Dean, one at a time, and he would then ask each one to dance. Shannon alternated between dancing with Dean herself and selecting one lucky girl for an introduction to her partner. Within an hour the large room was completely full of teenagers who had drifted by in response to word-of mouth advertising via cell phone.

The Rangerettes

"Don't look now, Dean, but two Rettes have come to check you out!" The din died down as two statuesque young women strode proudly into the room.

"Rettes?"

"Yeah, you know. Rangerettes!"

"Kilgore College Rangerettes?"

"Yeah, see? They have on their Rangerette T-shirts."

Founded in 1940, the Kilgore Rangerettes were the first women's dance/drill team, and they set the pattern for modern cheerleading. Since that time the group has become famous for precision and showmanship and has performed all over the world. They are particularly famous for extreme high kicks and the "jump split," where they jump up and land in the split position.

"Ooh! That brunette is a Lieutenant, and the blonde is her little sister."

"They don't look all that much like sisters."

"No, Silly! Every freshman gets a sophomore as her big sister. It's a tradition." The two girls started chatting with their hostess and glancing at Dean and Shannon. They were elite, and they knew it.

"Those girls are hot shit, Dean," Shannon advised. "It don't get no better than Rangerette!" She paused. "We call 'em 'kick chicks,' 'cause they can kick the light bulbs out of the ceiling fans."

Lou Ann brought the two visitors over and introduced them to Shannon and Dean. "This is Ashley," she said, "And this is Cookie."

"Pleased to meet you, Ladies," Dean said. "You Rangerettes do a fantastic job."

"You guys are skaters?" the older one asked.

"That's right," Shannon said briskly. "We skate senior pairs. We expect to compete at USFSA Nationals next year."

"Ashley's an officer," Cookie said, and we're going to New York to march in the Christmas parade!"

"That sounds like fun!" Dean replied. "I just hope your legs don't get frostbite." The girls laughed.

The four chatted for a time, comparing dance/drill to figure skating and talking about college life. Dean danced with Ashley once, then again later.

"That Lieutenant has the hots for you, Dean," Shannon remarked on the ride back to the Foster farm. "You gonna fuck her?"

"It wasn't discussed," Dean replied with a condescending tone.

"It'd be really hot. You oughta do it. Rangerettes are about as cool as it gets! All the guys want one. They're all stuck-up and snotty."

"It would be a lot of trouble, Shannon. Those girls are high maintenance, and Kilgore is a long drive for a date."

"I still say you oughta do it. It'd be worth the drive for a high-class girl like that. Way better than the trailer trash that lives at the Piccadilly!"

"Hey! Don't insult my neighborhood!" He feigned shock.

"Those girls are sleaze, Dean," Shannon replied in a knowing tone. "Trust your partner on that one!"

The Return Home

Dean and the Fosters loaded up the Cadillac and headed back toward Houston on Friday morning. "Where did you come up with that shootout idea, Dean?" Shannon asked after they had made their way back out to highway 59.

"Yeah," Millie said, "What possessed you to challenge Daddy Buff to a gunfight at the OK Corral?"

"It was payback time," he replied.

"What?"

"I saw it on the Discovery Channel," he replied.

"What are you talking about?" Shannon said, thoroughly puzzled.

"Sure. They run it all the time."

"Run what?" She was exasperated.

"You know, the brash young male challenges the older alpha male for dominance of the herd. They grunt and growl, and then they fight it out. It's all very anthropological."

"You wanted to dominate the Foster herd?" Millie inquired from beneath her eyebrows.

"I lost, didn't I?"

"You mean . . . you lost on purpose?" Shannon asked.

"It wasn't easy shootin' first like I was. I had to shoot a wide enough pattern the second and third time to make sure he'd win."

"You let Daddy Buff win?" Shannon asked. "Why?"

"Because he's the patriarch of the family. He needs to reassert his dominance periodically. It keeps the females in line. I just gave him the chance to roar again. If I had beat him, it would have undermined his position as leader of the clan. It's all right there in Anthropology 101."

"So, my family is a tribe of gorillas?" Fred asked.

"No, orangutans are closer to humans," Dean replied, "Or maybe chimpanzees." Fred and Millie looked at each other and chuckled.

"You're a nut case, Steele," Shannon said, grinning.

"'Daddy Buff' went home happy," Dean responded. "I needed some way to pay him back for all the groceries I ate."

"Well, you paid Marybelle back too," Millie said. "She's real taken with you. I've never seen that woman warm up to somebody that quick."

"I guess it's my boyish charm," Dean said, grinning smugly.

"You're an animal, Steele," Shannon said, grinning. "You flirted with my grandmother!"

"Well, I didn't score too big with your aunts, Kiddo. I doubt they'll be joining my fan club anytime soon."

"Too bad," Millie quipped, suppressing a grin. Fred gave her a cautionary look. He did not permit her wholesale criticism of his sisters.

"Are you disappointed that I didn't make a better impression on your sisters-in-law, Your Grace?" Dean asked.

"Oh, you impressed 'em," she said. "I expect they'll be gossiping about you for the next millennium. That's about the best we can expect from those two."

Fred reached over and gave his wife a slap on the thigh—a blow that purported to be punishment but came off more like a love-pat. They grinned at each other. Millie always reserved her right to take pot shots at her sisters-in-law, and Fred continually threatened punishment for the offense, but seldom delivered.

A few minutes later Millie noticed a grin on Fred's face as he glanced repeatedly in the rear-view mirror. She raised a cautionary eyebrow as she awaited his risqué comment. "You know," Fred said, "In most parts of the world, you have to sleep with a woman to keep her happy. In East Texas, all you have to do is brag on her cooking." This time Millie gave him a slap on the thigh.

"Works like a charm!" Dean said, grinning.

"Ooh, gross!" Shannon said, giggling. Then she took Dean's hand and squeezed it. "I'm real glad you came with us this year," she said. "I just knew it'd be cool!"

---

1. Spread—size of the pattern of bullet holes in a paper target.
2. Pool bank—a ridge of dirt pushed up by a bulldozer when digging a pool for the cows to drink from.

Chapter 15

The Zoo

Shannon Pouts

Shannon was sitting on the bench with her skates on when Dean came out of the boys' locker room. Her toe picks, digging into the black rubber mat, supported her knees, which, in turn, supported her elbows, which, in turn, supported her chin. A pleated skirt flowed a short distance downward from her waist barely covering the end of the bench.

"Time to hit the sheet, Tiger," he said. The girl didn't move. Her long honey-colored hair hung strangely unmoving in a pony tail behind her head. "Come on, Hot Shot. We got work to do!"

"I'm not skating with you anymore," the girl said. She sat with chin in hands and a pouty look on her face. Her lower lip protruded more than normally.

"Excuse me?" Dean said, walking back over to her. "Did I get off at the wrong subway stop? I'm supposed to be on Planet Earth."

"You heard me," she said, her voice aimed only vaguely in his direction. Then she deliberately took her attention off him. "I'm not skating with you anymore." Her words bounced off the low wall in front of her and dispersed randomly throughout the cavernous arena.

"OK," he said, conjuring a pensive look, like a wolf picking up a subtle scent from the air. "Do I perceive that something may be amiss in your world? Why have you come to such a weighty conclusion?"

"You're a liar and a cheat, Dean Steele!" Her voice carried the mixture of frustration and disgust that only a spoiled teenager can synthesize.

"Oh, that!" he said. "I can explain." She turned her face away from him, ignoring his attempt to joke her out of her pique. "Isn't this where I ask what the fuck it is I'm supposed to have done?" his submerged exasperation working its way to the surface.

"You said you'd take me to the zoo, and you didn't, and I hate you!" Her face reflected the pain of someone brutally wronged.

"Screw the zoo, Shannon! We've got a pairs program to work up here."

"You promised. You said if I'd skate with you, you'd take me to the zoo, and you lied." She glared up at him, fixing her gaze directly on him for the first time. "I don't skate with liars!" It was an announcement and an accusation in one compact verbal package.

"It was a figure of speech, Shannon!" He exhaled a disgusted sigh that silently screamed "Why me?"

"It was not! It was a promise, and I believed you, and you broke my heart, and I'll never forgive you!" She turned away in the appearance of abject pain.

"Wow!" he said, turning up his palms, widening his eyes, and bringing a surprised look to his face. "Who knew?"

He stepped back and looked at the girl. She sat in a black cloud of disgust and self-pity. He stepped through the opening in the boards and skated a leisurely lap around the silent arena that had been emptied for their use. Then he stepped out and walked up to Shannon. He sat down beside her on the bench. "Excuse me, Miss," he said, "But I've been thinking." He spoke as if confiding in her some intimate secret. "I've been spending too much time around humans lately. I swear it's been a month of Sundays since I've had the opportunity to fellowship with some of God's less evolved creatures."

The girl stared straight ahead. Only a near-imperceptible twitch of an eyelash suggested she might have heard him. "I was thinking about taking off tomorrow afternoon and spending time among the species that share this planet with us." The girl's face began to brighten up slightly. "Could you . . . find someone else to skate with tomorrow so I can go to the zoo?"

"Dean Steele, if you go to the zoo without me, I will feed you to the lions!"

"Well, then, Shannon, would you like to go to the zoo with me?"

She grabbed him in a bear hug. "Radical, Dean!" she exclaimed. "Too cool!"

"But I'm not interested in just walking around and saying, 'Duh, I wonder what that funny-looking critter is.' I want to hear a five-minute lecture about at least one of the animals."

"You want me to give a lecture? About an animal?"

"I insist. Zoos are supposed to be educational places."

"But I don't know anything about animals."

"You have an Internet connection, don't you? You have an encyclopedia on CD-ROM, don't you? It wouldn't take any time at all to prepare a five-minute talk on the vertebrate creature of your choice. You could call the zoo in advance to see exactly what species they have in the offing."

"I could do lions . . . , no, tigers!" She exclaimed. "I could do tigers!" Her ponytail bobbed up and down as she spoke. Her face radiated excitement.

"OK, just make it interesting and informative," he insisted.

"This is so cool! Can we take Jennifer with us? And Jayme? Radical!"

"Look, I'm not a Den Mother, here. Try to keep it down to three giggly little twits, no more. And everybody lectures. No tickee, no laundree!"[1]

Millie

"Guess what, Mom! Dean's taking me to the zoo! Isn't it just too cool?"

Millie looked at Dean from beneath elevated eyebrows. "You're taking my daughter to the zoo?" Her tone was suspicious, thinly disguised as merely inquisitive. Millie automatically looked for subterfuge in any out-of-the-ordinary event, possibly because she knew herself so well.

"Believe it or not, Madam," Dean explained, "This turns out to be a vital part of the pairs skating program." He accentuated this to sound like a revelation of great significance.

"And how, pray tell, did that come about?" Millie's voice was ripe with skepticism.

"Perhaps you could get the young lady to brief you on that," he said. "She explained it to me, but I didn't quite get it." He faked a confused embarrassment.

Millie gave him a knowing grin. "The little brat conned you, didn't she? It happens to her father and me all the time."

"I'm gonna give a talk on tigers, Mom. Jennifer's doing boa constrictors, and Jayme's doing flamingos. It's way cool!"

"You've got those girls lecturing at the zoo?"

"I was at least able to extract my pound of flesh," he said. "I insisted on having trained jungle guides."

Millie laughed. She was impressed by how he had managed to trick the girls into learning something. "You'll probably draw a crowd," she said, grinning knowingly.

Shannon stayed up late researching tigers on the Internet. She prepared an outline of the lecture on her computer and printed it out. The next day they skated early and again after lunch. Then the other two girls showed up, and they piled into Dean's mustang and went to the Houston zoo.

They came to the aviary first, and Jayme gave her lecture on the flamingos. A crowd of people gathered around her as she spoke, and when she finished, they started asking her questions.

When they reached the reptile compound, Jenny similarly enthralled an assembly with details about the life and times of the boa constrictor. Finally Shannon gave her dissertation on the Bengal tigers. Dean praised them each one for their worthy efforts. They ate popcorn and went home happy.

---

1. "No tickee, no laundree," A Chinese laundry operator in San Francisco is reputed to have said this, meaning, if you do not produce your laundry ticket, you cannot pick up your clean clothes.

Chapter 16

Dean's Lecture

The Request

"Would you do me a favor?" Shannon asked coyly.

Dean looked at her suspiciously from under his right eyebrow. "This sounds ominous," he said.

"Would you talk to the pairs and dance boys? I mean, give them some advice, seeing how you're older and wiser." She partially suppressed a grin at this subtle jab about his age. Dean frowned. "I mean, there's a lot of bitchin' going on about the boys, and you're kind of a celebrity here, and they might listen to you."

"Is this your idea?"

"Well, a couple of the pairs girls asked me if you'd give their partners some pointers. They're facing competition, you know, some for the first time, and they could use a . . . pep talk."

"I'm not an instructor. Why me?"

"Because you see things like a boy pairs skater, not a coach. That's what they need. Like, some inspiration, or psychological counseling, or something."

"Since when did I become a parish priest?"

"You know what I mean. Some of those little pricks don't have any discipline. They keep messing around and screwing up out there. You could talk some sense into 'em." She grinned mischievously. "You're . . . a father figure." She giggled.

"Bless you, my child!" He waved an invisible scepter at her. Then his face responded with mock disgust. "The dance girls put you up to this, right?"

"Come on. Do it for me. Please do it. Please, please, please!"

"You already told 'em I would, right?"

Shannon looked at him sheepishly, then rolled her eyes and bobbed her head from side to side as if to say, "Well, sort of."

"OK, I'll do it. But you owe me."

"Oh? And what's your payback," she asked coquettishly.

"I think a bizarre and dangerously unnatural sex act would probably suffice."

Shannon paused. "Deal!" she exploded. "How about . . . right now? Over behind the Zamboni!"

"Methinks thou doth protest too little, Fair Lady," Dean scolded.

"Just trying to keep my debts settled," She replied, innocently.

"I'll meet with the boys in that last little party room down there right after the pairs session, if you want to go ahead and set it up."

"OK, I'll tell 'em," she said, fidgeting excitedly.

"One other thing," Dean added. "Boys only. No girls."

"What? Come on. The girls need to hear it too!"

"No, they don't. This is a guy thing. It's a macho-type male bonding ritual. No girls allowed."

"Just me, then? I'm your partner. You'll need me there . . . for demonstrations and stuff."

"Are you a girl?"

"No. I'm a woman!"

"Close enough. You're out of there!"

"Aw, shit, Dean," she whined. "I need to hear this!"

"Don't press your luck, Lady. It's only by a thread I'm doing this at all."

"I'll go as your secretary. I'll take notes!"

"Wrong!" Dean said. "No documentation required."

Shannon's face wrinkled as she tried to think of some approach that might work. Dean glared at her. She knew there was probably none.

"I'll be the waitress," she said in desperation. "I'll serve beer and pretzels to the macho guys. Just like in the TV commercials. Please let me come!"

"You're skating on thin ice," Dean said, holding up a thumb and forefinger one-eighth inch apart.

Shannon sighed and relented. "Damn!"

The Meeting

An ungainly group of boys slowly wandered into the small concrete block room that was used for birthday parties and other, less important meetings. Dean was sitting at one end of the table.

"OK, guys," Dean said, standing up and glaring at the assembly of young men like a drill sergeant at boot camp. "There's one thing you gotta know about pairs and dance if you're gonna survive out there on the ice. Pairs skating and ice dancing are more dangerous than playing ice hockey." The boys exchanged puzzled looks. Most of them were constantly being teased as sissies by their hockey-playing peers.

"In hockey," he continued, ignoring the disagreement that painted their faces, "All you get is cuts, scrapes, bruises, and the occasional broken bone. Those all heal up pretty quick." After a pause he continued. "In pairs skating you can get hurt a lot worse." Wrinkled brows populated the small room. The unspoken question was, "What planet is he from?"

"You can get your ego crushed, your self-image bashed . . . and, worst of all . . . ," he paused, "You can have your will broken." There was another pause. "You can lose your confidence and get the self-esteem kicked right out of you, and that can leave you crippled for life." He had their attention, but they were still puzzled.

"Let me explain one of the facts of life for you. There's not much you can do to make a girl look better than to dress her up in a 10-inch skirt and send her scooting off across a sheet of ice. Girls on ice are automatically beautiful, graceful, breathtaking, and magical. The problem is . . . ice don't do all that much for a guy."

"If you try to compete with that, all you'll do is look sissy. So you have to settle for an automatic second prize in the popularity contest. Basically, you're not going to . . . enchant anybody. If you can't accept the fact that you are merely the pole she swings on, then you better start working on your singles act, or pick up a hockey stick, because you'll always be second banana in the eyes of the audience, and, yes, the judges too."

"And when you turn pro," he paused for effect, "Nobody will pay fifty bucks a seat to watch you skate by yourself. It just ain't all that pretty."

"You have to realize that your job, as the male member of a pairs or ice dance team, is to present the lady to the audience." He made a palms-up offering gesture with his hands. "If you keep that in mind, you just might salvage your pride in this otherwise no-win situation."

He paused to let it soak in. "Figure skating is a woman's sport," he continued. "Men are second-class citizens, tolerated here only because we serve a purpose." He paused. "Why do you think they call it 'ladies' and 'men?' Why not 'women' or 'gentlemen?'" Another pause. "So your only job is to make the girl look good. The judges and audience are watching her anyway, not you. If she looks good, the team looks good, and if the team looks good, then you look good. But that's the only way you are ever gonna look good. It's just that damn simple."

"But if you get concerned about making yourself look good, you'll just get your ego crushed, because as long as there's a girl on the ice, nobody . . . gives a damn . . . about you."

"So when you compete, you're trying to make your girl look better than the other guys are making their girls look. That's all there is to it."

"Now the biggest thing you have going for you is your strength. You should work out with weights regularly and take dietary supplements to build up your strength and stamina. I know they say weights don't build stamina, but they do, at least where a two-and-a-half-minute program is concerned."

"You need to be able to hoist her bulky little body like it was a feather, and don't ever let 'em see you strain. That breaks the 'magic' of the moment. Just grin like it's sooo easy to hold a girl who weighs almost as much as you do over your head with one hand."

"Any questions?"

"Yeah," one boy said, "Why do it? I mean, if it's that bad, why skate pairs at all?"

"I didn't say it was bad. I said it was dangerous. I said you can get hurt, badly. But if you do it right, it can be fun. It can be great."

"Then, how do you do it right?"

"You just have to get your enjoyment a little bit . . . indirectly. You have to realize that everybody is admiring her, but that you're the reason she looks so damn good. If you can take your pleasure indirectly like that, then you can have a great time. You're the one who makes the magic happen."

"But, don't they ever notice the guy?"

"Oh, yeah. If anybody stumbles or falls, the eyes immediately go to you. You're first in line to take the blame. If she falls, they feel sorry for her because she's trying so hard. If you fall, they feel sorry for her because she has a clumsy idiot for a partner."

"If you're lucky, though, there might be one or two other times in the program where the eyeballs are pointed at you. But if you live and work for those brief moments, you're just wasting your time."

"So, what's the answer, quit pairs and go back to singles?" one asked.

"Maybe. If what you live for is the roar of the greasepaint and the smell of the crowd[1], then pairs and ice dance are losing propositions. But you can set your goal on making your partner the most beautiful and graceful woman ever to glide across a sheet of ice, Sonya Henne, Peggy Fleming, and Dorothy Hammil all rolled into one, then take your pleasure from the success of the team, and it can be great. But you have to know who you are, and you may be the only person in the arena who realizes you're the reason she looks so damn good."

"But doesn't that mean we're just dorks standing around out there?"

"Maybe. That depends on your attitude. The fact is, though, the score you get for the program depends more on what you do than on your partner. It's just that you're working in the background while everybody's looking at her. You have to be mature enough to accept that. If you have some insatiable desire for attention, you will never be happy playing this game. And if you don't love it, it'll eat your heart right outta your chest."

"You mean we have to put up with being bitched at by our partner just so we can be ignored by the judges? Shit!"

"Ignored, yes; bitched at, no! You have to put a stop to the bitching."

"How? Carrie is always on my ass when we're skating."

"OK, here's an important point. Remember it's ten to one girls to boys in this sport. Since you are the ugly duckling, holding her bulky little bod up in the air so she can be the beautiful swan, she's got no right to give you anything but praise, respect, and eternal gratitude."

"Yeah, right! Go tell her that!"

"No, you tell her. But do it in a subtle way." He paused for effect. "Set her butt on the ice at twenty miles an hour a couple of times . . . just until she . . . gets the hint."

"Are you kidding? Drop her on purpose? She'd kill me!"

"No, killing you is what she's doing now, by bitching at you during the program. Don't underestimate the psychological effect it has on you. It can cause you to screw up, and then you get the blame for ruining the program. It can ruin your act, and it can ruin your life. It's gotta stop."

"She needs to mend her ways" Dean continued. "She needs to lose that habit and start treating you like a partner, not a hired hand. You can help her by reminding her that you're the only thing standing between her and a nasty collision with that cold, hard ice. And an occasional such collision serves as a pretty good reminder."

"Seriously, guys. I've seen several pairs teams where the girl was always bitching at the guy. They almost never win anything, and it's always the guy who screws up and gets the blame. Not the girl. So don't play that game. Teach your partner some manners. You owe it to her."

"Wow! I can just see Tiffany, mad as hell, sliding across the ice on her butt, with everybody laughing at her."

"Look, you don't have to drop her on her head from six feet up. Just remind her from time to time that she only flies like an eagle because you're down there working like a horse. You won't get much respect from the audience, but you darn sure should get it from your partner. If you don't, there's something awfully wrong . . . and you can fix it. Just set her on her butt a couple of times." He paused to grin. "Just remember to say, 'Oops!'"

"What if she gets mad at me and quits?" the boy asked.

"Then you're better off. If she can't be a part of a team, then you two have no future skating together anyway. Better to end it now than to waste a couple of years of frustration, 'cause it'll never work. Find a new girl who can be a partner, and there are lots of 'em out there. Or . . . you can take up stamp collecting."

"So those are the two problems I see when I watch you guys skate around here. Overactive male egos and bitchy female partners. You will do yourselves a favor if you fix both of 'em."

One boy spoke up. "Have you ever dropped your partner, I mean, on purpose?"

"Yes," Dean answered. "The first time it was like the Tuesday night bowling league. I scored a perfect strike on a beginners class using her as the ball. Took 'em all out, including the instructor."

"Wow! Was she mad?"

"Eventually she got around to mad. She went through several more severe emotions first, but she finally calmed down and just got mad."

"What did she do?"

"Let's see . . . screamed, cried, pouted, quit the team, threatened a lawsuit, tried to poison me, vowed never to speak to me again . . . just the usual stuff. But she did stop eating ice cream."

"That was over ice cream?" one of the boys asked, incredulously. "You dropped her because she ate ice cream?"

"Yeah. I don't like lifting lard over my head with one hand!" The small audience was wide-eyed. Shannon Foster was the senior girl skater at the rink. They rarely saw her fall, and they had difficulty imagining her sliding into a group of kids.

"So, guys," Dean concluded, "You gotta instill discipline and respect in your partner. That's the basis of a good pairs or dance team. So I expect to see some female butt bouncing on the ice out there from time to time."

The group pondered what he had said in silence. Then Dean spoke again. "There's one more thing that is especially important in pairs skating. It has to do with lifts." he paused again. "When she's up in the air, she's as helpless as a newborn baby. She has put her trust in you to keep her safe and sound until she gets a blade back on the ice. If you screw up while she's in the air . . . she pays for your mistake." The room was still and silent.

"You have to make a pact with yourself. You have to promise yourself two things. First, that you will never lift her feet off the floor unless you are totally confident in your ability to control her flight and get her back down safely. That means, don't try a lift you aren't sure you can do, except in the lift harness. And it means if your position isn't good going into a lift, then don't pull her off the ice. Comprendo?"

"What's the other one?" a boy asked.

"If you lose it while she's up in the air . . . you gotta get her down. You put her up there, so you gotta get her down." The room was as silent as a tomb.

"When you start falling, you've got to do one of two things. You've got to either push her clear so she can plan some kind of a landing, or you gotta put yourself under her."

"No way, man!" one of the boys said. "Those skates are sharp. I'm not gonna just let her fall on me!"

"If you put her up there, you gotta get her down, one way or another. That's the rule. If you don't follow it, you'll have more grief than you ever imagined."

"Did you ever drop one?" a boy asked, reading the look on Dean's face.

Dean inhaled, then sighed. "Yes, I did," he said softly. The room waited in silence for him to continue. "I once tried a platter lift on a girl I hadn't skated with very much. I had never practiced it, or even studied up on it. We weren't in the harness, and she wasn't wearing a hat. I hoisted her up, and I lost my balance." He inhaled. "She fell off behind me, and I couldn't reach her to break her fall." Another pause. "It was awful to hear her crashing into the ice behind my back. It seemed like she fell for about ten minutes." He paused. "She got a cracked wrist when she hit. She could have gotten a busted skull."

After a pause Dean brought the group back to reality. "OK, guys. Get out there and make it happen!"

The small group of boys filed out slowly, each member deep in thought.

Shannon

"How'd it go?" Shannon asked. "Were you able to corral those little farts?"

"Oh, yeah, I think I talked a little sense into 'em," He responded. "They should be easier to control now."

Shannon smiled proudly. "So, what did you tell them?"

"To always brush their teeth, shine their boots and do as they're told."

"You mean, act just like you do!" She playfully jabbed him in the ribs with her elbow and took off across the ice giggling. Dean recovered and raced after her. She squealed when she saw she was being pursued, skating as fast as she could. The other people in the arena looked up. After two high speed trips around the arena, he embraced her from behind, lifted her skates off the ice, dug in his blades, and brought their momentum to a halt in a shower of snow. Dean took her in the tango position, and they skated away. The eyes that had attached themselves to the pair gradually drifted away.

"By the way," Dean said as they whirled on the ice in an impromptu dance routine, "You might do some of the girls a favor if you mentioned to 'em it's not polite to curse your partner during the long program. I mean, you being a celebrity at this rink, and all, they might listen to you."

"Have you been watching what those little assholes do out there? No wonder they get bitched at. They're lucky the girls haven't killed 'em by now!"

"OK," Dean said. "Don't worry about it, then. It's not a problem." He smiled to himself.

---

1. "The smell of the greasepaint and the roar of the crowd," a statement of the excitement of being a circus performer, deliberately reversed here for effect.

Chapter 17

Millie's Moves

A Warning from Fred

"Since you and Shannon will be working together so much," Fred began, "Her mother and I wanted to go over a couple of things with you. Things that might be . . . important."

"OK," Dean said, still unclear why Fred had managed to get him alone after dinner at the Foster home.

"Shannon is a sweet kid . . . and smart, too. But she's also an impressionable girl. I mean, Hell, she's only sixteen, Dean. Kids that age don't know nothin'." Dean nodded. "And girls that age . . . well, they aren't emotionally mature. She's . . . well, she's still just a child in many ways." Dean began to see which way this lecture was headed. "She'll be going through a lot of changes during the next year or two as she matures," Fred said. "You'll need to be ready to deal with that."

"Thanks for the warning," Dean mused to himself, having already dealt with some of the girl's mood swings.

"We want y'all to succeed at this skating thing, and we wouldn't want anything to interfere with that." He was clearly uncomfortable with his assignment. "Sometimes kids will get a crush on an older person, you know?" He didn't look for an answer to his question, and Dean offered none. "Hell, I had the hots for my seventh grade teacher." He collected himself. "So it could happen here. If it did, then it would be up to you to handle it in an intelligent, mature fashion."

"You mean, don't screw her, Dad?" Dean said to himself.

"Millie and I know that you're mature enough and stable enough that you'll make a fine partner for Shannon. It may not be easy all the time. I mean, Shannon can be difficult. She takes after her mother." He gave Dean a knowing look. Dean listened attentively, but without acknowledgement. "So you, being older, would have to take it all in stride. Your maturity would have to make up for her . . . lack of maturity." Dean nodded pensively. "Hell, Dean, she's under age," he blurted. "And if anything went wrong, there'd be Hell to pay. You know how the laws are in this state."

"You mean you'd send me to jail, Dad?" Dean asked silently.

"Millie and I are tickled pink that you're skating with Shannon. I mean, you're just the right thing for her right now. It's a good deal all around."

175

"And when I've outlived my usefulness," Dean said to himself. "I'll be unceremoniously heaved over the gunwales, right, Daddy?"

"We just don't want anything to come up that might spoil it."

"And besides, Dad, Millie wants me all to herself!" Dean added under his breath. "Did she mention that?"

"So," Fred breathed a sigh. "I hope we understand each other better now."

"Sure," Dean muttered to himself, "My instructions are to screw your wife, but not your daughter."

Fred gave him a pat on the shoulder. "We like you, Son," he said, "And we know this thing is gonna work out real good for everybody."

Dean gave him a smile and a nod. "I understand your situation, Fred," he said. "If I had a teen-age girl, I'd be afraid to let her out of her room. I can't say I can be much help in the child-rearing department, but I do have a vested interest in keeping Shannon healthy and happy. I'll keep an eye out for anything that might throw a monkey wrench in the works, and I'll let you know if I spot any problems."

"I knew I could depend on you, son," Fred said. He was greatly relieved that his job was done.

Millie

"Fred gave me his 'Don't screw my daughter,' speech last night," Dean said, "But I guess you already know that."

"He said you two had a man-to-man talk," Millie admitted, "But he didn't say what it was about." Her face implied curiosity.

"Well, he told me he was speaking for both of you."

"Well, he would put it that way, if he were talking about something he thought was important."

"Yeah, well I guess he did."

"Did he upset you, Honey?" Her brow wrinkled with motherly concern.

"Not really," Dean said, "But there were a couple of things I thought a bit odd, to say the least."

"What?" This time her concern was real.

"Well, first, I'm twenty-six. I don't need to be told not to mess around with underage girls. Hell, I don't even screw married women, remember?"

"I see," Millie said, obviously insulted by his remark.

"And second," Dean continued, "Why didn't you just tell me yourself? You gave old Fred a pretty uncomfortable assignment, there."

"Dean," Millie began, "Whatever Fred said was his own idea. I never . . . ."

"Save it, Millie!" Dean interrupted her. "I could see your arm up his ass, making his lips move." He made quick use of Shannon's metaphor.

Millie inhaled and exhaled. "Dean," she said, "Fred and I talked about that subject a while back. Knowing him, I thought he might speak to you about it sometime, but I wasn't sure. He is a concerned father, you know." Dean gave her a silent, cynical stare. "Dean," she softened. "We just want what's best for our daughter, and for you too. If we go a little overboard sometimes, it's just because we care about you both." Dean looked at her, unaffected by her remark. Millie smiled softly and took Dean's hand across the table. "I'm sorry old Fred insulted you," she said, as if consoling an injured child. "He's not very good in that role, but he means well."

Millie looked warmly into his eyes. His face refused to give up a clue to his thoughts. "You're amazing," she grinned at last. "You can see right through me, can't you?" She threw her head back in wonder. "I'm always confessing to you," she sighed. "And now you've caught me again. I can't get away with anything around you." She smiled sheepishly. Dean knew that a well-timed confession was the big gun in Millie's well-stocked arsenal of manipulation weapons. She braced herself. "I put him up to it," she admitted. "I thought it would be better as a man-to-man thing. Besides, he needs to do his part in the raising of our child. He has a teen-age daughter, now. He needs the experience. It was as much for him as it was for you."

Dean made no reply. Soon the thundering silence again prompted Millie to fill it. "I knew," she continued, "That there was really no chance that anything improper would develop between you and Shannon. But you two will be spending a lot of time together, and she is a charmer." His continued silence pried another comment out of the woman. "But if something did happen, it would be disastrous. It would just ruin everything."

"And send me to jail, right?" This time it was Dean who couldn't fight the silence.

"Did he say that? Oh, my God. He can be so tactless!"

"He just put the cards on the table," Dean said. "It's a term in the contract. Right there between the new skates and the cushy job. Paragraph 21: Fuck my daughter and you go to jail." Millie closed her eyes and exhaled, frantically searching for a way to salvage the conversation. "Millie," Dean said, raising a palm, "It's OK. I understand. I would feel the same way if I had a daughter." Millie opened her eyes, but she still had not put together a response. "The only thing that pisses me off, besides your behind-the-scenes chicanery, is that . . ." He paused to inhale. "I probably know, better than either one of you, why it is such a bad idea to get emotionally involved with my partner. I just thought it ironic that I would get the lecture—that you thought me so stupid that I needed to hear it. Especially since I've shown proper restraint, even where you're concerned."

"Our relationship," Millie lectured, "Whatever it may or may not involve, is a totally separate matter." Her voice took a scolding tone. "It has nothing whatever to do with Shannon or Fred or anybody else. It's a private matter between you and me."

"I wish it could be that simple," he said.

"Well, it is!"

"I'm the only one who can define my relationship with my skating partner," he said, "It's part of the job."

"Go chase after college girls, or gym rats, or trailer trash if you must, but keep your hands off Shannon!" A harsh look of anger suddenly took control of her face. "I will not have my own daughter as a rival!" she snapped. Almost immediately her eyes registered surprise at what she heard herself say.

Dean looked at her, nodding slowly. His eyes said, "That's what I thought." He had gotten what he wanted from her. She had unintentionally given up the real reason for instigating the lecture he got from Fred.

"Dean, I'm sorry, OK?" she said, quickly returning the conversation to its original topic. "I didn't mean that."

"You didn't?" he asked from beneath skeptical eyebrows.

"I misjudged the situation. I insulted you, and I didn't intend to. Can you forgive me?" She gave him a soft, vulnerable look.

"How could I resist you?" he said, visibly melting. "You're the Ice Queen."

She smiled. "Give me a hug." They rose and he obliged. Millie held tightly to the younger man. "You're a rascal, you know that?" she whispered hoarsely into his ear. He held her silently, waiting for her to finish her thought. "You've got me wrapped around your finger. You can work me like a crossword puzzle."

"I think you overestimate me," he said. "Nobody controls the Ice Queen."

"Oh, God!" she said, hugging him more tightly. "I love being in your arms." She sighed audibly. "I just melt! You make me feel like a giddy teenager."

"I wonder," Dean thought, "Would Fred send me to jail for sleeping with you too, or would he just shoot me?"

Millie's Liaisons

The next afternoon Millie and Dean had finished working out some costume ideas at his apartment when the conversation waxed personal, about Millie and her relationship with her husband. "As for Fred," Millie said, "My liaisons over the years have not hurt him in the least. He believes I'm faithful. He wants to believe I'm faithful, and he doesn't press the issue."

"Your liaisons?"

"Are you shocked? There have been only a few, very well-placed, and each for a purpose."

"Oh, to close a deal or something?"

"Oh, Heavens no," Millie replied. "That's fatal. Once you ever fuck to close a deal, the word gets around like wildfire. I wouldn't be able to buy a Chronicle without blowing the paperboy."

"I see."

"So I maintain a good reputation," she continued. "But I will flirt and tease to close a deal. That's just being a woman. Every man thinks he'll be the first to break me down, but they never do, although I let him think it. I'll make him want it so bad he'll do anything, but I never let him have it."

"So, was it romance, then? These liaisons?"

"Oh, so you're curious about my dalliances, then?" She was grinning.

"Somewhat," Dean admitted, smiling. He wondered just how candid she would be with him.

"Well, there are . . . six gentlemen in the Houston society pages who have tasted Millie's charms over the past eighteen years," she said. "You'll forgive me if I don't mention names, but you needn't be burdened with their secrets."

"Please spare me," Dean said. "And it was . . . romance?"

"Oh, no. It was . . . business . . . you might say."

"But what about your reputation?"

"These are gentlemen who have much more to lose than I if anyone ever found out."

"How's that? I thought the system generally forgives powerful men who . . . mess around."

"Not these men. Each one stands to lose millions if there were a breath of scandal. That's my protection."

"So, do you have an affair going on now?"

"You don't understand. These were not affairs. They were transactions. Something of value traded for something of value. They had something I wanted, and I likewise. It was all very professionally done."

"Does this happen a lot?"

"Very rarely. In fact, there are only four gentlemen who are even candidates for such a transaction at this point. And nothing has happened for more than two years. I don't know when, or even if, there will ever be another."

"So, how does it work? I mean, how do these deals come about?"

"Hearing about Millie's naughty behavior turns you on doesn't it, Dear Boy?"

"I just like to learn about life when I get the opportunity," he said, with a grin.

"Then why the lump in your levis, young scholar?" She smiled knowingly, pleased with herself. Dean grinned sheepishly, admitting to his arousal so as to keep her talking.

"It usually starts with a gentlemen taking an interest in me. Very dignified, very discrete. I respond innocently. We chat. The conversation becomes more suggestive, but nothing is mentioned directly."

"I indicate an interest in something he owns, or something he can do for me. He indicates that he would do it for me if we were 'very close friends.' I gradually become more friendly. I weaken, I should say, allowing him to seduce me. Gradually I become more responsive to his suggestive remarks, although sex is never mentioned by name."

"Eventually he will suggest a business meeting on a Friday or a Monday in some exotic location. He will ask me to attend the meeting and to plan to be there for the weekend so we can work over the details. I accept, and I pack every sexy garment I own. After the business meeting he wines and dines me. I am eventually overcome by his charm and we shack up for the weekend. I proceed to fuck his brains out, very methodically and quite thoroughly. I give him the full-blown Millie treatment and leave him gasping, in a crumpled heap. By the time I get home, he's walking funny, and I've received whatever it was I wanted."

"Such a deal!" Dean said, grinning.

"Well, it has allowed me to establish financial independence for myself, and it has put smiles on a few of the furrowed brows on the top floors of the Houston skyscrapers. These are powerful men, taking advantage of their position. I'm a prize they have earned by all their hard work. I keep the price high, and I make sure they get their money's worth." She paused. "And the best part is, they don't tell anybody. They can't tell anybody. They would lose their board seats and management bonuses if there were a hint of scandal."

"Doesn't this make you a potential treat to them?"

"If I were a waitress or hairdresser, sure. But they know they can trust me. They know I have a secret to keep too. I have a family and a career at stake. I wouldn't risk all that for some tacky blackmail plot."

"I see."

"Now, isn't it time for you to call me a whore? Isn't this where Dean says what I do is prostitution, just in low volume and at a high price?"

"Is that what you want? Would it turn you on if I called you a whore?"

"Yes, actually, I think it would. And it wouldn't hurt me, either. I've totally reconciled my actions with my conscience." She looked at him from beneath a cocked eyebrow. "But I'd be very interested in your honest opinion."

"Well, for what it's worth, I'd have to say . . . I'm impressed. Technically, you're exchanging sex for money, I suppose. But you've raised it to such an art form that it bears no further resemblance to prostitution. It falls under the category of . . . big business."

"You're much more charitable that I ever imagined you'd be, Young Man."

"It's like watching a master artist at work, I suppose."

"But you don't consider me . . . cheap and tacky?"

"Somehow those two words don't seem to fit into the same sentence as 'Millie Foster'."

"You understand why I do it, then?"

Dean assumed she had worked up some justification that salved her conscience. He neither knew nor cared what it was. He sensed, however, that she had a need to share the rationalization of her misdeeds with him. "I have an idea," he said, "But I couldn't say exactly." This gave her the intro she needed.

"The world is unfair, Dean. It's out of balance. Men have all the advantages . . . all the opportunities. Just because you have three almost useless organs dangling between your legs, you get all the breaks."

"Hey, wait a minute. I wouldn't say useless. I can drown a gnat from ten feet away!"

"Touché! I'm sure you and your little fire hose make a great team. But the fact remains that, unless your parents passed you a Y chromosome, you have to work twice as hard for half the pay."

"There is enough truth in what you say that I'll not bother to dispute."

"But there is a flip side. Along with the many advantages of the male gender comes one serious drawback."

"Male pattern baldness?"

"No, Dean . . . sex. Men are positively helpless where sex is concerned. They are babes in the woods."

"So you use that to even the score, right?"

"Most women don't, really, but I do." She paused to prepare for her next speech. "Men are suckers for flirtation. They are easily charmed. They can't help it. It's endemic to the gender. So charm is a currency, and I spend it like cash. Flirtation is a commodity, and I have a boundless supply." She paused to grin at him. "I use the tools, Dean. I have the weapons, and I take deadly aim. It levels the playing field. It gives me a fighting chance." She paused for his response.

"You are heavily armed, oh mighty warrior, and skilled in the art of combat."

She smiled from beneath an elevated eyebrow. "So you don't begrudge me the use of my arsenal? You don't think me coarse for not leaving my sword in its sheath?"

"You're a successful woman, Millie, both at home and in the workplace. You have achieved that success without treachery. I can only admire you." A grin developed on his face. "Besides . . . you wouldn't be Millie Foster if you didn't bend hapless men to your will." She returned a suspicious grin.

"I'll tell you a secret, Madam, about those 'helpless victims' you leave strewn across the battlefield. The flirtation of a beautiful woman is no painful assault. Nothing makes a man's pulse, or his mind, race like the kind attention of a charmer such as yourself. You may be picking his pockets, but you do wonders for his self-esteem." He paused to inhale. "We're wired that way, we brutes. Our primary purpose is procreation. Everything else is a side issue. So you play right into our hands when you tantalize us with the possibility of a reproductive opportunity."

"So, I'm the victim now?"

"Not at all. But it's difficult, knowing the nature of men, to pity one who has been granted the temporary affection of a charming woman. The injury is very difficult to locate."

"Well, I appreciate your generous understanding, Young Man, and I hope you harbor no disgust, now that you know of my . . . methods."

Dean chuckled. "Don't faint of surprise, Madam, but I knew of your methods on day one. It took only seconds to determine that you are heavily armed, and it quickly became obvious that you are very skillful in their use."

"So you figured me out that first day at Starbuck's?"

"Not so much by what you did as by the effect you had on me."

"And what was that?"

"I found myself doing inappropriate things for reasons I didn't understand—like fondling your leg, for example. That was one of many tip-offs that your magic was working on me in full measure." She displayed a pleased grin. "So I can't feel sorry for the gentlemen with whom you transacted. They got a Hell of a deal!"

"Well, I'm offering you an even better deal, and at no cost. I want . . . and it will happen eventually . . . I want to have a romantic relationship with you. Regular liaisons. I'll give you what these gentlemen paid so dearly for, three times a week for free. You'll get the best I have. The best there is. I'll even cover the related out-of-pocket expenses. All you have to do is show up and bring your body. Millie will do the rest."

Her face moved close to his. "Millie will take good care of you, Dean," she said. "Millie will keep a smile on your face. No more of those painful nocturnal yearnings or messy emissions. No more embarrassing, inopportune bulges in your clothing. Millie will drain off your excess energy and keep the beast that lives within as tame as a kitten. Believe me, Dean, I can fill all your needs and satisfy all your desires."

"You paint a picture of sensual enslavement, Millie. It's straight out of 'Samson and Delilah.'"

"Don't be so melodramatic," she responded. "Try it for a week and see if you have any complaints. No slave ever had it so good!"

She put her mouth to his ear. "Give in, Dean," she whispered. "It's going to happen . . . and you're gonna love it!"

"We need to work on your self-confidence as a woman," he said. "Now go home to the man who deserves your . . . considerable charms."

Millie smiled knowingly, and she left.

Chapter 18

$\mathcal{D}e\text{-}\mathcal{D}e$

A Chance Encounter

Dean had to visit an Accumedical Data Systems customer in Dallas as a final obligation to his company. He flew up from Houston on a crisp December morning. He was checking into the Wyndmere Hotel on the Stemmons Expressway when he heard a familiar-sounding female voice. "Don't I know you, young man?" it said.

Dean turned to look at the elegantly dressed woman standing beside him. He recognized her as De-De Lindstrom, Millie's friend whom he had met at the Halloween party. "Yes, I'm . . . ," he began.

"Dean Steele, right?" she interrupted him.

"That's right. And you're Mrs. Lindstrom, right?"

"The very one," she said, smiling. "What are you doing in Dallas?"

"I have a business trip," he said, "Installing some software. I'll go back to Houston tomorrow. You?"

"Oh, I'm here for a bridal shower for a friend's daughter." She stood there while the desk clerk gave him his key and instructions to his room. "Dean," she said with a thoughtful look on her face, "I hate to sit in my room by myself all night. Would you like to join me in the lounge for a while? I hate to go in there alone. I get hit on by so many salesmen. I'm sure I'd be left alone if I were accompanied by a gentleman. Besides . . . ," she gave him a look of significance, "You're such a wonderful dancer, as I recall."

"Well, I could do that," he replied. "I'm not committed for the evening. I'll be finished at the hospital about six."

"OK," she said, "My shower will be over by four, and I'll do a little shopping. Why don't we just meet for dinner? I know a wonderful restaurant downtown. It's my treat since you're being so chivalrous."

"OK," Dean said.

"Let's meet in the lobby at, umm, . . . six forty-five. OK?"

"I'll be here," he said.

Dean thought it odd that the wealthy and socially connected Mrs. Lindstrom would not be staying with friends, and that she would have an evening free of social obligations. He thought the meeting with her might be amusing for a while, but he normally shared few interests in common with people from that strata of society. It would be a refreshing break from working the ADS customer through the installation and setup of their new computer programs.

Dinner

De-De was fashionably late, arriving in the lobby at five till seven, looking like a New York model. Dean smiled and shook her extended hand. "How was the shower?" he asked.

"Boring!" she answered. "She's a sweet girl, and I love her mother to death, but these Dallas society hens bore me to tears." She regarded him. "And how was your day?"

"Fine," he responded. "We got most of it up and running. I'll spend tomorrow training their operators." They got in his rental car, and De-De directed him to the restaurant.

Dean found the woman's conversation surprisingly interesting. She was not as shallow and vain as he had been led to believe. She was intelligent and articulate, with well thought out views on a variety of topics. Her attitude was only moderately cynical, and there was a well-concealed warmth underneath. She saw being a wealthy socialite as a game she had gotten herself stuck in, and she tried to make the most of it. Her parents were affluent, she had married well, and her first husband died, leaving her a fortune. She was now married to another wealthy older man, and the arrangement gave her considerable freedom.

They had finished the main course and were awaiting desert before De-De finally mentioned Millie. "How did you meet the charming Mrs. Foster?"

"She hunted me down like an animal," he replied, grinning. "She was familiar with my skating history, and she selected me to skate with her daughter."

"Lucky boy," De-De grinned.

"We'll see about that," Dean responded. "Sometimes I wonder if it was the luckiest, or the most tragic day of my life."

"I expect working with Millie can be a challenge," De-De said, attempting to coax a comment out of him.

"I expect you know her a lot better than I do," he said. "You've been friends since childhood."

"I love her to death," De-De said. "I just know she can be a cantankerous bitch." She looked at Dean for confirmation. He offered nothing.

De-De grinned. "I think she likes you, Dean," she said. "I know her like a sister. I've seen the way she responds to you. I think you may be something more than a skater to her."

"Like what?" Dean asked innocently, curious to derive additional insight into his mentor's motives.

De-De smiled. "Millie is a complex personality, Dean. There's a lot to her. She has ideas and ambitions that go far beyond River Oaks wife and mother."

"Like what?"

"I thought you might tell me."

"Did you bring me here to ask if she and I are . . . involved?"

De-De grinned. "No, but I could understand it if you were. She's an attractive woman. You could be forgiven if . . ." She paused to study Dean's face.

"I know y'all tease each other about things like that. It's an ongoing game of one-upmanship. Right now you're accusing her of an involvement with me. She denies it, but she keeps dropping hints just to keep you on the scent. You'd score a point if you got me to confirm it for you."

"Or deny it," De-De said. "Perhaps you don't like being used as a pawn in our little game." She looked at him expectantly.

"Y'all are so good at this game," he said, "And it means so much to you, I wouldn't want to ruin it by injecting any boring old reality into it."

"So, you're just going to sit there and keep the secret? Does he or doesn't he? Only The Shadow knows!"

"No," he said, reaching across the table and taking her hand tenderly. "I'm going to tell you . . . candidly and honestly . . . that it's none of your damn business." he spoke in a tender, intimate tone. "And that you're a very charming, very beautiful, very nosey bitch." He smiled sweetly at her.

"You're a rogue, Mr. Steele," she said. "I can see why Millie likes you so much. You're just the right target for her particular brand of dominant female obsession." Dean didn't respond. "So, I can tell you this. If she hasn't made a pass at you yet, she will. And if you haven't slept with her yet, you will. She wants you . . . and . . . she'll have you."

"You make me out a helpless victim," he said. "Am I without choice in the matter?"

"Not at all. You have free choice in the matter. I just know what a determined bitch she is. She can make a man want her very badly." Dean refused to let his countenance tell the woman anything.

The Club

There was a club in the building, and they went there and danced to the romantic music of a dance band. The woman softened her "take-charge" disposition, showing Dean her tender side. She pressed herself close to him as they danced. She allowed her feelings to flow more with each dance.

"When we get back to the hotel," she whispered in his ear as they danced, "Will you invite me to your room?"

"We'll have to wait and see," he said, "But I would be tempted. Would you accept?"

"We'll have to wait and see," she said. "But I would be tempted."

"Was there a bridal shower, Mrs. Lindstrom?" he asked.

"No, Dean, there was no shower," she confessed. "I'm a fraud."

"How did you find out where I'd be?"

"I have a friend who's in the business of finding out things," she said. "I simply made a phone call."

"A PI?"

"A very discreet one. He helps me out occasionally."

"So, you went to all this trouble just to find out if there was anything between me and Mrs. Foster?"

"Not really. I just wanted to get to know you . . . since you are obviously so important to my best friend." She paused. "And anything I found out about you and Millie . . . well . . . would be a bonus."

"And perhaps go to bed with me yourself?" he asked.

"That question has not been resolved, now has it?"

"But wouldn't you like to tell your 'best friend' that you've slept with me? Wouldn't that score a touchdown, or a home run, or maybe a slam dunk in your game? And if Millie and I are involved, you could 'horn in' on her action. And if we aren't, you could say you got me first."

She looked into his eyes. "Do I detect that you're a bit disgusted by my tawdry behavior?"

"No, Ma'am. I'm just trying to keep up with the action in this fast-moving drama, which is not easy, seeing as how I play the role of puck in your hockey game."

"No, I think I've put you off! I think you consider me cheap and tacky."

"You're anything but that, Madam." He softened. "I think you're charming, and I love to dance with you. So much so that I'm going to do it again, right now!" He pulled her to her feet and onto the dance floor. He held the woman in a loving embrace as their bodies swayed to the romantic music. He knew that dancing was her weakness. It softened her and brought out her vulnerabilities.

"Dean," she whispered. "You were right about me. I did plan this thing so I could get you in bed and then lord it over Millie. God help me, I'm such a slut!" She paused. "But now it's different. After spending this wonderful evening with you, and finding out who you really are, I don't care about Millie anymore. I just want us to be friends . . . close friends." She pressed herself against him and sighed. "I like you," she whispered, "Very much."

The Hotel

De-De was calm on the ride back to the hotel, like a schoolgirl in love. They spoke of light topics of mutual interest. Dean accompanied her to her door. "Make yourself comfortable," she said as she used her key. "I'll just need a minute."

"I won't be coming in," he said.

She went wide-eyed. "What?"

"I'll say goodnight here. I really enjoyed the evening, and I hope to see you again sometime."

She grabbed him and pulled him inside the doorway. "What are you doing?" she asked incredulously. "Surely you aren't going to just walk away!"

"Yes, Ma'am," he said, "I am. I'm not going to have a one-night-stand with a married woman that I've only known for a few hours."

"Dean, please. Just come inside and let's talk for a moment."

"No, Ma'am. I'll be leaving now."

Anger and frustration flared in her. "So, I guess you'll tell Millie you had me begging for it, right? She'll love that! Shit!"

"I won't tell Millie anything about this."

De-De inhaled and sighed. "Very well," she said. "You must think me an awful slut. I can't blame you for not wanting to shack up with this crazy woman." She looked at him. "I just thought you found me . . . attractive."

"Very much so," he said. "I would like nothing better than to spend the night rolling in your loving embrace. I just consider that to be extremely unwise, under the circumstances."

"Then, you'll at least give me a good-night kiss?"

"I'd be charmed." He took the woman in an embrace, and they engaged in a long, passionate kiss. "Good night Madam," he said, and he left.

Millie

"Dean," Millie said, "De-De Lindstrom has all but stopped hounding me about you. It's not like her. Do you know anything about that?"

"I know absolutely nothing about the wealthy and charming Mrs. Lindstrom, except what you've told me, and precious little of that do I believe."

"I can't believe she would just stop teasing me about you. She was absolutely ruthless for a while, then she just went quiet!"

"Maybe she suddenly developed good taste."

"Not De-De Lindstrom! She thrives on scandal."

A few days later Millie met Dean at his apartment. She looked at him knowingly. "Guess what," she said. "De-De came clean with me. She told me about your little encounter in Dallas."

"Fascinating," Dean said. "I must have forgotten."

"Don't be coy with me, Dean. She told me all about it. Now I want to hear it from you."

"I told you, I don't remember seeing Mrs. Lindstrom anywhere except at that Halloween party, and then it appeared she was a mere peasant, so I took no notice of her."

"Save it, Dean! The Wyndmere Hotel on Stemmons Expressway. Dinner at the top of Reunion Tower. Does that refresh your memory?"

"Oh, yes. Now I remember. I ran into her at the car wash. We had sex on the hood of a Toyota, covered with bubbles. It was really fun until that big rotating brush started whipping my ass!"

"I'm not amused, Dean. Just tell me what happened that night."

Dean gently took her chin in his hand and looked lovingly into her eyes. "Fuck you, Mrs. Foster," he said softly but firmly. "I ain't tellin' you shit!"

"All right, Dean. Be a jerk if you must. I'll tell you what you did."

"I can hardly wait," he said sarcastically.

"You took her out to dinner and dancing, You charmed her pants off. You took her to the hotel, and you fucked her brains out, you ungrateful little shit!"

"Damn," he said. "You'd think I'd remember something like that! And I thought I just installed some software!"

"No, Dean. You installed your hardware in my best friend! Now what do you have to say for yourself?"

"Absolutely nothing! Zero! Nada! Zilch!" he inhaled. "If you and your so-called 'friend' want to play silly mind games on each other, you can leave me out of the equation!"

"Dean, you have to respond to this. She told me some very horrible things!"

"I don't have to give you shit, Madam! Has it occurred to you that little De-De might just be yankin' your twine? On the other hand, has it occurred that it's none of your fuckin' business if I do shack up with her, or anybody else, for that matter? Do the world a favor and butt out of my life, Millie."

"Dean, she's my best friend! If you're involved, that changes everything!"

"I'm not playin', Millie! Leave me out of this ridiculous game. And get the fuck outta my house while you're at it."

"You must feel guilty, Dean, or you wouldn't get so upset."

"Not guilty, Millie . . . ashamed. I'm ashamed I was stupid enough to get involved in a skating project with a neurotic housewife who has psychotic friends!"

"Very well, Dean." Millie inhaled. "I'll tell you what she really said. She didn't say you slept with her. She said you had dinner and danced. She said you were a perfect gentleman, and she was an absolute slut. It was a kind of confession for her."

"OK," he said, "So now we have story number two. In case I don't like this one either, what's number three gonna be? We ran off to Vegas and got married?"

Millie inhaled, then continued. "She said she went up to Dallas to 'run into' you so she could find out if you and I are involved. She also thought she might possibly sleep with you, and then she could give me a hard time about it. But she said you were so charming, and such a good dancer, that she decided she wanted you as a friend. She said she invited you in, but you left her with just a goodnight kiss."

"A touching story, Millie. It ran on 'Days of Our Lives,' two seasons ago."

"Just tell me what happened, Dean!" She was frantic. "Is De-De lying to me?"

"Fuck you, Mrs. Foster! Haven't you left yet? Your curtain call was five minutes ago!"

"Dean, this is important to me, can't you see that?"

"Yeah, you'll get two points for a safety if you can block her punt, and a fifteen yard penalty for illegal use of the mouth!"

"It has nothing to do with that silly game!"

"It has everything to do with that silly game! You two have some kind of weird, bullshit thing going on here, and I want no part of it! If she tells you she fucked me, then OK. Maybe she gets a touchdown. I don't give a flying gopher turd about your stupid game! And I'll sleep with anybody I please, and I won't tell you about it, before, during, or after! Is that clear enough, or do I have to send you a fuckin' E-mail?"

"Don't be angry, Dean. I just care about you, that's all."

"Save it, Millie! You're the Ice Queen,. Ethylene glycol in the veins."

"I have feelings, Dean."

"Well deal with 'em, and get off my ass. I won't be dragged into this stupid game of 'Dueling Bitches'."

Millie pouted. "Then you refuse to tell me what happened in Dallas?"

"Congratulations! You finally got one right!"

"Very well. She said she wanted you, but you didn't give her anything but a goodnight kiss. I believe her Dean. Maybe I'm a fool, but I believe her." He looked at her in stony silence. "Am I a fool, Dean?"

"Careful, Millie! I could write volumes on that topic."

"Why won't you answer me?"

"I've got things to do, Millie," he said. "Return to home and family."

"Give me a hug first."

"Bad Ice Queen! No hug! Vaminos!"

"Please, Dean." She pouted like a child. "Just a little hug. I feel all insecure right now." She batted her eyes.

"Your lease has run out, Lady. Vacate the premises!"

"A little goodbye kiss then?" She smiled sweetly.

"Your visa has expired. You're deported!"

She gathered her belongings and left.

Chapter 19

A Rangerette Christmas

"Guess what, Mom!" Shannon bubbled. "Dean's going to the Rettes Christmas party!"

"The who?"

"The Kilgore Rangerettes!" She took on a knowing tone. "Lieutenant Ashley invited him! Isn't it just too radical?"

"How do you know all this?"

"Well, I did some checking! See? First I saw this pink letter in Dean's pile of mail, and it smelled like perfume, and it was postmarked Kilgore, Texas. So I called Lou Ann, and she didn't know anything about it, but I got Cookie's phone number from her. That's the Freshman Rette I met at Lou Ann's house at Thanksgiving. She's pretty cool. Anyway, Cookie told me Ashley invited Dean to the big Rangerettes Christmas bash, and he accepted! Isn't it just too freaky?"

"So, have Dean and this . . . Ashley been . . . ?"

"Yeah. See? One of the other Rettes, Amanda, is from Houston. She graduated from Deer Park. Anyway, her boyfriend, Joe Bob, lives in Pasadena, not too far from Dean. So Ashley liked what she saw of Dean at Lou Ann's house Thanksgiving, so she goes home with this girl, Amanda, the next weekend, and they call up Dean, and they get together for a double date. Dean, and Ashley, and Amanda, and Joe Bob. Well, Ashley really likes him, see? I mean, Cookie says she's gone totally taffy-ass over him. Anyway she invites him to take her to their big Rangerettes Christmas ball!"

"So, that's why he's been so vague about the 19th!"

"Yeah. He doesn't want us to know he's dating a Rette, for some reason."

"So, what is little Ashley really like?"

"Well, duh! She's a big sophomore at Kilgore college and a Lieutenant in the Rangerettes! She's a hopelessly stuck-up bitch, of course! She treated me like slime at Lou Ann's house. She looked at me like I had some disease! But she was real impressed with Dean. She thought he was way cool." She paused to think. "I told him he ought to date her because she's a Rangerette, but I was just teasing him. I didn't know she was gonna come scratchin' on his door like a stray cat!"

"But he's seen her several times, right? He's . . . dating her?"

"Oh, yeah! And he's fuckin' her too. I'm pretty sure."

"Shame on you for saying that, Shannon! . . . but how do you know?"

"Well, Cookie is her little sister in the Rettes, and they're real close, and she says Ashley has gone totally ape-shit over our Mr. Steele. I mean, he's older and wiser, and she thinks he's radically cool, and all, so she just totally daydreams about him! So Cookie figures Ashley's not a total virgin anyway, and she's really changed since she met Dean, so she's probably puttin' out. Besides, you know Dean. He has serious moves. If he wants her, he'd have no trouble gettin' in her pants, no matter how high-and-mighty she thinks she is."

"Remind me to wash your mouth out with soap, Young Lady!"

"Oh, lighten up, Mom! I'm not in kindergarten anymore!"

Shannon

Two days later Shannon approached Dean. "Hey, Mr. Studly, can Kyle and I ride up to Kilgore with you on the 19th? It doesn't make any sense for us to go in two cars."

"What are you talking about?"

"The big Rangerettes Christmas party, Silly! Kyle is taking me. I figure he and I can ride up with you and Joe Bob."

"All right, Miss Nosey-Face. What do you know?"

"Huh? Well, everybody knows that Lieutenant Ashley invited you to the Rangerettes Christmas Ball, and you and Joe Bob are going up there on the 19th and coming back on the 20th. And I'm going with Kyle, so maybe we can ride up with y'all."

"It's by invitation only, Shannon! You can't go!" Dean's disgust level was high and rising.

"Sure I can. I'm invited! They always invite a few really cool high school girls who are hot prospects for the Rangerettes. It's part of their recruiting."

"Wait a minute! You got yourself invited by conning them into thinking you are a prospect for the Rangerettes?"

"It was easy! I just sent Cookie my resume, and she did the rest. I got this real nice letter from the Director."

"You're a fraud, Foster! You have no intention of going to Kilgore College! I'll talk to your parents. This is not a suitable outing for a high school girl."

"No, Dean, you can't! They already said I could go!"

"Joe Bob and I are staying overnight. I do not want to baby-sit two teenagers!"

"Sorry, Dean. I'm invited to the party, and I'm going. Mom and Dad said I could go, since you'd be there. So, there!"

"This is crazy!"

"You know why she's doing it, don't you, Dean?"

"Doing what?"

"Why Ashley invited you! She just wants to show off to her fancy friends! She'll be so cool with a hunky graduate student from U of H, who's also a USFSA medalist, as her date. It's just so gross! I can't believe you fell for it!"

"Maybe she just enjoys my company. You ever think of that?"

"Gross, Dean. Read my lips! You'll be a laughing stock."

"Taking a Rangerette to their big Christmas party?" he said. "An officer, even? How cool is that?" Shannon scoffed.

By the end of their practice session, Dean had calmed down. "Why did you do it, Shannon?"

"Do what?"

"You know what! Get yourself invited to the Rangerettes Christmas party. You're a skater. You have no interest in that cheerleading stuff."

"Well, I was really impressed by those two girls I met Thanksgiving, and I really think I can make a good Rangerette, and I just wanted to meet them all and see what it's really like with them."

"Bullshit!" Dean's patience faded. "You're playing some stupid game, trying to ruin the first date I've had in a decade. You're an insufferable little twit!"

"No, Dean, honestly. I'm really looking forward to meeting all those cool girls, and dancing with Kyle. They're gonna have this really cool band."

"Save it, Dipshit! You'd never go within a hundred miles of Kilgore if you hadn't found out I was going up there to that party."

"No, honestly. I've been planning this since Thanksgiving. I only today found out you were going too."

"Kiss my ass, you little liar!"

"Come on, Dean! What will it hurt? We'll have fun! Take us with you. Please, please, please!"

"First, I'm going to try to get your invitation revoked. If that doesn't work, I'll report Kyle's car stolen, so you'll both be arrested before you make it to the Beltway."

"Come on, Dean! Don't be an old Fudd! It'll be fun! You'll see."

Millie

"I hear my daughter horned in on your Christmas celebration, Dean."

"You mean Kilgore?"

"Yes. She was quite devious about it I'd say."

"More than a little. I don't even know how she found out about it, or how she was able to get herself invited. The Rangerettes Christmas party is a pretty hot ticket."

"Deviousness runs in the family, Dean, on the female side." She grinned.

"I suppose it does." He grinned. "You sure didn't jump to my aid and try to salvage my outing by keeping her home."

"It wouldn't have worked. She was dead set on going to that party." Millie paused to inhale. "Are you going to take her with you?"

"Would you make her stay home if I said, 'No?'"

"Probably not."

The young man sighed. "Then I guess I'll let 'em ride up with us. I'll need to keep and eye on her anyway. She doesn't do parties very well, as we've seen."

"This girl," Millie began, "This Ashley. Isn't she a bit . . . young for you?"

"She's twenty. She's a sophomore. It's legal." His irritation showed.

"I realize she is 'of legal age,' but I just might think she would be too . . . inexperienced to interest you very much."

"She is a bit inexperienced," he replied with sarcasm, "But I offered to help her with that." He couldn't resist firing a warning shot across Millie's bow.

"I'm sure you could do wonders for her . . . lack of experience," Millie laughed, "But I just think you might find the whole thing a bit . . . childish."

"It will be the first party I have attended with a date since I was conscripted into the Foster Navy. It will be a great pleasure, even if we only play patty-cake and bob for apples all evening." He paused to focus on her. "Besides, the Lieutenant has some intelligent thoughts of her own."

"Not to mention a well-rounded derriere, I suppose."

"A requirement for the regiment. Only gorgeous gets in."

"Well, spend your spare time as you wish, Dear Boy." Millie dismissed him in an irritating, flighty way.

The Ride Up

Shannon was quite animated on the ride up, being the only girl in a car with three boys. By the time the 160-mile trip was over she had related most of her childhood experiences at least once and in considerable detail.

The Party

Dean was able to stay away from Shannon and Kyle, spending most of his time with Ashley and her upperclass Rangerette friends. Early in the evening he danced with the Captain and the other Lieutenants, and chatted with some of the faculty members in attendance. Later he spent most of his time with Ashley as their conversation became increasingly intimate.

The After-Party

After they left the ballroom Dean and his entourage went to Ricky's home to change clothes, and to continue the party. Ricky had graduated Kilgore college two years before and was working for an oilfield service company located outside town. He had rented a house in Kilgore with a co-worker. Ricky's date, Angela, and Joe

Bob's girlfriend, Amanda, were both sophomore Rangerettes. Cookie, a freshman, was there with her date, making five couples.

The punch at the party was only lightly spiked, but the drinks at Rickey's house were not so restricted. Rickey, Dean and Joe Bob changed into jeans and T-shirts, but Shannon and the four Rangerettes still had on their party dresses. They quickly decided to peel off their formals and panty hose and strip down to bra, panties and high heels. After a couple more drinks they decided they wanted to jump in the Jacuzzi. Shannon argued that the venue was sufficiently private that they could go in naked, and the Rangerettes agreed. Just as the girls were about to remove their remaining garments, Dean and Joe Bob produced some "emergency bikinis" they had brought in anticipation of just this development.

"They're kinda brief," Dean remarked, "But they'll keep you from getting kicked out of the Rangerettes."

"Why didn't you tell us you had bathing suits for us when we took off our dresses?" the girls inquired in disgust. The young men exchanged knowing looks.

"We just wanted to wait and see if you had any class at all, and . . . we find . . . you are totally without!"

"Jerks!" The girls put on the bikinis and got into the Jacuzzi.

As the evening wore on, the couples paired off, and Dean and Ashley disappeared into one of the bedrooms. Shannon and Kyle spent some time kissing, but mostly Shannon talked. Dean had promised the boy a date with one of the Piccadilly girls if he would keep Shannon occupied and out of trouble for the evening. Kyle took his duty seriously and ended up mainly as a target for the girl's sharp wit.

The three sophomore Rangerettes had signed out of the Gussie Nell Davis Rangerettes Residence Hall for the weekend and did not have to return to campus until Sunday. Shannon returned to the dorm with Cookie at 1:00 AM and spent the night there. Kyle slept in Dean's Mustang. Dean and Ashley occupied one of the bedrooms. By 3:00 AM all the partygoers had found a place to sleep.

The Ride Back

"What's it like, Dean?" He and Joe Bob were chatting about cars, but Shannon projected her inquiry from the back seat.

"What is what like, Princess?" Her catty tone had alerted his suspicion.

"Fucking a Rangerette. Are they better in bed than regular girls?"

"Time to shut your face, Shannon!"

"No, really! Did she bring her pom-poms to bed? She didn't kick out the ceiling lights while you were on top of her, did she? Did she yell, "Go! Go! Go! while you were humping her?"

"Shannon I'm going to let you out at the next truck stop. Tell the nice man in the 18-wheeler that you'll do anything for a ride to River Oaks. He'll get you there in a few days—when he gets tired of your mouth!"

"How 'bout you, Joe Bob?" Shannon asked. "Are Rangerettes really good in bed? They can do those really wild jump splits. Does that make it better?"

"Well, uh . . ." the boy began his answer. Dean tapped him on the shoulder and shook his head. Joe Bob went silent.

Then Dean addressed Kyle. "Maybe now you can see why I advised you to stay as far away from this psychotic little bitch as you can get. She is terminally tacky with no hope of redemption."

"Well, I . . ." Kyle stammered.

"Do yourself a favor, Kyle. Don't even talk to her at school. She's poison. Avoid her like gorilla shit."

"Ooh, sensitive!" Shannon cooed. "There must really be something special about fucking a Rangerette to make you so touchy! And don't try to tell me you didn't do her either! It was written all over her this morning. You must have kept her up all night!"

"Shannon, shut the fuck up, right now, or you're walking!"

"She's just a bitch, Dean! Did you see they way she was using you? Hanging on you like she was your steady squeeze, and bragging about it to all of her friends. You'd think she has names picked out for your kids already!"

Dean swerved the Mustang off onto an exit in a maneuver that tossed the passengers around. He stopped the car on the side of the service road. He opened the door, got out, and dragged Shannon out after him. "We need to talk," he said as he dragged the girl forcibly toward a nearby tree.

"Are you mad at me?" Shannon asked sheepishly when they reached the tree.

"What makes you ask?" He forced a calm tone.

"Well, you dragged me out of the car, and . . ."

"Yes, I'm upset! You're way out of line, Shannon! You're insulting my date and embarrassing me in front of those guys!"

"I don't see why! I just . . ."

"Then you're an idiot too! It's none of your business what I do on a date. Ashley's a nice girl. Keep you nose on your face, for a change!"

"But, Dean! Surely you can see she's just . . ."

"End of discussion, Shannon! Ashley is fine, and what we do is none of your business. If you say anything more, I'll give you an ass whipping right here!"

Shannon judged that further conversation would be ill-advised. "OK, we'll talk about this sometime when you can be more rational." She turned on her heel and returned to the car with her nose in the air.

Ashley

Ashley spent the next few weekends in Houston to be able to see Dean. "Dean, I'd like for you to come home with me, to Gainesville, some weekend. I just know you'd like my dad, and Mom would love to meet you. I've told them all about you."

"I have to practice every day, Sweetie, but maybe we can work it out."

The girl's face saddened. "I guess you're not ready to meet my family." She looked down.

"No, I'd like to do that. It's just having the time to make the trip that's the problem. I don't have much freedom right now."

Ashley sighed. "I know I'm not . . . exactly what you want." She looked at him. "My tits aren't very big, and my ass is too little." Dean's jaw dropped. "But I'm still filling out, and I'm working out in the gym. My butt will get bigger. Mom's did. And I can get implants after I graduate. I know some girls who did, and they look really great." Dean blinked incredulously. "I just think I can be the girl you want . . . if you'll . . . give me a chance."

"Ashley . . . what are you talking about?"

"I really like you, Dean, and I'm willing to do whatever it takes to be the girl you want . . . if you'll just give me the chance."

"Ashley, listen to me. Your ass is perfect. Your . . . boobs are just fine. Great, as a matter of fact. You . . . You're a charming woman, and I would love to meet your folks." He paused to study her face. "So where did you come up with this . . . nonsense?"

"Well, I just know that you're older, and all. And you've been around a lot. And you have a lot of . . . girls around you. And I'm just a sophomore, and I haven't ever done much, and all."

"Who have you been talking to?"

"Huh? Oh, nobody. I just know what your . . . situation is, and all."

"Who . . . have you been talking to? Who upset you? Who filled up your head with bullshit?"

The girl sighed. "Well, I've been trying to find out as much about you as I can. Joe Bob told me a lot about you."

"And . . . Shannon? Have you spoken with Shannon . . . or her mother?"

"Oh, not her mother. I've never met her."

"But Shannon then. Have you spoken with her recently?"

"Well, we did have this one phone call. She called me the other night."

"Come here, Sweetheart." He took the girl in his arms. "I want you to tell me everything Shannon said about me, one preposterous lie at a time. We're going to sort this all out. What did she say?"

"Oh, just the usual stuff. You're really smart, and a great skater, and you've got lots of discipline."

"Let's get on to the bad stuff. Tell me something that you found disturbing."

"Well, she said you live with a bunch of girls, and you have really wild sex with them all the time, and you like a real . . . experienced and . . . adventurous lover. I don't really know all that much about . . . you know . . . ."

"OK, let's call that bullshit pile number one. I live in an apartment house with all kinds of people. I'm not dating anybody right now, except you, and I do not have orgies in my apartment."

"But you do . . . ."

"I'm not a saint, Sweetie, but my social life is very dull now that I'm working on the skating project. You are the one bright light on a very bleak horizon."

She smiled. "Really?"

"What else?" His face bore a firm and disgusted look.

"Oh, um, she said you only like girls who have really sexy bodies, with big tits and really big butts."

"Ashley, I like pretty girls, and pretty comes in all shapes and sizes. You, for example, are very well put together. Your tits and ass are very well proportioned to your size. You're a Rangerette, for Pete's sake! You wouldn't be here if you weren't beautiful." Ashley grinned self-consciously. "But I look deeper than the skin, Sweetheart. I enjoy talking to you. I like to hear your perspective on things. Let's call that one bullshit pile number two."

"OK, so she also said you're a genius, and you get bored with dumb girls really quick, and you just use 'em for a while and then get rid of 'em."

"OK, genius, maybe." He grinned. "And dumb girls do bore me." He nodded his head. "But I don't use 'em. I don't even date 'em in the first place."

"You don't think I'm dumb?"

"You're a sophomore at Kilgore College. What's your GPA?"

"Uh, three point eight out of four."

"See? No dumb chick, this!"

"No, but I mean, I'm not . . . widely traveled."

"You've already come from Gainesville to Kilgore, and you've even been to Houston! Not a bad start."

"Well, I've been a lot of other places too. We marched in a parade in Chicago."

"See? You're practically a jet setter!"

"Yeah, but it was all with the Rettes." She shrugged.

"Hey, you're an officer of the organization that started the whole dance-drill cheerleading phenomenon! Don't ever put that down. This is not some local drill team we have here. You're world-famous!"

"I know. I was thrilled when I got accepted!"

"OK, bullshit pile three. What else?"

"She said you were destined to be an international figure skating star, and you would probably marry an Olympic champion or something, and you'd never settle down with a mousey Texas girl who only knows how to kick." Her face reflected immense sadness.

Dean paused for a moment to clench his fist and grind his teeth. "Ashley . . . Sweetheart, I know a few Olympic champions, and they are just as flawed as anybody else. They do not walk on water, unless it's frozen. In fact, they can be more conceited and cantankerous that most other folks can be. I'm not setting any such requirements on my search for a mate. That's bullshit four."

"OK, Dean," she said. "I guess I got a little down for no good reason." She cuddled under his arm.

"No, you had good reason, and I'm gonna fix that!"

Shannon

"I have something to tell you, Shannon."

"Oh, yeah? What's the big deal, frog-face?"

"I'm through. I'm quitting, and I never want to see you again. This has been the biggest mistake I have ever made, giving up a career for a neurotic housewife and her psychotic daughter."

"Ha, ha, Dean. That's cool." Shannon laughed.

"No, I mean it. That was a really shitty thing you did to Ashley!"

Shannon became more serious. "What are you talking about?" She tried to conceal her whirring thoughts.

"Telling her all that stuff about me. My God! It was hideous!"

"I hardly ever talked to Ashley!"

"Phone call last week, remember?"

"She told you about that?" Shannon was becoming worried.

"Every word, you vicious little bitch!"

"Hey, I was just trying to help you out!"

"Bullshit! You were trying to break us up! And break that girl's heart in the process." He paused as his anger flared. "You are evil! You're some kind of a fuckin' demon! You deserve your own dorm room in Hell."

"Dean, what is the matter with you? She just wanted to know about you. I think she likes you."

"Who placed the call, Shannon?"

"I . . . don't remember."

"Bullshit. You called her up and fed her a line of crap a mile long!"

"Dean, I was just trying to help her understand you better. It was for her own good!"

"Save it, Foster! Every word was calculated to cut like a knife! You'd pour water on a drowning man! Shit! I can't believe this!"

"Dean! I don't know what she told you, but I was just trying to help!"

"Yeah? Help who? Certainly not Ashley or me!"

Shannon's face hardened. "She's jealous, Dean. She wants you all to herself. She's trying to break up our skating team!"

"Well, she's too late, because you beat her to the punch! I don't even want to be in the same arena with you, ever again!" Shannon began to cry and left the room.

Millie

"I hear you're having second thoughts," Millie said. "Or maybe it's fifth or sixth. I've lost count."

"You daughter's a vicious bitch, and I'd be an idiot to skate with her."

"You state that as if it's some kind of news!" Her voice had a "so, what's new?" tone.

"The enormity of it! She tried to cut that college girl's heart out!"

"She didn't realize what she did was so . . . tacky. She's young and naïve, and she's trying to protect her skating partnership."

"By killing an innocent girl?"

"Oh, it's done all the time in this female-dominated sport! The sheet is lined with the bodies of the innocent." Dean realized that Millie was patronizing him. "I can understand your being upset. Shannon misbehaved. But it's nothing to ruin a partnership over. It's just . . . girl stuff. They brutalize each other all the time, just like boys do. Only with words, not fists."

"All the more damaging."

"I expect you're right. The scars go deeper." Millie's understanding seemed to calm Dean down. He exhaled a sigh. Millie smiled at him softly as she sensed her charm was working. "You sorted it all out, Mr. Smooth. No harm done. The majorette is all put back together."

Dean scoffed. "She'll never see me the same again!" He grinned for the first time. "She thinks I'm a satyr who runs a sex palace full of big asses and huge boobs."

"She was bound to find out sooner or later!" Millie laughed at her own humor. Dean chuckled as well. "Seriously, Dean, Shannon has learned her lesson. Ashley will recover from her wounds. Your relationship . . . with both of them . . . is back on track."

"With Ashley, maybe, but with your daughter . . ."

"She's no different than she was the day you asked her to skate with you. She's still the same talented, hard-working skating partner you had. That hasn't changed." She paused to sigh. "And she's still a bit of a bitch. That hasn't changed either." She paused. "Apparently it's a genetic thing."

Dean was silent for a time. "I guess it would be a waste," he said after a sigh, "To shit-can the whole thing after this much investment of time and effort."

"You're probably right, Honey. Besides," she grinned, "You wouldn't want to lose me in the deal!"

"Ha! To be free of the tyrannical Ice Queen! Now there's a tempting prospect!"

"You know your life would dull down to a boring soap opera without my . . . influence and . . . participation." She wore a sly grin.

"Influence? How about interference? Interruption, perhaps? What about interdiction?"

"What about intercourse?"

"Social, of course."

"Whatever." She gave him a seductive grin.

The fact that Dean knew Millie was using sexual flirtation to calm him down and bend him to her will made it no less effective. The upset was all but gone, and the incident seemed much less significant. He felt his thinking aligning with hers. "It comes as natural to you as breathing, doesn't it?"

"What's that?" She pretended not to know to what he referred.

"Seducing men to get your way."

"Why, the very idea! I would never stoop to using sex to influence your decision." Her sly grin exuded extremes of self-confidence.

"I am . . . disarmed by your . . . grace and charm."

"Then get back to work!"

"As you command, Milady!"

The Breakup

"Hey, Dean! I hear you broke up with the Rangerette."

"News travels fast."

"Yeah, Cookie told me all about how you dumped her. She's all busted up about it. I hear they have her under a 24-hour suicide watch at Rangerette Central."

"Kiss this, Moose-face!" He touched his hip pocket.

"But really. Why did you break her heart?"

"You wouldn't understand."

"No, try me. Why did y'all break up? Did she find out you're an asshole?"

Dean sighed. "I realized it wasn't fair to her. I can't even do justice to a girlfriend in Houston, much less one that far away. She was . . . wasting her time on me."

"And you too, right? She isn't wild enough for you."

"She's fine, Shannon. I like her a lot. It's just not a good idea. That's all. She needs to date somebody younger and more accessible. And I need to focus on skating."

"Well, you're better off, Dean. She wasn't really all that cool. Not actually."

"Shannon, you wouldn't recognize cool if it was wearing a sign."

"So, OK! You're free! Let's do some spins!" She skated away. Dean shook his head and sighed.

Chapter 20

Dogtag Dance

A Request

"Dean," a woman's voice said, "Can I have a minute?"

"Sure, Susan," Dean said as the woman walked up to him grinning self-consciously.

"I need to ask you for a favor. I'm giving a birthday party for Allison in two weeks, here at the rink, and I'm trying to line up the entertainment for it." Dean stopped what he was doing and looked at the woman. "Allison, she's fourteen—will be—just raves about you. She thinks you're just about the most beautiful man alive, and the best skater in the world." The woman blushed. "I was wondering if there was any way I could get you to skate a number for her party." She looked at him with pleading eyes. "It would mean so much to her."

"Susan, I think it's too early for Shannon and me to skate any kind of number in public. We're not far enough along skating together yet."

"Oh, I know. I just know you used to compete, and Allison is so taken with you and your skating . . . I know she would just love it if you skated a solo number at her party."

Dean's face registered shock, so much so that the woman thought she must have spoken out of line. "I don't know," he said.

"I'm sorry, Dean," she said, "You're a pairs skater now. I had no right . . ."

"No, it's OK. I just need to think about it, that's all. Can I let you know tomorrow?"

"Sure," the woman gushed. "Just let it be our secret, OK?"

"Fine," he replied.

The Deal

"Susan," Dean called out.

"Oh, there you are, Dean," the woman said. "I've been looking for you."

"I want to talk to you about this party thing."

"It's just an idea, Dean. I'll understand if you don't want to do it. I really shouldn't ask."

"No, it's OK, but there is really only one routine I could possibly have ready in time. One I used to do a long time ago, but it might not be appropriate."

"What is it?" The woman's interest was piqued.

"It's kind of a 'bad boy' routine I used to do in jeans and T-shirt. It's kinda like 'Grease' or something."

"Oh, Dean, that would be perfect! Allison an her friends watch that movie all the time!"

"This dance is . . . kinda intense."

"Intense?"

"Yeah. It has some kinda wild, kinda disco moves in it. It might not be suitable for younger audiences."

"Oh, it can't be as bad as what's on the cable these days. It would be great!"

"OK, but, in case anyone gets offended, remember you were warned."

"I'm sure it will be perfect," she said. "Oh, thank you, Dean, so much." She paused. "Will a hundred be enough?"

"A hundred what?"

"A hundred dollars? I know it's not much, but having a daughter skating is so expensive . . ."

"Susan, you don't have to pay me. I'll do it for Allison, for her birthday."

"Oh, Dean, that's terrific!"

The Performance

After the cake and punch, the kids went out to the arena to watch some skating. Several of the students skated their routines. Then the announcer said, "Get ready, girls. Next we have Dean Steele doing his famous dogtag dance!" A shriek went up since none of the party-goers even knew Dean would be there. Allison's mother made the embarrassed girl go out and stand on the ice. One of the boys had set up a row of small orange traffic cones in a straight line angling across the arena.

A murmur of excitement went through the assembly as they asked each other what this was all about. The music started with a heavy rock beat. It was "Bad to the Bone," and it was very loud. Most of the young girls were standing along the rail, looking into the arena through the Plexiglas. After the music started most of them began to dance to the beat.

Dean skated out wearing an olive drab undershirt, blue jeans and military dogtags. He looked like a US Marine on leave. His pants were fashioned of thin stretch denim, but cut and sewn like Levis jeans. They had been made years before, when he was smaller, and they were quite tight. His hair was slicked back and his muscular chest and shoulders protruded from the thin undershirt. He wore a playfully arrogant and conceited look as he chewed on a match. The girls started gasping, screaming and jumping up and down when they saw him.

He skated a very masculine, sexy routine with "Saturday Night Fever" moves combined with very athletic jumps and spins, including an impressive series of Russian split jumps. The Russian split is more difficult for a man to perform due to the different shape of the male pelvis, but it looks more impressive for just that reason. At one point he skated behind the birthday girl, lifted her ponytail and exhaled hot breath on her neck.

The music faded into Kathy Mattea's "455 Rocket," a hard driving rock tune about an Oldsmobile with a very large engine. He picked up a steering wheel and skated as if driving a car. The crowd was truly impressed by spins, double jumps and even a back flip executed with a steering wheel in hand. Dean punched his fist into the air on the word "rocket" each time it occurred in the song.

Dean was doing a spread eagle on outside edges during the line in the song about "what I got underneath my hood." It was suggestive to say the least.

During the line in the song where the Rocket "hit the curb" Dean skated into the boards with a loud bang, bounced off and went down on his back. He slid through the row of traffic cones, scattering them to the four corners during the line about "taking out the safety rail." Then he jumped up and acted out the role of the puzzled cop. This section included the most provocative moves of the entire program.

Encouraged by the enthusiastic response of his young audience, Dean got fully in character and interpreted the music with full force. The teenage girls never stopped screaming. Some were even crying, like the audiences at the Beatles concerts in the sixties. Even the moms in attendance gave their undivided attention to the ice.

Shannon

"I hear you skated at Allison's party," Shannon said coolly as she put on her skates for their afternoon practice.

"Yeah," Dean replied. "It was a hoot."

I hear you did your famous 'dogtag dance' that Liz North was so hot about."

"I don't think it's actually 'famous'."

"It is now. Everybody's talking about it. I hear it was pretty disgusting."

"Really?" he replied, suddenly irritated. "Nobody I talked to used that particular adjective. Who said it was disgusting? And I'll check it out."

"Well, judging from the descriptions I heard . . ."

"Yeah, and what was that?"

"Well, I hear it was pretty raunchy. Lots of bumping and grinding and stuff."

"Well, you must have heard about someone else's routine. That wasn't mine."

"Why did you do it, Dean? Why did you skate in public without me, and why didn't you even tell me you were gonna do it? How could you be such a shit?"

"Well, you and I don't have anything that's even close to ready for prime time, Kid, and besides, Susan asked me for a solo number."

"So? Why did you keep it a secret from me?"

"It was a surprise for Allison's birthday! We kept it a secret from everybody."

"I wouldn't have told anybody."

"There was no need to bring you into the conspiracy."

"For Pete's sake, Dean, I'm your partner!"

"Indeed, you are. You're my skating partner, not my mother, my owner, my employer, or my priest."

"Oh, so you just think you have the right to sneak around and skate at other girls' parties and not tell me about it, huh?"

"Of that, there can be no doubt," he said, matter-of-factly.

"It sucks, Dean!"

"Why?"

"Because!"

"You got anything more specific in the way of a reason?"

"Well, for one thing, I would have gone to the party if I had known my partner was skating a solo number!"

"You had school."

"I would have cut class."

"Not smart, Einstein."

"I just think it was a shitty thing to do, not telling me about it before you did it. It means we're not very close."

"It was no big deal. I just did the number for the party, and it was OK."

"It was more than OK, from what I heard. You had those little girls creaming in their jeans."

"I think 'screaming in their jeans' is more accurate. They were just acting silly, as young girls will sometimes do."

"How many of 'em have offered to go to bed with you?"

"Well, now, let me see . . . Can I borrow your calculator? It was, ahh yes . . . exactly . . . none. That's how many."

"Just wait, then. They'll be all over you by tomorrow."

"I seriously doubt it."

"I'll put out the word they have to keep their hands off of you."

"Thanks, Shannon. I feel a lot safer now," he responded with sarcasm in his voice. "Maybe I won't get gang-raped by a dozen twelve-year-olds."

"But wait," he continued, "I'm a single guy with no steady girlfriend right now. Maybe I'll get me a girlfriend out of this thing, if it was as sexy as you say it was. Maybe I'll have my pick of the gum-poppin' thirteen-year-olds in the club. This could work out OK!"

"Fuck you, Dean Steele!"

"Personal attacks on your skating partner are unbecoming, Shannon."

"Well, fuck you anyway. I don't care if you shack up with all the girls in the club at the same time. It would serve you right!" She stomped out.

"Well, thank you, partner," Dean mumbled to himself.

Millie

"Well, Dean," Millie said, "I hear your performance was quite a hit."

"Somebody must have liked it," he replied.

"All the females in the audience, at least," she said. "I hear you had them screaming your name."

"Screaming something," Dean said. "Girls that age will scream at anything. I think they were just having fun."

"Well, you had an effect on some of the older girls, too, Young Man. I hear you caused quite a stir among the adult females."

"I didn't hear them yelling," he said.

"They weren't yelling, Dear Boy, they were quietly plotting how to get their hooks into you."

"Oh, come on, Millie! Those ice moms are so deep into the mother/daughter/ school/skating thing, their libido has long since died an unlamented death."

"From what I hear, you woke it up, Sonny-boy, with all that hip-swiveling and pelvic thrusting you did out there."

"That's funny, I didn't realize you saw the number."

"I didn't, you sneaky little rat! But I've heard about it in great detail, from numerous sources."

"Well, you can't believe everything you hear. Surely you realize the tale gets embellished with each retelling."

"Tight undershirt, tight jeans, muscles and dogtags? My God Dean, that would make Whistler's mother's hormones bubble!" He looked at her. "You were practically naked from the waist up, and those jeans came out of a spray can!"

"Are you disgusted by my unseemly behavior in front of the skating club, Madam?"

"No, I'm mad as Hell you didn't tell me about it before it happened. I would have crawled across the Antarctic in my underwear to see it!"

"Does that mean you approve of my reckless behavior?" He grinned.

"Your behavior was great. You just should have done it for me, you little shit!"

"I see. Then I'll not be punished?"

"Not unless you refuse to do that dogtag dance for me. That's a capital offense, punishable by a slow and painful death!"

"Well, Ms. Foster, I'm glad you don't hold a grudge over my indiscretion. Unlike your dear daughter."

"Oh, she's just mad because you didn't skate with her. And a little jealous of Allison too, I expect. After all, Dean, she is your partner."

"I tried to explain to her 'partner' is not the same as 'owner.'"

"She'll get over it. But if you ever skate that dogtag dance again without me being there, I'll break both your legs."

"I'll keep that in mind. I'm not sure I could land a triple Lutz wearing two casts."

"And another thing. You'll be getting a lot of invitations and offers from the ice moms as a result of this. You need to make sure you routinely turn them down."

"What kind of invitations do you think I'll get?"

"Oh, things like, 'Hi, Dean, I baked you some cookies,' or 'Oh, Dean, would you like to come to a little get-together I'm having at my house,' or 'Dean, can I blow your horn till your eyes roll back?'"

"You've got a wild imagination, Millie. Ice moms aren't quite that aggressive."

"Just keep your pants zipped up, Dear Boy. Messing around with anyone in the skating club would make for some very messy business."

"Thanks for the warning," he chuckled. "I would never have figured that out on my own."

"If you get any offers, whether it's for cookies or . . . whatever, you just let me know who it was. I'll scratch her eyes out on the spot, and put an end to it right there."

"Damn, I'm lucky to have such protection!" Millie looked at him somewhat puzzled. "Your daughter also offered to warn the twelve-year-olds to stay out of my bedroom."

"I don't think the twelve-year-olds are the problem," Millie said. "Its those thirty-year-old bitches that worry me."

Brat

At practice the next day Shannon was distant and aloof. She twice broke out of synchronized spins early, and then she popped the first jump of a double toe/double Lutz combination into a single and didn't even attempt the second jump. She skated over to the rail, hopped up and sat on it. Dean finished the combination alone then skated over to where she sat. She looked away from him, idly swinging her skates back and forth. He stood beside her quietly for a while, gazing nonchalantly across the rink. "Shannon," he said in a soft, inquisitive voice designed to gently coax her attention onto himself. "What the fuck's wrong with you?" The latter sentence came out harshly enough to make her flinch.

"Why do you do that, Dean? Why do you treat me that way? 'What's wrong with you, Shannon? Why are you such a bitch, Shannon? Kiss my ass Shannon!'" She used a deep, dim-witted voice inflection in a very cold and mocking way.

"I was led to believe I had a dedicated athlete for a pairs partner," he said. "Now I find that's not always the case. I'm not your Daddy, your Mommy, your teacher, your psychiatrist, or your priest, Kiddo."

"Or my brother!" she added.

"Or your brother. Actually, I'm your worst fuckin' nightmare—your pairs partner. We have a one-in-a-million chance to do something worthwhile, and your immature little fits of pique just reduce it to zero. I don't have the patience of Job, I'm afraid. I'm too old and too cynical to put up with cheap bullshit from a spoiled teenager."

She hissed and looked away from him in anger. Vibrations of rage emanated from her body.

"Besides," he said, speaking very close to her ear, as if telling a secret, "You love skating, and you love skating with me. You can't help it."

"You're an asshole!" she snapped.

"Be that as it may, you still love to skate with me."

"You're a jerk and a shithook . . . and you're mean!"

"But you knew that. It was all in the disclosure papers."

"What papers? What are you talking about?"

"The full disclosure form you signed before you agreed to skate with me."

"What? I didn't sign any form!"

"The lawyers didn't give you a document laying out what a shithead I am?"

"No!"

"Oh, boy! Have you got a lawsuit, or what? You won't have to wait 'till your parents die. You can get all their money right now!"

"Are you making a point, Steele?" Her voice was cold and disgusted.

"I'm asking you to get over whatever miff you have today, pull the burr out of your ass, and act like an athlete. Take control of your emotions for a change."

"Fuck you, Dean Steele!" She turned away.

The young man sighed and shook his head. "OK, Kid, let's take a break. I'll buy the Gatoraide."

Sullenly, Shannon followed Dean to the gate and across the mat to the cold drink machine. He put in three quarters and pulled out an orange colored can. He pulled the top and took a swig. Then he offered it to her. "Don't I get my own?" Her voice was cruel and icy.

"Can't afford it on my salary, Sweetheart." He cocked his head as he looked at her. "Afraid you'll catch something?" She snatched the can from his hand with a disgusted movement and sucked down a mouthful of its contents. Then she glared at Dean.

"Now," he said. "What's bothering you?"

"You." She gave him a cold, victorious look.

"Ah! And what about . . . 'me' is bothering you?"

"The way you do." Her response was tinged with disgust.

"And what about . . . 'the way I do' bothers you, Princess?" He was clearly forcing a calm attitude of solicitous understanding through gritted teeth.

"The way you never skate with me in public. You'll skate your ass off for some nobody little twit's birthday party, but when you and I skate together, everybody gets locked outside! Are you just ashamed of me, Dean, or what? Are we ever gonna let people see us skate together?"

"Ummm, I see your point," he said, easing up a bit. "You got a minute?" She answered with a bored, disgusted look. "Lemme give you a little background information here," he said, placing his hands together as if he were a professor preparing to launch a lecture on thermodynamics. "I needed that little birthday party thing. I hadn't skated a planned performance in front of real people in almost ten years. I didn't know if I could do it anymore. I was afraid I'd freeze up, or blank out and forget everything, or fall down all over the ice." Her jaw dropped as she gazed at him in disbelief. "But I did have one routine I could do: 'Dogtags.' I had done it enough before. I knew it cold. If I was ever gonna perform in public again, this was where I had to start. I desperately needed to get this step behind me before I could ever skate a pairs program with a new partner. I had to take my professional rehabilitation in stages, and that was step one."

"I still think it was a shitty thing to do though, not telling me about it before you did it. It means we're not very close."

"Why do you say that?"

"Because! It was important to you to perform again for the first time, and you decided to do it at Allison's party, and you didn't tell me. I wanted to be there with you, to share the experience."

"Maybe I didn't need the additional pressure."

"Pressure? You think I'd put pressure on you? Shit, Dean! I'd support you! Don't you know that?"

"It was just easier this way. I did the number and it went off fine. If I had known it would work out well, I would have invited you. It's just, if I had fallen on my face, then I wouldn't have wanted you there to see it."

"Dean . . . ," she said, softening markedly.

"Once I got out there, it all came back to me. Lucky for us! When I heard the music and the response of the crowd, I got right back into it. But before the music started, I was scared to death. I wanted to jump the rail and run out through those big old front doors, skates and all."

"I can't believe this! Dean Steele scared of a little girl's birthday party?"

"Afraid of failure, Shannon. Afraid of screwing up. That's the big bad wolf, here." The girl shook her head in wonder. "But look," he continued. "You and I don't have the basics of skating together worked out yet. We have to pay our dues by working out all the basic pairs moves before we can even do a simple program in public." He looked at her. "You could do a singles program, though. In fact, that would be nice. It would be good for you to get some more performing experience. Every little bit helps, while we're waiting to get good enough to perform together."

"As if, Dean," she said blandly. "Everybody's seen my Juniors program a hundred times. And I can't just whip up a new dance routine to some old cowboy song the way you do."

"Sure you can. I'll help you. We can work you up a cute dance routine to one of the country songs."

"Dean," she said, looking at him with doe eyes, "I'm sorry I'm such a bitch. I always regret it when I have one of these fits, but I can't help it." She took his hand. "Can you forgive me?"

"It's OK, Sweetheart. I should have told you why I wanted to do that party. I guess I just thought you'd know. Or maybe I was afraid to admit I was scared."

She hugged him. They finished the shared can of electrolyte fluid, and then they finished their practice.

Chapter 21

Millie's Plan

Millie and Dean were sitting in the upstairs lounge at the Texas Ice Stadium, waiting for a meeting with the manager. "You know," she said, "Since you've been skating with Shannon, I've become mighty popular at the skating club. Most of those women treat me like a long lost friend. I can't count the number of boring hen parties I've been invited to."

"Yeah, you told me. So, why so many warm new friends?" he asked.

"Because they know my daughter's not going to beat them out of a singles medal at a contest anymore. A short time ago they were scheming to cut my heart out with a dull butcher knife."

"They really get mad at you, just because Shannon was competition for their daughters?"

"Oh, Hell yes! When Shannon first started skating here, I was welcome as could be. But when she started placing well in the contests, I got the cold shoulder from some of the moms all the time. It didn't bother me, 'cause I don't care what a bunch of silly housewives think, but it's just comical how they've warmed up to me since Shannon has moved over to pairs. There aren't enough days in the week to accept all the lunch invitations!" She grinned. "There are three women, though, who just recently started hating my guts."

"Yeah? Who are they?"

"The moms of the pairs girls. You and Shannon will be unbeatable, and they know it. They know second fiddle is the best they can hope for now, and they hate me for it. I could get a salad fork between the ribs at any time. If you find my lifeless carcass under the Zamboni machine, you'll know what happened."

"Gee, Millie, I didn't realize being the Ice Queen was so fraught with danger."

"Well, there's only one gold medal in each event, Dear Boy, and if my daughter gets it, then their daughter doesn't. And that makes me pretty unpopular."

"Maybe you should start wearing a Kevlar SWAT vest to the rink."

She laughed. "No, but I do enjoy it, particularly when they look at me and see their hopes of fame and glory going up in smoke. You can read it in their eyes. Just when they thought they had a chance to win something, Millie Foster comes in with a blockbuster."

"That's kinda your style, isn't it, Ms. Foster?"

She grinned. "Yes, Dear Boy, it is my style."

Faux Pas

At a club ice session Shannon and Dean were chatting with members of the figure skating club. Millie was standing nearby as a group of young skaters and their mothers walked by. "I think you're beautiful," one admiring little girl said to Shannon.

"Well, thank you, Courtney," Shannon said brightly.

"But my mom says you're not very feminine," she continued, with wrinkled brow. "She says you're too big to skate like a girl."

Millie's eyes went sharply to the girl's mother, who promptly began turning colors. "That's OK, Honey," Shannon replied, giving the little girl a squeeze. "You're feminine enough for both of us!" Then she added her eyes to the glaring scrutiny of Courtney's mom.

The woman tried to formulate a response, but was unable to do so. "Kids say the strangest things," she finally mumbled, and walked away, dragging her daughter by the arm.

"She's dead meat," Millie muttered. "I'll have her heart on a silver platter."

Dean, who overheard Millie's comment, moved close to her. "And what shall you have done with her, Your Highness?" he asked. "By what means shall the villainess be dispatched?"

An evil grin slowly engulfed the woman's face as she turned to look at Dean. "She has committed the unforgivable," Millie said, "She criticized a club member who is a competitor. She will never have stature in the club again." The grin became more sinister. "I'll see to it."

"Couldn't you two just duel it out with hatpins at sunrise, or something?"

"No, Dear Boy, she replied coyly, "I'll simply use this little *faux pas* to cut her off at every turn. She'll soon be dog shit in this club."

"But won't the little girl suffer?"

"Sure, but that's how the game is played. You score points, and you lose points in the joy, and the anguish, of your daughter."

"Still, it seems a shame if the little girl gets hurt by her mother's careless remark."

"She'll probably just give up skating," Millie said, "Or maybe find another club. Those are the breaks. The daughter is the tool I use to punish the mother."

"Millie, life in the Amazon jungle isn't that cruel!"

"Listen, Dean, she'd do it to me in a heartbeat if she had the chance. She's a vicious bitch, and she's going to get what she deserves." Millie paused. "As for the little girl, she just made a poor choice of parents."

"Millie, you'd pour water on a drowning man!"

"Now, wait a minute, Dean. Let me explain something here. Let me contribute to your education, you naïve young man." She inhaled, "The competition here, the real competition, is not between the skaters on the ice. That's just the facade. The real competition is between the moms. It's that good old, 'My daughter is better than your daughter,' kind of a catfight that forms the cornerstone of this little society. And when Sheila brought her daughter into this fray, she came to play as hard as anybody else. Well, she made a mistake, and she got caught at it. Now she has to pay the price. This is where I run up my score in the game. When little Courtney is cut from the toy soldiers dance or doesn't get a part in one of the group numbers, that's a point for me." She regarded the young man from beneath raised eyebrows. "That's the game, Dean. She wouldn't hesitate to do it to me."

"You actually think she'd try to knock Shannon out of a medal, just to score some sort of points against you?"

"You're damn right she would, without even thinking about it! A snide comment to a judge, an upsetting remark to Shannon just before she skates. You bet your ass she would!"

"And this is the progress of civilization? Mothers using their daughters as pawns in a vicious contest of one-upmanship?"

"Well, Dean, if you're not comfortable with it, I'm sure you can find some other planet where all is sweetness and light. But this is here and this is now, and I play the game by the rules." She smiled. "And I usually win."

"And you leave the shattered dreams of little girls in your wake."

"Don't be so hard on me, Dean. Do you pity the Rockets, or the Astros so tenderly when they lose a game? Figure skating's a sport, too, for Christ's sake."

"When the Astros take the field," he responded, "They know who the opposing team is, and they know the rules by which they'll win or lose. But when that little girl goes out on the ice and practices her spins, and dreams of skating in the Olympics, she doesn't know that her mother's thoughtless remark might piss off the Ice Queen and put an end to her skating career before it gets off the ground!"

"What do you want, Dean?" Millie asked in frustration. "What do you want me to do?"

"Punish the mother without punishing the little girl! Gouge out her eyes or put her salad forks on the wrong side of the plates, or something. Just let the little girl skate, if she has what it takes."

"But punishing the girl is *how* I punish the mother. Don't you get it?"

"You're a clever woman, Millie. I'm confident you can find ways to embarrass and humiliate that woman without crushing that little girl's hopes and dreams. You just don't have to be that fuckin' cruel to an eight-year-old innocent bystander!"

"One more time, Dean. Do you think it's cruel if Craig Biggio strikes out, or if Hakeem misses a lay-up shot? It's a game, for Pete's sake!"

"One more time, Millie. There's something wrong with a game in which you have to crush a little girl's dreams in order to score points against her mother. So either play the game by reasonable rules, or don't play it at all!"

"You've got your share of gall, Young Man, telling the Ice Queen to back off when she moves in for the kill."

"Perhaps," he replied, "But I'm just concerned that there might be a shred of conscience buried deep behind Her Majesty's cold, hard eyes, and this glorious victory of yours might someday become tarnished by the salt of a little girl's tears."

"You're soft, Dean," she said. "You don't have the heart of a competitor."

"If I enjoyed the sound of breaking ribs and the sight of some kid's blood on my cuff, I'd be a fuckin' hockey player. But I don't, so I'm not. I'm a figure skater. And I don't want to win medals by sabotaging the other skaters, or bribing judges. I just want to work up a good program, and skate it well. And if nobody does any better, then maybe I'll win something. In this sport you 'compete' by doing your best, not by smashing the other guy's face, or filing his edges."

"All right, Dean. I see your hopeless idealism can't be quashed. You're a lost cause."

"OK, so what about little Courtney?"

"She's toast, Dean. I have to take her out. It's the way the game is played."

"It's a mistake, Millie, trust me. Find a way to blow up the mom without splattering the daughter."

Millie gave him a tired and exasperated look. Then she brightened up. "There might be a way," she said.

"I thought so."

"Maybe," she continued, "If you came to the Queen's chambers, late at night, and pled the little girl's case." She grinned. "The Ice Queen can get very generous when she's given something she really wants."

"You're suggesting I might have to sacrifice my honor just to obtain justice for one of your subjects?"

"History is replete with such instances, Dear Boy. It was all the rage a few centuries back."

"You mean, I'd have to capitalize on Her Majesty's weakness in order to obtain mercy for a helpless little girl? That sounds pretty disgusting."

"On the contrary. You'll enjoy it thoroughly, I promise."

"Hmmm."

"I think you should do it. You'd save that little girl's skating career. You'd salve the Ice Queen's conscience . . . if she has one, and you'd get your horns trimmed quite thoroughly in the process. Everybody wins!"

She grinned as he looked at her in mock disgust. "Come on, Brave Knight. Ride to the rescue of this tiny damsel. It's the honorable thing to do."

"More appealing than that," he said, "Would be to punish the evil Ice Queen by fucking her brains out. Now there's a worthwhile mission for an honorable knight!"

"I think you're right," she said. "And if anyone can fuck some sense and civility into this degraded monarch, it's you, Sir Studly." She grinned. "I'll receive you in my chambers this very night." She paused. "Actually, I'll be at your place around ten." She leaned close to his ear. "And if you give me what I want . . . ." She exhaled into his ear. "Little Courtney will live to skate another day."

By saying nothing at that point, Dean agreed to meet Millie secretly at his apartment that night.

The Meeting

Millie arrived at ten sharp, wearing a short, clingy minidress. She walked over to the couch, then moved over to sit beside Dean. Her face came close to his. "You really turn me on, Mr. Steele. You know that?" she asked, coyly. Dean was embarrassed and slightly uncomfortable. She looked into his eyes and began to close the gap between their lips. Soon they touched.

It began as a soft, gentle pressing of lips, but soon Millie sighed and began to press harder. As she became excited, her lips parted and began to pull at his. Soon his tongue slipped inside her mouth.

Millie moaned as she pressed herself close to Dean. She began to lie back, pulling him down on top of her. Instinctively, his left hand found her abdomen and started slipping downward. It moved to her thigh, slipped under the hem of her skirt and began moving back up. Millie parted her thighs, and Dean's hand came to rest on her panties at her pubic mound.

Millie pulled away from the kiss and trapped Dean's left thigh between hers. Then she pressed her pelvis against him and began a slow serpentine gyration.

Dean began to have second thoughts about what was developing. But Millie was falling deeper into the throes of passion. Her moaning became louder as she pressed her groin into his leg more forcefully. His fingers, now trapped between her pubis bone and his muscular thigh, began to manipulate her gently through the thin silk.

Soon her moans turned into gasps as her sexual energy built toward a release. The desperate grinding of her hips became more forceful, and her body became increasingly tense as passion took control of her. Not knowing what else to do, and fascinated with this new facet of the Ice Queen, Dean continued to manipulate the sensitive organ he held. Suddenly Millie's body went rigid, as she let out a long, low moan. For long moments she gasped and moaned as passion ruled her existence. Finally her body began to relax slowly. The process continued until it left her limp and panting. Gradually her breathing slowed toward normal.

"Oh, you rascal!" she said at last, smiling at him. "See what you do to me? I can't believe you made me do that!" She took a deep breath and exhaled a sigh. "I haven't gotten off like that in . . . forever!"

Dean didn't have a response, so he looked at her in silence. She smiled when she realized he was more embarrassed than she.

"I told you, you get me hot," she said in a shy voice. "Now you know how much."

Finally regaining his composure, Dean responded, "OK, but I thought you just liked to watch me skate."

"Sometimes . . . ." she said, looking into his eyes as if trying to decide if she was going to finish her sentence, "When I watch your tapes . . ." again she paused for courage, "When I'm all alone in the house . . ." another pause, "I get really turned on, and I fantasize about making love with you." Her eyes widened a bit. "Are you shocked?"

"Surprised, a bit, perhaps," he replied. "Not shocked. Except I always thought it was guys who fantasize about sex."

"Not exclusively, my naïve young friend. Some of mine get pretty steamy."

"Oh, like what?" Dean found himself suddenly interested.

Millie smiled. She was visibly pleased by his curiosity. "One of them starts off with us ice dancing in an empty arena. We skate a beautiful and erotic program, and then you take me right there on the ice."

"Do we get frostbite?" he asked, grinning.

"Just your knees and my butt," she laughed. "You know?" she said after a pause, "Here I am telling you my most intimate secrets, and I enjoy it. It really . . . turns me on to tell you how hot I get watching you skate." She shook her head slowly in amazement. "I never dreamed I would actually get the chance." Dean smiled softly at her. "OK," she said, "Give me a couple of minutes in the bathroom, and I'll meet you in the bed. Ladies have to be fresh, you know."

"Uh, what? Are you . . . ?"

"Yes, Dear Boy. I'm staying over with you tonight—at least for a while. You win the prize. The Ice Queen belongs to you, tonight, Stud."

"But, shouldn't we take a look at that before we decide?" Dean fought to keep his thoughts on a rational plane.

"Dean! I got off in your hand just then. I'm ready for some serious lovemaking right now. You've got me thoroughly seduced. What happens next is . . . you get to fuck my brains out!"

"But, what if . . . it turns out to be a bad idea?" He attempted to put his desire for the woman in the background of his thoughts.

"That's what tomorrow's for, Dear Boy. We can sit around all day and ask ourselves, 'Oh my God, what have we done?' But tonight the heart rules the head. Tonight is for lovers." Standing in front of him, she raised the front of her skirt and pressed her bare abdomen against his face.

"Are you sure you want to do this?" He asked, feeling himself weakening.

"Wild horses couldn't drag me away. I want you inside me. I want to feel your power flowing through me, sweeping me away. Tonight, the Ice Queen is your love slave."

Dean saw something vaguely frightening about her attitude toward adultery. If anyone were to be thinking long-term, it would have to be him. "One question, though," he said as Millie impaled her navel on his nose. "If it's a bad idea tomorrow, after we've done it, isn't it a bad idea tonight, before we've done it?"

"There's a whole ritual of remorse we'll go through the morning after. But I'm in no mood to worry about that now." She unzipped her dress and let it fall to the floor. "I want to lie next to your warm body between those cool sheets." She reached behind her back and unsnapped her bra. It quickly slipped off her shoulders and onto the floor, exposing her ample bosom. "I want to feel the vice-like grip of your arms around me, squeezing me." She stood before him, displaying her femininity in full view. Then she went into the bathroom.

Dean thought about what had happened. He wanted this woman, and she certainly wanted him. But an affair with his skating partner's mother had a huge potential for disaster. Besides, he had only known her a short while. She was a complicated woman. Her stated reasons for the affair were questionable at best. There could be other, darker motives for her interest in him, motives that might not come out until much later.

The pairs skating partnership made some kind of sense. A lot of time, effort and money was about to go into it. A relationship such as Millie proposed could blow it to smithereens at any time, particularly toward the culmination, when the pressure on everyone is greatest.

Dean was still on the couch when Millie emerged wearing nothing more than one of his white dress shirts.

"I thought you'd be warming the bed for us," she said.

"It's a bad idea, Millie," He said. "No matter how much we might want it, it's a recipe for disaster."

"Come on, Stud. You can handle a little extra pressure. Besides, you'll love it, I promise." She smiled seductively. "I'll make sure you do."

"No doubt, Madam. But we can't let it happen. Not now, anyway . . . with so much at stake. If we do have a chance at a medal, and I'm not saying we do, I'm not going to put it at any unnecessary risk."

"Are you serious? You're actually going to . . . kick me out of your bed? I can't believe it!"

Dean looked at her, as if to say, "You might as well believe it."

Anger and frustration flared in Millie's eyes. She started to make a cutting remark, but stopped herself just in time. Dean wondered what the unspoken insult was. It occurred to him that he would probably never know. Millie walked over to the window and stared out at the city for long moments. Finally she came over and sat down beside Dean, her borrowed shirt inadequately concealing her voluptuous anatomy.

"I have wanted you as my lover for years," she said. "Ever since the first time I saw you skate. I've worn out one VCR, two heavy duty vibrators and no telling how many batteries watching you skate. And now, here I am, in your apartment, naked, and horny out of my mind. The time is right for us, Dean. You can have me. You deserve me, and I deserve you. We deserve this moment. We owe it to ourselves. We can deal with whatever complications arise."

"If it were just you and me," he replied, "I would agree completely. But we're a part of a larger whole, here. If we were to indulge our personal desires, we would be letting down several people who trust us and depend on us. Your husband, your daughter, my partner, my sponsor."

"But they'll never know!" Her frustration showed itself.

"But I'll know, every time I look in the mirror. And you'll know, every time you look at your husband or your little girl. It's just too much to risk."

"Are you sure that's the way you want it?" she asked. His expression assured her his decision was final. "OK, she said. We'll play it your way. Hell, maybe you're right. We might have just messed everything up anyway."

"It's not that I don't want to . . ." he started.

"I know," she interrupted. "I saw the lump in your pants, and I felt it. You have a more analytical mind than I do, that's all, and you're probably right." She came closer to him. "But if you're not going to fuck me, I at least want you to know what you've won." She moved closer. "There are two reasons I want to make love with you," she continued. "First, I need it. I need to feel like a woman, and you, Buster, do make me feel like a woman. I'll be forty in a little over a year, and my beauty will begin to fade. But in your arms, I can be twenty again."

"Millie, I . . ."

"No Dean, don't worry. Just let me get out what I have to say." He sat back. "The second reason is for you. I think you deserve better than what you've been getting." She paused to think. "Do you know how many men would jump at the chance to lick my boots if I'd let 'em? They number in the hundreds. But I've never given the slightest chance to any of them. Millie the untouchable. Millie the unapproachable."

"But you." She shook her head. "I melted like a snowball in Hell under your touch. You got me off with a kiss, for Pete's sake! You put your tongue in my mouth, and sent me to orgasm city!" She looked into his eyes. "What all those guys want so badly, but can't have, is yours for the taking. Hell, I can't control myself around you. I don't even want to control myself around you. I want you to control me and tease me, and torment me . . . just to prove you can. I love the way you make me admit my darkest secrets. I'm hopeless where you're concerned." She paused. "Such power," she mused. "Such power."

She paused again, and then continued. "So my gift to you, is just this. I want you to know that you have conquered the Ice Queen. With almost no effort, you have made me your love slave. Just by being you. I wanted to show you that in bed. I wanted to show you the helpless, conquered, sex slave Millie Foster. But if I can't show her to you, at least I can describe her to you."

She looked out the window for a time. Then she came back to Dean. "You need to know this," she said. "You need to understand the effect you have on me, because you affect other people too. Not in the same way, of course. But your skating inspires people. You have a tremendous talent. You speak to the audience with your skating. You stir their souls. So use that gift, and don't let any vindictive judge deter you from it." She paused. "Are you following all this, or do I sound like a lunatic?"

"It's very . . . eye-opening," he said. "You have been extremely . . . candid with me. It must be hard to admit to such personal feelings."

"Well, yes. It's not like me to put my cards on the table quite like that."

"Just, please clarify one point. Are you saying you wanted to sleep with me to . . . build up my confidence, so I would skate better?"

"Oh, my God" she gasped. "I've messed it all up. No, no, no, that's not what I'm saying at all."

"I'm sorry if I didn't hear it correctly."

"Well, maybe there is some truth to the way you said it." She inhaled, then sighed. "You've had a very profound effect on me, Dean Steele, and I'm a tough nut to crack. I think it's important for you to know that. That's all. Sometimes I think you underestimate yourself—your power over people. I just hoped that seeing how thoroughly you have conquered the Ice Queen might make you more aware of your gift, and encourage you to unleash your power on the audience and the judges. That's all."

"I see. I had misunderstood you."

"No, you were right. But that was reason number two, remember? Reason number one was, I wanted it. I wanted you to excite me and control me, and give me those feelings that I've missed for so many years. Feelings I've never even experienced." She came over to him and cradled his face in her palms. "And I still want it. I ache to grip you between my legs and feel you pumping your power into my helpless body. You are the giver, Dean. I can only be the receiver. Your have the power. It comes from within you. You generate it. I can only absorb it for a time."

They embraced, and then Millie dressed and left.

Chapter 22

A Houston Christmas

"Dean," Millie said, "It's all set. You're spending Christmas with us. All of Fred's relatives are coming down from East Texas. It'll be a total zoo. You'll be miserable, but it's mandatory. Shannon would slit her wrists if she didn't have you there to brag about. So plan on spending Christmas eve and Christmas day in River Oaks."

"It sounds as though I am without option."

"Oh, absolutely! Even a notarized death certificate wouldn't get you out of this engagement."

Dean sighed. "Seriously, Millie, wasn't Thanksgiving punishment enough?"

"Forget it, Dean. You've been sentenced, with no hope of parole. Just try to grin and bear it." She gave him an understanding smile and a hug.

Dean spent the afternoon of Christmas eve chatting with Shannon's relatives and enduring her outlandish and embarrassing assertions about him, his apartment, his car, his motorcycle, and what they do skating together.

"Dean," Millie said, "I'm running out of space to put people up for the night. "Would you mind to take Bradley and Boyd home with you, just for tonight? Y'all can come back over here for breakfast. Surely they won't be too much trouble just for that little while. You can stick 'em anywhere you have room."

Dean groaned. Bradley and Boyd were Shannon's cousins. Bradley, from Corsicana, was fifteen and Boyd, from Gilmer, seventeen. "OK," he said. "I guess I can stand it."

"Oh, my God!" Shannon exclaimed when she heard of the sleeping arrangements. "You boys are gonna have to be real careful. It's a jungle over there, and you're raw meat!"

The two boys' jaws dropped. "It's nothing but really wild, really tacky girls over there. You better stick close together so you don't get raped!"

"It's just an ordinary apartment house," Dean protested.

"Oh, as if! Like they don't lose two or three guys a week over there!" She grinned at Dean. "Seriously," she continued, "If you get attacked by a gang of tacky girls, just start yelling at the top of your lungs. You won't be able to fight 'em off. There's too many. You'll just have to hope help arrives before it's too late." The two boys were wide-eyed.

"Shannon," Dean said. "Could you stuff a sock in your mouth for us, please?"

"And stick close to Dean when you walk in from the parking lot. And don't unlock the door for any reason. It's probably just a trap."

"Are you finished, Foster, with this B movie script of yours?"

"Just trying to take care of my cousins, Dean. I'd hate for anything bad to happen and mar their Christmas in the big city." She grinned mischievously.

"You are truly cruel," he mumbled.

After supper, the electrical power in River Oaks went out due to an ice storm. Dean and the boys brought in a car battery and rigged up a power inverter to supply electricity for the electronic grand piano in the living room. Marybelle Foster played gospel hymns on the piano while Dean accompanied her on the guitar and Buford on the banjo. The whole group sang gospel songs by candlelight. Marybelle sang harmony and Buford sang bass. The old standard "I'll Fly Away" was perhaps the most moving experience. Buford's banjo picking enthralled the group.

After an hour of singing Shannon lit up and said, "Guess what, Mamaw, Dean's a clogger! You've got to clog for us!"

"Oh, pshaw! I haven't done that in years! Besides, I don't have my Mary Janes."

"Yes you do," Buford said, holding up a pair of shoes with taps on them. "I brought 'em."

"Y'all ganged up on me!" the elder Mrs. Foster said.

They plugged a CD player into the inverter, and Dean and Marybelle clogged to John Denver's rendition of "Thank God I'm a Country Boy," much to the delight of the assembly.

Shannon followed Dean and her cousins to his car as they left, still offering the boys advice on how to avoid excess intimacy with the predatory female inhabitants of the Piccadilly apartment house.

The Piccadilly

The two boys rode with Dean to Clear Lake City, where the power was still on. "You guys wait here a minute," Dean said as they entered his apartment. "I gotta pick up my mail."

He stopped at apartment 106 where there was a party going on. He made his way to Kristin, one of the girls who lived there, and gave her a hug. "Merry Christmas, Dean" She said, grinning. "I never dreamed I'd see you at our party."

"I just dropped by to wish you a merry Christmas," he replied grinning. "Listen," he said, "I've got a couple of country boys staying over with me tonight. They're cousins of my brat skating partner. She's been filling their heads with wild tales of how . . . friendly . . . the girls are here at the Piccadilly. I thought it might be funny if you and one of your roommates dropped by for a minute and made a fuss over 'em. You know, say they're cute, and stuff like that. Would you mind to do that?"

"Heck no, Dean! Karen and I'll drop over in a while. It'll be fun."

"OK, no big deal, though. Just give 'em something to talk about on the way home, OK."

"Right," she said. He gave her a kiss on the cheek and left the party.

About fifteen minutes later there was a knock at Dean's door. "See who that is, will you?" Dean yelled to his two guests who were watching the Playboy TV channel while he checked his E-mail. Boyd opened the door, revealing two girls in party clothes. "Oh, Hi," Kristin said. "We ran out of limes for the Margaritas. We were hoping Dean could spare us one."

"Who is it?" Dean yelled from his office.

"Uh, it's two girls who want to borrow, uh, a lime," Boyd replied.

"OK, let 'em in," Dean said. "I have some limes in the fridge."

The two girls pushed past the young man and entered the apartment. Karen had never seen inside it before, and she was curious. Kristin had some history in that unit.

"Who are your friends, Dean?" Kristin asked. "They sure are cute!"

"Oh, uh, Bradley and Boyd, cousins of my skating partner. They live up in East Texas."

The girls said hello to the two awkward boys and began to chat with them. Kristin latched on to Boyd, and Karen sat down beside Bradley on the sofa. The girls gushed and giggled and flirted. When Dean figured the boys had had enough, he emerged from the kitchen with a lime. "Here you go, ladies," he said.

"You know," Karen said, "There's a party in 106. Y'all could come over. It'd be fun." She grinned at Brad.

"Thanks, ladies," Dean said, "But we need our beauty sleep. We didn't get this good looking by stayin' up all night." The girls said goodnight and left.

Dean Steele was something of an elder statesman in his apartment complex. He was older than the majority of the residents, and he had been there longer than most. Unlike many of them, he had a college degree and a steady job. He was the de facto assistant manager since the apartment manager occasionally sought his help on policy issues as well as electrical repairs. Unit 201 was the largest apartment in the complex, and it had attained almost legendary status among the young female residents. Only a select few of them had ever been inside it. Most people in the complex knew that Dean skated with a brat from River Oaks. At the Piccadilly, gossip travels at the speed of sound.

Soon another knock came at the door, and two more girls presented a flimsy excuse to meet Bradley and Boyd—and to see the inside of Dean's apartment. These two were soon followed by another flirtatious pair. Finally Dean turned off his porch light as a signal that the occupants had gone to bed.

"OK, muchachos," Dean said. "I'd be lynched by the Foster clan if I let you go to that party. So pull off your boots and bed down for the night." The two young men reluctantly complied.

After a while Dean heard a noise in his living room. He got up and peeked in, only to find his two guests, fully dressed, with boots in hand, preparing to leave. He watched the two boys make their silent exit and then dialed a number. "My ponies are out of the barn" he told Kristin. "Don't let anybody ride 'em, and send 'em home at 1:30." The laughing young woman agreed.

Bradley and Boyd were warmly welcomed at the party in apartment 106, where they made a number of new friends. At 1:30 Kristin pulled then away from the girls they were kissing and said Dean just called, looking for them. "I told him you're not here, but you better get home before he comes looking for you." The boys hastily left the party and snuck back into Dean's apartment. Dean, of course, was sound asleep.

Christmas Day

"Oh, my God!" Shannon exclaimed when she met her two cousins as they were getting out of Dean's Mustang. "They both got raped. I can tell by looking!"

"If you don't get off that particular line of questionable humor, Princess, it's gonna be a very long and tedious Christmas," Dean said.

"Were you hurt?" she asked the boys. "Did you get all scratched up?"

"Maybe if you ignore your cousin, she'll do us a favor and fall in a deep hole somewhere," Dean said to the boys.

"It wasn't too bad," Boyd said. "They let us go after about an hour." He grinned at Brad.

"Yeah," Brad added, "They said they wouldn't hurt us . . . as long as we gave 'em what they wanted."

"I thought we were going to deny all that, Guys," Dean said, faking alarm at their admission. "We're gonna tell everybody we just read the Bible a while, said our prayers, and went to bed early."

"OK," Boyd said. "They won't believe Shannon if she tells the real story. Not if we all three deny it."

"Good plan," Dean said.

"I can't believe this!" Shannon said. "You just stood by and let my cousins get raped by seven or eight tacky girls?"

"Look, Shannon. You don't know what we were up against. It was like a CIA operation. One of 'em distracted me while several more snuck in and kidnapped the guys. Once I figured out what had happened, it took me half an hour to find out which apartment they'd been abducted to. Then I had to do the Rambo thing to get 'em out of there alive."

"And just how did she distract you, Dean?" Shannon glared at him.

"She had a fascinating theory on the basis of the Arab/Israeli conflict. I was simply enthralled by her analysis of the historical differences between the two cultures."

Bullshit! You were making out with some trashy girl while my cousins were getting raped!"

"That came after the discussion of the Middle East."

"I can't believe you! All you had to do was keep Bradley and Boyd for one night! And now they've probably got some hideous disease!"

"Oh, shit!" Dean said. "We'll need a story if you guys come down with a dose of the clap." He paused to think. "I know a doctor," he said. "He'll treat you in confidence. Just let me know as soon as it starts hurtin' to pee."

"OK," Boyd said. "We'll be cool about it. Right Brad?"

"Yeah," the other boy said.

"I'm gonna tell!" Shannon said. "I'm gonna tell Aunt Linda and Aunt Earlene their boys had wild sex with tacky girls and now they've got VD!"

"We'll all three deny it, Shannon," Dean said calmly. "They won't believe you." Dean and the boys started toward the house. "Don't worry about the gonherria," he said, so Shannon could hear. "Penicillin clears it right up."

After breakfast two of the younger children distributed the gifts, and everyone opened them. "Oh, my God!" Shannon said, "Dean gave me jewelry! What is it? Earrings? Cool!" She examined the small gold items. "It's a word or something. Look! It says, 'T-U-O.' What does that stand for?"

"Turn it over, Shannon," Millie said, grinning at Dean.

"Oh, OK. Now it says, 'O-U-T.' What's that stand for? Something University of Texas?"

"What does it spell?"

"Oh, O-U-T, uh, out?"

"Look at the other one."

"Uh, it's different. It says, 'N-I,' no, it's 'I-N.'"

"Oh, my God!" one of her girl cousins said."

"What?" Shannon said. "What is this 'out,' and 'in' business?" Her three female cousins looked at her in horror. "Oh!" she said, beginning to laugh, "In one ear and out the other!"

"Somehow it reminded me of you," Dean said.

"I'll wear the 'IN' on my left ear and the 'OUT' on my right ear," she explained, "'cause he usually skates on my left side," She went over and gave Dean a kiss on the cheek. "You're a rascal, Steele," she whispered. "Thank you for my earrings!"

Later Shannon received another small gift from Dean. "You better open that one in private," he warned her.

Unable to wait, Shannon began to rip at the paper. The small box contained a gold chain necklace that held the words "SEXY BITCH" in gold. Delighted, she showed it covertly to everyone in the room.

Epilog

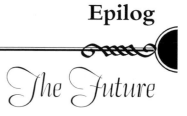

The Future

Now Dean and Shannon have gotten their skating partnership underway. The initial hurtles have been cleared, and the bulk of the work lies ahead. Dean is determined to give the skating project as good a chance of success as possible. Shannon is on board with the pairs team, and Millie has stated her intentions, both for the skating endeavor and for her and Dean. Fred is committed to support the effort financially. Walt is prepared to handle the media.

The Baton Rouge Skating Club will be putting on an exhibition before long, and they may invite Shannon and Dean to skate there. The Bluebonnet Open in Austin will be the first actual contest they could compete in. After that, the USFSA contest series begins with Southwest Regionals in Denver and Midwest Sectionals in Detroit, leading up to the US National Championships in Cleveland.

So, what lies in store for this determined team that is attempting to overcome almost impossible odds and accomplish something truly spectacular in the annals of figure skating?

Will they be able to work up truly inspiring skating programs to compete with the established pairs teams? How will the contest judges respond to their unusual style? How will the media commentators and the audiences respond? What about falls and injuries? What about sabotage by other skaters?

Can Dean and Shannon hold it together? Will Shannon's work ethic overcome her selfish immaturity? Will her crush on Dean cause friction between them? With her mom? Will Dean be able to fight the frustration and withstand the pressure of guiding the team? Will Fred stay the course and provide all the necessary support? Will Walt be able to control the media when they begin to compete and attract national and international attention?

And Millie—will she succeed in her quest to conquer the Ice Man? Can Dean find ways to resist the temptation to be drawn into a dangerous relationship? If not, can he and Millie keep the beast under control?

The next phase of this adventure is covered in the second book of this series, *Ice Dance—On The Ice*.

Kent Castle
Houston, Texas
July 4, 2013

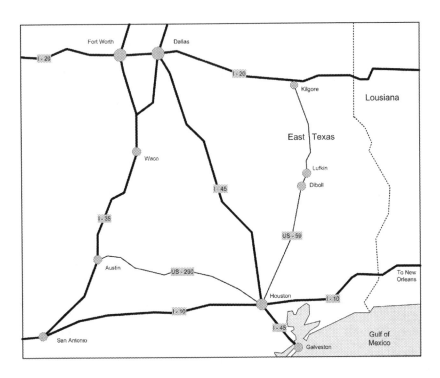

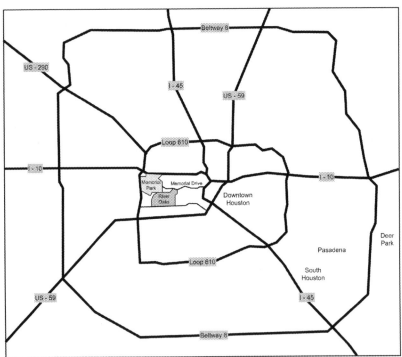

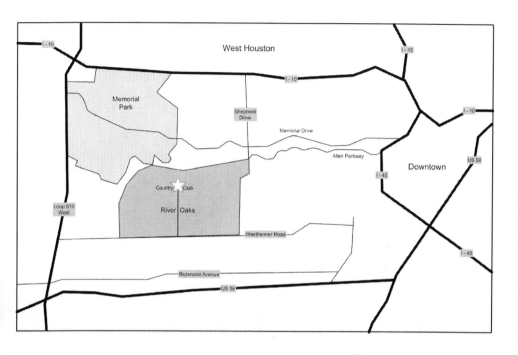

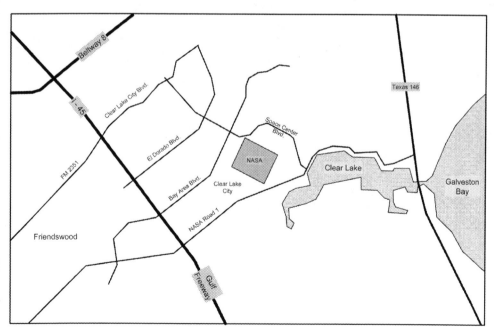